SCARCITY

RANDALL WOOD

SCARCITY

For information contact:
Tension Bookworks
PO Box 93
Nokomis Fl, 34274
www.tensionbookworks.com

Book and Cover design by Derek Murphy
Formatting by Jayne E Smith

Cataloging-in-Publication Data is on file at the Library of Congress

Wood, Randall, 1968-
Scarcity / Randall Wood—2nd ed.
ISBN-13: 978-1-938825-23-1
First Edition: November 2012

10 9 8 7 6 5 4 3 2 1

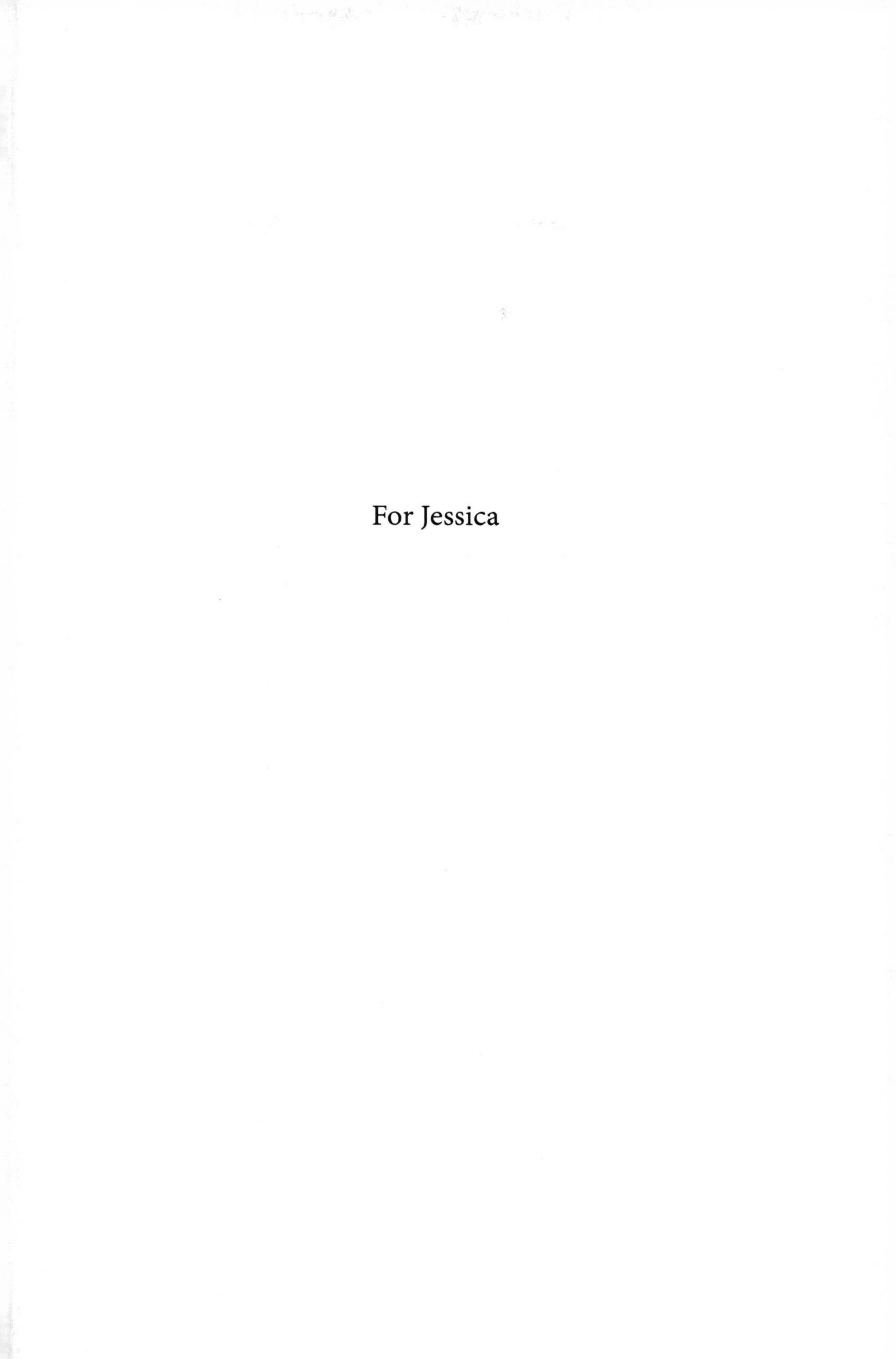

For Jessica

scar·ci·ty |'sker sə tē|
noun: insufficiency of amount or supply
rariety of appearance or occurance.

The doctor sees all the weakness of mankind.

– *Arthur Schopenhauer*

...under conditions of scarcity...justice demands that those who have consented to be posthumous organ providers, i.e., those who have fulfilled the moral duty to consent, be given first priority access to the cadaver organ pool in the event of need. Non-consenters are to be given second priority access.

– *Michael J. Booker, August 1990*

Service to others is the rent you pay for your room here on earth.

– *Mohammed Ali*

FOR MORE OF MEXICO'S WEALTHY, COST OF LIVING INCLUDES GUARDS

November 16, 2008—New York Times

—ONE—

"ANITA! BREAKFAST!"

"I'm coming, Papa!"

Anita ran the brush through her dark hair three more times before standing and examining her wardrobe selection again. She had changed four times, somewhat of an average for her, before deciding on the new jeans and loose shirt. It was a far less provocative choice when compared to what she had worn to the nightclubs the previous night. The tight dress, high heels and makeup would not have met her father's approval, and she had been forced to sneak out of the house to avoid him seeing her. While she loved him dearly, he was having a hard time letting his little girl grow up. Her teenage figure was growing in all the right places and she enjoyed the attention she attracted from the boys at the clubs, attention she knew her father would frown on. So she would dress down for him today as she was only going to the mall with her friends. She added some jewelry to her wrists and ears before grabbing her cell phone and running down the stairs.

She bypassed her mother at the stove and rounded the table to reach her father. He lowered his newspaper for her kiss and his smile was genuine as she continued on to buss her mother's cheek while she scrambled eggs at the stove.

"Good morning, Papa." She smiled her sweetest smile.

Mr. Perez frowned slightly at that as he examined her clothes. She was obviously going somewhere this Saturday morning and that usually meant a request for money. But she was fifteen years old and still called him Papa. He knew he was being manipulated, but he also admitted that he let it happen.

"The mall?" he asked.

"Yes, Papa, with Consuela and Maria, just for fun."

"Should I call Juan to drive you?"

"No, Papa. Maria has a new car. She is driving us!"

"Maria drives now?" He turned to his wife. "When did this happen?"

"She's sixteen now. Did you not notice?" His wife laughed as she set the eggs in front of him. He folded the newspaper and tossed it aside before biting into them and burning his tongue. He examined his daughter while she ate some banana with her fingers and tapped the screen on her phone. The bracelets jingled with every bite.

"I would prefer that you not wear so much jewelry. It attracts the wrong kind of attention. We talked about this, remember?"

Anita rolled her eyes before smiling at him. "Papa, it's the mall. They have security, and I won't be alone, I'll be with my friends."

Mr. Perez opened his mouth to say more, but a look from his wife cut him off and he added more eggs to it instead. His daughter's teenage sense of invulnerability was well established. She felt that her father's wealth would shield her from the dangers of the world as it always had. But her father knew better. That same wealth could make the world more dangerous. It was his fault really. Maybe he had protected her too much. But like any parent, he hoped that such lessons could be avoided.

A honk from outside caused her to flip the phone shut and stand. She shoved the last bite of banana in her mouth before starting for the front door. She made it around the corner before returning with a grin. Her father already had his wallet out and was extracting a credit card. She took it with the smile that he loved before planting a kiss on his cheek.

"Good-bye. I love you!"

Her mother sat down with her own eggs and poured herself some orange juice before smiling and shaking her head at her husband.

"What?"

"Pushover."

He picked up the newspaper again and hid his grin behind it.

* * *

Anita's friends had shown up only a half hour late, which was somewhat early for them. She piled into the convertible and they immediately become engrossed in a rehashing of the previous evening, what boys they had met, which ones they wished to meet again, before half-arguing over who had seen which one first.

None of the girls noticed the two men following in the new, somewhat ambiguous car. The two men were not alone, but part of a six-man team who constantly rotated their surveillance of the girls. They were experienced men, as this was their trade and they were long past their first time. They switched every hour with the other two-man crews hovering around the outdoor mall at a five-block radius, ready to move in when the first good opportunity presented itself.

Three hours later Anita dropped her bags around her feet and collapsed into a chair at the mall's outdoor café. Her feet were sore from the new heels she had bought and she set about changing back to her old ones after the waitress took her drink order. Her friends were also equally burdened by their morning of shopping. Now the café was growing crowded as shoppers looked for a place out of the sun and a cool drink.

"Four pair of shoes, Maria? Really?"

"I couldn't decide what color!"

Anita sipped her drink as she took in all of their bags. Still tired from their previous night out, she was ready to leave right now, but she knew her friends weren't close to being done. She was done spending money on herself. She would find something nice for her mother next. But she didn't want to lug all her bags around for another few hours.

"We should take these to the car."

"Yeah, but we'll lose our table if we do."

"I have to pee."

Anita rolled her eyes before standing and shifting her foot in her shoe for a better fit. The new blister was rubbing, but not as bad as in the new shoes.

"Give me the keys. I'll take our stuff out."

"Then I will pee," Maria added.

"And I will sit here and do nothing." Consuela smiled and stretched.

Anita took the keys and stuck her tongue out at them before gathering up all of the bags. It was quite a load, but it proved to be more bulky than heavy when she started walking. She left for the car as Maria darted off to the bathroom. Neither of them noticed the man at the next table dialing his phone.

"She's leaving the other two and going to the car alone. Move in now."

"Okay."

The leader in the car immediately relayed the information to the others before sitting low in the seat just as Anita emerged from the mall. He watched her struggle under the bulk of the multiple bags as she approached, oblivious to her surroundings. The van pulled into the lot and slowly circled closer.

"Wait till she's done and on her way back in," he ordered.

He couldn't have her locking herself in the car should she notice them in time. If they had to break into the car to get her it would slow things down, possibly enough to cause them to abort. The van pulled away and cruised through the lot as if in search of a better parking spot.

He watched her fumble with the key fob and door before unceremoniously dumping the load of shopping bags in the back seat. She then stooped to check her makeup in the outside mirror, removing her sunglasses and squinting at her reflection in the bright afternoon sun.

"Get ready, move in slow."

"We got her."

He had just given the order when he was startled by the passenger side door opening as the man who had been tailing the girls flopped onto the leather seat beside him.

"This is a good time, no?"

"Yes, Jesus Christ, you scared the shit out of me."

"Sorry…look, she's moving."

They returned their gaze out the window to see Anita finish her primping and start walking back toward the mall, dismissing the van approaching from behind.

"Look around."

"Looks clear on my side, nobody looking our way."

The lead man grunted before speaking into the phone.

"Take her."

There was no reply other than the immediate speeding up of the van. The side door slid back to reveal two men dressed in face masks and gloves. The girl turned her head at the sound of the revving engine and caught sight of the approaching van.

It was already too late to run.

Frozen with terror and disbelief, Anita held agreeably still as the two men grabbed her with practiced moves by the arms and legs and had her on the floor of the moving van within seconds. Only then did the shock succumb to reflex. She managed one scream before the duct tape secured her mouth shut. Her kicking legs and flailing arms were soon defeated by even more tape, and it accumulated, binding her body tighter and tighter until the movement to breathe was all she could voluntarily perform. Her face was kept toward the floor until a dark cloth covered her eyes and was secured around her head along with her long hair. Only then was she flipped over.

A voice hissed in her ear, "Relax, pretty, there's nowhere to go now, and in case you haven't figured it out yet, this is a kidnapping."

She whimpered and tears flowed under the scarf over her eyes and she barely noticed the straps being tightened around her body, securing her to the hard board. The van took several turns and the men were forced to hold the board in place as they worked to prevent her from sliding around the metal floor.

After what seemed like forever to her, but was actually only a few minutes, the van turned down a narrow alley and came to a sudden stop. After the noise and violence of the last few minutes, she found herself surrounded by silence as the men left the van as one, slamming the doors shut behind them. She struggled against the straps and tape but soon accepted defeat. An attempt to rub the cloth from her eyes also proved futile. She forced herself to calm down as she was dizzy from the lack of air and her rapidly beating heart. She listened intently for any sound of someone passing by. The distant sounds of traffic were all she could make out. She had no idea where she was or how long she had been gone. Did her friends even know what had happened? Were they calling her father? The police? Why was this happening to her?

Her thoughts were interrupted by the rattling of a key in the lock of the driver's side door. Anita yelled against the tape across her face and struggled in vain against the straps. The van rocked as a heavy man entered and sat behind the wheel in the still warm seat. Her hopes of rescue died a quick death when he spoke.

"Sorry to disappoint, little girl, but I'm just the chauffeur."

The van was started and put in gear and Anita slid across the floor to impact the side of the wheel well as it took the turn out of the alley. She heard the horns of rush hour traffic as the van weaved in and out, cresting hills and bouncing through potholes. The board absorbed most of the impacts with the walls of the van, but it did nothing to prevent the tape from tearing at her skin where it had been so quickly applied. Anita ground her teeth against the pain until the ride smoothed on what could only be a freeway. The relief was short-lived as the van pulled off after a few minutes and bounced down a poorly maintained road. The sounds of loud music could be heard along with equally loud voices. Eventually, the van briefly stopped before pulling into a small garage. Only when the door was down did the engine shut off and the driver exited. Anita lay in silence once again for a moment until more voices preceded the opening of the back doors. Hands grabbed the board, and she was lifted out, only to be carried inside and up some stairs, before being roughly deposited on the floor.

"You two get out."

Anita felt their footsteps as they left only to then hear the voice again.

"Listen closely. You've been kidnapped. You do as we say and follow the rules, you'll live to go home someday. If not, life will become very unpleasant for you. Do you understand?"

She managed the slightest of nods.

"My knife is sharp. Don't move while I cut the tape. I'll place a towel over your head. You'll cover your face completely when we knock on the door and keep it covered until we leave. The radio stays on at all times, you will never touch it. We're always watching. You understand?"

Despite her fear, Anita managed another nod without crying. The knife made rapid work on the tape and she felt the pressure decrease as her body was freed. The towel came down on her head as promised and all light was blocked out. The straps were removed except for the ones holding her feet. She heard a heavy grunt as the man got to his feet and walked to the door. A radio came on, blaring loud music and startling her, yet the volume could not cover the creaking of the door as it opened and closed. The sounds of several locks being thrown quickly followed and only then did she dare attempt to move. Her shaking hands covered with tape managed to find the towel and pull it and the scarf from her eyes. She found herself in a small room with an equally small bed.

One heavy door appeared where her ears had said it would be, another showed a small and filthy bathroom beyond it. A window covered in a tattered blanket let in just enough light around the edges and through the thin fabric that she could make out the grid-work shadow of metal bars. A tile floor long in need of cleaning matched the peeling paint on the walls. The sounds of a busy street could be heard three floors below. Her fingers and manicured nails found the tape on her mouth and she pulled it free only to let out a pent-up sob. She stifled it in fear it would anger her kidnappers. Undoing the leg strap, she rose on shaking legs and walked to the bed. Sitting down, Anita began crying softly and picking the tape free from her skin. Surely this wasn't really happening to her. Any moment now her father or the police would come through the door and take her home.

Wouldn't they?

* * *

"Khalid, let's go!"

Hanni gave Tariq a look that shut him up before turning to check on his friend Khalid. While only a few months younger, his friend had trouble on the steep climbs, always falling behind as they neared the top. The other boys laughed at him and his weakness, but such remarks drew the wrath of Hanni, whose size was enough to ensure his friend was left alone.

"You okay?"

Khalid nodded and caught his breath.

"It's your turn tonight?"

"Yes."

"You want me to come with you?"

"No."

Hanni grimaced at his friend's sharp reply. He should not have asked and hurt his pride. He looked away and listened as Khalid caught his breath. It only took him a moment, as it usually did. He never got winded on the road, no matter how far they walked. Only on the climbs.

"Ready?"

Khalid nodded and set off after the other boys and the small group of goats they were after. Hanni followed his friend without a word, automatically adjusting his pace to match his.

Khalid eyeballed the far ridge to the west as he and his friend fetched the goats down from the highland grazing site. Squinting against the setting sun, he could just make out the American firebase and its many satellites. Soon he would break away from the goat herd and his friend Hanni to sneak off to the hiding place of the AK-47 the village boys all shared. Tonight it was his turn to fire at the Americans. Something they were paid to do by the Taliban soldiers who occupied the valley. As far as he knew, none of his friends had ever hit any of the soldiers. But his family was poor and the Taliban commander had promised two dollars a day for any boy in the village who would do so. Khalid had actually come to like the Americans, as did his father. They had paved the road during the winter lull in the fighting, and now a truck traveled twice a week to the neighboring villages to make trade easier. The existence of the road also took the percentage of each trade out of the hands of the village elder, something he did not agree with. So, while the elder may have wanted *some* Taliban influence to keep him in his position of power, the people themselves were leaning toward the Americans.

As a result, Khalid's short ration of ammo would not really come anywhere close to the fire base. The Taliban paid him to shoot, not to necessarily hit anything. It was merely to harass the Americans, to remind them that they were far from home and not wanted here, at least by some.

It was dark enough now and the human eye had a difficult time adjusting between the still sunlit sky and the dark ground, something he had learned at a young age. He waved to his friend and broke away through the cypress trees, his teenage legs adjusting to the rugged terrain with no thought. Moving from shadow to shadow he kept the trees between himself and the always watching eyes on the far ridge. Working down a small draw he reached up under the exposed roots of a tilted cypress and retrieved the rifle. An old can sat next to it and he pried the lid off to reveal twenty 7.62 rounds for the AK. Ten fewer than last week. Perhaps the Taliban were rationing for a big attack? Or maybe they were running out of money? Either way, it was not much of a concern to him. He'd been born in the Korengal valley, and he would most likely live there until he died. He had never known a time when his country wasn't at war.

He pulled the empty magazine from the rifle and with a callused thumb slowly pressed the rounds in, one by one. The magazine was old and the spring did not offer the resistance it should. The rifle would often jam when he fired it, but twenty rounds would only take a brief moment to discharge. He would fire at one of the outposts tonight before hunkering down behind some cover to wait out the return fire. Then a long nap before the early morning chill would wake him. He would then make his way home, circling wide to enter his village from the opposite side. It would be a long night, but he had taken the money.

Tonight he would use the wall. Sometime before he was born, the previous occupants of the village had a logging operation in the valley. It had long since been shut down, first by the Russians and then by the Taliban. The small mill had been surrounded by a low wall to prevent erosion, and it had since fallen to rubble, leaving only one long stretch still standing. Khalid left the draw on his belly and crawled his way through a spur before reaching trees he thought thick enough to hide him from the Americans. He knew they could somehow see in the dark and had been warned to keep something between himself and them at all times. Feeling safe now, he picked himself up, and holding the heavy rifle, made his way up the ridgeline.

* * *

Specialist David Zemmler had been in-country for eight months and had tracked over the same ground Khalid was now traveling more than once. It was very familiar ground. As a result, he knew just where to train the new LRAS night scope they had mounted yesterday morning.

The new scope was a vast improvement over the old one. Despite the fact that it ate batteries at a rapid rate, the sensitivity and range were worth it. The first night they had used it they had almost called everyone out to stand to. Every night-crawling animal prowling the valley had glowed like a beacon, making them think the Taliban were massing for a full assault. Fortunately, cooler heads had prevailed. Now more familiar with the new scope's capabilities, Zemmler scanned the valley for people. The law in the valley was that anyone seen outside the village after dark was considered the enemy. He turned the scope to scan toward the sawmill again, but before he got to it he noticed a large heat source moving slowly up the ridge in its direction. Playing with the zoom, he focused in closer to see one man with the familiar walk of one toting a rifle. His arms moved as if connected, or holding something with both hands, and he did not reach out to the trees to help him up the steep slope.

"Hey, Johnson."

Johnson picked up his head from where it had been resting on his arms and rubbed the stubble on his head. Two of their platoon were assigned to each shift, but only one could use the scope at a time, so the other usually banked up some sleep. Now his was being interrupted and he was annoyed. He leaned his head back against the wire cage full of dirt and rock and gazed up at his partner.

"What?"

"Wake up the sarge. I got a hadjji sneaking up the ridge toward the sawmill."

"Rifle or radio?" If the man was carrying either one, the rules said he was a fair target.

"Rifle."

"Okay, I'm on it."

He rose from his spot behind the hesco and walked toward the main bunker. Less than half a minute had passed before Sergeant Daly was gazing through the scope. He watched silently for a few moments while Zemmler and Johnson waited.

"I'd say he was heading for the sawmill, too. Probably likes the cover of the wall. We took fire from there a couple weeks ago and the mortar crew has it preset in their computer now."

"Should we light him up?"

Daly thought about it for a few before he replied. "Let's wait till he gets there and then have the Charlies drop some HE on him. The captain will want us to go up there and tear down that wall if the hadjji's use it for cover again. Be easier to just drop some rounds on it and save us the climb and a lot of work."

"Okay."

Zemmler exchanged a look with Johnson. No fun for them tonight. The mortar crew would get all the fireworks. But the sergeant was smart enough to get the job done and save them some work at the same time.

"I'm going back to my rack. Wake me up if you need anything." He walked away, scratching his ass through his boxers. Even at night it was hot here, they all wore as little as possible. He stopped before he had gone three steps and turned.

"Hey, Zemmler."

"Yeah, Sarge?"

"Don't need to wait for him to shoot our way. Soon as he gets there, just drop it on him."

"Okay."

* * *

Khalid had gained the position he wanted and was surveying the wall from behind a tree before he moved out into the open. The corner was the best spot he decided. It would give him cover from two directions.

Not wanting to crawl anymore, he sprinted across the open area and flopped down behind the wall. Fumbling with his clothes, he pulled up his sleeves and prepared to lay the rifle over the top of the wall.

A strange whistling sound moved through the trees to his ears. The wind was blowing, but he had never heard it sound like that before.

* * *

"He's there, whenever you're ready."

After waking up the mortar crew with the radio and telling them the target, the last few words were their sole contribution to the night's activities. They watched for the flashing impact of the high explosive rounds already on their way to the sawmill.

They didn't have long to wait. The rounds crumped into the target with blinding flashes and heavy thumps that reached their ears only a few seconds later. They quickly had a group of armed men in boxer shorts, flip-flops, and chest armor gathered around them.

"What we got?" one of them asked.

"Hadjji with a rifle at the sawmill. Sarge said to use the Charlies," Johnson replied before speaking into the radio to the mortar crew. "Your range is good, spread it around some."

Some watched as the mortar rounds pounded the area around the sawmill for the next minute before Johnson spoke again and cut them off.

"That ought to do it. Thanks, guys."

Most of the men wandered back to their racks. Nothing they hadn't seen before. Zemmler was scanning through the scope. The others waited until he pulled his head back.

"Couple of small fires, but no sign of him now."

"Probably in pieces, or halfway to Pakistan by now. Either way, he's done. Score one for the Infidels."

The rest nodded agreement before disappearing behind the hescos in search of their bunks and more sleep.

Another day in the valley.

* * *

Khalid had never known such pain or terror. The explosions had come without warning and never seemed to stop. He had dropped the rifle and cowered behind the wall for an eternity, screaming as fast as he could suck in the air and force it back out. Until the sudden pain in his chest had come. It had burned into him like fire and his breath was taken from him. The explosions ceasing had not even registered in his mind as he rolled onto his back. The stars shining brightly down on him through the smoke were the last thing he remembered before the darkness descended. The fires burned around him for the rest of the night.

SEARCH MOUNTED FOR BOY BELIEVED
KIDNAPPED BY DRUG GANG

October 17, 2008—New York Times

—TWO—

ANGEL PULLED HIS EYES from the captivating view of the setting sun and returned his gaze to the inside of the plane. A Cessna Citation II, it was small enough for him to touch both walls with his outstretched arms. While it was configured for air medical transport, there were no patients on board today. There was just himself, the two pilots, and the cargo.

Today the cargo was not unusual. While the medical cot held everything required to sustain a patient for a long flight, this one also contained a few modifications. Under the cot and in the overhead areas were several hidden compartments used for smuggling cocaine. The heavy nylon equipment bags with their multiple zippers also held medical supplies if one did not dig too deeply. The bottoms of each were false and also packed with cocaine. It was proving to be one of Angel's best ideas and he had exploited it for some time now. The medical flights occurred every day, and it was normal for them to go to small, rural airports. As a result they raised little suspicion with the authorities or customs officials. They were even given a special designation prefix in their call sign. Any plane flying under "Lifeguard" status enjoyed priority takeoff and landing privileges as well as the briefest of customs inspections. After all, weren't lives at stake?

His eyes fell on the cooler strapped to the cot. It was something that had started about a year ago and so far it had proven to be quite lucrative. Today the cooler was worth more than the entire amount of cocaine on board.

Glancing out the window he could see the lights of the west coast of Florida coming on in the darkness. He pulled the blanket around him tighter as the altitude chilled the interior to a temperature he was not accustomed to. His handheld GPS told him they had another forty minutes or so to go. That meant they would probably start a descent from their current altitude for the landing in Orlando in about ten minutes. He killed the cabin lights so they would not reflect off the cockpit windows before closing his eyes and settling in to wait.

He actually smelled it before the pilots and jerked his head up to sniff again. He looked toward the cockpit in time to see the warning lights and hear the alarm. The smoke coming from the air vents caused him to jump up only to be yanked back in place by the seatbelt. He quickly thumbed on the overhead lights and now clearly saw the smoke entering the cabin. Releasing the belt, he slid down the bench seat and knelt in the cockpit door.

"What the fuck is going on?"

The pilot ignored him while he hit the firewall shut off valve and spoke to the copilot through his headset.

"Venice or Punta Gorda?"

"PGD has a longer runway!"

The pilot flipped switches and turned dials on the GPS navigation system until he saw the graphic for Punta Gorda airport. He then turned to watch his copilot flipping switches, each one shutting off a different electrical component. Despite his efforts, the smoke continued.

"It's not working!"

"It's that damn engine! I told that bastard mechanic there was a vibration and the oil pressure was low. He told me they would get it next month at overhaul!"

The copilot only ground his teeth and continued to flip the switches. The smoke just kept coming, forcing Angel to cover his mouth and nose with his sleeve. His eyes were also beginning to burn and water. The copilot stopped to don his oxygen mask before pulling out their book of checklists. Angel tried his question again a little louder.

"What the hell is happening?"

The pilot turned as if just noticing him.

"There's a fire in the number two engine. We can't stop the smoke so we're going to have to make an emergency landing!"

"We can't do that! Not with this cargo!"

"We don't have a choice, you idiot! Now go strap in and pray that we all live!"

Angel watched the pilot and gripped the cockpit door frame as the plane swung into a right turn. The pilot keyed the button on the yoke and tried to speak clearly into the microphone.

"Miami center this is Lifeguard seven-two-eight-Charlie-David. Mayday-Mayday-Mayday. We are inbound PGD. Fire in engine two with heavy smoke in the cockpit. Three, repeat three, souls on board. Fuel state 4200 pounds. Requesting you roll trucks."

"Eight-Charlie-David, Miami center. Copy your Mayday. We are clearing traffic and contacting PGD. Repeat fuel state and souls on board."

"Miami, Eight-Charlie-David. Fuel is 4200 pounds and we have three souls on board."

The smoke became too much for Angel and he felt his way back to the bench seat. The oxygen masks had been removed to make way for more drugs. A great idea of his at the time. It may kill him now. Idiot. Through watering eyes he struggled with the seatbelt. Before he could fasten it he saw the oxygen port on the cot in front of him. He *was* an idiot. The answer to his problem was right in front of him! He quickly felt for the equipment bags and pulled an oxygen mask from one. Stabbing the tubing onto the Christmas-tree fitting, he reached for the tank valve. Would the oxygen aid any explosion if they crashed? Didn't really matter if he suffocated before they got there, he quickly decided. He cranked the knob until the oxygen hissed into the mask. Slapping it on his head he pressed it tight against his face and took several deep breaths. Only then did he notice that his inner ear was telling him they were in a steep descent. He quickly found the bench seat and strapped himself into it, scooting to the limit of the seatbelt to be near the exit door when the time came.

The lights below them were coming up quickly, but the pilot forced himself to ignore them and concentrated instead on his instruments. The smoke was to the point where it was forcing them into an instruments-only landing. He used the rapidly vanishing view to verify what the GPS was telling him. He made a note of matching the large blue expanse of Charlotte Harbor on the display with the large black area a mile short of the runway. If it all went to hell, he would try to put the plane in the water. It was theoretically a more survivable choice if the landing gear failed to come down. The area around them was too developed, and in the dark he couldn't tell between what was a farmer's cleared field, and what was heavily forested. Either way, it was going to be one hell of a landing. At least the runway was an old military training base from World War II. It should be plenty long enough for what the plane needed. Now if he could just see it through the damn smoke.

"Checklist," he prompted.

The copilot responded with a series of items and they both worked to verify them in what little time they had left. When they got to the landing gear, they both held their breath until the three little green lights came on, granting them a chance at the runway. The pilot allowed his muscles to relax a fraction before leaning forward to see out the cockpit window. They were passing over the harbor and he could see both the runway lights and those of the rescue vehicles speeding down the taxiways.

"Gear down."

"Flaps extended."

The pilot made a few corrections, fighting the single operating engine with the rudder to keep the nose pointed where he wanted it to go. Unfortunately, the strong cross-wind was also a problem as it often was at sunset near the water. He would have to set down the rear gear and then point the nose down the center line before allowing it to touch. Something hard enough to do in the dark, let alone with a cloud of smoke in the cockpit. His eyes were burning and watering heavily.

"You're off heading," his copilot prompted.

"I can't see."

The copilot reached over and wiped the man's eyes with his tie.

"Better."

He felt the burble of ground effect air as it rose off the warm ground and pulled the throttles back more as they crossed the end of the runway. But the smoke had robbed him of his vision and he misjudged the altitude to the point that the plane hit hard and bounced back into the air. He struggled to put it back down but in his haste the nose slewed left before hitting the concrete. Feeling the weight of the aircraft transfer from the wings to the landing gear, the pilot quickly engaged the thrust reversers and brakes while the copilot shut off the remaining engine and pulled the lever for the extinguishers. The thrust reverser engaged as it was designed to, but with only one engine dialing down the result was a further slew to the left. Before the pilot could correct, the gear on that side caught the edge, pulling the small plane off the runway and into the grass.

Angel pushed against the ceiling of the plane with both hands and braced his feet on the medical cot as the plane slid sideways through the turf. The loud cursing from the cockpit only added to the terror of the impact he felt was surely coming.

A loud crack and the scream of tearing metal announced the failure of the left gear. The wing on that side fell into the turf and caused the plane to spin as it continued its journey across the airport grounds. After another fifty meters it contacted a taxiway and the rest of the gear was torn away from the belly of the plane. The plane left the ground again only to come down hard and a large crack in the cabin opened with an explosion of sound. Angel felt himself doused with hot hydraulic oil. Fortunately his thick flight suit protected him from the worst of it, and he yanked his hands away from the opening crack in time to keep them attached to his arms. The smoke quickly cleared as it was sucked out the new opening and Angel was treated to a violent tumbling view of the airport lights before the cabin finally spun to a stop.

He opened his eyes to find himself lying on his back in what was left of the cabin. He soon heard loud diesel engines and voices shouting outside the plane. He moved to try to get up, but was stopped by a sharp pain in his leg. Pulling the oxygen mask away and looking, he saw that the angle of his right foot was not as it should be. Amazingly, it didn't really hurt that much. He gaped at it in wonder until a voice brought him out of his stupor.

"Don't move, buddy, we'll get you out in a minute!"

Angel looked up to see two firemen gazing in through the crack in the side of the plane. He also saw white powder flowing from a crack in the overhead. It settled on his hair and coated his flight suit.

Twenty minutes later he sat on the gurney and watched as the firemen swarmed around what was left of the aircraft. The pilot and copilot were severely injured and had already been flown away by a helicopter. He waited for the inevitable and it didn't take long. Watching as the bags were taken from the plane, followed by the cooler, he barely noticed the needle as the medics started an IV and took his blood pressure. He held the oxygen mask over his face and watched as a state trooper walked around the wreckage with what looked like a plain-clothes detective. The trooper eventually approached the ambulance and without a word handcuffed Angel to the gurney. The detective produced a digital camera and took his picture before speaking to the paramedic.

"We'll be sending somebody in with you."

"Anything I need to know?" the medic asked.

"Cocaine in the cabin with him. A lot," the trooper replied. "We also have this cooler, it's marked Human Organs. I doubt it's for real, but will it hurt anything if we open it?"

"I doubt it. Just close it quick if it's what it says it is. Want me to do it?"

"Sure." The trooper was a bit squeamish about what might be inside.

The medic reached down to his boot and produced a switchblade, something only people in his occupation were allowed to carry, and quickly sliced through the seal. He popped it open, and looking inside, saw two small plastic bags on ice, each holding some dark tissue. He held it open for the trooper and detective to see.

"What are they?"

"Kidneys."

"No shit?"

They all looked at Angel, but he chose not to meet their gaze. He contemplated his deformed ankle instead and silently cursed his luck. The detective took a few shots of the cooler's contents before moving away to have a short conversation with the trooper. Angel watched from his seat on the gurney and stewed. His mind was already looking for a way out of this jam, but the damn leg and the handcuffs were limiting his options.

"You can take him in now. We'll be right behind you."

They called him the Major, despite the fact that he had long ago retired. But in Afghanistan everyone seemed to have a rank or title, and that was his. He now worked for one of the many subcontractors that handled a number of jobs the military didn't wish to. His years in the army had made him fluent in the local language and customs, so he had been hired and given the task of liaison between the Afghan soldiers and the Americans here at this remote base on the Pakistani border. He also looked after their wounded, and if necessary, their dead.

The Major watched through the Plexiglas door window of the multi-bed ER. The building they were in was constructed from a large prefabricated kit. It had been flown out to this remote location in the Abbas Garr by a series of Chinook helicopters and erected in only one day. Its six-bed operating room was tending to only one patient at the moment. A teenage boy who had been brought into one of their remote outposts by his father and a village elder. On first exam the boy was dead, but a more thorough check by the medic in the field had revealed a faint pulse. A collapsed lung and a large amount of bleeding had him close to death before the sucking chest wound was corrected. His strong heart, conditioned by the daily climbs in the mountainous Afghan terrain, was the only thing that had kept him alive through the night. The X-ray on the wall showed some metal in his chest, right up against the aorta, and some extensive lung damage. His odds were not great, but the surgeon was skilled in chest trauma. It was sort of his area specialty.

The metal was most likely American in origin. The report said the only action last night was some mortars being dropped on a suspected insurgent. The boy's clothes reeked of carbon, telling them he had been either firing a rifle, or had been around something exploding. Maybe both. Either way, they had an opportunity to gain some favor with the villagers if they were able to save the boy. If not, they were required to dress and package him for a quick return to his village, where there would be a burial before sunset as their custom demanded.

This custom was something the Major exploited every chance he got. What better way could one ask for to dispose of evidence? He fingered the boy's blood test readout he had pulled from the chart. He would soon enter its information into his computer and email it off. Within a few minutes he would get an answer, along with the plane's availability. He turned to look through another Plexiglas window into the morgue to see his colleague waiting. They exchanged a silent look. They would know soon.

Turning back, he saw the surgeon peeling his gloves and gown off and tossing them into a waiting hamper. The rest of the team were performing a count of all their instruments before two of them would close the boy's chest. The surgeon pushed his way through the door, only to find the Major waiting.

"How's it look?"

"Well, there was a lot of damage. I'm amazed he lasted the night up on that mountain. But the kid seems to have a strong heart. If I didn't know better, I'd say he was at least sixteen. We managed to sew everything up, and as long as the aorta holds, I think he'll make it. We'll know more tomorrow."

"Okay, I'll go talk to his father. What's the kid's name?"

"Khalid."

The doctor turned to leave and the Major looked through the morgue window again to shake his head at his partner. The man silently picked up his blades and put them away. Perhaps tomorrow.

Despite his disappointment, the Major forced a smile on his face before he went outside to talk to the boy's father.

IN EARLY 2011, MORE THAN 110,000 PEOPLE WERE ON THE NATIONWIDE WAITING LIST FOR AN ORGAN. AN AVERAGE OF NEARLY 20 OF THEM DIES EACH DAY WHILE WAITING.

March 2011—News in Health

—THREE—

DR. MATTHEW DAYO PICKED up the chart from the desk in his small office and tucked it under his arm. The chart was thick, as were most of his patients, and he held it under his arm with a practiced motion while reaching for his coffee. He savored the rich brew as he left his office. Coffee at work was a rarity for him as he was usually in surgery on most days and could not afford the slightest tremor in his hands from the caffeine.

Days without surgery were few and far between and he felt odd when not in scrubs. Not one for worrying about appearances too much, he had thrown his white coat on over a golf shirt and a pair of jeans that morning for a day spent in the office pushing paper. But after a few hours he needed to move around and decided to visit a patient or two. As he rounded the corner and stepped from the carpet to the tile floor, his Nike's squeaked loudly, drawing a few looks from passing staff. He ignored them, as his mind was on his patient.

A short walk down the corridors of Johns Hopkins' cardiac wing brought him to a series of glass-walled rooms. He nodded to the charge nurse who was on the phone and got a smile in return. The fifth room held Mr. Hernandez and, as usual, his wife in a chair nearby.

"Good afternoon."

"Hello, doctor."

Dr. Dayo's eyes automatically rose to check the monitor hanging from the ceiling. His patient was still showing a wide rhythm with no signs of improvement, and his blood pressure was lower than he would have liked. He flipped the chart open to the trending graphs and confirmed what he saw. His patient was deteriorating. Despite his poor color and obvious weakness, he managed to put on a show of strength for the doctor. He straightened up in bed and in defiance of his shortness of breath, spoke forcefully, with an attempt to hide his South American accent.

"No news today?"

"I'm afraid not. You've only been on the list a short time. I know telling you to be patient sounds rather foolish, but that's what I need you to be. I have your name in every database there is. Your new heart will come, you must have faith."

"I understand. But…I have always been…a man of action. This waiting…it's not in my nature."

"I can understand that. Just one day of paperwork is about all I can stand. A businessman like you, I would never survive. I don't know how you do it."

"I get out…as much as I can. My company…has many branches. Travel is the…boss's prerogative, no?"

Dr. Dayo had to smile at that. While he was considered among the best in his field, he was still tied to the hospital. Once his youngest was out of the house, he and his wife had some plans to do some traveling, but right now his practice required the majority of his time.

He placed the chart on the bed and donned his stethoscope. Mr. Hernandez leaned forward without asking and took the obligatory deep breaths, getting to number four before collapsing in a fit of coughing, the fluid in his lungs plainly heard. His wife looked away as he spit into a nearby basin before falling back into the bed. The color of his face slowly returned to his current gray and he took the offered mask from the doctor and placed it over his face. Dr. Dayo waved off the nurse who appeared at the door. She checked the monitor before returning to her paperwork.

Dayo waited patiently for his patient to regain his breath. His pulse oximetry rose slowly to the low 90s but no higher. He finally dropped the mask and offered a crooked smile to the doc.

"Not yet."

"No, not yet," the doctor echoed. "I may put you on the bi-pap machine for longer periods though. It will help with the fluid in your lungs."

"Whatever you say, doctor," his wife answered for him.

Doctor Dayo held his patient's gaze until he got a small nod of consent. It had been hard to get his patient to agree to it while he slept, but he seemed to be more pliable now. He picked up the chart to make the required orders. He flipped it shut with a snap.

"I'll check on you again this afternoon. Just don't go anywhere okay?" It was their standard joke.

"I will…be right here," Mr. Hernandez managed with a grin.

"Good man." He patted his patient's leg and with a light touch on the wife's shoulder, left the room.

He stopped at the nurse's station and handed her the chart.

"Some changes, Terra."

"Okay."

As he left, he passed two men entering the unit. They nodded to the doctor and he simply returned it as he knew their English was very limited. Mr. Hernandez's brothers. He was told they visited at least once a day for several hours. All the way from South America. It was good to have close family at a time like this.

He decided to hit the coffee kiosk on his way back to his office. His current cup had gotten cold.

*　　*　　*

Mr. Hernandez nodded to his subordinates as they entered the room. The first approached the bed and looked carefully for any new equipment they had not seen before. The other examined the room closely for anything that could be a camera or listening device. After a nod to each other, the first "brother" spoke.

"One of the medical planes crashed in Florida last night. The shipment was compromised and the courier was arrested."

"Who?"

"Angel."

Hernandez grimaced at this. His best man was in federal custody. He thought for a moment before replying. "Where is he?"

"We're looking right now. We've seen Federal Marshals at the local hospital. I'm sure they will move him soon. He already faced charges in Maryland and the District of Columbia. Most likely he'll be moved there to face a grand jury, or they'll try to cut a deal with him."

"Angel is a good man...but he knows too much. Get Jimmy...have him...take care of this."

"*Si.*"

"The shipment...it contained organs?"

"Some kidneys."

He just nodded before shaking a finger at them. That meant hurry.

"Get me my fucking heart."

One of them left to make a phone call. Any attempt to do so in the room drew the wrath of the charge nurse, and they did not wish to make trouble that would call attention to themselves.

Hernandez sucked on his oxygen while cursing his sick heart and rotten luck.

* * *

Jimmy sat under the shade of the umbrella and nursed a beer. The sun was bright and shining off the multiple wet and constantly moving bodies of the children in the pool. He unconsciously did a count every few minutes as he couldn't keep them all straight. The dog ran circles around the pool for awhile before joining him in the shade for a rest. Like Jimmy, he was too old to keep pace for long. The dog nudged Jimmy's hand for some attention, and he shifted the beer to the opposite hand to accommodate.

One of the boys broke away from the pack long enough to assure he had Jimmy's attention for his next dramatic entrance to the pool. The splash was actually quite impressive while the entrance bordered on painful. But the boy had the energy of a seven-year-old, and was not about to let a little pain stand between him and his fun.

The dog tired and slowly sank to the ground to rest his head, yet he stayed vigilant of the children, and the boy in particular. Jimmy shared lifeguard duty with the dog and knew he could watch the kids by watching the dog if need be. Something he did when he was distracted by other things.

His favorite distraction emerged from the house with two fresh beers in her hand, and Jimmy quickly drained his before allowing it to be replaced. His free hand wrapped around her waist as she glided into his lap.

"He's happy. Thank you for that."

"No problem, you said he earned it."

"He's never had a real birthday party with all his friends before. We never had the room or the money."

"It wasn't hard. I'm just glad I could make it."

"Well I'm glad you could make it, too. Maybe there'll be a chance to show you how much sometime after the party." She leaned in for a kiss.

The kiss was interrupted by his cell phone ringing. She immediately pouted and slid off his lap. He was forced to stand and dig in his pocket to reach the phone. She smiled over her shoulder as she walked toward the pool to check on the kids.

"Stay," he told the dog before walking toward the house. He managed to enter and shut the door, making it much quieter before answering.

"Yeah?"

"We have a job."

"Now?"

"Right now. I'll see you at the garage in an hour?"

Jimmy checked his watch before returning his gaze out the windows. She was sitting on the edge of the pool with her long tan legs in the water. The kids were splashing water and getting her wet. She didn't give it a second thought and played along with them.

"I'll be there."

"Okay."

Jimmy sighed before setting his just-opened beer down on the counter and walking to the window. She soon saw him there and rose to walk around the pool. Before she reached it, she knew. He opened the door for her before moving to where he could see the dog.

"You're leaving?"

"Yeah, I have to go. I'm sorry."

"I understand. He won't though."

"I'll talk to him."

"No, I'll do it. Cody knows what work is, he sees me leave every day. He just doesn't understand how it works all the time. He's too caught up in the party right now. I'll tell him later when he notices you're gone." She rose up on her toes and wrapped her arms around him for a long kiss. He returned it with all he had. She just smiled that smile he couldn't resist before turning to resume her spot with the kids. They never said goodbye. It was something they seemed afraid to do.

The dog watched him leave, but instinctively knowing he wasn't going, he made no move to follow. Jimmy walked through the modest Florida home and retrieved his bag from the bedroom. After adding a few items from the bathroom, and one from under the bed, he left quietly through the front door. Once outside he could again hear the shouts of the playing children. He drove it from his mind long enough to get into the six-year-old Chevy he was driving today.

Twenty minutes later he pulled into a parking garage for long-term vehicle storage. In the back corner he parked the older car next to a new Mercedes AMG. He quickly had the bag swapped into the new car and, popping the trunk, he produced a fresh set of clothes in a higher price range. Once the clothes and shoes were swapped out, he returned to the driver's seat and dug into the glove box. Here he found another wallet that he transferred what cash he had on him into. Pocketing it, he then pulled a newer Rolex out and secured it on his wrist. The last item was hidden in a secret panel in the door, and after triggering the hidden switch, he pulled the black Sig Sauer automatic free. He had just verified that it was loaded and stuck it back in its hiding spot when a black Porsche pulled in next to him. He thumbed the door locks open and waited.

Manuel leaped from the Porsche, wearing a high end casual suit and deck shoes. His hair contained enough gel to hold his curls in place and Jimmy's sharp eyes could see a lipstick smear on his collar. He was fifteen years junior to Jimmy, young, fit, good looking, and thus far the only partner Jimmy had ever worked with that he liked. While still a little cocky and too sure of himself, Manuel was wise enough to see that Jimmy was the only man over forty in their line of work who was still alive. Jimmy also had the respect of the bosses, which was a rare thing. In the last two years that they had worked together, Manuel had learned a great deal, while also developing a healthy respect for Jimmy and his abilities.

He jumped into the passenger seat and tossed a bag into the back seat as Jimmy put the car in gear.

"Got your ID?"

"Yeah, my newest one. Let me adjust this before we go."

Jimmy waited while Manuel tightened the strap on his ankle holster. Only when he was through and they both had their seatbelts on did he pull the car out of the garage.

"Where we headed?"

"North, up the east coast, Baltimore or DC. I'm not sure yet."

Jimmy turned the car in the desired direction and headed for the highway.

"What's the job?"

Manuel tilted his head forward to look at Jimmy over his expensive sunglasses.

"You're not going to like it."

Jimmy said nothing and gripped the wheel tightly with both hands, the blood leaving them made the multiple scars stand out.

* * *

Lenny Hill had been a cop since he was five years old. At least that's when he remembered getting his first badge and gun. A gift from his father, he had worn it for weeks, roaming the neighborhood, arresting his friends and the occasional dog, writing tickets on a notepad and issuing them to neighbors as they drove down their suburban street, and chasing down his friends and having shoot-outs till they were all dead. Born into a family of policemen, he had sat quietly and listened to them talk of investigations and captures, stakeouts and chases, even the occasional shooting. It was no surprise to anyone when he graduated college with a criminal justice degree and applied for the Detroit City Police. A year with the SWAT team and a few more of hard experience followed. Somehow he found the time to complete a master's degree and with his father's encouragement applied for the FBI. Excelling in languages, he soon found himself stationed in the Miami office and working with other government agencies in all types of investigations. A natural diplomat, Lenny was often called upon to negotiate with foreign police forces when their help was needed on a particular case. His linguistic skills expanded to include Spanish, French and German, and he soon caught the interest of Interpol. With some pressure from above, he accepted the position of liaison with the international organization, which ironically involved a move of only a few blocks. That was several years ago and he had worn out four passports since. But the job was never boring for long, just sometimes inconvenient.

"Why does this crap always have to happen at night?" Lenny asked himself.

Even as he grumbled, he knew it wasn't true. The late night calls just seemed to stick in his memory more. He could also argue that the later the call came, the bigger the headache that came with it. Most of his colleagues would readily agree. He was into his twenty-second year as a cop and it was definitely showing. His once dark hair was now peppered with streaks of gray, and the stubble on his face had long since matched. Despite regular trips to the gym, his muscular frame was now showing the beginnings of a spare tire. The scars had weathered a little from the years, but still served to remind others of his days on the force. Despite the damage, he retained the weathered-yet-rugged look that suburban moms found enticingly attractive. Something he would have been surprised to know if he ever took the time to meet one. Work as an Interpol agent just didn't leave much spare time, and after a failed marriage, Lenny had accepted the truth—he was married to his job.

He now gazed through the glass at the man seated alone on the other side. He was the reason he had been awakened at home by both his pager and phone going off simultaneously. That was over three hours ago and Lenny was now on his third cup of coffee. The file he held was thick and still warm from the printer. He had taken all the time he needed to review it carefully while the Marshals, state, and local cops had watched him impatiently from across the room. What they were in such a hurry for, he didn't know. Was he supposed to burst into the room and run a good-cop-bad-cop approach or something? He'd ignored them while he took careful notes on a legal pad. A cigarette burned on the desk next to him despite all the no-smoking signs. It was three in the morning and they had called him, not the other way around. Besides, the man in the interrogation room wasn't going anywhere, at least not soon.

He now took careful stock of the prisoner. The file he had in his hand wasn't entirely new reading to him. He had read it once or twice before. Unfortunately, there were several of its kind and the review was necessary before he spoke with the man.

Angel Sanchez was one of the higher-ups in the Cali cartel. Born in California to illegal immigrants, he was first arrested at the age of fourteen for drug possession with intent to distribute. Getting the usual slap on the wrist three more times before finally serving some time, he eventually graduated to smuggling. Low on education but very street-smart, he was soon moving more product across the border than most men twice his age. Recognizing early that greed is what doomed most of his fellow smugglers, he spread his money around, buying protection and information. When the Mexican Army joined the fight, he was pulled out of the trenches by Oscar Hernandez, head of the Cali drug cartel. He was elevated to chief negotiator with the Mexican gangs that moved product across the border. He also developed the many new methods the DEA had discovered the cartel using over the last couple of years. Tunnels. Cruise ship employees. Submarines, even. The man had a capable mind, which also meant he had to know the depth of his problem right now. Lenny watched him closely. Angel sat quietly without fidgeting. No drum of his fingers on the table or tapping foot under it. The cast on his lower leg was apparent, sticking out of the oversize prison jumpsuit. He had reportedly refused any pain killers after the leg was set. He didn't gaze around the room at the bare walls or stare into the mirror with his tough-guy look as the ignorant gang members often tried. He was simply waiting, Lenny decided, for him.

"Said nothing to nobody huh?"

"Not a word, not even to ask for his lawyer."

"Camera running?"

"Yup."

Lenny took a healthy swig of his coffee before opening the door and walking in. He shut it behind him and nodded at the prisoner as he sat down.

"Hello, Angel."

Angel took his time sizing Lenny up. Even bending down to see what kind of shoes he was wearing. Evidently Lenny passed whatever test he was being subjected to, as Angel chose to speak.

"Who are you?"

"Lenny."

"Lenny," Angel repeated with a smile. "I guess I should say what are you, you don't work here."

"Here? No. You could say I work everywhere. Kinda like you."

"DEA?"

"Interpol."

Angel swallowed that information and Lenny let him digest it for a minute. He could see the wheels turning. He looked at his watch before turning his wrist to show Angel.

"It's been six hours since you crash landed. You think Oscar's worried?"

"Fuck you," Angel deadpanned.

"Not me. You know who's gonna get screwed here, and it sure as hell isn't me. You've had a few hours to think about it. I don't need to explain your options to you, you already know 'em. That's why you didn't ask for a lawyer. You're in the States, so they get you first. After that it's Mexico and then Columbia. But you and I both know you won't last that long. Oscar knows what he has to do. Question is, do you?"

Angel broke eye contact and Lenny had his answer. He kept his poker face on until Angel met his gaze again.

"You've got that kind of pull?"

"Yeah, I can have a federal prosecutor here within the hour and we can cut the deal. You get retirement in witness protection. A new face probably. Some cash. That's it. Beats the alternative by a long shot."

Lenny had the prosecutor sitting outside the door already. The smart ones knew when they were caught. They also knew they were major liabilities for their bosses. Talking down to Angel would just irritate him and really served no purpose. He could already tell that Angel had come to the same logical conclusion that he had. Cutting a deal was the only way that Angel had any hope of living. Even if he were held in solitary, somebody could always be found to get to him. He had to eat. He had to sleep. If he went to jail for any length of time he would quite simply be dead soon after, and he knew it.

Angel stewed for a minute before raising his head to ask a question.

"My wife?"

"Get a new one."

"My money?"

"Gone."

Angel stewed some more.

"I have to stay in the States?"

"That's how it works. the Marshals will take care of all that."

Some more silence. The people on the other side of the glass held their breath.

"What do you want?"

Lenny smiled. "You know what we want. We want Oscar."

It was Angel's turn to smile.

"You already have him."

ORGAN TRANSPLANT WAITING
LIST REACHES HIGH IN U.S.
April 11, 2008—Medical News Today

THE SUN WAS JUST beginning to show in the eastern sky when the cars descended on the hospital from every direction. Officers entered every entrance and fanned out down every corridor. The parking garage and doctors' lot were blocked off by city police, while the Federal Marshals and FBI agents, plus one, entered the main entrance. A bewildered security guard rose from his position behind a desk full of monitors to see multiple badges thrust in his face and a parade of windbreakers bearing the letters of every law enforcement agency he could think of flowing past.

"Critical Care?"

"Fourth floor." He reflexively pointed.

"How about you take us there?"

"All right."

The man led them away through the twist and turns of the old building until they reached a bank of elevators. They filled two cars to capacity, leaving two men behind, and rode up in silence.

"Can you tell me what's going on?" the guard asked.

"You'll know soon enough. Is your hospital chief of staff here yet?"

"I doubt it, but I can call him if..."

"Not yet. We'll tell you when."

"Okay."

The doors opened and they followed the man past another desk and through some double doors. A small waiting room was seen with two Hispanic men sleeping in chairs. The lead man just pointed and four men broke away from the group to detain them. They woke with a startle and the looks on their faces gave them away. The group hurried on, and after several twists and turns came to another set of double doors. Here the security guard hesitated.

"Do all of you really need to go in?"

The lead man pushed past him without a word and they all entered the darkened ward. He was met by several staff members who stopped and stared. The names of the patients and their doctors where written on small dry erase boards outside every glassed-in room. He began scanning the names as he walked along, comparing the picture in his head with the faces behind the glass.

J. Hernandez

M. Dayo

This was it. He looked inside to see a rather ordinary man of about fifty sleeping comfortably in the bed. The monitors hanging from the ceiling providing proof that he still lived. He spotted the man's wife sleeping in a chair off to one side. Pulling a picture from his pocket, he held it up as he slid the glass back. The men followed him in and the wife awoke with a start to see the room full. One of the men motioned for her to remain silent. She did.

The man on the bed seemed to sense their presence and slowly opened his eyes. They were all the proof the lead man needed. It was always the eyes. Surgery could change some things, but the eyes were always the thing that gave them away. The man didn't blink or speak, he simply looked from man to man as if he had been expecting all of this, and they were late.

The lead man reached out and grasp the man's chin, turning his head to the side. The scars behind his ears were plainly seen. He smiled.

"Hello, Oscar. I've been waiting to meet you for some time."

Oscar Hernandez said nothing, but the look on his face was one of intense hatred. It was all he was capable of and he ignored the technician who moved forward and began taking his fingerprints. He instead focused on the man who had addressed him by his true name.

Lenny returned the look without a word.

* * *

Tessa ran the hairbrush through her hair while also talking on the phone and picking out what shoes to wear. Her Facebook page was open in front of her and she stopped brushing long enough to scroll through the new pictures on her friend's page.

"He's so cute! You sure he's not with that bitch Megan anymore?"

This produced a long explanation of the steamy and very public break up witnessed the night before. All caught by someone's smart phone and uploaded soon after. The pictures were making their way around the web at lightning speed.

"Has he updated yet?"

"No, his page still says he's hitched. He may not have gotten on yet today. He works for his dad, you know."

"He has to work? That sucks. I would just die if my dad made me work. Where's he at?"

"You don't know? At the grocery store on Vogle Avenue. He like, stocks shelves or something."

"Yuck, his dad makes him work *there* ?"

"Well duh, his dad owns the place, and about a thousand others just like it."

"Oh, I get it."

"So come pick me up and we'll get some groceries."

"No way."

"Why not? You better get there before that slut Jennie does. You know she'll just flop on her back in front of him if she decides she wants him first."

"I know…she thinks she's Paris Hilton or something."

"So come get me and let's go!"

"It's the opposite way, why don't you come get me?"

"My dad took my keys. I scratched my BMW."

"Again?"

Tessa grabbed the keys to her Mustang and bolted from the room. She still had her iPod nubs in one ear with the phone to the other. The hairbrush stayed in her hand long enough for her to check the results in the hallway mirror before she stuck it in a back pocket and ran down the stairs, through the kitchen, and out to the garage. Her travels did nothing to stop the conversation.

"Okay, that's like twice in two months you've wrecked your car. You've only had your license what, five months?"

"It was the damn mailbox. I didn't see it in the dark, and the garage door thing was not my fault. I didn't know my brother had closed it!"

"Right."

"Like you can talk!"

Tessa ran past her father's Mercedes and her mother's Volvo before getting to her new Mustang. It was blue with a white leather interior—just like she had asked for. Her mother had insisted they buy her the car despite her father's reservations. Her mother had actually tried to talk her into a BMW or a Mercedes, but she'd had her heart set on the little convertible ever since she saw one in a music video. Tessa didn't understand that her mother was trying to keep up appearances through her daughter. So her daughter was now being seen in an American-made car. It was disgraceful.

"It was parked. I didn't hit anything!"

"That's what you told your parents, maybe."

"Shut up!"

She jumped in the car and impatiently waited for the door to open. She used the time to check her makeup in the rearview mirror. The breeze blowing in the open door whipped her long blond hair around her face, and she had to pull the stray strands out of her eyes before putting the car in reverse and backing out. The Maryland suburb was quiet as she pulled around the circular drive and through the gate at the street.

As usual, the car's CD player came on despite the phone in her ear, and she raised the volume of her voice to be heard over it. Turning it off never crossed her mind. She punched the accelerator to get to the stop sign at the end of the street in record time, as was her usual driving habit. After a rolling stop, she punched it again and sped through the curving streets on the way to her friend's house.

"So what're you wearing?" her friend asked.

"My Lucky jeans and those new boots I got last week."

"That'll work. If not, he's blind. He's always checking out your ass in the hallway."

"No way!"

"Yes he does! You're so clueless sometimes."

Tessa laughed and pulled more hair out of her face. The wind was whipping it around constantly. She fumbled with the phone while she searched for her sunglasses in the center console. She braced the steering wheel with her knee so she could use both hands.

* * *

Carl was just pulling his truck up onto the curb to park. It was his fifth year in the landscaping business and he was doing well. So well that he had been working Saturdays just to keep up with the workload this summer. He parked his truck halfway over the curb and lowered his ample frame out with the use of the handle. At least all the extra work was burning off a few pounds, something his wife had commented on yesterday. He stood with the door open while he reached under the seat for his clipboard. Finding it all the way in the back, he was forced to stretch to reach it.

"Let's go, Carl. I told Dawn I'd be home by two," he heard his partner Nick call from the grass on the other side of the truck.

"I'm coming, just a second."

Carl pulled back and looked up the street as he straightened his sweat stained hat. Another truck was approaching from around the curve. It was Kurt Johnson, his competition. They had a friendly rivalry, as there was plenty of work to go around in this upper class neighborhood. They would often get a beer together after a long day and do a little under-the-table price fixing. He waited for him to get closer so he could give him the finger and a smile. It was their traditional greeting.

* * *

Tessa looked up just in time to see the truck parked up on the curb with the driver's door open. She let the car drift to the left to pass without letting up on the gas. Her hair flipped into her eyes once again, but she was too busy with the phone to bother with it.

* * *

Johnson flipped Carl the bird as he rounded the curve. He punctuated it with a honk of his horn as Carl returned the gesture. He returned his gaze to the road, but it was already too late.

* * *

Tessa shook the hair out of her eyes in time to see the approaching truck. Her driving reflexes were not developed enough to avoid the collision. She dropped the phone and grabbed the wheel in time to overcorrect. The Mustang responded instantly to the steering command, and the car slewed to the right, barely avoiding the head on collision.

But there was no where else to go. The car impacted the parked truck straight on, the nose diving under the high rear end and defeating the airbag sensor. The force lifted the rear wheels off the ground and shoved the truck forward several feet. Tessa's size and weight worked to send her chest into the steering wheel before she was thrown down and under the dash. Her head struck the shifter, and she mercifully lost consciousness before the car collapsed around her. Ironically the phone survived the crash and her friend could be heard calling out to her from somewhere in the backseat.

"Tessa? Are you there? How long till you get here?...Tessa?"

* * *

Carl and Kurt pried the door open with a shovel far enough for Nick to squeeze into the opening. Nick's brother was a paramedic, and he knew enough from him to hold the girl's neck straight while he checked her out.

"She's breathing."

"Ambulance is on its way," Carl informed him. He was still shaking from the near miss. He could have easily been between the car and his truck if Kurt hadn't been driving by.

Tessa coughed and blood trickled from her mouth. Nick wasn't sure what to do about that, but he remembered that he couldn't let go of her neck.

"Hope they get here quick. She's bleeding from her mouth."

As if they had heard him, the sirens sounded in the distance.

"Couple of minutes, Nick, just hold on."

Nick looked down at the broken girl in his hands. "You hear that, pretty girl? Just hold on, they're coming," he whispered.

* * *

Senator Remington Lamar of Maryland sat on one side of the large conference room table surrounded by aides. A tall man with steel gray hair and dark intelligent eyes, his name suited him. He looked exactly like what he was—an old money politician from New England. His family had been in politics since the Civil War. Currently, his younger brother and uncle both worked for the State Department, while his nephew was soon to graduate from the naval academy. All of them were ensuring the family tradition would live on for the next generation. Due to this legacy, the senator held power and influence few in his profession could match, which was the reason he had the task before him. It kept him a very busy man. But he had always been busy, first in school, and then in the military. He had followed his years of service with a successful chairmanship of the family business that had made his family even wealthier. He had since traded the business world for government work, first as a governor, and now as a senator in his fourth term.

The pile of paper on the table in front of him had been several months in the making and was nearing the point of being ready. As the head of the committee in charge of overseeing, and now revamping, the Department of Homeland Security, he was putting in the long hours. Projects of this size required help, and the senator liked to surround himself with younger versions of himself, like the man sitting across the table from him.

Although several years younger, Special Agent Jack Randall of the FBI had a career path similar to his. After leaving a family business behind him to join the FBI, he had quickly gained some fame chasing down Mafia heads, serial killers, and terrorists, before advancing to his latest position as FBI liaison to Homeland Security. Senator Lamar had asked Jack only once to come on board, and his combination of law enforcement and business experience had proven him to be the perfect man to help him with the giant undertaking.

"Tell me what we have so far, Jack."

"Well, if we go with the current plan to combine the Border Patrol, Coast Guard, ICE, the TSA, and a big chunk of the DEA, we look to remove several layers of bureaucracy and save billions in the process. We'll have to retire a lot of brass, but that'll free up even more funds for more troops on the ground."

"They're going to argue that it'll create more bureaucracy."

"The old way it would. Whenever they shuffled two decks of cards together, they always kept every one, no matter how many duplicates they had. Nobody wanted to relinquish their kingdom. The plan is to axe all the dead weight during the shuffle and streamline the process, compartmentalizing things for greater efficiency."

"What about the military side?"

"I've been able to find several National Guard and Reserve units that can tie their yearly training in with real-time Homeland Security operations, mostly MP units, Search and Rescue operations, and airborne radars from the Air Force and Navy. The Army Corps of Engineers will be working on the fence for a few years. Border crossing points are being reduced by 20%. The remaining points will be upgraded with more space and equipment. More sniffers, X-ray machines, and dogs. We'll be relying less on point of origin clearances and doing it more at the border. The timeline for the construction phase is three years. That's with projected overruns."

"The drones?"

"Until the question of arming them or not is laid to rest, it's still on the table. Once that's been dealt with, I don't see much of a problem. The cost is minimal for what they do, and it's proven technology. We see about two dozen being deployed. Most on the Mexican border and the Gulf states, less on the Canadian side."

"I'll need the hardware orders to help get it past Congress," the senator mused. "What about the rest?"

Jack pulled another printout from a stack of paper in front of him.

"Looks like at least four new cutters, eighteen V-22 Ospreys, two hundred and four Hummers with the night vision periscopes, thirty-eight Blackhawks, twenty light observation helicopters, a few radar towers and blimps, the two floating oil platforms we got for a song, and the rest is miscellaneous support equipment."

The senator was silent as he scanned a copy fetched by an aide. Jack waited patiently. He knew what the next question would be."

"The budget?"

"Even with the newest additions, if we use the incentive/fine contract I'm proposing, they would have to come in nine months early before we went over budget. I have a spreadsheet that breaks it all down." Jack looked to one of his aides and the man pulled a large printout from his briefcase and placed it on the table.

The senator eyed the two-inch thick document and quickly chose to ignore it for the moment. The restructuring of Homeland Security was a huge project, and he had pulled some of the best people in government to help him with it. He chose to trust his people, but he would review the document later when he was alone and verify what he was being told.

"What about the sectors? Are we still thinking the same number?"

Jack was quickly handed a map with another being sent across the table to the senator.

"Yes. Sector One. Michigan to Maine and down the east coast to Virginia. Sector Two is Virginia to the Florida border. Sector Three is Florida, around the Gulf to the Texas-Mexico border. Sector Four runs the border from Texas to California. Sector Five is the entire west coast plus Hawaii, and six is the Canadian border back to Michigan, and Alaska. All have separate budgets based on need, with a general fund for assets used by all. There will be liaison officers in every sector to ensure the flow of intelligence and communication, as well as coordination with the military and other government agencies."

The senator let his chair fall back as he examined the maps. It seemed like such a simple solution, yet he knew the fight he faced. But this was the time to do it. The American people had let the current president know they were tired of the crime, the drugs, the free social services, and the terrorism all associated with an unsecuredd border. Congress had been dealt a devastating blow in the last election, and as a result, a slew of long-term representatives had been shown the door. The new House and Senate had a lot of young faces who had campaigned on the promise of reform. It was his job, as a veteran of the Senate and head of the committee on Homeland Security, to lead them to the completion of that task.

"Have we forgotten anything, Jack?"

It was Jack's turn to sit back in his chair. His answer was blunt and made the eyes of the senator's aides bug out. It was not an answer one heard in the political arena.

"Yes, sir, a ton of things. We just don't know what they are yet. We'll have to confront those problems when they come up."

Senator Lamar smiled at both the answer and his aides' reaction to it. It was the kind of answer he wished he got more of and the very reason he had asked for Jack's assistance in the first place. When dealing with a task as large as he had, you needed men with integrity that weren't afraid to tell him like they saw it. Jack had integrity in spades.

"Yeah, I'd say that's an understatement."

They each had a good laugh and the aides all looked at their counterparts with unease before the senator stopped and addressed them all.

"Would you all mind? Mr. Randall and I need the room."

Jack placed his hand on his briefcase so one of the aides wouldn't add it to his pile and watched as the table was cleared before they all filed out. The afternoon sun seemed to flood the room now, and Jack relaxed as the senator stood to remove his jacket.

"We need to talk about the political battle for a moment. Don't worry, you won't have to fight any of it. Just leave that to me. First thing I want to hear about is this cartel leader you busted this morning. Is it true he was just over in Baltimore at Johns Hopkins?"

Jack smiled. He knew the senator could use the bust for political points, and at the moment had no qualms about helping him. The man was cleared for the information, so Jack was not in violation by filling him in. He pulled the file from his briefcase and slid it across the table to the senator, who opened it long enough to see the face of a man lying in a hospital bed, before snapping it closed to listen to Jack.

"Oscar Hernandez, head of the Cali cartel. We found him in the critical care unit waiting for a heart transplant. He'd had some serious facial surgery and was posing as a businessman from Mexico. Apparently he has some form of an enlarged heart and will die without a new one. He's been here for a few weeks under another identity."

"Amazing. Desperate times call for desperate measures. I guess his options were pretty limited."

"Not too many places to get a new heart. Kidneys maybe, but not a heart. His blood type is rare, also. AB negative. So I guess he calculated his chances and made the trip."

"How'd he get here?"

"Looks like a chartered air ambulance flew him out of Mexico City. That's as far as we've traced him so far. We're looking into the company, for several reasons."

"Oh?"

"The reason we caught him is that another plane from the same company crashed in Florida. The man on board was Angel Sanchez, a major mover of drugs into the States from Mexico, and a higher-up in the cartel. The plane had some cocaine on board, and some other disturbing items."

"Such as?"

"A cooler with a pair of kidneys inside—human kidneys. The cooler even had the seal of Doctors Without Borders. Calls to them showed no knowledge of the kidneys. The plane was bound for Orlando where two people were waiting to receive them. The doctors were questioned and from the looks of it, they and the hospital all had reason to believe the kidneys came from legitimate sources."

"So what did they do with them?"

"The surgeons did the transplants. But the recipients are under arrest for now. Once they recover, they have some explaining to do."

"The surgeons just did the transplants?"

"Hippocratic oath. You treat the patient in front of you. The kidneys would have been wasted if they had waited much longer. This way the patients live, and we get to question them."

The senator slumped back in his chair for a moment before it dawned on him that Jack hadn't answered his question.

"So how did that translate into Oscar being our guest?"

"Angel gave him up. We cut him a deal and the Marshals have him in witness protection. He's feeding us information on the cartel."

"Just like that?"

"Well, he gets to live, and we give him a new face."

"Worth it," the senator agreed with a frown. "Who turned him over?"

"One of our guys...kinda. His name's Lenny Hill. Since this involves Mexico and Columbia and a few other Central American countries, Interpol had dibs on him. Lucky for us, it happened not far from him. I know Lenny, he helped me with some international law questions I had after the terrorist bombing in Africa. Good guy, good record. I heard he talked to Angel for all of fifteen minutes before he agreed to flip. Now he's picking his brain with some of our DEA guys. If I know Lenny, we'll have all that Angel has to offer before he's done with him. I'll make sure you get copies of the transcripts."

"And then what?"

"We get Angel his new face and stick him somewhere in west Nebraska."

The senator thought about it for a moment. It seemed like a deal with the devil. But he was a politician and he knew that you sometimes had to get in bed with some bad people in order to move forward. It didn't mean that he had to like it, though.

"Can we at least have the surgeon make him butt-ugly?"

Jack smiled at that.

"I'll see what I can do."

"All right."

The senator swept the file up and placed it in his briefcase for review later. He had other things to talk about.

"Let's go down the list of congressman and see where their votes are on our little project."

They were only fifty names into the list when an aide entered the room holding a cell phone.

"What is it?" the senator asked.

The aide approached with a pale face and handed the senator the phone. He and Jack both saw the look, and it was apparent that something was very wrong.

"What's the matter, Susan?"

"It's your wife on the phone, sir. Your daughter...she's been in an accident."

PARENTS PUSH FOR
TEXTING AND DRIVING BAN.

February 2011—CNN

ANITA SAT ON THE floor in the corner of the room as she had become accustomed to doing. She faced the door and its three locks and listened to the noise on the street below, mostly drunk voices, passing traffic and barking dogs. She had tentatively searched the room the day before, holding her ear to the walls and floor, and creeping in her bare feet, praying she would not be heard. Straining to hear over the radio, she heard nothing beyond the talk of her kidnappers in the room next door, and the faint voices coming from the street below.

She had no watch. The only way she had to track the time was the shadow of the window bars from the window slowly crawling across the floor. She sat on the pillow and watched the men's shadows move around under the door. The empty plate and cup sat on the floor by the door, and she waited for them to bring her more food and drink. She'd had nothing but some fruit and a small tortilla the day before, with one glass of water that she had dared to refill at the sink in the small bathroom. The water was not on all the time, something she had learned already. Her captors controlled everything.

Her gaze moved to the bed. She had examined its filthy sheets and blanket and discovered what could only be spots of blood on both. This had sent her into a fit of crying that she had somehow stifled so as not to anger her captors. She could not bring herself to sleep in the bed, and instead curled up on the floor in the corner of the room. What if they came in while she slept in the bed and took it as an opportunity to rape her? They were constantly drinking, and their voices would get louder the longer they did so. Occasionally an empty bottle would strike the door, sending waves of terror through her, but so far they had left her alone. The only questions they had asked were the names of her relatives, and as she answered them one by one, she heard the beeping of her cell phone as they looked the numbers up and wrote them down. After that they had ripped the remaining lengths of tape from her skin and stripped her down to her panties and shirt. They had laughed as she cowered in the corner with the towel over her head, crying and shivering in the night air.

The towel sat on the floor next to her now, and she kept it within arm's reach at all times. She had been warned to immediately cover her head when they knocked on the door and to stay that way until they left. Failure to do so could result in her seeing their faces, and that would mean a certain death. The radio was not to be touched and was on at all times, the constant noise serving to cover any noise she may try to make, as well as keep her nerves on edge.

It worked too well. The previous day she had done nothing but sit in the corner and cry, rising every so often to vomit in the toilet. She retched until she could produce no more, her fried nerves and adrenal glands keeping the torture alive until she had finally fallen asleep from sheer exhaustion.

A loud knock caused her to jump, and she quickly threw the smelly towel over her head before the last lock was thrown open. She heard two sets of feet enter. One stopped and the sound of the dish being collected was heard. The other crossed the room until they stopped in front of her. A hand suddenly grasped her arm at the elbow and she gave an involuntary flinch.

"Relax, I'm not here to hurt you."

The voice was new, younger, and the hand was soft, not rough and callused as the others. A faint scent of aftershave met her nose, and his breath did not smell of alcohol. His hand moved into hers and she allowed herself to be pulled up to her feet.

"I've brought you some gifts."

She allowed herself to be led to the bed, and she sat with apprehension on its edge. Was this to be when they raped her? Her hands trembled.

"I know you're scared, but you shouldn't be. As long as you follow our directions, you'll be fine. As long as your family pays, you'll go free."

"Why are you doing this to me?" she whispered.

"Your father has money, yes? We want it, that's all," the voice replied.

The heavy footsteps returned, and the young man dropped her hand to stand.

"That's everything?"

"*Si.*"

"We're leaving now. The water will stay on for another hour. I suggest you make use of my gifts."

She never saw the man's gaze linger on her for a moment before he spun on his heel to leave.

She heard them leave the room and waited until the last lock was thrown. She smelled it before the towel was off her head.

Beside the door sat a plate of hot food and a large bottle of water. She examined it to find a large bowl of spaghetti and half a loaf of bread. An orange and an apple sat on the floor next to them. The water was still cold. Her mouth watered, and she ate as her hunger dictated and the food was soon gone. She forced herself to leave the fruit until later, and examined the contents of the box while she finished the bread.

Another towel, this one clean. A toothbrush and toothpaste. A bottle of shampoo and a bar of men's soap. A large and warm sweatshirt with a soccer team logo on the front. A pair of pants, too long, but close enough for her to wear. She dug into the box and checked every corner, but that was all she found.

Gathering the items, she stood and walked to the bathroom. At least she could wash the smell of sweat and fear and vomit from her skin. Her belly was full, and she would soon be clean and could maybe, for a moment, not feel like a caged animal.

Maybe.

* * *

Lenny watched through the glass as the lawyer spoke with his new client. The conversation was slow and often interrupted by the oxygen mask. Lenny kept waiting for the man to choke and drop dead, but his wish was never granted. He smiled and waved when Oscar indicated him with a bony finger through the glass. The lawyer followed the gesture and offered a toothy grin to Lenny.

"Smug little bastard, isn't he?" the current Federal Marshal guarding the door commented.

"Yes. That he is," Lenny agreed.

"It's almost like he doesn't believe that he's caught."

"He doesn't. He and his kind know how screwed up our justice system is here. He thinks he can beat this and walk away. They all do. They've been buying judges and lawyers and politicians their whole lives. He thinks that he can throw some money at the right people, threaten a few others, and this will all go away. He may be right. His little finger pointing gesture was just another veiled threat. Pretty soon that lawyer will try to come out here, in his million dollar suit and fake teeth, and threaten me with all kinds of legal action. He doesn't care, as long as he gets paid. But I got a little surprise for him."

"What's that?"

"Patience, grasshopper."

* * *

A few hours later Lenny sat across from Jack in his office at the FBI. They both had their feet up on the desk.

"So he's talking?" Jack asked.

"He's singing loud. We've been arresting people by the droves. We have names of dealers, wholesalers, pilots, boatmen, guards, drivers, mules, lab men...you name it. Tunnel locations, ship's names, money launderers. We've got a grand jury working extra shifts, and the FBI and DEA have every interrogator they have pounding them with questions. Everyone gets the when, where, why, how, and from whom they moved or produced the drugs. The tree has a lot of branches, but the key is Angel. Without him it would all be hearsay. He ties all the others to Hernandez. The transcripts are going to be in the tens of thousands of pages. We may have to cut down some more trees."

"Excellent. I understand Oscar has a new lawyer?"

"Yeah, the Attorney General felt he deserved expert council, so he called Gordon Liebowitz and asked him to serve. He jumped at it. Flew down in his private jet and met with Hernandez this afternoon. It didn't take long."

"I know him. He represented the Mob bosses I dealt with a few years back. He's slick. We'll have to watch him carefully."

"The key will be how the jury comes to view Hernandez. When you look at him, he looks like your ordinary forty-something male. I mean he's even less threatening. He's short, he's got a belly on him, and he's going bald. On top of all that, he's going to die of heart failure soon if he doesn't get a transplant. That's going to garner some sympathy right there. Not to mention he's up against the entire U.S government. Americans love an underdog. How do we convince twelve good men that he's the Spanish Al Capone? And if we do, how do we keep them from being too scared to find him guilty? We're going to present evidence of murder, extortion, assassination of government officials, human trafficking, drug production, and smuggling. This guy had an airliner blown up just to kill three people! He had a soccer player killed for missing a goal in the World Cup! If anybody deserves to rot in hell, it's him. If the jurors aren't scared after hearing all of that, then they're too stupid to be on a jury in the first place."

"So what do you suggest? Send him back to Columbia and let them try him?"

Lenny sighed and reached for his drink on the edge of the desk without taking his feet down. He almost lost his balance, but after grunting with the effort, managed to retrieve the scotch. He knocked it back before replying.

"Three years ago they caught Ruiz, the head of the Medellin cartel. He had a mistress he couldn't stay away from and they caught him with his pants down. He had two judges killed and blew up the courthouse before he miraculously escaped. He sits in his mountaintop mansion now and never leaves. Evidently some kind of deal. We'll never know."

"Mexico?"

"Even worse. So far we have three names in the AFI, the Mexican FBI, and a few more in their government all involved with protecting shipments or outright assistance. Their government is so heavily infiltrated by the cartels they've become a joke. The Mexico border states are like the old west, the only law there are the cartels and their gangs."

"It's a battle," Jack acknowledged. "I'm working on some changes you'll soon see proposed in some bills."

"I hope they're serious changes. Anything else is just a waste of time and money."

"What do you think of the legalize drugs theory?"

Lenny grimaced at that and leaned even farther back in the chair. He sat for a moment before dropping his feet to the floor and sticking out his empty glass.

"I'm gonna need more scotch if you want to talk about that."

Jack poured another finger in his glass without a reply.

Lenny squirmed in his chair while he formed his thoughts. He had known Jack for a little over two years or so, but they had developed a good friendship and a mutual respect for one another. This wasn't their first time drinking in his office, and he'd had dinner with him and his wife a few times. It was long enough to know that Jack wasn't a political creature. All of which meant he could speak freely and it wouldn't leave the room.

"We're going to have to legalize dope."

Jack's expression didn't change. He had come to that same conclusion himself since he had gotten involved in the homeland security project. To those who had never really educated themselves on the problem, it was blasphemy, an idea so outrageous it was immediately dismissed as ludicrous. To those in the know, it was the only way to win the so-called War on Drugs.

"We have to get the big money out of the equation, and the only way to do that is to legalize it, tax the hell out of it, and stiffen the penalties for offenses related to the use of it. Once the money is no longer a factor, you lose the turf wars, the gang warfare, the theft and robbery associated with it. The purity levels can be regulated, and that'll diminish the threat of overdose. We could take the forty-plus billion we waste every year fighting the war and put it toward education and treatment. We could fund testing for employers, and they can keep their policies on hiring anyone found to be using. If we mirror the alcohol laws, it would be hard to set any court precedence that didn't already exist. It's actually hard to find a reason *not* to do it, other than the associated stigma and the general lack of knowledge on the subject by Joe the voter."

"How much would we gain by taxing it?"

"It's estimated to be as high as forty billion a year. Add that to the forty billion saved in police and prison costs and you have a sum that gets the attention of the politicians. And right now the country could use an extra eighty billion or so."

"Wouldn't there be an increase in the number of users?"

"A very small one, maybe, comparable to the slight increase in drinkers following the repeal of Prohibition, but people aren't going to run out and start shooting heroin just because it became legal. The recovered addicts will say we're idiots."

"And the treatment centers will say they're treating them anyway.

What would the cartels do?"

"Fight it. It's the last thing in the world they want. They would funnel all the cash they could to anyone willing to speak out or vote against it. It would destroy their business overnight and they know it."

"Wouldn't there still be a black market?"

"Nah, do you see a black market for beer? How about liquor? Legalization would just pull the price so low that there would be no reason for a black market. There'd be no profit in it, a waste of time. No huge profits means no business. There's no need for dealers, no more shoot-outs over territory, no cops or judges being corrupted. All of the inner city kids who fall into the business now have to find legitimate employment. And we could refocus the prison system to boot."

"How so?"

"The last numbers I saw said something like sixty percent of federal prisoners were in for drug-related offenses. But you and I both know that hardly any of them serve their full sentence due to overcrowding. With the drug related prisoners out of the way, the rapists, murderers, robbers, sex offenders, child molesters, drunk drivers, and thieves can actually serve their full time. We can also make the penalties for drug related crime really stick. Driving under the influence of drugs or alcohol can now have a penalty that's worthy of it. Commit a crime under the influence and some time can be added. It would work to change the mindset of the casual user, which should have been our target all along."

"You think we should hit the demand side of the equation more?"

"Absolutely. Even if we don't end up legalizing dope. We've been gearing everything toward the supply side since we started. The casual user accounts for the largest portion of drug money by far. They're the people putting the big money into illegal drugs. You will *never* make any headway if you ignore the demand side. If the casual user knew he'd lose half his assets, his car, his career, and a serious chunk of his freedom, he'd think twice about those few lines he does on the weekend."

They sat in silence for a few moments and sipped their scotch. Both of them were thinking the same thing. The politicians would never have the balls to propose it.

"Sucks, doesn't it?" Lenny stated, not really expecting an answer.

"Yup."

"If it was 1920, we'd both be committing a federal offense right now."

They both fell silent as they contemplated the drinks in their hands. It seemed silly, yet it was true. Jack broke the silence.

"What do you think we should do with the extra eighty billion?"

Lenny didn't have to think about it.

"Spend it fighting big tobacco. Fucking things are killing me."

* * *

The Major watched through the window again as the nurse injected something into the boy's IV line. Miraculously, he was still alive and even showing some signs of improvement. He made a note in his ever-present notebook before spinning on a heel to return to his small office. There he saw the company mortician waiting for him. He shut the door behind him and rounded the desk to his chair.

"What is it?"

"Do we have anything?"

"Not right now. What's your hurry?"

"I only signed up for a year in this mountaintop hell. I'd like to make my pile before the time runs out."

"You and me both, but the customers just aren't placing orders. This isn't fucking McDonalds here, ya know."

"I know that. But you're telling me we got nothing pending?"

The Major pulled out the notebook and leafed through it.

"We need a liver, type A, but the only one we got in there is damaged. If he dies we can harvest what's left and sell it maybe. But the customer is at the edge of the time allotment. It'd be a gamble. The kid is AB negative and I've got a few customers with that blood type waiting. We need a heart and two kidneys. Problem there, is he's improving also. There're only five Afghans on the ward right now. Not a lot to choose from."

"There're about a dozen Americans."

"No way. Don't even think it. Every troop that leaves here dead gets an autopsy as soon as he hits the ground at Dover. Afghans are our only choice. I want to be able to enjoy my money when I get back to the world."

"Yeah...I guess. Just hate the waiting."

"Look at it this way. It's a war, you shouldn't have to wait long."

The mortician thought about it while he contemplated the notebook lying on the desk.

"Maybe we can speed up the process another way."

* * *

The senator and his wife waited in the surgical waiting room with all the other worried people. Most were there for surgeries that had been planned for some time. They read magazines and watched the TV mounted on the wall. A corner table held a large puzzle, and a father and his son worked the pieces together while they waited for news of the boy's mother. There was little conversation, and the elderly volunteer sitting in the corner quietly fielded call after call from family members looking for updates on the progress of their loved ones. He was an expert at telling them nothing, as the new privacy laws prevented him from easing their tension and worry over the phone, but he managed to do it in a way that was both polite and respectful.

Rita Lamar contemplated the carpeted floor while she waited and managed to form the opinion that it was the most dreadful pattern she had ever seen, before her thoughts returned to her daughter lying in the room down the hall. She had gotten the call from the paramedics who had found the number in her daughter's recovered cell phone. Thankfully she had been out shopping with a friend who drove her straight to the hospital. There she had not even seen her daughter as Tessa had already been rolled away for emergency surgery. Rita had clung to her friend until her husband's arrival, and despite who he was, they were unable to get any more information. The nurse had simply replied with what she could read off the chart—chest and head trauma. Just what did that mean? The hours crept by agonizingly slow, and their cell phones never stopped ringing until they both finally just turned them off.

The phone in the corner rang again, and after a short and quiet conversation, the volunteer hung up and approached them.

"Senator Lamar?"

"Yes?"

"Your daughter is out of surgery. The doctor will be here shortly to talk with you. If you would just follow me, please?"

They rose silently and were led away. The others waiting all watched with stoic faces, as if they were being led to their own deaths. The fear gripping their hearts tightened as they were placed in a small private room by the volunteer. It was a room where one received bad news and Rita gripped her husband's arm as they sat on the cheap couch.

A polite knock preceded the arrival of the doctor. Rita's first thought was that he was too young, barely thirty years old, until she saw his eyes. They revealed an age beyond his physical years. He looked tired, both mentally and physically. The scrubs were sweat stained, and the booties he wore on his feet over the tennis shoes revealed blood stains. He crossed the room and offered a hand and a smile. Her heart leaped at that. Her mind screamed for information, while her heart dreaded what news this man was about to bring.

"Mr. and Mrs. Lamar? I'm David Balzano. My team and I have been working on your daughter."

She's alive! She felt the fear that gripped her lessen slightly. She forced herself to wait while the man fell into the chair across from them.

"Your daughter is alive, but her injuries are quite extensive. She was brought into our trauma unit by helicopter and we quickly moved her to emergency surgery due to her injuries. She was unconscious at the scene, and we've determined that to be from a head injury. The CT scan showed a concussion with only minor injury to the skull, a nasty cut and some bruising. We ran a complete head injury protocol on her and found nothing to be overly concerned about. We don't feel that the injury is a danger at this time."

He paused as he tried to stifle a yawn and they waited again.

"I'm sorry. Both of her legs are broken." His hands became animated and pointed out the areas he was describing on his own body. "The right leg has a mid-shaft femur fracture that will require surgery at a later date to set. The left leg has both the tib and fibular bones fractured. Both legs are immobilized and we also feel they will heal just fine."

The doctor paused to take a deep breath. He removed his skull cap and used it to wipe his hands. They braced themselves for the worst news.

"The medics at the scene estimate she was traveling over thirty miles per hour when she hit the truck. Evidently it was parked up on the curb and the car wedged itself under it for a few feet. As a result, the airbag did not deploy in time, and your daughter was thrown forward into the steering wheel. She wasn't wearing her seatbelt, and without the restraint, she suffered major chest trauma."

Rita let out a sob at the news and her husband gripped her hand tighter.

"All of the ribs on the right side are fractured as well as five on the left. It's what we call a flailed chest. She suffered extensive internal bleeding, a punctured lung, and a ruptured spleen. She coded shortly after arrival due to blood loss, but we were able to replace it and restart her heart. She can't breathe on her own, so she's currently intubated and on a ventilator. We removed the spleen and stopped all of the internal hemorrhaging, but what worries me now is her heart."

"Her heart?"

"Yes. She suffered what we call a myocardial contusion, essentially a hard blunt impact to the heart, and it's now severely bruised. Like any muscle that suffers such a blow, it swells. Right now it's functioning enough to keep her alive, but the injury is severe. The swelling may interfere with the normal beating of her heart, as well as its chemistry while her body works to repair the damage."

"How bad is that?" the senator asked.

"It can cause heart attacks or dysrhythmias if the muscle is damaged enough. It can also lead to bleeding into the pericardium, the sac surrounding the heart, which would have to be drained as the blood would place pressure on the heart, as well. She'll be closely monitored around the clock. If she starts showing signs of heart failure, the only option may be a transplant. Let's just hope it doesn't progress to that. On the plus side, she's young. Kids have a miraculous healing ability. One of my teachers used to say if the pieces are all in the same room, you still have a chance, and he's right. We'll know more in the next twelve hours or so. Until then, we wait."

"Can we see her?"

The doctor shook his head. "Not right now. She's in the recovery unit and we keep it as sterile as the operating rooms. Once we move her out of there and into the ICU you'll be able to visit for short periods. There'll be a strict protocol for you to follow to keep her safe from infection. My nurses will walk you through it."

Dr. Balzano looked them over as they absorbed the news. The father looked like he was okay, but the mother was barely keeping herself together. He decided he'd put in a call to Susan, the hospital's grief counselor, and have her pay them a visit.

"Folks, I know what you're going through. Nobody is ready for a day like today and I know I've painted a pretty bleak picture here, but I want you to know that your daughter is getting the best care there is. This hospital pioneered trauma medicine decades ago, and it's still the leader today. She's getting the benefit and experience of all those years."

The senator and his wife perked up only slightly at that. He managed a nod.

"I'm sharing care of your daughter with Dr. Fong. He's one of our cardiac surgeons and very experienced. He's also a good friend. He'll be contacting you shortly."

"Thank you, doctor."

"Okay, well I'm going to go check on her progress. Someone will be here soon to get some information from you and set up some contact numbers so we can stay in touch. We offer a website that you can use to give out information to those you give a password to. We find it helps keep family informed without you having to spend all your time on the phone."

"Can you get some security to keep the press away?"

The question caught Dr. Balzano off guard.

"I'm sorry?"

Out of habit, the senator stuck out his hand. "I'm Senator Remington Lamar of Maryland."

Dr. Balzano shook the hand automatically.

"I'm sorry, sir, I didn't have time to read your daughter's file, and I just didn't recognize you."

The senator waved it away as irrelevant.

"I'll notify security to keep an eye out."

"Thank you."

Rita's self control finally ended and she broke down crying. The doctor left them alone in the room and walked down the hall toward the recovery unit. His fist tightened on the surgical cap in his hand.

A senator's daughter? Add that to the drug kingpin upstairs and this place was becoming a real zoo.

He changed directions and found his way to his office. He needed to unwind a little. The five hours of surgery had put a crick in his neck and he wanted some time in his chair. As he passed through the outer office he was surprised to see Janice still there. She gave him her questioning look as he walked past.

"Can you call security and have someone keep the reporters away from the senator and his wife, please? We'll need someone outside the ICU also. I just need my chair for twenty minutes."

She didn't bother answering. She had been there long before him and knew each doctor's routines. She had already picked up the phone by the time he closed his door.

He ignored the clutter that dominated his office and pulled some files from his chair and tossed them on the floor next to his Box. The chair had heat and massage, and he'd had it delivered on his first day to everyone's amusement. Soon they were envious and a few more just like it could be found throughout the building. After arranging himself and turning it on, he felt the stress beginning to subside.

While his body relaxed, his brain was not in the mood. He found himself looking at the Box on the floor. He liked to keep the things he pulled from peoples' bodies—he used them when he taught classes to young surgeons. Mostly metal, they ran the gamut from lawnmower blades to street signs. There were a couple of arrows. A piece of fence. A carabineer. A fork. A prop from an RC plane. Some rebar. An axe handle. They all had their own unique story of how they got to be inside a living human, and how he had gotten them back out.

Today was different. Nothing had penetrated the girl's body today, yet the damage was just as severe. The patient would take some close watching from both him and Dr. Fong, if she was going to make it. He forced the thoughts from his mind and leaned the chair farther back. He needed twenty minutes of rest before he went back to the ICU. He made sure his pager was on his chest before he allowed himself to fade out.

REPUTED COLUMBIAN DRUG CARTEL LEADER
IS ORDERED DETAINED BY JUDGE IN N.J.

February 3, 2010—The Associated Press

—SIX—

ANITA'S PARENTS FOLLOWED THE detective through the madhouse that was the headquarters of the Mexican AFI. Despite the many ceiling fans hanging over them, the air was thick and humid with the smoke of multiple burning cigarettes. Dressed in a cheap suit, and already stripped of his tie and jacket, the detective wove through the crowd with a practiced ease until he arrived at his desk. Here he stole some battered chairs from his neighbors and offered them to the harried couple. Rounding the desk, he fell into his own ancient chair and let it fall back to the limit of its capabilities. The chair complained with a loud squeak that they barely heard over the multiple conversations and ringing phones echoing in the large room.

"You say your daughter has been kidnapped? How do you know this? Are you sure she's not off somewhere with a young man, perhaps?"

The father felt his blood pressure rise, but fought to keep his cool.

"I know my daughter. She's not one to take off on her own, and there was no boy in her life. Her friends tell us there was no one she was seeing. They say she left them at a café in the mall and went to the car and never came back. A man saw her get pulled into a van. We've been calling for two days and no one has bothered to come by. The police haven't even questioned the witness. What the hell are you people doing?"

"I am…not surprised."

"You're not…what the hell?"

"Mr. Perez. I can tell you this, you are far from being alone in this situation. Across Central and South America kidnappings happen by the thousands every year, over five thousand in Mexico alone last year. If this was Columbia it could be for propaganda, or to fund terrorist purposes. Maybe they wish to have one of their own released from prison? You are not a politician but a businessman, so I am comfortable telling you that your daughter was taken for one thing only. Money. This is nothing but a business deal for them, and one that has become very profitable. That is good news, as they'll be reluctant to kill her. She is worth nothing to them dead."

"So how do we get her back? Who do we talk to here?"

"Here? You are talking to me now, yes? As for what we can do for you, I'm afraid there is very little."

"Very little? You could have people out looking for her!"

"That is what you don't want anyone doing. If we were to somehow stumble onto where they were hiding her, they would most likely kill her before any rescue could happen. No, you don't want that."

"The army?"

The detective smiled at the man's ignorance.

"The army is rather busy fighting the narcos. They have no time for one girl. And if they did, they would go in with guns blazing. Your daughter would not survive. Besides, most kidnappers are tied to the cartels. It is sort of a side business for them."

"Why haven't they called?"

"Most likely they are still on the move. They're asking her questions to get a better idea of how much money you are worth. When they're ready, you'll get a call, and when it comes, you need to be ready."

"I don't understand. How can we be ready? You've told us nothing, and you say you can't help us. How're we supposed to be ready?"

The detective let his chair fall forward and opened the top drawer of his desk. It was as cluttered as its surface and he rooted around until he found a stack of business cards wrapped in a rubber band. He rolled it onto his wrist before fanning them out in his hand. After a quick search, he pulled one from the pile and offered it to the father.

"What is this?"

"His name is Luis. He's a negotiator. I've worked with him before and he's very good. Call him, he'll tell you what you need to do. If he needs my help, tell him to call me and I'll do what I can."

"That's it? That's all you can do?"

"Look around you, Mr. Perez. Do we not look busy enough for you? Call the man. He can help you more than I."

Accepting the fact that they would get no further help here, the couple rose and with a look of disdain, the man took the card before leading his wife away through the crowd. Once they were lost in the confusion, the detective reached for his phone.

"Yes?"

"The parents just left. I gave them the card and the usual story. I would expect a call very soon."

"Good."

"They're worth more than the last one. I can expect my share to increase?"

"You'll get what we agreed on and no more. Send the medic to the house tonight. Tell them we need the full package."

The detective's happy tone was checked by the rebuke. For a moment he had forgotten who he was working for.

"I'll call him right now."

The call ended without a reply and the detective dialed a new number from memory.

"Yes."

"They need you tonight. He wants the full package."

"I understand."

* * *

The Major watched as the team stopped their actions and the doctor checked the time.

"16:42."

The nurse wrote it in his notes at the same time as the Major. The doctor shook his head in disgust. He had thought the man would pull through. He turned to see the Major waiting.

"He's all yours now. Sun will be down in a few hours, you'll have to hurry. I'll go talk to his commander."

"We'll get him ready quick."

He watched as the team removed all the debris left behind after they ran a code. The tube was pulled from the man's throat and the syringes all counted. The Major moved in to roll the man out on the gurney and the team made room for him, all of them wanting the evidence of their defeat gone as soon as possible.

He pushed through the double doors of the medical unit and quickly entered the morgue. Here he found his partner waiting with the autopsy table already set up. They quickly moved the Afghan soldier's body to the table and positioned him with his head in the clamp. The man wasted no time and placed a cooler full of dry ice on the floor next to him. He pulled out a scalpel and began the Y incision. The body wasn't even cold yet, but he was already behind.

"Time of death?"

"16:42."

The man glanced at the clock on the wall between incisions and speeded things up.

"The plane is already on its way. It was at another base north of here. Should be about thirty minutes."

"Just the liver and the kidneys, right?"

"That's it. His blood type isn't a match for the heart we need."

The mortician did some quick calculations before speaking.

"It'll be close. Get the funeral linen ready. We'll have to wrap him quick if they want him tonight."

"The doctor's talking to the guy's commander, but his village is close. They probably will want him tonight."

"Well then quit jawing and get your hands dirty."

He sliced his way through to the abdominal cavity and began removing bowel. The smell was overpowering, but the man had gotten past that years ago. He would slow down when he got to the liver, as it required some finesse.

The Major locked the door behind him and pulled the shade down over the window before moving to one of the cabinets against the wall. He pulled out a sealed package of white cloth that had been approved by the Afghan government for the wrapping of the bodies of their dead soldiers. Unlike the Americans, they received no embalming or dress uniform before burial. While their religion didn't forbid an autopsy, it did call for a simple cleaning of the body before being wrapped in clean white linen for burial without a casket. Something his company was contracted to do.

The Major opened the package and spread it out on an adjoining table. It had to be applied in a certain way, so as not to show the large crude stitches left by the mortician's handiwork.

Despite the air conditioner, he started to sweat. A glance at the clock showed only twenty minutes left until the plane arrived. He preferred to meet them on the tarmac, but today they may have to wait for him. Waiting meant a greater chance of conversation with the ground crews. It was better if they just landed, fueled, and took right back off, the shorter the time on the ground the better.

He looked across the room to see his partner elbow deep in the body of the Afghan soldier. He was sweating as well.

It was going to be close.

* * *

Anita sensed a change in the conversation outside the door. Normally loud and brash, it had been hushed for the last hour. The TV they watched constantly was also louder. She strained to hear what they were saying over the sound of the radio, but was unable to make it out. Clearly it was something they didn't wish her to hear, and this set both her mind and stomach in motion. The fear ratcheted up as her mind filled itself with thoughts of what they could be discussing. Where they planning her death? Her rape? Was she going to be moved as she had heard them discuss before? It dawned on her that they had not been drinking today, and this only added to the mystery.

The sound of a door slamming shut on the lower floors made her jump and she heard the men scramble to their feet. Someone was arriving, someone important.

The squeaky steps and heaving footfalls announced the presence of not one, but two men. They were greeted with respect and another hushed conversation took place near the blaring television.

"...take at least three of each."

"...after I...what I need."

The sound of a weapon being cocked sent her stumbling back from the door and she retreated to the far corner with her towel. Her heart raced and she fought back the bile rising in her throat. The urge to gag had just subsided when a loud knock on the door caused her legs to fail her. As the locks were turned one by one, she managed to grope for the towel and throw it over her head.

The door opened a few inches while the first man peered in to see if the towel was in place. Once he saw her cowering in the corner, he entered, and she heard several footsteps follow. She trembled as they approached.

The lead man smiled at her fear. He enjoyed this part.

"Stand up."

"W-What do you want?"

"Stand up!"

She rose on shaky legs. The tears flowed from under the towel.

He grabbed her arms and roughly spun her around till she faced the wall. She cried out as he twisted her wrist.

"Be quiet! We are going to remove the towel and put a smaller blindfold on you. You will shut your eyes and not open them until we say. Do you hear me?"

"Y-yes."

A hand roughly gripped the back of her neck and she felt the towel pulled from her face. She didn't dare turn her head, and held as still as she could while hands placed thick wads of cotton over her eyes before a long strip of black cloth was wrapped around her head and tied.

"Tighter."

The blindfold was given another yank and knotted off before the hand on her neck was removed. The pain remained, and she knew her neck was bruised from the rough treatment. She hoped that was the end of it as one of them turned the radio volume even higher.

She was lead toward the door, but halfway there hands seized her and a rag was stuffed into her mouth before she could cry out. She felt herself lifted and flung onto the bed.

This was it, she thought. They were going to rape her.

She struggled futilely against their grip until she felt something round and cold against her head. She immediately stopped as the barrel of the gun pinned her head to the pillow.

"Hold still, little girl, or I will make you very dead, very quickly."

To her surprise and confusion, her clothes stayed on, and she only felt the odd sensation of her arm being exposed as someone ripped the sleeve of her sweatshirt open to her armpit. She felt a gentle hand caress her arm before the others tightened around her biceps.

The sting of the needle caused her to flinch, but the movement was checked by the strong hands holding her. The needle burned for some time as the hands performed their task. She heard the ripping of tape and felt the needle being removed, only to be replaced with a small bandage.

What were they doing? Why did they want her blood? The thought died as she was again yanked to her feet and walked to the wall.

"Are you ready?" she heard the man ask another.

"Yes."

The rag was yanked roughly from her mouth and she had time to take half a breath before a fist slammed into her stomach, driving the wind from her. She sank to the ground and gasped for breath only to have her head snapped back by another blow to the face.

"Again!"

The unseen fist came from the right this time and connected with her eye beneath the blindfold.

"Again!"

The fists continued to rain down on her face and head and she rolled on the floor in a futile attempt to avoid the blows she could not see coming.

"Enough."

She was allowed enough time to regain her breath and she sucked in the cool night air in deep ragged breaths before being dragged back up against the wall. They left her seated and the unseen hands worked to prop her against the wall, turning her toward the room.

The leader approached and grabbed her swollen face in his hand, turning it left and right as he examined his handiwork. A trickle of blood poured from her nose, as well as her mouth where she had bitten her lip. The bruises were already beginning to swell her eye shut.

"We wait one minute," he announced.

Anita could not help but whimper at the remark. One minute until what? Her death? Further beating? What did they want from her? The adrenaline and fear soured her stomach and she vomited onto the floor. The men stepped back to avoid the mess. One of them laughed at her reaction.

"Stand back. Move that light over here. Be still, little girl, and hold this."

She felt something thrust into her hands. Despite her confusion, she recognized it immediately as a newspaper. She was guided by their hands into holding it against her chest with her bound hands showing. The barrel of the gun was back against her temple, and she held still as ordered.

The sound of the camera sent waves of relief through her body, and it was all she could do to hold herself up for the six quick shots. The gun was soon removed and the men filed out of the room. She collapsed onto the floor and sobbed uncontrollably.

Part of her stayed alert enough to hear the return of footsteps and she froze in place, awaiting another blow to the face. Instead she smelled the cologne of the young kidnapper who had spoken to her previously. She felt his hands as they cut the tape from her wrist and sat her up. He wiped the vomit from her face and hands before placing a towel full of ice in them.

"It's over. They won't be back."

He guided the towel to her face, and she held the ice there until the pain subsided.

"I want to go home," she whispered to him.

"I know, I know. With luck, this will be over soon. They won't hurt you again. They just needed the pictures."

"Why did they have to hit me?"

"The pictures must be…convincing."

They sat in silence for a moment and he reached out to stroke her hair as she quietly cried behind the blindfold. He pulled his hand back as someone entered the doorway.

"That's enough. Let's go."

"I'm coming."

The young one grasped her hand and placed two small objects in it before he silently departed. She kept her fist closed until she heard the three locks engage and only then did she slowly untie the blindfold and pull the multiple wraps away from her eyes. She was blinded by the light of the lamp that they had aimed at her for the pictures, but averted her eyes to reveal what was in her clenched fist.

Pills.

For pain.

She held them in her hand and wept. The tears continued as she crawled across the floor to the bed and pulled the blanket down to her. Wrapping it around herself, she curled herself into a ball and cried some more. The tears continued until sleep finally overcame her, and she slept the deep sleep that only a survivor knows.

The ice melted on the floor beside her.

MEXICO HOLDS DRUG SUSPECT
ACCUSED OF GRISLY TACTICS
January 13, 2010—New York Times

—SEVEN—

THE APPROACH INTO MIAMI airport was uneventful and they gazed out the window of the plane as it banked over the neon glow of South Beach. As usual, they did not wait for landing clearance as their Lifeguard call sign, used by all air-medical planes, placed them first in line. They could see several airliners circling like vultures as they waited for their turn to land, but the small plane ducked under the mob and lined up on their approach vector quickly.

Their biggest delay was the fault of the wind. The planes were landing from a direction that put them a long taxi away from the customs offices, and they readied themselves as they bumped over the expansion joints of the still warm taxiway. The scream of jet engines sounded repeatedly over their heads as the heavy traffic continued.

But their Lifeguard status even worked on the ground, and they didn't even slow as a 747 stopped on its way to the runway in order for the small plane to taxi past. Soon they passed the freight haulers where FedEx and UPS fought for space. Once past them, it was a short trip to the Customs ramp.

Nothing more than a small modular structure, it sat on the apron like an afterthought. There was plenty of room tonight, and the pilots had no problem turning the plane all the way around so it faced the taxiway they had just come from.

"Everybody ready?" the crewman asked as he stuck his head in the cockpit.

"We're good up here. Just pop open the door and sit on the floor. It's the only way they'll see you from this distance."

"All right, just be ready."

The crewman retreated back into the plane and pulled the pin out of the door handle before working the two-step lever to open the door. The seal cracked with a pop and the warm humid Florida air quickly sucked what remained of the air conditioning out the open door and into the night. The crewman sat on the door step and adjusted his surgical mask. He couldn't help scanning the area for approaching DEA officers, but soon shook himself out of it and focused on the presentation he was trying to project.

"Ready for what?" the pilot wondered out loud to his partner in the cockpit. "We're bingo on fuel. We can't just hop over to the runway and fly away. They'd be all over us before we got to the first taxiway. This is all on him. We've got nowhere to run. Either this works or we're screwed, that's all there is to it."

The copilot just offered a loud sigh for a reply. Their job right now was to just keep the cockpit lights on so the customs man could see them when he approached. That was all for right now. He was aware of the dangers, and bitching about it wouldn't help.

The crewman tried to be casual and do some paperwork while also keeping an eye on the customs station door. It soon opened, and an overweight, tired looking agent emerged and started their way. As the crews were not allowed to exit their planes until they had been inspected, the agent had no choice but to go to them. So he covered the distance with long strides, looking to get the inspection over with quickly so he could get back to the movie they had playing in the office.

"Come on, you fat idiot, just look over here," the crewman muttered as he watched him approach.

Eventually the agent did just that. Cautiously he slowed his pace and changed directions in order to better see the men in the cockpit. What he could make out stopped him in his tracks.

The plane's crewmembers were all wearing surgical masks on their faces. Something he dreaded seeing as it seemed to be happening more and more lately. He circled to the right and held up his clipboard to shield the airport lights from his eyes. There was a crewman sitting in the door wearing one, too. That usually meant that the patient they had on board had some kind of nasty disease. Something he wanted no part of. He stopped and filled out the form on his board without getting closer. After that he pulled a pair of latex gloves from his pocket and slipped them on.

"Atta boy, you dumbass." The crewman grinned behind his mask.

The customs man was angling for the front of the plane where a small pop-out window was used by the pilots. He silently took the forms the pilot offered, and with barely a glance copied down some numbers before quickly handing his own form back. With the noise on the apron as loud as it was, he would have had to get close to the window to converse with the pilot. Obviously that was not going to happen tonight.

The customs man finished their silent transaction, and with a salute of his clipboard waved them on, heading back to the office to find a bottle of hand sanitizer. The crewman wasted no time in closing the door to the aircraft as the pilot slipped the brakes and headed for the fuel point. They all shed their masks as soon as they were clear of the customs ramp.

Another load of drugs and organs had just entered the United States.

* * *

"That's him."

Jimmy took a good look at the man crossing the street toward the parking ramp and compared it to the picture in his hand.

"I think you're right. Say hello to Lenny."

Jimmy squirmed in his seat to get the blood flowing back into his sore ass. After the long drive up from Florida, he and Manuel had found a decent hotel for the night and caught up on their sleep. The envelope with the picture and a short file on the man had been waiting for them at the front desk when they had checked out. He didn't know who had sent it, or where it had come from, and he really didn't wish to. The information had always been accurate in the past and that was all he needed to know. Manuel had filled him in on the rest in the car on the way here. His ass was still complaining about the drive, but they'd really had no choice. It was not like they could get on a plane with the items they had in the trunk.

Jimmy looked up at the hospital as Manuel started the car. If they moved, they would be out of the dead space between the security cameras, and he wished to delay that for as long as possible. They had spent the morning both walking and driving around the hospital and its surrounding neighborhood. They made notes of exits and fire escapes, loading docks and parking ramps, security guards, and cameras. Only after they had compared notes and made a detailed map over the one conveniently offered by the hospital's website, did they pick their spot to wait.

Jimmy went over the printout again while they waited for the man to emerge. Oscar was on the fourth floor, and he had already ruled out any chance of springing him. Besides, that wasn't the mission he had been tasked with. He just knew he would be asked sooner or later.

"We follow for no more than a mile or two, depending on where he goes."

"I got it," Manuel replied, his eyes never leaving the entrance of the ramp.

Jimmy set down the printout and palmed the digital camera in his lap. It was already on and ready to go. The picture was necessary, after that they could go to work.

The first and second cars were driven by an elderly woman and a hospital employee still wearing his scrubs. The third car was new but very plain. It screamed government ownership.

"There he is."

"Give him a few."

They watched Lenny turn toward them and pull up to the corner light. After a slight pause, he turned again and drove away from them toward the highway. Manuel let a car pass before pulling out to follow. The Mercedes didn't fit the neighborhood they were in, but coming from the hospital they weren't too out of place.

Jimmy reviewed the pictures he had snapped as the car pulled away. He had managed four as the car turned the corner.

"Pictures are good. Let's see where he goes."

They followed from a distance until traffic picked up, forcing them to move in closer. They almost lost him at a red light, but skinned through just as it turned. Manuel braced for the rebuke, but Jimmy held his tongue. Soon they were in moderate traffic heading west on Lombard. Jimmy pulled out a street map and consulted it.

"What do you think, boss?"

"He's heading toward the convention center or the ball parks. Both of them are next to the business loop that takes you to I-95. There's also a bunch of hotels. I like this traffic. Let's stay with him a little longer."

"You got it."

They followed the car for another few blocks until it turned left on South Eutaw Street and pulled into the parking garage of the Marriott Hotel. Manuel drove past the hotel and continued on down the street till he hit the red light at the corner.

"I'm out here. Circle around and meet me right here in six minutes."

"Six," Manuel echoed, checking his watch.

Jimmy grabbed a small bag from under the seat and opened the door. Stepping out on the curb, he made a show of waving to his partner for appearance's sake before turning and striding toward the hotel. Bypassing the front entrance, he walked at a normal pace toward the parking garage and entered the dark interior. Scanning the cars behind his sunglasses, he walked the ramp, looking for the plain car with the license tag he had memorized only minutes ago. Level two proved to be the charm and he found the car parked close to the entrance to the stairwell and elevator—a high traffic area. He looked for cameras as he approached and seeing none, made his decision. Lenny was nowhere to be seen, and the car's engine creaked as it cooled.

Reaching in the bag as he approached, he pulled the device free, knelt down, and fixed it to the frame of the car under the rear seat. He was back on his feet without seeming to break stride and made for the stair entrance. Two minutes later, he was back on the street and managed to make it to the curb just as the car pulled up to the light. He made a subtle hand gesture that moved Manuel on and continued on across the street and down another block. Finally satisfied that he wasn't seen and followed, he stopped and bought a newspaper from a box on the next corner. He stood and gazed over the top of it until he saw Manuel approach again. This time he quickly folded the paper and walked to the curb. He was back in the car with the smallest of stops, and they were soon moving down Eutaw once again.

"What now?"

"Well. I'm wondering where he'll go next?"

"I can find a place to park and we can fire up the laptop?"

"Somewhere between the hotel and 95."

"I don't think there's anything except the two stadiums and the Federal Reserve Bank. You don't want to park there, do you?"

"No, probably not a good idea." Jimmy checked the map and saw that the kid was right. His protégé had done his homework.

"How about this bar right here?"

"The Pratt Street Alehouse?"

"Why not?"

"Think they got beer?"

"Aren't you funny today?"

The kid just smiled as he pulled the car in.

The three-story building had one Baltimore Oriole blue wall that stuck out from a distance. The inside boasted brick walls with arches dividing the room, and a long bar down one side. More Baltimore team colors were predominant in the decor, and multiple flat-screen TVs occupied most of the wall space.

It was slow and early for lunch, but they managed to find a corner table where they could view the laptop without anyone looking over their shoulder. It only took Jimmy a couple of minutes to pull up the software and find the signal. Despite the car being in the garage and surrounded by concrete, the signal was strong. It held agreeably still as they gazed at it.

"So what do you think?"

"He could leave in ten minutes or ten hours. Who knows?"

"So what do we do?"

Jimmy looked up and eyeballed the many taps behind the bar. He was somewhat of an expert. He consulted the beer list before he signaled the waitress.

"I think I'll try the Ironman Pale Ale. What are you gonna have?"

Manuel just shook his head and smiled as he watched the young waitress approach. He preferred other indulgences over beer.

Fifteen minutes later, the dot on the screen began to move.

"There's our boy. What do you want to do?"

Jimmy chewed slowly and watched the dot move toward the business loop. The range of the tracker covered most of North America, so he wasn't worried about losing him. After a few minutes, his suspicions were confirmed.

"He's heading south toward DC. Let's just watch him and see where he goes. If he stays in DC today, we'll move down there, too. I want to track every address he goes to for more than twenty minutes. One of them should have our target."

Manuel nodded in agreement. Jimmy had taught him to work smarter, not harder, and this was another lesson. This way they could track the Interpol agent right to the target without the risk of being seen. It was so simple it was stupid, as Jimmy liked to say.

Jimmy pulled his eyes from the screen and drained his beer. Since it looked like they were staying for awhile, Manuel signaled the waitress for another round.

"Thirsty work?" the waitress asked.

"Yes, it is." Jimmy smiled.

The waitress saved her smile for Manuel before she turned and walked toward the bar. Manuel enjoyed the view while Jimmy's eyes returned to the screen.

* * *

The target they spoke of was being treated to a fast food meal at a small row house in suburban DC. It was one of many since his late night trip to the house, and he was far from happy about it.

Angel sat at the table and ignored the bag of cold tacos that had been dropped in front of him and instead contemplated the two Marshals sitting across from him. The younger, muscular one, Jake, added hot sauce to his pile before crossing the room and flopping into an old recliner in front of the TV. The older and fatter one was Charlie, and he ignored Angel's stare while he ate. He had been paired with these two for the last few days, ever since his midnight flight into Andrew's Air Force base. A half dozen vans had all departed the base at once, heading in all different directions. The one carrying him had been cleared of tails and after a two-hour wandering trip around the DC area, it had deposited him in this row house. He had been remotely visited by several agents who questioned him for hours in the basement in front of a camera. The video feed had landed him in front of a grand jury for another few hours, and he had been led through the questions by the federal prosecutor. It had just gotten worse every day. He was ready for it to be over so he could get away from his handlers, especially when they insisted on feeding him this slop.

"Enjoying this are you? Think this is funny?"

The old Marshal chewed slowly and contemplated Angel from the other end of the table before replying. "Yeah, I do."

Angel sneered and shook his head.

"How long you been a Marshal?"

"Eight years. Twenty years in the army before that."

Angel looked to the younger one sitting in the chair.

"How about you, kid?"

"What?"

"How long you been a Marshal?"

"Four years."

"And how much you make a year?"

"Sixty k."

Angel shook his head again. The older Marshal put down his taco and glared at him. He had made it clear to Angel from the start of all this that he didn't like him, and he wasn't in the mood for his condescending questions.

"So go ahead and tell us how stupid we are, asshole."

"I didn't say that. I'm just thinking that since we're both working for the same people, I sure got the better end of the deal."

"I don't work for any drug dealer, and I sure as hell don't work with you."

"I didn't say you worked with me. I said we both work for the same people."

The younger one didn't take his eyes off the football game on the screen, but he couldn't resist taking the bait. "How you figure that?"

Angel was genuinely shocked. He looked from one to the other in disbelief until the young one turned to see what had silenced him.

"You two just don't get it do you? Follow the damn money, it's that simple. You work for the government. That means you get paid by the American taxpayer, the same taxpayer that spends billions on drugs every year. You think I make money selling drugs in Mexico? Honduras? Hell no. It's *all* American money, guys. Your government spends forty billion dollars a year pissing in the wind trying to stop it. Excuse me for picking the profit side of the business. I'm a fucking millionaire several times over, and you're pulling down a lousy sixty k a year? You can look down your nose all you want, but you both know I'm right. We're all working for the same people."

"You're not so rich anymore," Charlie pointed out.

"You think so?" Angel shot back. "Only if you guys find it all, and I can make in one week what you'll make in your whole wasted life!"

"Fuck you."

"Fuck you?" Angel laughed. "Is that all you got? Come on, you can do better than that. You should be thanking me for showing you the light! Congratulations! You work in the drug trade! Welcome to the club!"

Jake turned back to his football game. "I don't see it that way. You're peddling poison to kids. I'm on the right side."

"You think so? You gonna tell me that there's all these people out there that have no idea that drugs are bad for them and against the law? I'm not buying that. What about alcohol? How about cigarettes? They all know and they choose to do it anyway. There's not one person in this whole country that didn't know and did it anyway. People spend forty billion a year on drugs. They want them. Nobody's innocent. They're *all* guilty."

Charlie tossed down the remainder of his food and swept it up into a ball before standing.

"You need to shut the fuck up."

"Or what? I'm your only tie to the Cali cartel. You're just a damn babysitter. Kiss my ass."

The Marshal bit his tongue until he walked past, before turning and kicking the chair out from under Angel. He was about to follow it with a kick to the ribs when Jake engulfed him in a bear hug and walked him back.

"Run your mouth some more, asshole!"

"Let it go, Charlie, he ain't worth it. Just cool off. He's just trying to push your buttons. Don't let him get to you."

Charlie let himself be pushed down the hallway before Jake let him go. He spun on a heel and stalked into the bedroom he had chosen before slamming the door. Jake waited till he heard the bedsprings creak before turning and walking back into the kitchen. Angel had picked himself off the floor and was rubbing his shoulder.

"Your partner's a real ass."

Jake was across the room in two strides and quickly had Angel up against the wall, with a forearm across his throat. Angel struggled, but Jake just increased the pressure.

"Look at me, motherfucker," Jake said quietly.

Angel stopped struggling and did as he was told. Jake's face was inches from his and he could feel his breath on his face.

"If you ever run your mouth like that again, you're gonna have a little accident. You hear me?"

Angel saw the look in the man's eyes. He meant what he was saying. He managed a small nod. Jake held the pressure a couple seconds longer to drive the point home before releasing him. Angel slid to the floor and coughed until he regained his breath. Jake had already dismissed him and returned to his chair to watch the rest of the game. Angel rubbed his neck and hobbled to the kitchen table. Eventually his stomach won out and he gathered his food and took it to the microwave. Once it was warm, he found a spot in the chair across from Jake. They watched the game in silence, each ignoring the other.

POLICE: ACCUSED DRUG LORD MOVED TONS OF COCAINE TO U.S.

August 31, 2010—CNN

—EIGHT—

RITA LAMAR SAT IN the chair and watched her daughter's chest rise and fall with each cycle of the ventilator. Tessa's swollen eyes were taped shut and the bruising on her face had regressed to a yellow-blue stain along her jaw line. Her legs were propped up with pillows and traction was provided to one leg to aid the pins holding her femur together. The ugly stitches and bandages covering her chest could be seen peeking out from behind the collar of the hospital gown, and Rita reached out to adjust the garment, being careful not to touch any of the many wires that crossed her chest. The pumps and IVs constantly dripped bag after bag of fluids into her daughter's bruised arms, and she had lost count of the many changes in their names. The fluids went in, and the catheter in her bladder showed a steady output. Something the nurses in attendance constantly monitored.

She had come to view them as angels. They constantly hovered nearby, keeping a quiet distance and intruding only when necessary. Most had taken the time to get to know Rita, and they had provided a comfortable chair that extended out into a sleeper so she could spend the nights with her daughter as well. It had been decided by Dr. Fong that visiting hours did not apply in this case. Rita was grateful.

She paused to grasp her daughter's hand again and applied a slight squeeze, hoping to get one in return, but it did not come. She fought back the tears and pulled herself together. Her husband was on his way and she would hold her emotions in check, for both him and her.

The loud click of his shoes on the tile floor announced his arrival before she saw him. He looked quite foolish in his mask and gown over the business suit and office shoes. He leaned down to buss his wife's cheek through the mask before sitting next to her on the arm of the chair.

"Any change?"

"No. The doctor came this morning and said her heart had not improved. He said something about a balloon pump, whatever that is. I couldn't really follow."

"I'll ask before I go. You look tired, dear. Did you sleep at all here last night?"

"No, not really. The nurses are so kind, but this is a busy place. They brought in two new patients last night and one of them...his heart stopped not long after they got here. They worked on him for an hour but...he died. It was so sad, like they had lost a battle. There was no family here, so they had no one to ask anything. It went on for so long. Finally two of them just rolled him away."

The senator didn't know what to say to that, so he just held his wife's hand while they watched the ventilator breathe for their daughter.

"I want you to come home tonight. You need your sleep."

"I don't want her to be alone."

"She won't be. I'll stay tonight. You need to go home and sleep."

"No, you need to sleep. I know you can't leave work." She held up a hand to silence him before he could protest. "It's important that you stay at work. I understand, just please stick close. If something should happen, I'll need you here quickly."

The senator bit his tongue and just offered a nod. He would placate her for now. But soon he would have to make her go home. He had called the hospital several times and received updates from the nurses about his daughter and his wife. He knew sooner or later he would have to force the issue. But not right now.

They sat in silence for a few moments before a nurse appeared on the other side of the glass. She held her hand to her head in the universal sign for "You have a phone call." The senator rose and exited the room.

"One of your aides outside," the nurse offered before going back to her monitor screens. He walked the length of the unit and punched the button on the double doors to let himself out. Striding down the short hall, he entered the waiting room to find two of his aides sitting in chairs with other patients' family members. They looked horribly out of place.

"What is it?" he demanded, clearly irritated.

"I'm sorry, sir, the speaker called for you." The aide held out a phone.

Before he could get it to his head he heard a scream from the unit. He recognized it immediately as his wife. Dropping the phone, he turned to rush back in, but was brought up short by the coded entry door. He slammed a fist into the wall in frustration before a yell from behind him turned his head. He turned to see two men running toward the unit. He managed to flatten himself against the wall as they rushed past, one of them tripping the door code with his ID card.

The doors parted with a hiss and the senator leaped after them to follow. He rounded the corner to see his wife being physically restrained by a large nurse while others crowded the room around his daughter. The first thing he noticed was the monitor over their heads. His daughter's heartbeat was erratic and one nurse stood poised over her chest, ready to start compressions. The nurses were all talking at once and the gown was ripped from his daughter's body as others slapped large patches with wires connected onto her chest and side.

"She's in fib!"

"Stand by, we're charging."

They waited tensely while the capacitor whined up. A beep announced its readiness.

"Clear!" the nurse called out.

Everyone held up their hands for her to see. She scanned once before pushing the button. Tessa's body shivered on the bed, and Rita turned and buried her head in the nurse's chest. The group stared at the overhead monitor as the rhythm returned to its previous steady beat.

"Sinus."

"Do we have a pulse with it?"

"I've got a femoral."

"Sixty systolic…it's rising."

"Get a blood-gas. I want it repeated every five minutes."

The nurse holding Rita pulled her gently away from his chest before speaking. "It's okay, she's back."

Rita looked up at his face before turning to see the staff around her daughter. They were relaxed. Her tension dialed down a bit. The senator joined her and took the place of the nurse.

"She's okay," he told her. "They got her back."

They watched silently as the team worked.

"Her PH is down."

"One amp of bicarb," the doctor ordered. "Repeat the gasses every five for now, and let's start her on a drip."

Rita sank into the chair and the voices faded around her as she focused on her daughter's face. Her husband's hand found hers and gave it a comforting squeeze, but her eyes never left her daughter.

She would give anything to save her.

* * *

Anita's days had become routine. She woke when the sounds of the street below her reached a volume that overpowered the sound of the radio and announced the start of the day. She listened and waited until breakfast arrived, usually a breakfast roll and some eggs. Some fruit maybe. Nothing beyond water to drink, but she dared not ask for any juice as she was accustomed to at home. The men outside the door would change soon after, and she had learned to recognize their voices. Most were serious drinkers and would start on the first bottle soon after they arrived. The TV would come on and the voices would get louder to be heard over it. She would wait until they were settled in before attempting to bathe, always with an ear tuned to the sound of the locks. Her nails and hair were long and unkempt, but she had no way to fix the problem. She would spend hours running her fingers through it in a vain attempt to keep it untangled while she counted the hours off by songs on the radio. Lying on the floor, she would let her mind wander, trying to place herself anywhere but where she currently was, the constant noise both her tormentor and only companion.

A new noise broke through and she heard the men fall silent as one of them answered the cell phone. A brief one-sided conversation prompted a flurry of activity on the other side of the door. She braced herself for the unknown and her fear leaped to her throat as a hard knock was heard on the door. She barely managed to get the towel over her head before the last lock was thrown and the door burst open. Several sets of feet entered and she was yanked to her feet only to have the towel tightened around her face. She struggled to breathe as she was forced down onto the bed. Her hands were pulled behind her and she felt the towel being rolled up her face.

"Shut your eyes!"

The towel cleared her mouth and she had time to suck in one good breath before the tape came down across her mouth. The towel was tied tightly across her eyes and she was flipped over onto a hard board. The tape came around her quickly, and she was soon wrapped to the point that she was immobile. The straps came next and she was again a package ready for transport. They stopped to catch their breath before hoisting her up and carrying her from the room. They almost dropped her twice on the steps, but after some cursing from the older one, they slowed down enough to get her to the bottom were she was roughly dropped on the floor.

She forced herself to calm down as she took deep breaths through her nose. The fear of suffocation soon passed and she listened to her surroundings.

"How long?" one asked.

"He said within twenty minutes. Be ready by the door and keep her out of sight."

One of them ascended the stairs and the sound of empty beer bottles being disposed of could be heard. The others waited in silence. The board grew cold on the bare concrete beneath her.

"What happened? Why are we moving?"

"How do I know? We just watch her. If the man on the phone says move, we move. Now shut the hell up."

They were moving her? Anita's heart leaped at the news. Had her father paid the ransom? Was she going home, or were they taking her somewhere else? Were the police closing in? Was she going to be rescued and the kidnappers somehow found out? What was happening?

A horn sounded outside the garage and the men moved around her to open it. A blanket was thrown over her and she heard the sound of the spinning chain as the door was cranked open. The van entered, only to stop just inches from her spot on the floor, and the door was hurriedly cranked down once the van was inside. She could feel the heat of the engine on her face even after it was shut off. The doors on both sides opened and more footsteps joined the others.

"She is ready?" the new voice asked.

"Right there."

The blanket was yanked from over her and she sucked in the fresh air. She listened and flinched as the board she lay on was nudged by a foot.

"Good, get her loaded up."

Hands grabbed the board and she felt herself roughly loaded into the van. She couldn't help but cry out through the tape as her head bounced on the board.

"Be quiet, little girl. I won't tell you again."

She was shoved across the floor of the van until she met the wall and the back of the driver's seat. She felt a boot holding the board in place as blankets were piled onto her. She struggled to remain calm, but soon the lack of air forced a panic and she struggled and cried against the restraints.

"I said be quiet!"

"You idiot! You want to kill her? She can't breathe."

The blankets were pulled away until her nose was exposed and she sucked in the cool air in rapid breaths.

"Calm down. You can breathe now," she heard a voice tell her. She recognized it as the young one. She soon smelled his cologne.

"Just pile them on but leave her head exposed. I can cover it quickly if we get stopped. Stack the laundry bags around her."

A grunt was the only reply. She heard the men labor and felt the impact of several soft bags hitting the floor of the van. The smell of bleach and detergent was evident.

"That's good enough, let's go."

The van was started and put in gear before the sound of the rattling chain raising the door was heard once more. The van pulled out into the street and was soon in heavy traffic. After several turns, she lost all sense of direction.

She smelled the cologne stronger before she heard a whisper from the young one in her ear.

"Open your mouth as wide as you can and pull your tongue back."

Not understanding, she did as she was told and soon felt the blade of a knife pierce the tape. She sucked in the night air through the narrow slit as a thirsty man drinking water. She heard him chuckle.

"You're welcome. Now be still until we get there. It is not far."

The muffled sounds of Mexico City traffic made their way through the layers of blankets, but she had no idea where they were. They traveled on a highway for some time, but soon were back on the city streets where the bumps and turns had her in pain on the hard board. Some of them severe enough to produce involuntary grunts of pain that prompted a tap of a finger on her arm as a warning. The tape began to pull on her skin. Her legs, which hadn't been shaved for some time, felt as though they were on fire.

"Almost there," she heard.

It was the reverse of their departure. The van stopped and sounded its horn. A door was opened manually this time before the van pulled inside and was quickly shut off. This time only three sets of hands grabbed her, and she was once again set on the floor and covered as the van departed. The remaining hands grunted as they hoisted her up and soon she was swaying as they mounted three flights of stairs. This time she was placed on a bed. Two sets of feet left the room. The young one spoke to her.

"Hold very still. I don't wish to cut you."

He quietly cursed the tape as he cut her free with rapid slices of the knife. She froze in fear as she slowly felt the pressure ease. Next the straps were undone and she lay free but still blindfolded.

"You are in a new room. The same rules apply. Don't break them, Anita. These men, they are worse than the others. I'm sorry for the tape. I don't know why they have to use so much. The lotion works to get it off your skin."

She heard him walk across the room and there was a pause as he turned on the ever present radio. The music barely covered his footsteps as he left the room. This time she heard only two locks being thrown before the steps continued on. Only when she heard the sound of the TV coming on, did she dare to move.

She first peeled the tape from her mouth and took her first unlabored breaths in over an hour. The towel came off next and she gazed about at her new prison. It was smaller than the previous room, but cleaner and with fresh paint. She lay on a double bed that was pushed up against the corner. A single window, with the now familiar blanket nailed over it, let in the cool night air. She saw a small bathroom in the opposite corner—surprisingly cleaner than the last. Searching the bed coverings for blood, she was relieved to find none. A box on the nightstand contained some toiletries and a bottle of lotion. She remembered what he had said and pulled the lotion from the box. She set about pulling the tape from her skin.

She held the sobs back for as long as she could. The pain of the tape removal was nothing compared to the pain in her heart. If he heard, the young man never said a word.

MORE THAN 8,000 PEOPLE ARE WAITING FOR ORGAN TRANSPLANTS IN THE NEW YORK ORGAN DONOR NETWORK'S SERVICE AREA.

New York Organ Donor Network

ANGEL SHIFTED IN THE chair and re-crossed his legs. The panel before him on the large TV screen was made up of three men and two women, each of them better dressed and sitting in a much more comfortable chair than he. He had no doubt his handlers had given him the metal folding chair on purpose. It was just another petty way for them to kick him again. He had been in the chair for two hours already and was growing tired of the questions. He had already given them every name and address he could think of. Tunnel locations. Corrupt government officials. Ship's names. What more did they want? Didn't they realize it would all be replaced within months? It was an exercise in futility. A total waste of time. But he really had no choice did he? So he sat in front of the camera in the basement of the row house and spilled his guts.

He watched two of them have a whispered conversation while they chose the next topic for their endless questions. He had shocked them a number of times when he reported the actual quantities of drugs crossing the border and had to smile at their naïveté. They really had no clue. He had thrown out the figure of eight hundred tons of cocaine and they had simply refused to believe it. He had simply shrugged. Screw 'em. He didn't really care if they believed him or not. Reality can be a real bitch when you're on the losing side.

The older woman, with her hair pulled back so tight it seemed to raise her eyebrows, loudly shuffled some papers and brought everyone's attention back to her. She hadn't made any attempt to hide the fact that Angel repulsed her, and he had decided to treat her in kind. He braced himself for her condescending tone. She talked to him like he was a child and she had caught him misbehaving.

"Mr. Sanchez, we would like to steer away from the drugs for a moment and talk about the human organs you had on board with you. Our information says that you had a total of two human kidneys on board destined for people in an Orlando hospital. The cooler had the seal of Doctors Without Borders and the transplant was in the UNOS computer, yet they claim to have no knowledge of the transplant organs' origin. What can you tell us about this?"

Angel took a deep breath. They were gonna love this.

"The smuggling operation needed a legitimate cover to get the product through customs. We noticed that medical flights are hardly looked at, and even receive preferential treatment. So we started an air medical company and used animal organs at first to get through customs. The seals on the coolers were easy to forge and the paperwork was even easier. People wanted the organs so bad they were willing to believe anything. Somewhere along the line someone needed a real kidney, so they found a donor, some peasant farmer down in Oaxaca, and a doctor that would do the operation. The recipient paid a fortune for it. So we saw it as a bonus. It gave the flights credibility and another source of income. Sometimes the cooler was worth more than the drugs we brought in. We could pay some farmer five k for a kidney, and sell it for a hundred times that in the States. The problem was always time."

"Time?"

"I don't know a whole lot about the science end of it, but evidently a kidney is only good for so long once it's taken out of someone. On top of that, it has to match the person it's going to. We didn't really have a source that would provide us with a list of people and their blood types. It was kind of a custom-order type business."

"So you found a solution? How?"

"The surgeons we had weren't really top of the line and there were a few deaths, so the peasants weren't really eager to take the money, no matter how much we offered. The bosses needed to find another source. Evidently they did, because we soon had all we needed coming out of Mexico City. I wasn't privy to the source myself, but I would meet the plane, load it with product, and an ambulance would just show up with the cooler and a legitimate destination. I just wore a flight suit and acted the part. An ambulance would be there to meet us when we landed, and that was it."

"So where did the organs come from?"

Angel squirmed again. Drugs were bad enough, but this was really unsavory. At least he had immunity.

"I can't say for sure, but I have an idea."

"Go on."

"The cartels are tied in with a lot of Mexican gangs. It's mostly just to move product and buy influence with the police and government. Most of these gangs have a kidnapping business going, also. It's become a big money maker for them. They're mostly small, very compartmentalized sections. One group does the actual kidnapping, another transports the victim to a safe house, another guards and takes care of the victim, and another makes contact and negotiates the ransom. These people never see anybody else within the group. If one is caught, the trail ends with them. It's very hard to catch them, and the police have basically given up on it."

"They've given up on it? You mean they don't even look for the kidnappers?"

"Exactly. They refer the families to professional negotiators. Most families with money in that part of the world have K and R insurance. The kidnappers count on it."

"K and R?"

Angel rolled his eyes and shook his head with a smile. These people were truly naive.

"Kidnapping and Ransom. Most of the big insurers are out of London these days."

He paused while they all made notes on their ever present legal pads. He felt as if he were giving a lecture on the true nature of the world to a group of children. He played with the laces on his cheap shoes until they were ready.

"You were saying that the police do nothing?"

"A kidnapping negotiation is a month's-long process. The police have neither the time nor the resources to pursue kidnappings. They're too busy chasing drug runners, eh? And the army is now engaged with the gangs on the border. They have no time either. It has become a rather safe and profitable business."

He watched them as they once again had a whispered conversation among themselves, each of them holding his hand over his microphone. Angel shifted in his seat again and fetched the bottle of water, now warm, from the floor beside him. Finally the uptight woman in the power suit took her hand off her mic.

"So how do these kidnappers get the organs?"

Angel traded a look with his handlers sitting against the wall. My God, were these people really that stupid?

"I would assume from some of their victims. Maybe they somehow know their blood types before they snatch them, or maybe they test them after they have them, but since not everybody gets released, even after the ransom is paid, I'm guessing that's where they come from."

"You're saying that people are being kidnapped just for their organs?"

Angel shrugged. "I guess I am."

"How do you know this?"

"I don't for sure, but I can tell you that a couple of the gangs have grown very brutal in the past year. The police think they just had bad negotiators, or that the gangs killed a couple of them just to prove that they would and force the other families into higher ransoms. I don't know. But the bodies that were found were never complete. It was always just a head in a box, or a hand or something, never the full corpse. Makes you wonder."

"And these gangs work for the cartels?"

"They're independent gangs, but yes, they work for the cartels. *Everybody* works for the cartels. If the cartels need someone kidnapped, the gangs do it for them. I think the organ thing is just a bonus, so to speak."

He waited again while they made more notes and talked with each other. Angel scratched an itchy spot on the side of his head. The damp basement made his skin crawl.

"You have names and addresses? Phone numbers?"

"Yes. The names will be aliases, but the addresses will most likely be the same. They really have no reason to change them. Like I said, they aren't really in any danger from the police. The phone numbers change daily, but I had a contact at Mextel who would give me the updated numbers. Most of them have criminal histories. You should be able to find them in a computer somewhere, I would think."

"Are there any names within the government tied to this?"

"...a couple."

Angel spent the next half hour listing names, addresses, and phone numbers for the camera. The written transcript had grown to over forty pages today. It was about their usual and Angel was tired. Soon the panel had determined they had heard enough for that day and they left his view on the screen. Angel rose and silently followed the Marshals up the steps and into the main floor of the house. He grabbed a pack of cigarettes left on the table by one of them and hurriedly lit up before flopping into one of the old recliners. The two agents regarded him with contempt.

"You're gonna burn long and hot, Angel."

Angel waved the remark away with his cigarette.

"Yeah...tell me something I don't know."

* * *

"This is all of it?"

The negotiator's name was Luis, and he stood in the family's living room, examining the documents the father had provided. He paced while he read and they watched from the couch while he did so. The wife sat on the edge, hanging on the man's every word, while the father sat back with a drink in one hand. He was not pleased with the prying questions being asked by his newest employee.

Luis stopped and dropped the papers on the pile already stacked on the coffee table. He ran his hands through his hair in exasperation before stopping in front of the couple.

"This is not enough. They'll demand several times this. We must be able to negotiate from a point of strength. If we offer this, they'll think we're playing games and we'll get nowhere. I need a figure we can work with."

"That's all I can get right now!"

"Right now? Right now? I don't think you heard me before. This'll most likely take months. We'll start talking with them soon, and it will be once or twice a week if we're lucky. You have time to get more money. If they think we're not negotiating in true faith, you'll get her fingers in the mailbox! Do you understand?"

The father shook his head in disgust. "I don't like this. How do we know they'll even give her back once we pay them?"

"They'll give her back. If they don't, no one will ever pay them again, and they know it. This is nothing but a business deal for them. You are a businessman. You must look at it from that point of view. We both have something that the other wants. There is only the matter of price to settle. But you must be willing to work with them, or they'll make an example of her and that is what we don't want."

The father drained his drink and fingered the empty glass. His wife gripped his hand and he relented.

"I...I will find more money."

"Good. They'll be calling soon. We must be ready."

"And if they demand money up front?"

"We give them nothing. First we'll demand proof of life. We'll do nothing until we get it. We give nothing unless we get something in return. They'll expect this, and it will show that we are professionals, also."

"Professionals? They're fucking animals!"

"This is true. But they're very smart animals. We must be careful."

"Where do you think she is?" the wife asked.

Luis softened his tone for her. The woman looked ready to break down crying at any moment.

"She's somewhere in this city, to be sure. They most likely have her in a house where they can keep her confined and quiet. She'll be moved periodically to other places, but no one but her captors will see her. She'll be fed and clothed and kept healthy. Most of them who come back were treated well. You must understand that she's worth a lot of money to them. It's in their best interest to take care of her. Other than being quite scared, I doubt that she's been harmed."

The wife just nodded as she tried to wrap her mind around the situation. The father was still pissed and couldn't let it go.

"Those useless police. If she's in the city like you say, they should be out looking for her."

"If we try to locate her, we put her life in danger. Anytime the kidnappers have been cornered by the police, it has not worked out well for the victim. The police go in shooting and the victim...they tend to get caught in the crossfire. Something we don't want."

"So how long will this...negotiation last?"

"With luck, maybe two or three months."

"And if we have no luck?"

"I can't say."

"Why so long? Can we not just pay these bastards and get it over with?"

"If we pay too fast they'll see it as a sign of weakness and just demand more. We don't want that either. This is a game to them, but we both want the same thing. You have to trust me to see it through."

The father contemplated his empty glass further and Luis watched him closely. Finally he saw the man's muscles relax in surrender.

"Very well, we will do as you say."

* * *

Luis drove away from the family's gated home and entered the crowded streets of Mexico City. Once he had determined he had no tails, he found his way to the freeway circling the city. Only then did he open the glove box between the seats and select a cell phone from the many present. He dialed the number from memory.

"Yes?"

"I've met with the family. They're not ready yet. I want them to wait two days before they call so I can work on the father some more. The money is there, he's just reluctant to show me it."

"Good. He's worth more than the financial reports say, I'm sure. Do you have a figure in mind?"

"Between eight hundred thousand and one million."

The detective was ecstatic but tried not to show it. His question still revealed his greed.

"My cut will increase?"

"Your cut will remain as agreed! Do not try to alter the agreement or I'll find a new employee, you understand?"

"Yes, yes, I understand."

"Good. Now do as I said, and tell them to have the damn picture ready."

"It's already been done. They moved her to the second location, as we discussed."

"All right, do nothing else till you hear from me. Wait for my call."

"*Si.*"

ILLEGAL KIDNEY TRANSPLANT CASE EXPOSES HUMAN ORGANS BLACK MARKET

October 29, 2011—Health

RITA LAMAR WAS WIDE awake. She had finally relented to both her husband's and the doctor's wishes and gone home for a night to get a shower and some needed sleep, but after tossing and turning for several hours, she had stopped fighting it and gotten up. She fixed herself a small meal and was now wandering the house with a drink in her hand. Her robe hung loosely around her, and she could tell she had lost several pounds since the accident. She now ventured down the hall, forcing herself to avoid her daughter's room. Her husband had closed the door for the night before going to the hospital, so it would not draw her eyes as she passed, and she soon found herself on the stairwell.

It proved to be just as bad. Her only hobby was photography and the walls of the stairwell were adorned with hundreds of pictures of her family—her daughter predominant among them. Birthdays, sports, class pictures, family reunions, all of them together on the campaign trail with her father, they chronicled the life of a successful and loving family. Her daughter's prom pictures were the latest, and she saw her smiling face next to the young man in his rented suit. One of the few boys her father had approved of, she had somehow found a flaw in him a few months later, and was soon dating another. There had never been a shortage of boys.

At the bottom of the stairs she turned toward the kitchen, but after a pause continued on to the garage door. After turning the lights on and gazing out at the empty spot where the little Mustang used to be, she flicked the switch and returned to the house. The streetlights painted the walls with dark shadows and she gazed out the picture windows to see the deserted streets. Still several hours until sunrise, she expected to see nothing. Sipping the drink, she wandered down the hall toward the library. A bit of motion caught her eye as she passed her husband's study and she entered to investigate, only to see the neighbor's cat sitting outside on the windowsill.

"Hello, Calvin."

She touched a finger to the glass and was rewarded by the cat nuzzling the window in return. He soon lost interest and scampered off in search of whatever cats do.

Turning from the window she was presented with her husband's desk, messy as usual as he had no aides at home to keep it tidy for him. Her husband was not a morning person, although he rose before six each day for a full day of work. He was fonder of burning the midnight oil and had been known to forget the time on occasion and call an aide or lobbyist at two in the morning.

She noticed his briefcase sitting unlocked on the credenza next to some papers. She picked one up.

It was a transcript of an interrogation. She scanned it quickly and was about to put it down when the words "organ trafficking" caught her eye. She settled in to read further. The drink was soon set down and forgotten as she dug into the briefcase for more.

Two hours later she turned on the senator's copy machine.

* * *

Dr. Dayo left his office after a few hours of paperwork. His stomach had informed him an hour ago that it was empty, but he had overruled it until he had finished the last patient chart. He only got stopped twice on his journey, once for one of his nurses who had been out on maternity leave, and again for a quick consult with a colleague. The line in the cafeteria was short, and he eyeballed the sandwiches before picking one to go with his salad. He needed to lose a few pounds, or so his wife had informed him. He scanned the crowded room for a table, hoping to spot some of the residents. He liked the questions he got from them in the informal atmosphere.

Off to one side, he noticed two men in suits sitting alone in the sea of scrubs. Despite the crowd, their large table was devoid of any company, and when he saw who they were he wasn't surprised. The two lawmen just didn't belong, and as curious as his people were, they knew they wouldn't get any answers from sitting with them.

The younger one made eye contact and waved him over, so he found a seat and unloaded his tray.

"Busy day, Doc?" Jack asked.

"No more than usual."

"How's our guest doing?" Lenny inquired.

Dr. Dayo played with his salad a little before replying. "About the same. His heart is failing, but it's doing so slowly. Nothing from the donor registry yet. We're waiting."

"What are his chances of getting one?"

The surgeon shrugged. "No way to know really. The organ procurement business is a black hole. We have a board here that decides if the patient qualifies as a recipient or not, but once that determination is made, it goes out to several organizations that find the organs and match them up to people on the list. At that point, it's really out of our control."

"Just how does the whole thing work anyway?"

"How does one get a new heart? Well, two years ago it was fairly simple, but now it's kind of complicated."

"The simple version will suffice, Doc."

"Obviously the first thing you have to do is get sick or injured. Most of the people on the list are suffering from an advancing disease that's leading to the failure of an organ. A smaller group is there because of some form of injury that's damaged the organ beyond its capacity to function. Whatever the reason, it's been determined that they need the transplant to continue living."

Dayo paused to chase down a stubborn crouton. The two cops waited patiently until he finally speared it.

"It basically follows a simple path. Patient A gets sick and goes to see his doctor. The doctor runs a few tests, and either discovers the problem himself, or refers patient A to a specialist who does. This leads to more blood work and tests until a diagnosis is made. The severity of the problem is determined, and the need for a transplant is established."

"Who makes that call?"

"By this time a lot of these patients are hospitalized. Some aren't, but that doesn't change things a whole lot. Each hospital has a board that meets when needed to determine a patient's eligibility. The criteria are pretty strict. The patient has to be healthy enough, aside from his organ failure, to survive the surgery. They have to have sufficient financial means to afford the follow-up care and drugs required to retain the organ. They need a healthy support system, preferably family, in place. We look for destructive behaviors also. They can't have a history of drug or alcohol abuse. They need to have lived a somewhat healthy lifestyle. We look for smoking, obesity, eating habits, education level, marital history, job security, everything. The organ from a donor is considered a great gift, and it's not going to go to someone who won't or can't take care of it."

"Sounds pretty harsh. But I guess you have no choice."

Dayo pointed his fork at Jack before swallowing another bite of his meal.

"It is harsh, no doubt about it. But with over 100,000 people on the list waiting for organs, we don't have a choice. A lot of those people die while they're waiting. We have to take into account everything we can when we make a decision. I've seen patients get moved down the list on the basis of how well they care for their teeth. If you can't be trusted to brush your teeth, how can you be trusted to take care of a new liver?"

Dayo let the question hang while he moved on to his sandwich. Both cops couldn't help but look into their coffee cups and wonder how clean their teeth were at the moment.

"So what happens at the committee meeting? Are the doctors there to lobby for their patients?"

"Sometimes. Most of the cases are pretty clear, though. There's a scoring system here that we use. I can't tell you how they might do it elsewhere. It's a constantly evolving process."

"So let's say the patient makes the list, then what?"

"We send all the information to UNOS. That's the United Network of Organ Sharing. They're the ones who keep the master list, so to speak. All fifty-eight recovery regions in the United States check the list when they have a donor, and if they find a match they make what's called an electronic offer to the transplant center. The transplant center will decide to either accept or reject the organ. If they reject it, then the next transplant center on the list gets the offer, and so on until the organ is accepted."

"Why would you reject an offered organ if they're so rare? I would think you'd want every one you could get?"

"Sounds simple, but it's not. There are actually several reasons an organ can be rejected. Most of them are just due to compatibility issues. The patients have to be compatible as far as blood type. Height and weight have to be similar. For kidneys, there are what we call markers. Six of them total. We do what's called a histo-compatibility study and the more markers that match, the less chance of rejection by the recipient's immune system. For hearts we don't have to be so precise. Blood type, height, and weight are usually enough. Transport time used to be a big factor. A heart was only good for about five hours outside the body. So we basically drew a circle around the hospital and the new heart had to come from inside that circle."

"Used to be?"

"Remember when I said it was simpler a couple of years ago?"

"Yeah?"

"Let's just say that sometimes technology works for and against you at the same time."

"How so?"

Dayo swallowed his last bite of sandwich and looked around for any eavesdroppers before sipping his drink and continuing.

"You won't read about it or hear anybody involved in the process claim that it's true, but there was always a battle among the transplantation centers for donated organs. The shortage forced the large volume centers and locations with a low supply to compete against the small transplant centers with a large population base. Sometimes there was even a barter system going on. We'll take this heart and we'll owe you a kidney, that type of thing. Then you had the government trying to set rules as to whether to transplant the sickest patients first, or the less sick first as they had a better chance of surviving the procedure and the post-transplant period. It failed simply because each patient was different, and it was too easy for the doctors to change the definition of how sick their patient was. But that's all in the past now."

"How's that?"

"About two years ago this company out of Indiana comes out with this new transport device for organs. They call it the POPS machine. Stands for Portable Organ Preservation System. It's turned the transplant community on its ear. In the old days we recovered the organ from the donor, placed it on ice, then applied as much gas and jet fuel as we could to get it to the hospital in time to place it with the receiving patient. This new machine mimics the body's natural functions. Instead of cooling the heart, they keep it at normal body temperature. They also withdraw a liter of blood from the donor and mix it with some anti-clotting drugs and some nutrients and hook it up to the machine. The machine circulates the blood and oxygenates it. They can even hook up electrodes and keep it beating. They've kept a human heart on the machine for over twenty-four hours, and the heart was still viable for transplant. The POPS machine expanded the circle of donors from a few hours flight time to include the whole world."

"Amazing."

"True. Until you realize that the technology has outpaced the system. Before the machine came along, one of our surgeons would fly to the donor, recover the heart, and fly back with it. Now I get a phone call with the message that a heart was found in Mexico or Europe or somewhere and it's on its way. The heart shows up at the airport where a flight crew hands it off to one of our people. A chart about the donor may come with it, but unless you speak Spanish, and I mean medical Spanish, it's basically worthless. So we really have no way of verifying anything about the organ we receive. Other than some papers we can't read, and the assurance of the organization that handled the recovery, we're basically operating in the blind."

"So set up a system to verify the organs?"

"From what I'm reading, UNOS and Doctors Without Borders are working on it, but it takes time and a lot of connections. In the meantime, we just can't turn down organs that show up on our doorstep, so to speak, just because we don't have as much information as we would like about where they came from. How do I tell a patient that he's going to die because of red tape? I'm not. I'm a surgeon. Someone else is going to have to come up with a solution."

They all sat back and contemplated the doctor's position. A heart transplant was obviously a far cry from swapping out an engine in a car. Lenny and Jack had no idea.

"So how did our boy Oscar get himself in the system?" Lenny asked.

"I don't know, but he is. Everything checked out. There's nothing in his chart that would make him ineligible for a transplant. Trust me, I know it frontward and back."

"I can answer that one," Jack cut in. "I've got a computer wiz on my team. He's only 23, but whatever I ask him for, he always gets it. Sometimes it's through normal channels and, I suspect, sometimes not. I prefer not to know. Anyway, one day I asked him how secure our computers were. He just shrugged and said they weren't. He tells me a secure computer is an oxymoron, like child-safe plutonium. It doesn't exist and never will. You said there were fifty-eight different recovery organizations in the U.S. alone? I'm sure they all have a hundred or so employees. That means there are plenty of computers to hack. Oscar just determined what he needed to get his new heart, created a profile that perfectly fit the bill, threw some money at it and inserted himself into the system. I wouldn't even bother trying to track it down, be just a waste of time."

"Yeah well, I have some people with time to waste. Not my call anyway," Lenny replied.

Jack just absorbed the answer while he swirled the remains of his coffee around. It was an odd situation, one that he wasn't sure how to approach. His thoughts were interrupted by the doctor.

"Is there any way we can keep this quiet if he does end up getting a heart? If it becomes public the whole organ donor program will be damaged. The campaign they have going to increase the number of donors is working, and I'd hate to see it take a hit because of this."

"I don't know, Doc. Is he going to get a heart?"

"No way to answer that. He's at the top of the list, but he has an uncommon blood type. His chances are fair. I can't take him off the list just because of who he is, or for the fact that he'll probably be in prison soon. If anything, it gives him a guaranteed support system. Ironic, huh?"

"Paid for by us," Jack echoed.

"Just who is this guy, anyway? I mean, is what I see in the papers true?"

Jack exchanged a look with Lenny. Getting a nod, he sat up to face the doctor directly.

"Who is Oscar Hernandez? The papers call him the Colombian Al Capone, but that doesn't even scratch the surface. We think he killed his first man at age fourteen with some help from his brother. The two were a brains and muscle pair growing up in Medellin, and they quickly made a name for themselves. Oscar went from entering the cartel to running it in less than five years, and he's been running the show for over ten now. He's taken over one rival already when their leadership all died from a car bombing at the boss's house. The bomb took out twelve women and children, too. He's been tied to the deaths of three federal judges. They've tried to arrest him a few times for trafficking, but the witnesses always end up dead or just disappear. Flight 206 out of Cartagena blew up with 62 people on board back in 2002. There were three witnesses and their families on board coming to the States to testify against him. The papers never put it together, and we blamed it on the FARC to keep the reporters happy, but it was Oscar taking care of business. The goalie from the last World Cup team was murdered a week after they returned from Africa. Shot multiple times while walking down the street. Broad daylight. Evidently Oscar is quite the soccer fan and didn't like the goal he let by in the finals. No witnesses, of course. We estimate he's responsible for sixty percent of the cocaine that enters the U.S. annually. He has ties with the Zeta's and the other Mexican gangs you're hearing about in the papers. That enough for you, Doc?"

Dr. Dayo just nodded slowly as he absorbed the information.

"Yeah...Yeah, that's enough."

The two of them watched as the doctor bused his tray before standing.

"Gentleman, I should be getting back upstairs."

"Thanks for the information, Doc."

"Anytime."

Lenny watched as the doctor made his way through the tables to the trash bin. He quickly dumped his tray before stuffing his hands in his pockets and weaving through the crowd.

"What do you think?" Jack asked.

"I'd say that's a man with a lot on his mind. Can't say I'd want to be in his shoes right now."

"Yeah...me either."

DRUG CARTEL LEADER ESCAPES
FROM COLOMBIAN PRISON
January 12, 1996—The Washington Post

—ELEVEN—

"HE'S AT THE HOSPITAL again."

Jimmy just grunted and made a notation in the notebook they were keeping. GPS was a godsend. They had moved to a second-rate motel just outside the District and had watched Lenny move about the city for a couple of days now. The room was unkempt as they had refused the services of the maid since their arrival. Empty pizza boxes and dirty clothes adorned the vacant chairs and every horizontal surface. The window was open as they were on the third floor and high enough to avoid any prying eyes. Jimmy sat in his boxers with the laptop on the bed in front of him. Manuel sat similarly clothed at the small table. They wanted to keep what clothes they had clean for as long as possible. So far they had three sites picked out as possible locations for their target, and Manuel had driven past a few of them. Nothing they could pin down so far. One had turned out to be a new restaurant that wasn't in the GPS system yet, hardly anything to complain about.

They would change hotels again in another day to keep up appearances. Something with room service this time, as they were already sick of takeout. The days had become monotonous, but Jimmy kept them busy with contingency plans and scouting expeditions. While he had been to DC several times in the past, his partner had not. It was important for both of them to know the basic layout by heart if they had to make a rapid exit. Not to mention that security here was higher than what one would find anywhere else. So Manuel had spent several hours driving around town.

Jimmy had spent his time watching the tracker and surfing the internet. While information on Lenny was hard to come by, he had managed to find some bank accounts and had tracked the flow of money in and out of them. One of them had led him to an ex-wife. The money flowing into her account didn't stay long. Most of it left within a day or two and moved on to an account in Raleigh, North Carolina. The name on the account was Mellissa Hill.

Lenny's daughter.

While Lenny had no internet presence, his daughter was all over it. He soon had a complete profile of her including her class schedule, her position on the volleyball team, and even a copy of her last grades. Her Facebook profile provided an in-depth look into her social life. He knew who all her friends were, the name of her boyfriend, and all of her professors. He knew what bars she and her friends frequented, and even what her plans were for the upcoming weekend. Cracking her Twitter account provided a constantly updated monologue of where she was and what she was doing. It was almost too easy. He had already made a one page cheat-sheet of all of this information, as well as several downloaded pictures. He saved it to his thumb drive for printing next time they went out, before forwarding the information to their respective phones.

Manuel absorbed the information on the small screen in his hand and lingered on the pictures. Mellissa was a very pretty girl, a little on the young side for him, but nevertheless. He especially liked the pictures of her in her volleyball shorts.

"She's a looker, huh? Maybe I'll get lucky and get to meet her?"

Jimmy frowned at that. His partner had much to learn. Every man had his weakness. For some it was booze, others blow. For others still it was power and money that were an addiction. For Manuel it was women. While his partner was a man of questionable moral compass, he kept his addiction confined to willing participants. Something Jimmy accepted as he had no room to talk. But he had started to think of the man as a younger version of himself, and the comment was not something he approved of.

He sat back and fixed Manuel in his gaze. Manuel felt the look and turned his head from the screen. Seeing the expression on Jimmy's face, he sat up.

"Let me tell you something kid. This job you and I have? It requires a major character flaw. For better or worse, you and I both have it, and let me tell ya, it's nothing to be proud of. You know the ones who came before you? My previous partners? They all let it consume them. The flaw that let them do the things we do took over, and they started to think they were special. That they were *allowed* to do the things they did, just because nobody held them accountable for it. Hell, they were even praised for it. Some ugly-ugly things. Pretty soon the things they did defined them. They became animals. That thing you just said? Don't let those kinds of thoughts enter your mind. If they do, it tells me you're heading down the same path as they did. And you know what? They're all dead. They lost focus and became careless. This is just a job. Don't let it become the definition of who you are."

Manuel held his gaze and absorbed the words. He knew better than to make an offhand remark. The truth of the words rang true, and he had no choice but to accept them. The man was teaching him a lesson, one he had learned the hard way. His respect for Jimmy rose another notch.

"I understand. It won't happen again."

"Good man. Now tell me what you think we should do next."

Manuel had already been thinking along those lines, and Jimmy joined him at the table so they could compare notes. Some points on the map were listed and a few visits to Google maps provided them with pictures of the addresses. Manuel game-planned each one, and then discussed how they would get away. Jimmy accepted most of his plans, and modified or rejected the remainder, explaining the flaws and giving him a chance to fix them. The sun was going down before they packed it up to leave.

It was time for a better hotel.

* * *

The box had arrived in the mail as any other package would. Luis had snatched it from the maid's hands and set it on the table before ordering her out of the room. He took a long minute examining it from all sides while the parents impatiently watched. The address was written in plain blocked letters as if done by a child just learning to write. No return address was seen and the post office mark was that of Mexico City. There was nothing to distinguish it from any others.

On opening it, they found three items: a pre-paid cell phone and two envelopes. The negotiator quickly grabbed the envelopes before the father had a chance to.

"A moment please!"

The parents watched as he held the envelopes up to the light and examined them closely before selecting one to be opened. He pulled a small knife from his pocket and carefully slit the end open. Moving the other out of reach of the father, he shook the paper out onto the table and unfolded it by the corners. A quick examination showed it to be a list of dates and times and nothing more.

"What is this? I don't understand. Why do they not tell us what they want?"

The negotiator spoke quietly and calmly, the better to keep the parents from getting emotional. "This is the way we will talk with them. The phone can't be traced and doesn't have a caller ID option. It's pre-paid, so there's no bank account or check number to track down. The police could attempt to trace any calls made to it, but they're most likely on the move when we talk. It would take hundreds of men to do so and they know it. We'll buy a charger and extra battery tonight and keep the phone ready. The list is the times we can expect them to call. As I expected, they'll call three times a week. They may skip a day just to show us they are in charge. Do not get discouraged, this is how it's done."

The father just nodded and gripped the end of the table with both hands. He watched Luis reach for the other envelope.

"What is that?"

"I have to warn you first. It is a picture of your daughter."

The father thrust out his hand. "Let me see it!" Luis held it out of reach. His size allowed him to keep the father at bay.

"Since we are alone, I will show it to you. But I feel I have to warn you. These men never send a good picture. It is meant to provide proof of life, but it is also to intimidate you, to play on your emotions. If you let it affect you, then the kidnappers win. You understand?"

The two of them steeled themselves, and when Luis had gained as much as he could from the moment, he placed the picture on the table. The father picked it up with trembling hands and sank down into the chair next to his wife.

She took one look and let out a cry, burying her head in his shoulder and closing her eyes. The father did better, muttering a prayer as he gazed at the photo.

Luis gently took the photo from his hands and viewed it with a magnifying glass. He took in the girl's bruised face and bloody nose and mouth, and stifled a grin. The photo was perfect. He could clearly see the girl's beaten face with the tears coming from under the blindfold. The paper in her hands was easily identified as a popular market tabloid, and he pulled a folder from his briefcase and made a show of comparing it to printed copies of the front page from the last few weeks.

"This was taken three days ago," he announced. "She appears damaged, but otherwise unharmed. You must understand that they did this just for the picture. It is meant to draw a certain emotion."

"How can you tell?"

"The injuries are all new. If they were beating her, she would have some older bruising. The gun is not even cocked and the safety appears to be on. It could not even fire if they were to pull the trigger. This photo is staged to scare you."

The father took the photo from his hands and examined it again, looking for the things the man had mentioned. On verifying them himself, he saw the man was right. He nodded before laying the picture on the table in front of him.

"Unfortunately, there is nothing in the background that provides us any clue as to where she is. The first phone call is scheduled for two days from now. We'll have to wait and be ready."

Luis reached across the table and gently took the photo from the father again. This time he gave another quick look before putting it back in the envelope and into his pocket. The memory of the picture would work better than letting them keep it. Something he had discovered some time ago. Let their imaginations add to the image that they saw instead. It would better serve his purpose.

The father's mind raced as he attempted to comfort his wife and rein in his own emotions. A man of logic and considerable intelligence, he soon saw the truth of the man's words and was nodding in agreement. He raised his eyes to meet the negotiator's and said the words Luis was waiting to hear.

"We will do as you say."

* * *

Senator Lamar and his wife sat once again in the critical care unit. The activity outside the door was steady and sometimes even rushed. The hospital staff came and went in their color-coded scrubs, performing tasks that they couldn't imagine. The nurses typed endlessly into the computers while others stared at monitor screens and tracked their patients' progress in thick charts. The binders snapped open and closed with sharp cracks, but soon even these faded into the background noise outside the thick glass doors.

The activity inside the room was directly opposite that seen on the outside. Their daughter's chest rose and fell with the hiss of the ventilator. The heartbeat on the monitor stayed irregular and the expressions on the attending nurses' faces was one of concern every time they documented it, although they quickly tried to hide it after seeing the looks of the parents. It was plain to them that their daughter was not improving.

The senator watched as Dr. Fong entered the ward and stopped to see another patient. He couldn't help but notice that his bedside manner was on par with that of a seasoned politician. The smile was reassuring. He always made physical contact, be it a handshake or a comforting hand on a shoulder or a patient's foot. He was a natural educator, also, and was not above using the dry erase board to explain a procedure or some anatomical mystery. It worked. The patient always smiled and the family sat a little straighter after his departure.

Dr. Fong caught the senator's gaze as he crossed the room toward the desk. He offered a quick smile and wave of acknowledgement before he grabbed a chart out of the rack and walked toward them. The chart was Tessa's, and it had grown to two volumes since they had arrived. He paused outside the door to flip through several pages and graphs, turning the chart sideways to take in certain pages. His brow creased as he absorbed the information. He turned to ask a question of the nurse at the desk that the senator could not make out. The reply was a jumble of numbers that meant nothing to them. The doctor simply nodded as if he had expected the answer before turning to slide the glass door open.

The senator rose and automatically offered a hand which Dr. Fong grabbed while switching the chart to his other hand with a practiced movement.

"Morning, Senator, Mrs. Lamar. How are you two holding up?"

"We're doing as well as expected."

He smiled and pointedly looked at his wife.

"Is that true? He is a politician."

She smiled a smile she didn't really feel to humor the doctor before replying. "I got some sleep last night, don't worry about me."

"Okay."

He walked in and sat on the edge of the girl's bed and rested a hand on her foot. The chart was laid aside while he formed his thoughts.

"I'm afraid I don't have any news good or bad. I had hoped to see some improvement in your daughter's cardiac output by now, but it seems to have plateaued off. Her ejection fraction is low and we're seeing some signs of ischemia."

"I'm sorry?"

"Ischemia. It means her heart isn't getting enough oxygen. I think it's time we talk about the balloon pump I mentioned earlier. Do you remember me talking about that?"

"I remember something to that effect mentioned."

Dr. Fong waved it away. "You had a lot on your mind. I'll give you a refresher." He stood and grabbed the dry erase marker and after taking a look at the board, erased it with the sleeve of his coat, something the senator thought showed some panache. A quick 2D drawing of the heart was soon on the board with the aorta protruding out the top and arching over the left side.

"Okay. If you can follow my lack of artistic ability, this is the heart and this is the aorta, the main vessel carrying blood away from the heart. This feeds the arteries that go out to the body. It's a high pressure system, and the blood is oxygenated at this point. That means this blood needs to feed the heart, also. However, the pressure is too high to feed it directly. It would eventually damage the vessels it was flowing to. So it does it by way of back pressure. Are you still with me?"

The senator and his wife followed the lines as they appeared, along with the lecture, and both of them managed to keep up. They nodded to the affirmative.

"See this valve right here? It has flaps that open and close with each beat. One of them blocks the arteries leading to the heart when it's open. Once the pressure drops a bit, the valve closes and the flap uncovers the opening to those arteries. The back pressure remaining in the aorta then pushes the blood into the heart's arteries. If the pressure is too low due to a weak heart, the flow of blood becomes inadequate. Still okay?"

The senator smiled. "Still with you, Doc."

"Okay, so what we do with the balloon pump is we go in through the femoral artery down here in her leg and we feed the balloon up and into the aorta right about here. Once it's in place we program the machine to sense her heartbeat and inflate the balloon, like this, at just the right time to increase the pressure in this area. That forces more blood to the heart and provides it with more oxygen. The more oxygen it gets, the easier it is for it to function and that, of course, helps it to heal."

Dr. Fong stepped back and examined his mess of squiggles and arrows and hoped he hadn't jumped over their heads with the explanation.

"Did that explain it okay? If not, I'll be happy to show you again. It's important that you understand it."

The senator looked at his wife and, getting a nod from her, he answered for them.

"I'd say we understand it okay. It sounds really simple actually. You can do all that with just a small wire in the leg?"

"I never say that it's simple, there's *always* a danger when dealing with the heart. The device has to be placed just right and monitored closely afterward. But for the benefit it provides, I would say it far exceeds the risk. I'll need your consent to have it placed. Don't rush. I'll give you a few minutes to talk."

He rose and left the room to talk with the charge nurse. Senator Lamar's eyes were drawn to the dry erase board. While he had talked, the doctor had again erased the board with his sleeve and re-written what was previously there. He marveled at the man's memory.

Turning to his wife, he saw her watching her daughter's chest rise and fall. She looked close to tears. He reached for her hand and gave it a comforting squeeze and was relieved to get one in return.

"Honey?"

"I don't like it. Another machine? But I trust him, and I don't see how we have much choice," she said.

"I think it's best, too. I'll go tell him."

The senator rose and left the room, closing the door behind him.

"Doc?"

"Yes?" Doctor Fong turned. "What did we decide?"

"If you think the pump will help her, then we both agree that it's what should be done."

"I do. It'll give her heart a little help, hopefully enough to avoid a transplant. That's the worst case scenario, but I have to remind you that it's still a real possibility."

"If you need me to sign something I'm ready to."

"Very well, Susan will get you the papers and we'll get it done this afternoon."

Before the senator could thank him, the doctor's attention was drawn away by the loud beeping from the monitor bank.

"Bed six is in V-tach!"

The senator stood tight against the counter as the staff rushed past him and into the room. He watched through the glass as Dr. Fong gave orders and the staff repeatedly shocked the patient as they had his daughter. Drugs were pushed and within a minute the patient was back to a normal heartbeat.

All of this went unnoticed by Rita Lamar. As soon as her husband had left the room her gaze had returned to the bed holding her daughter. This time she focused not on her daughter's chest, or her sleeping face, but on the chart left behind by the doctor. She squinted to see the tabs and their titles separating the three-inch thick binder into sections until she found the one she wanted.

With everyone's eyes diverted elsewhere, she pulled the chart into her lap and flipped it open to the section she wanted.

LABS

Tabbing through the papers she quickly found one labeled CHEMISTRY and another that said HISTOCOMPATIBILITY. She chose two others that seemed to contain the most information and pulled them from the chart. Creasing and folding, she had them stuffed in her purse within seconds and the chart was placed back on the bed just as her husband turned and reentered the room.

"They got him back," he informed her.

"Good," she said, her voice cracking.

He once again grasped his wife's hand in his own. He was surprised to find it sweaty.

TURKISH DOCTOR WANTED BY INTERPOL
IN SPOTLIGHT IN ORGAN TRAFFICKING INQUIRIES

November 9, 2011—New York Times

—TWELVE—

DR. DAYO RUBBED HIS eyes and sat up from leaning over the desk. There were still three charts waiting for his review on the right side of the desk. But the pile on the left contained twice that, and that was enough for one night. After a day of surgeries, including an emergency stab wound, he had given a lecture to some students, answered two requests for consult from other doctors, and then tackled the pile of charts. Since it was not long after the switch for daylight savings time, the sky outside was already dark, the only shadows being provided by the mercury lights in the parking lot.

He rubbed his neck as he made a halfhearted attempt at organizing his desk. Realizing it was going to stay a mess no matter what he did, he quickly gave up. Retrieving his coat from the rack by the door along with his helmet, he locked up on his way out. Christine had said goodnight hours ago and the outer office was dark. He navigated more by memory than anything else and managed to make it to the door without running into anything. Once out in the hallway, he looked both ways and saw no one but a night janitor polishing the tile floor at the other end of the hall. His shoes squeaked even louder now with no noise to compete with them.

Preferring to walk after sitting for so long, he made his way to the stairs. Two flights down he emerged into another hallway. This one showed some activity as the ER at Johns Hopkins was always busy. He passed an unconscious man being pushed on a stretcher heading for the CT scanner. His head sported a bloody bandage and his arms were red and scraped down to the raw tissue. A foot also stuck out at an odd ankle. The look from the tech who was pushing him said it all.

"Busy night?" Dr. Dayo asked.

"We're packed, Doc. Five car pileup on 95. They're still bringing them in. Better get out while you can."

"I plan to."

He left the man behind and continued on toward the ER entrance. He heard the chaos that was the Emergency Room well before he entered through the double doors. Here the noise quickly rose to a level that drowned out his squeaky shoes. The patients were stacked in the hallways, and he had to maneuver around the techs and ER nurses who rushed in every direction. An overdose chose to empty his stomach as Dr. Dayo passed, and he moved just in time to save his shoes. Approaching a trauma room, he saw a team working on a man in a similar state to that which he had seen in the hallway. The only difference was this man was still conscious and screaming in pain. The odor of alcohol could be smelled wafting off the man even from outside the room. The ER doctor looked up from his place at the head of the bed and caught Dr. Dayo's eye. He just shrugged and smiled as he made ready to intubate the man on the stretcher. Another drunk driver, nothing new to him. Dr. Dayo moved on before he got the urge to step in. He sometimes missed the excitement of the ER, but not tonight, he was just too tired.

Stepping through another set of doors, he passed through the triage area. The waiting room was packed with all manner and color of people. Some visibly sick, others bloody and injured. A few had the fidgety look of those close to withdrawal and others looked perfectly fine, calmly waiting and sipping their vending machine coffee. He made his way through the throng until he was able to step outside and was greeted by Harold, one of the hospital's longtime security people. While Johns Hopkins was one of the best hospitals in the world, it did not reside in the best part of town. Their security staff was larger than most hospitals of its size.

"Gettin' while the gettin's good, Doc?"

"You know it. Looks like a full house for some time in there."

"Actually getting better now that the snow's gone. Cuts down on all the homeless trying to get a bed for the night."

"I know I'm ready for mine."

"Give me a second and I'll have Jerry walk you out."

An approaching siren announced the arrival of another ambulance. The wail died as it rounded the corner.

"That'll be the last one from the pileup," Harold commented as he pushed buttons on the panel in his kiosk. The lights they triggered would tell the crew where to take their patient.

"You're busy here. Tell Jerry I can make it fine myself."

Harold frowned at that. He'd been a cop before taking this job, and he knew the area they were in all too well.

"Not safe, Doc. Jerry will be here in a few. What's a few more minutes?"

"It's all right. I'll be on my bike and out of here before he gets here, but thanks."

"All right, be careful."

Harold shook his head as he watched the doctor walk off into the shadows toward the employee parking lot. Doctors were all the same he thought. They all thought they were untouchable. He hoped this one never had to learn the hard way.

Dr. Dayo made it through the gate and was fumbling with his keys in the faint light when he arrived at his bike. A new Harley Davidson.

He had finally had the courage to ignore his wife long enough to buy it. He had secretly shopped for months before deciding on the make and model. One of the few pleasures he had was the occasional ride with a few of his surgeon buddies. He now paused for a moment to take in the lines of the sculpture of steel and leather. As much as he was a fan of the old-school Harleys, his love of cutting edge technology had won out and he had chosen the new V-Rod Nighthawk edition. Its black-on-black color scheme gave him a chill the first time he had seen it, and it still did today. Now that the weather had changed, he had taken every chance he could to ride it to work.

Still holding the helmet in his hands, he threw a leg over the seat and reached out with the key to start it up for a minute of warm up before he left. He was stopped short by something obstructing the key. He leaned over to see a big glob of something foul stuck to the ignition switch. Gum? Some damn kid? He poked at it. Wax. Someone had smeared wax over his ignition and it had dried there. He picked away at it with a fingernail and discovered it would come off. He had it halfway exposed when a voice interrupted his progress.

"Having some trouble, doctor?"

The voice had a condescending tone with a Spanish accent. Dr. Dayo straightened up to see two men watching him, one of them smoking a cigarette. He blew the smoke out forcefully before smiling at the doctor. He had greasy hair and a large tattoo on his neck. The other was just big and sported a Ravens Jacket.

Dr. Dayo looked toward the hospital, hoping to see Harold or Jerry walking toward him, but the lot was as empty as when he had arrived.

"Relax, Dr. Dayo. Nobody is going to hurt you."

"Do I know you?"

The one talking took a long last drag on his cigarette before dropping it to the ground. He crushed it out with a steel-toed boot before once again smiling that smile, as if he were a cat playing with a mouse. The other just glared before slowly walking a wide circle around them. He kept his hands in his pockets, and Dr. Dayo shifted in the seat to keep them both in view.

"No, you don't know me. But we know you."

"What do you want?"

"Nothing...nothing. Just to give you a message, that is all."

Dr. Dayo swung his leg over the seat and turned so he could still see the man who had now moved behind him. The man didn't stop, he merely continued to circle. Dr. Dayo tightened his grip on the helmet. The two men stood their ground, not impressed by his movements.

"And what message would that be?"

"You have a patient, a friend of ours, you might say. We want to be...reassured that you will do your best for him. You will do your best for him, right, Doctor?"

Dr. Dayo understood the Spanish accent now. Hernandez was evidently having second thoughts about his surgeon.

"The man's heart is failing. He'll die soon unless he gets a transplant. I have no control over that."

"We understand that...but if a heart should come?"

Dayo grit his teeth. "He'll get my best effort."

The greasy one lost his smile before reaching in his pocket. Dayo stiffened and the man watched him with his hand frozen for a moment before he slowly withdrew the pack of cigarettes. He took his time tapping the pack before extracting one and lighting it. The smile returned.

"Very good, Doctor. That is what we like to hear. This man...he is very dear to us, you understand. I would hate to think what his death would drive us to do."

Dayo just stood and waited, ready to swing the helmet if they came closer.

The smoker surprised him by clapping his hands and raising his arms wide as if to give Dayo a hug. The other one turned and started across the parking lot.

"I'm sorry to delay you, Doctor. I know you must be eager to get home to your wife, Anna, and your two boys. The older one can really swing a bat, yes? You should be proud."

He made an elaborate show of putting his hands together as if in prayer and bowing before flashing the twisted grin as he spun on a heel to follow his companion. Dr. Dayo watched them until they disappeared into the dark streets.

Once they were gone, the doctor considered going back to the hospital, but he realized it was over. The men had sent their message, loud and clear. But what should he do now?

He threw his leg back over the bike and scraped the remaining wax away with the key before inserting it. The bike started with a throaty roar and he quickly revved the engine a few times to warm it up. The helmet went on after a look behind him and he quickly worked the gas and clutch to move the bike onto the street. He took several turns as fast as he could and drove home at well over the legal limit. Parking the bike outside the front door, he bounded up the steps and into the house.

"Anna!"

He moved toward the sound of the TV in the family room. Empty.

"Anna!"

He strode into the kitchen. Also empty. He pulled a knife from the block on the countertop before moving through the kitchen on the way to the stairs. A door opened in front of him and his wife emerged holding a basket of laundry.

"Matthew? Is that you yelling?"

Dr. Dayo quickly hid the knife behind his leg.

"Just me, honey. House was empty. I couldn't find you or the boys."

"The boys are at a sleepover. Are you okay?"

Dayo recovered quickly. "Yeah, just tired I guess. I'm gonna go upstairs and change."

"Okay, come find me in the family room when you're done? I'll fix you a drink."

"That sounds good."

She pecked his cheek as she walked past with the laundry. He managed to keep the knife out of sight and climbed the stairs to the master bedroom. Pulling off the leather jacket, he flung it on the bed. The knife lay next to it and he stared at it for some time before moving it to the bottom of one of his drawers. He shed clothes as he walked to the shower. The water worked to clear his head, and he thought about what had happened and what he should do while the water flowed.

Eventually his thoughts were interrupted by a knock on the door.

"You still in the shower?"

"Just getting out now," he yelled.

"All right, I left your drink on the nightstand."

"Thanks, honey, I'll be down in a minute."

"Okay."

He quickly dried off and left the bathroom to pick up the drink. He drained half of it on his way back to the bathroom. He combed his wet hair back and examined himself in the mirror. He tossed back the rest of the drink before nodding to himself in agreement.

Walking out again, he quietly closed the bedroom door. Picking up his cell phone he scrolled through the numbers until he found the one he had just typed in a few days ago.

"Federal Bureau of Investigations, how can I direct your call?"

"This is Doctor Mathew Dayo from Johns Hopkins calling. I need to speak with Agent Jack Randall please."

"I'll have to page him, sir, is this urgent?"

Dayo ran his hand through his wet hair.

"Yes."

* * *

The ward was quiet as the medical teams moved about caring for the various patients. There were no private beds or different levels of care. All the men, regardless of age or nationality, shared the large room until they were either healthy enough to leave, or they succumbed to their wounds.

The Major was making small talk with the nurse at the desk. He had made it a point to get to know the medical staff as well as possible and they had become used to his presence. He would often walk the ward at all hours, claiming boredom or lack of sleep. He would visit the Afghan patients and flip through the charts so he could report to their superiors or the relatives on their progress.

He had also made an effort at observing the staff while they operated the various pumps and ventilators. Occasionally he would even venture forth a question, and the staff had proven to be eager to explain the equipment, as most professionals are. They enjoyed showing off their skills and he had developed a good working knowledge. He was at the point where he could hear a particular beep and know what piece of equipment had made the sound.

The desk was at one end of the long room with the most critical patients close to it and the rest spreading down the narrow hallway by level-of-care needed. As the conversation continued, he watched as the two doctors on duty made their way slowly down the line. The Afghan boy was about halfway down the right side and they were close. He cut the conversation off with a quick excuse and made his way to the boy's bed just as the doctors did. One picked up the chart and flipped through it.

"G'mornin, Doc."

"Morning, Major."

"Any good news I can tell the family?"

The doctor read a quick graphic before shaking his head. He flipped it shut with a practiced movement before resting his gaze on the patient.

"The only good news is the burns on his neck and face seem to be healing all right. I was worried about infection. If he was in the States he'd be in a burn unit, which is kept a lot more sterile than what we can do here. But he seems to be okay there. We'll keep the bandages on him for awhile longer just to be sure. As for the chest tube, I think it'll have to stay for another day or two at least. I'd like to keep him on the vent and let his body rest."

They both looked the boy over while the doctor spoke. With one eye showing through the bandages covering half his head and all of his neck, it was hard to tell what he looked like. The endotrachial breathing tube protruding from his mouth jerked slightly with each cycle of the ventilator. The bandages on his chest rose and fell in a steady rhythm, and the bubbling of the water seal servicing the chest tube sitting on the floor could be heard over it all. Two pumps served the IVs in each arm, keeping the boy sedated and paralyzed so the machines could do their work without interference.

"So what's the prognosis? Think he'll pull through?"

"I don't quote odds if that's what you're looking for. Is he better than he was yesterday? Hard to say really. He's not worse. If the burns keep healing and the chest does the same, we can hopefully remove the chest tube and start thinking about weaning him off the vent. My biggest worries at this point are infection and a P.E."

"P.E.?"

"Sorry. Pulmonary embolism. Basically an air bubble or a clot blocking blood flow to the lungs. With chest trauma like he has, he's prone to developing embolisms and clots. If he throws a big one, he could arrest or even have a stroke."

"So what can you do about that?"

"Not much. If it happens...at least it'll be quick. I wouldn't get the family's hopes up just yet if I were you. Kid's tough, and he's got a strong heart, but he's far from out of the woods yet."

The Major made a few notes while the doctor waited patiently for any more questions.

"Okay. Not worse, but no real improvement. I'll lay it out straight for them."

"That's all you can do."

"Thanks, Doc."

"Any time."

IN A POOR ECONOMY, BLACK MARKET ORGAN TRADE IS A BOOMING BUSINESS

October 27, 2011—International Business Times

—THIRTEEN—

RITA LAMAR WAS OUT of her element. She gripped the wheel with both hands and tried not to make eye contact with the people on the sidewalk as they stared at her. Why she was drawing such attention was obvious. She was a white woman in a Mercedes traveling through an area where she did not belong. She checked her progress on the GPS and the red line on the map had so far kept her true. She spotted a young boy sitting on a graffitied mailbox. He met her gaze and flashed a hand gesture at her. She had no idea what it meant. Another one, maybe in his teens, moved from his spot against the building and walked to the curb. He looked confused as she drove on by, but just shrugged it off and returned to his spot against the wall.

Soon the neighborhood changed and the parked cars spewing loud rap music gave way to Latin beats. More groups of men, some of them heavily tattooed, crowded the corners and sat in the parked cars. The signs were now all in Spanish and she started looking for her destination. The GPS guided her through a turn.

A stoplight held up her progress and she felt her heart beat quicken as she was eyeballed by the people around her. She kept her eyes straight ahead and prayed for the light to turn.

A loud knock on the window next to her made her jump.

"What you want?"

She just stared back. A young Latino man dressed in baggy jeans and a soccer jersey was standing next to the car. A bandana adorned his head, which was also covered by a baseball cap, while his neck and arms were covered in tattoos. He looked both ways up and down the street before repeating his question.

"What you want, lady? Rock? Powder? I got it all. Good stuff."

Her mind raced to catch up. Drugs. He thinks I want drugs. What do I do?

"Come on, lady, don't got all day. What you want?"

She just shook her head. He stepped back and glared at her in disbelief before breaking into laughter. He leaned back in till his face was inches from hers through the glass. Suddenly he punched the door of the car and she jumped in her seat against the seat belt. His laughter was loud and the crowd on the sidewalk joined in.

She quickly recovered and drove through the intersection despite the light still being red. She forced herself to calm down as the GPS took her around another corner.

Four blocks later, she found her destination. The bar sat in the middle of the street and sported a long line of motorcycles in front. A crowd of men and women dressed in leather sat around the entrance and in the street. Two of them stepped into the street and stopped her car. One looked in all directions as he approached. He leaned down to look at her before smiling. He tapped on the glass.

"Mrs. Lamar?"

She rolled the window down an inch.

"Yes."

"Pull your car around the back of the building. I'll come and get you. Don't be afraid, no one will harm you here."

She just nodded and rolled the window back up before following the pointed finger. The back of the bar's parking area held even more bikes and she only waited for a moment before the man was back. She unlocked the door and stepped out, quickly closing it behind her. She was about to lock it when the keys were snatched from her hand. She flinched.

"This way. Say nothing until we tell you to," the man said.

He indicated a doorway. She clasped her purse tightly and did as they asked. A swarm of men surrounded the car, checking every inch inside and out and even crawling underneath it. She forced herself to ignore them and walked through the doorway. A dark hallway led toward the front of the building where loud music emanated from an overhead set of speakers. Another man waited outside a door. A nod from the first man prompted him to open it and she was led inside. The room was lit by a pair of floor lamps and a small desk lamp. On the other side sat a man engrossed in some papers. Not dressed in the leather of the bikers, he instead wore a pair of khaki pants and a silk golf shirt. Unlike the others, his skin was void of tattoos. He looked up as if he were expecting them before shuffling the papers back into a file and putting them away. He waved them inside before stopping to light a cigarette. Rita Lamar met his gaze as he sized her up. When he had scrutinized every inch of her, he nodded a command to the men who had brought her. The guard from the door stepped forward. He pointed to her purse.

"If you don't mind?"

She pulled the purse off her shoulder and handed it to the man. He dropped it on the floor without looking in it. He then reached out with both hands and took hers. Gently turning her he placed her hands on the desk. She was treated to a very thorough and undignified search. He ran his hands through her hair and down over every inch of her body. He felt inside her bra and between her legs. He removed her necklace and bracelet and handed them to the other man. Her shoes came off and he examined them closely. The other man examined the jewelry under the light of the lamp before tossing it all on the desk. He then retrieved the purse and dumped its entire contents on the table. They all watched as he examined every item carefully, taking his time. He found a box of tampons and sliced each one open with a knife until he had a pile of cotton on the table. Once he was done with its contents he examined the purse itself, splitting the strap open with the knife and probing every corner. When he was satisfied there were no listening devices hidden anywhere, he raked the entire mess back into the purse and dropped it on the floor.

"She's clean."

The man behind the desk just nodded and the two left the room, one of them taking her cell phone with him. Once the door was shut, he gestured to the seat across from him. Rita summoned what was left of her dignity and smoothed her dress back down into position. She took the offered seat without touching her hair.

The man sitting across from her gazed at her face, and then at a laptop computer open on his desk. She waited in silence. When he finally did speak it was with a rich Spanish accent.

"Mrs. Lamar, you look just like your pictures."

He spun the laptop around to reveal a picture of her and her husband on the campaign trail. She stood beside the senator as they waved to the crowd. He spun the laptop back.

"When I got the message to come meet you I was somewhat surprised. My employer is not one who gets phone calls from the wives of senators. Just what is it that prompted your call?"

"I have an offer for you."

"Go on."

"How do I know you have the authority to make this deal?"

"Mrs. Lamar, I did not travel for twelve hours to waste my time. Do I need to remind you that you called us? Or that if this is some kind of play to make things...difficult...for us, my employer will not act favorably toward you? He is not a man who plays games. Nor does he like his time wasted."

"I understand."

"Then what is it you want?"

Rita talked for two minutes. The man's interest grew with each sentence.

"An intriguing offer. I think my employer would be quite interested. You have the information we need with you?"

Rita reached for the purse on the floor and rooted around in the mess until she found the hospital papers. She handed them across without a word. The man scanned them quickly before setting them down on the desk blotter.

"This should be sufficient."

"When can I expect an answer?"

"I must take some steps to verify what you have told me, but I think we will have an answer for you soon. This number is yours alone?"

"It's my cell phone number. No one else ever has it."

"Very well, I suggest you keep it close by. I will have these men escort you back to a…more familiar area. We wouldn't want anything bad to happen to you now, would we?"

The man's smile made her skin crawl.

* * *

"One hour, that's all I can stand."

"Jack, you're being ridiculous. Can't you just enjoy yourself for once? It's a cocktail party, not a board meeting."

"There's a bar right?"

Debra smiled and waved at a woman across the room as they entered, and without losing her grin, berated her husband.

"Jack, if you embarrass me here tonight you may not like how the evening will end."

Jack frowned at that, but knew better than to reply. He simply put on his best fake smile and followed his wife farther into the house. They made it inside without being announced like royalty, as had happened at the last one of these things she had dragged him to. The Washington cocktail party circle was a list he would rather not have his name on, but due to the press and the connections he had made, it was unavoidable. The invitations came to the house and were intercepted by his wife before he got home. She would spend hours debating which ones they were to attend, and then, of course, there was the shopping. She had a closet full of dresses, but always had to find something new for each party. Jack had finally put his foot down and limited the parties to one a month. The alternative was too unpleasant.

Tonight they were at a senior senator's home. The welcoming party for the new freshman congressmen who had just taken office was a much anticipated gathering. Some had been carefully selected and subsequently elected with the backing of the party. Others were in place due to massive campaign spending out of their own pockets. A few were radicals that had jumped on a vacancy left open as the result of a juicy scandal. Whatever the route they arrived by, there were a lot of new faces in the crowd. Tonight the established would be checking out the new class. Everyone was either on stage or one of the judges. Jack hated every minute of it.

Nevertheless, he shook hands and said the right things as they made their way through the crowd. His wife had snagged a glass of something bubbly off a passing tray, but he had yet to see anything to his taste travel by. Finally, he spotted what looked like a bar in the far corner. Skillfully passing Debra off to a talkative wife-of-somebody, he made his way there.

"What can I get you, sir?"

The man was older than Jack by twenty years and calling him sir with an island accent. Something Jack was never comfortable with.

He eyeballed the table and saw nothing but glasses of champagne and what looked to be several different wines.

"This it?"

"We have over thirty wines from the senator's native California, as well as several champagnes."

"Okay…what's your name?"

"My name is Marco, sir."

"Just Jack is fine, Marco. You have anything…else?"

Marco looked left and right before leaning foreword.

"The senator has a full bar in the butler's pantry. What can I get you, Mister Jack?"

"Some scotch?"

Marco nodded and signaled to a passing waiter. A whispered conversation led to his disappearing into the hallway behind Marco. He reappeared moments later with a towel covered tray. Marco placed it under his table before rising with a rocks glass full of amber liquid in his hand as if by magic.

"Macallan 12?"

"You're my hero, Marco."

"I have the bottle here, should you wish some more."

"I won't be far."

Jack saluted the man with his raised glass before returning to the crowd to find his wife. He was forced to stop and shake a few hands and endured having his picture taken with a few senators as he wandered the room. He soon found her in a small group of people. Two of the couples he recognized as a sitting senator nearing the end of his last term and the head of the Department of Agriculture. A fourth woman was in the group alone and was drawing the gaze of a few passersby. The hair was a little too blond and the makeup a little too heavy. The dress, while certainly stylish and expensive, just didn't seem to fit and barely contained the body within it. Despite her skinny figure, she sported an obviously augmented bosom that she apparently was quite proud of by how much of it was on display. She gripped the champagne glass like it was a hammer and laughed loudly at an unheard joke while she tottered on her heels.

Jack caught his wife's eye and raised a questioning eyebrow. She managed to roll her eyes before returning her face to its mask of politeness. Jack moved in to rescue her.

"Oh, is this your handsome man?"

"Yes, this is my Jack. He's the FBI liaison to Homeland Security at the moment."

"And doing a fine job I hear," the senator added.

"Yes, thank you, senator."

"Honey, this is Luanne Foster, Congressman Foster's wife. From Mississippi."

"Nice to meet you."

"And you too. I didn't know there were so many handsome men in Washington. Debra here better keep an eye on you."

"She does," Jack confirmed. He took a sip of his scotch so he wouldn't have to say more.

"Just where is our newest member anyway. He leaves you all alone?" the senator asked the woman's cleavage. His wife stewed, but kept her face impassive.

"Oh, he went to find the little boys room. I'm sure he'll find his way back soon."

As if on cue a young man in a new suit joined the group. He quickly retrieved his drink from his wife's hand before slipping an arm around her. His smile was full of white teeth and he radiated energy.

"Hello all, what did I miss?"

"Honey, this is Jack Randall and his wife Debbie." Jack felt his wife tense—she hated to be called Debbie. It had been Debra since high school.

"Hello, don't believe I know you. I'm Congressman Harry Foster of Mississippi. Nice to meet you."

Strike one, Jack thought. Never admit to not knowing someone, especially in this crowd. He exchanged a look with the senior senator as he shook the man's hand. He released it and sized him up while he shook Debra's hand a little too vigorously before returning his arm around the waist of his wife.

Strike two. Jack's eyes didn't miss much and he now focused on the small trace of white powder on his shirt just right of his tie, probably left there as he returned something to his inside jacket pocket. He checked the man's eyes as he listened to something the Cabinet head was saying and got the confirmation he was looking for. Jack waited until he was done speaking and before the young man could reply he spoke.

"You missed some."

The young man stopped with his mouth open before recovering and turning his gaze to Jack.

"I'm sorry?"

Jack leaned forward slightly and fixed his gaze on the man's shirt.

"I said you missed some."

His wife saw it before any of the others and quickly brushed at it, but the damage had been done. Jack took his wife's arm and led her away.

Debra allowed herself to be led to a corner before speaking.

"Jack, that was totally uncalled for."

"Uncalled for? The man is dumb enough to do that stuff here, in front of all these government people, *and* an FBI agent, and you think I'm wrong? It amazes me how anybody that stupid can get himself elected."

"Still, you didn't have to make a scene."

"*I* made a scene?" He fixed his wife with his gaze. Now it was him calling her out.

"Okay, maybe not. But do you have to be a cop all the time? Can't we just have a night without the FBI on duty?"

"All right. Not sure how I'm supposed to do that."

Debra just stewed and waved to a friend. Keeping up appearances. Jack decided to defuse the situation.

"Somebody should at least call the fashion police on that wife of his."

Debra face cracked into a grin. She couldn't help herself.

"Stop it."

"Well? How anybody can wear that much makeup and still be over-exposed is beyond me. She shrink that dress on with a hair dryer?"

Debra hid her grin behind her hand and stifled a giggle.

"I thought Senator Rosen was gonna fall right in if he leaned forward any more. Was she on that Real Housewives show?"

Debra let out a laugh, but managed to cut it short. She dragged her husband away till they were out of earshot.

"Oh, Jack. I think I've had enough for tonight. Take me home."

"Yes, ma'am."

Jack got a nod of approval from Marco as his wife pulled him past the bar.

The evening turned out better than they had both hoped.

MEXICO SUSPECTS EX-DRUG CZAR TOOK HUGE BRIBES FROM TRAFFICKERS

November 21, 2008—CNN

—FOURTEEN—

LUIS THUMBED THE REMOTE till he found the soap opera his wife liked. As long as it was on she was happy. And occupied. Without the TV she was constantly finding reasons to nag him. It was one of the drawbacks to working at home. He dropped the remote on the table and walked to the back bedroom. The kids knew not to bother their father when he was in the back room.

Closing the door behind him, he sat at the desk and fired up his computer. After a few security measures he was in his email account. An innocent looking message caught his attention and he clicked it open.

Anyone looking over his shoulder would see the message as a normal correspondence between two family friends. This one contained a brief update-on-the-family type of message and had a few pictures attached.

He clicked on the first one to see what looked like a birthday party for a young boy. The boy smiled at the camera with the cake full of candles in front of him. Another showed the boy with his mother and father looking on as he blew them out, while a third pic was of the three of them posing and waving into the camera.

Innocent pictures.

Luis quickly saved each picture to his hard drive and called up another program. He transferred the first picture to the new program and waited for the prompt. When the program had scanned the picture, the prompt appeared with no hint as to what was needed. Luis knew. He looked at the numbers he had jotted down from the text section of the message. Arranging them in order, he added and subtracted the first number to and from the remaining ones until he had the key decoded. He quickly punched it into the computer.

The picture became a mess of pixels as it was slowly decoded by the software into a text document. It was a lab report. He clicked on the icon in the corner and soon the printer was spewing the data out. He lit another cigarette while he waited and then repeated the process on the remaining two pictures.

Once he had all three printed out he exited the program and called up another file. His guest list, as he liked to call them. He eliminated most based on blood type alone. After narrowing it down to three, he settled in for a more detailed comparison. The cigarette burned down in the ashtray, ignored as he read the last file.

He had a match.

He fired off a return message to the sender before leaning back in his chair with a frown. The timeline was too quick. They would probably not be able to pull a double profit out of this one. But it gave him an idea.

He only had to wait a few minutes for the reply. The computer announced it with a beep and he eagerly clicked the mouse. It was what he expected. He copied down the times and sending instructions.

He clicked the computer off and stored the files in a locked file cabinet before picking up his cell phone. It was answered on the first ring.

"Yes?"

"I need you at the clinic tonight. I'm sending you the information. I'll need some additional items also." He went on to explain.

"I understand."

Luis hung up and selected a different phone from the many in the drawer. This one was also answered on the first ring.

"The package goes to the clinic tonight."

"The usual time?"

"Yes, don't be late."

Luis hung up and selected a third phone.

"We have a change in plans. We will be using the second script tomorrow."

"It's too soon. What if they ask for more proof?"

"I have an idea for that. Listen."

A minute later the man was chuckling.

"That just might work."

* * *

Half a world away, the Major had received a similar email. After checking his files he had also found a match. Now he sat in the makeshift morgue with his partner to discuss their options.

"A heart? Why couldn't it be a damn kidney? Even with the new transport machine, we'd be right on the edge of the viability time."

"How long do we have?"

"A kidney is good for forty-eight hours with the new machine, maybe more. A heart was only good for four to six maybe until they came along. If I harvest it while there's still blood flow I can get it on the machine immediately. Maybe twenty hours, but that's pushing it. It could last long enough to get it to the east coast. But the plane will have to be waiting on the damn runway ready to go."

"The plane's in Bangkok right now. I can get them here quick. We just have to time it right. If the heart is no good, we don't get the full amount, not even close."

"This can't be a cadaver harvest. The heart needs to come from a living donor."

"Living donor? The kid needs to be alive when you take it? How the hell are we supposed to do that? We don't get them until they're dead."

The mortician paced the room while he thought it out. It was a lot of money and he only had a few weeks left to make it. He could give a damn about some filthy little Afghan kid.

"The kid would have to be brain dead."

"I don't follow you."

"Brain dead just means the brain is gone but the body keeps going. There's no way to bring them back and they would die a few days later anyway. We just have to figure out a way to do it without the medical team getting suspicious."

"There isn't going to be an autopsy. The body and the heart will be gone before he has a chance to get cold."

"I know that," the man snapped. "But that doesn't mean the team won't notice something wrong! What did the doc say when you were in there with him?"

"Umm, he said the kid's burns were healing okay, and that he wanted to take him off the vent in a few days, if he could."

"So the chest tube is still in and the kid's sedated. Good, what else?"

"Something about him being worried about infection and a…P.E. A pulmonary something."

"Pulmonary embolism. It's an air bubble or blood clot in the lungs." The mortician continued to pace. "Does he have an infection now?"

"No, doc was real happy about that."

"Good. Lemme think a minute." He walked to the drug cabinet and rooted in a pocket for the key. Throwing the door open he gazed into the interior. He started thinking out loud.

"Potassium would be too quick. They could correct it during the code and it may cause the heart to infarct."

The Major had limited medical knowledge but he joined the man at the cabinet as they looked for possibilities.

"Histamine might do it. We could dump a lethal dose in his IV and wait for him to arrest. It would throw him onto a lethal arrhythmia. But they might give him drugs and counter that also. I don't want to risk damaging the heart."

"Insulin?" the Major ventured.

"It would drop his blood sugar and cause an arrest, too. But it's easy to detect and correct. You just give them some sugar and they bounce right back."

"I've never seen them check a sugar during an arrest."

The man thought about that for a moment.

"Never?"

"Not once."

"They probably never consider it. You can't join the army if you're diabetic. They'd have no reason to suspect it. That's an idea, but we need something to put him in brain death, not stop his heart."

The Major gazed around the room until his eyes fell on the rack of oxygen cylinders.

"I could charge an O2 cylinder with carbon monoxide and swap it out. Wouldn't that work?"

The mortician considered it for a moment before rejecting it. "It would do it. It wouldn't even trip the pulse oximetry sensor. But I'm still afraid of infarction. The heart's going to have to be as undamaged as possible if we want it to last fourteen hours."

The Major gazed back into the cabinet and let his eyes roam the shelves.

"Ketamine?"

"Yeah, it'd work, but not what I'm looking for."

"Then I'm out of ideas. Why don't we just put a round in his head?"

"Very funny. So he's on a vent, two IVs?

"One in each arm."

"Tell me about these burns."

"They cover half his head and his neck on one side. One eye is covered, but the doc says he'll probably never use it again. The hair will never grow back. The neck is ugly, but not too bad. Why?"

"You know where the carotid artery is, right?"

The Major automatically reached for his own neck and applied two fingers.

"Good, I think I found our solution. This is what you're going to do."

* * *

The Global Express 7000 was one of the finest business jets on the market. The owner of one could fly at speeds and distances unheard of just a few years prior. Most were owned by large corporations or wealthy individuals and outfitted to fit their every want and need. Many were equipped with multiple flat-screen TVs and fully stocked bars. Bedrooms were often found in the back so one could fall asleep in one country, only to wake up half a world away. For those who could afford it, it was the ultimate way to travel.

The crew in Bangkok often enjoyed the trappings of their plane. Too often, they would say. While the plane could hold up to fourteen people comfortably, they hardly ever had more than four on board. This, along with the unusually Spartan interior, only served to lighten the takeoff weight and increase the already impressive range and speed of the aircraft. They had been in and out of Bangkok on several occasions, and despite their recent arrival from the States, they were being sent out again the next day.

The medical crew had the POPS machine torn down and disassembled on a table in the hangar and were cleaning and replacing every part. This carrier was to be exchanged for one they would be picking up at their next destination. One of them worked on a smudge of something sticky he could only guess at on its eggshell white cover. He looked up as one of the pilots walked into the hangar.

"Back to China again?"

"Nope, your favorite," the pilot replied.

"Afghanistan? Shit. How long?"

"Long enough to top off the tanks and scoot back to CONUS."

"West coast?"

"East coast. Baltimore."

The other medic groaned. They were in for a long day. Despite the luxury and space of the plane, an 8,000 mile flight was still an 8,000 mile flight. And they had already watched all of their movies.

"What's the cargo?"

The pilot leafed through the paperwork he had until he found the ones he wanted. He handed them over without saying anything. The medic stripped off his gloves and scanned the documents.

"It's a heart going to Johns Hopkins. We'll have to tweak the harvest time maybe, but these papers look just as good as the last ones. We even have a new letter from Doctors Without Borders for verification. I don't know who prints this shit up for us, but it's good. I can't tell the difference from the real stuff. We even have a pre-approved customs clearance, complete with sticker. Should be easy."

"Easy? You don't have to stay awake for fourteen hours flying this thing there. Makes me wish I was still doing the Mexico flights. Down and back in one day. That was cake."

"So why did you switch?"

"The money for this is three times better, and I get to fly a Cadillac plane instead of a Citation taxi."

"Greedy bastard," the other medic chimed in.

"Yes I am," the pilot confirmed without hesitation.

The medic laughed as he stuffed the papers in a pocket and gloved back up to continue his cleaning.

The pilot picked up a piece to examine it closer before the medic took it out of his hands and placed it in a container of alcohol.

"Do I go up in the cockpit and just start playing with stuff?"

"Yeah, yeah. Just how does this damn thing work anyway? What's wrong with a cooler full of ice like we used before?"

"They still use it for short trips, but this machine will soon replace that, too, I'm sure."

"Why's that?"

"The machine mimics the body's natural functions. It circulates blood through the organ, feeds it nutrients, oxygenates the blood, and keeps it at normal body temperature. All the cooler did was slow down the dying process long enough for a surgeon to get it into a new body. With this thing it's like it never left. When we get the heart I'll just hook up the major arteries and veins here, here, and here, fill this reservoir with the donor's blood and turn it on. The machine does the rest."

"But now does it beat? Don't you need a real person for that?"

"No. I can set the machine to pulse the blood through the heart, or I can stick electrodes in it here, and here, and the machine will give it little shocks to make it beat."

"Like a pacemaker?"

"Yeah."

The pilot bent down and looked the machine over for a minute before straightening up with a shiver.

"Creeps me out. What's next? Frankenstein?"

"Maybe in a few more years," he said it with a straight face and his partner turned away to hide his.

"Think I'll stick to flying," the pilot replied before spinning on his heel and walking off.

The medic watched him leave until he disappeared through the door of the plane.

"Think he bought it?"

"Yeah...you got a sick sense of humor, you know that?

"Yes...yes I do."

DRUG CARTEL'S
SECURITY CHIEF CAPTURED
December 25, 2011—The Associated Press

—FIFTEEN—

LUIS PULLED HIS CAR up to the gate of the home and pushed the button through his open window. After a short wait the gate jumped and creaked as it parted, allowing him to drive through. He drove past the overgrown grass and untrimmed hedges on his way to the front door. It was amazing how quickly the grounds were deteriorating. The gardener had been given a vacation, as had most of the maids. Only Anita's former nanny, and now head housekeeper had been allowed to stay. The girl's friends and their families had been given a story to keep them quiet, while the immediate relatives had been sent a carefully worded email explaining that they were off on a business trip that they had decided to make into a family vacation as well, and they would call when they returned. The husband and wife had not left the house for the past week. The maid was venturing out for food and keeping the interior somewhat clean, but it was too much for one person and it was beginning to show.

He strode around the side of the home to enter from the back as it was closest to the dining room. The pool was full of leaves and he found the father sitting in a chair staring at it. He looked up as Luis approached.

"They have not called."

I know , Luis thought, *I haven't told them to yet.*

"They'll call tonight at the time stated in the letter. We're ready. I must however talk to you and your wife. Is Consuela here?"

"No, my wife sent her away for the day. She was…hovering. My wife wanted to be alone."

"I understand. Could we go inside?"

"Yes."

The man rose from the chair on tired legs. Luis eyed him closely. The shirt was new, but the wrinkled pants were the same ones he'd had on yesterday. His hair was also unkempt. The man was obviously not sleeping well, if at all. Good.

Luis followed him inside and they found his wife in the kitchen, sitting at the table. She was only steps outside the dining room as if afraid to get too far from the phone and its awaited call, despite assurances from Luis that it would not ring yet. She looked even worse than her husband, but at least she had some food in front of her, although little appeared to be gone.

"How are you today, Mrs. Perez?"

She attempted a smile before replying. "I'm still here waiting."

"Not much longer, let's hope."

Luis placed the box of equipment he had brought for appearances sake on the dining room table. They watched with anticipation.

He had visited the Perez family every day since they had hired him. Mostly just to put on a good show and build their trust. He always brought another piece of equipment, and the dining room of the large house resembled a busy office or communication room. He had speakers and microphones set up so they could speak with the callers hands-free, as well as a variety of recording equipment. Spare batteries and chargers for the cell phone were laid out and plugged in and a generator waited in the garage with cords trailing into the house, ready to be started and hooked up in the event that the city's power, notoriously unreliable, should be interrupted at a crucial time. This he had all explained to the family and their confidence in him had improved with every visit.

After arranging everything just so, he paused to open a bottle of water before turning the chair around and facing them.

"I expect the call soon, most likely in the early evening. I know better than to ask you not to be here when it comes so I must prepare you for what will be said. They'll be loud and threaten many things. They will demand an outrageous amount of money. Their language will be harsh and insulting. You must *never* let them get to you. Do you understand? If you cannot keep your emotions in check, you must leave the room. They would like nothing more than to hear you crying, Mrs. Perez, or to hear you get angry, sir. They work to play on your emotions, and we can't let them do that."

"You expect us not to be emotional? How can I not be? They have my little girl. Who knows what they're doing to her."

"I understand. But I not only ask this of you, I require it. It is the key to getting your daughter back. Can you do this? I need to know."

Mr. Perez sat with his wife and Luis saw the head come up and the shoulders go back. He spoke with a forceful voice.

"We will control ourselves. You have our word."

Luis was happy to see a little steel in the man's back. But not too much. It was a fragile situation. One he had to perform well through tonight.

"Will we be able to speak to her?"

"No. Remember when I told you that the kidnappers keep each part of their operation separate? The man we'll speak with tonight is just their negotiator. He'll be someone who is high up, perhaps even the man in charge, but he'll be alone in a room much like the one we are in now. He most likely does this almost every night, each time with a different family. Your daughter won't be anywhere near him. She's somewhere in the city, but where she is, even he may not know. We'll demand further proof of life."

"Will you know him...from before?"

"Perhaps. I've talked with many such men on the phone or over the radio in the last few years. I may recognize his voice, or the name he uses."

Luis reached out for a file on the desk and opened it. He removed a list of names and placed it on the table. Some of them were in groups and highlighted in various colors. He placed it on the table in front of them.

"These are all men you have talked to?"

"Most of them yes, some have dealt with others who work as I do."

"What are the colors?"

"The blue ones are amateurs, usually a low payoff and quick return. The yellow names are Colombian rebels who need money to support their revolution."

"And the red names?"

Luis reached out and took the list back from the man.

"Let's hope we don't talk to a red name tonight."

Hours later they sat as before, the husband and wife at the kitchen table and Luis in the dining room. Consuela had returned in time to fix a quick meal only to be politely sent away soon after. Luis sat with his feet up and thumbed through some papers. He hated the waiting, too, but it served to build the tension and that was what was really needed. The time had come and gone thirty minutes ago as planned, but when the phone rang it was still an expected surprise.

His feet hit the floor and he flipped several switches before picking up the phone. The husband and wife entered the room, but a pointed finger stopped their progress before they got too close. He picked up on the fourth ring.

"Hello?"

"You keep me waiting, Mr. Perez. That is not a good way to start out with me."

"This is not Mr. Perez. I've been hired to speak for them."

"What the fuck is this? You think this is some game? Put the father on or this is over right now!"

"That's not going to happen. If you want your money you deal with me. That's your only option."

"Bullshit! You think we're not serious? I don't have time for your bullshit games! If you want your product back, we do this my way. Now where is the family? Put the father on the fucking phone!"

Luis smiled at the use of the code phrase. It was a popular one. He used some in return.

"Relax, friend. If you want to see this through to a decent settlement, you deal with me. That's how we're doing this."

"And just who the fuck are you?"

"You can call me Tajo."

"Then Mister Tajo with the smart mouth, her blood will be on your hands!"

The connection broke and Luis sat back with a small smile on his face. He erased it as Mrs. Perez wailed behind him.

"Where did they go? We've lost her!"

"What the hell are you doing?"

Luis stayed calm as he adjusted the equipment. He spoke over his shoulder.

"Relax, that went well. He's bluffing. It went how I expected it to. Now they know you have hired a negotiator, and that I am serious. They have to change their plan now, but they're actually not upset either. These people prefer to work with people like me. An amateur would try something stupid, and then both parties lose. He also knows that if he's talking to me then the police are not involved. He'll call back." Luis settled back in the chair and again put his feet up.

The father stopped pacing and stared at the man sitting in the chair. His negotiator was relaxed and sure of himself. Luis felt the man's gaze but ignored it. The father soon gave up and left the room to check on his wife. This gave Luis a chance to smile again and check his watch. Fifteen minutes.

On cue the phone rang again. This time Luis engaged the electronics and let it ring. Four, five, six rings until he picked up.

"This is Tajo."

"Well Mr. Tajo. You are still there. I would think you'd have been fired by now, but since you are not, I guess we will speak."

"Very good. What should I call you?"

"You can call me…Miguel. *Si?*"

"Miguel, I am glad you decided to call again."

"Tajo, I have decided to hate you already, but we can talk."

"Also good. Are you ready to be serious? No more threats?"

"That depends. How much are they willing to pay for the package?"

"Three hundred thousand dollars."

There was a pause before the laughter of the man on the other end was clear. Luis smiled at the father while he waited.

"Is that a fucking joke? Are you a comedian? I thought you were a professional, Tajo? But this? This man and his company are worth millions, and we are not some charity asking for a donation!"

"The man's company is worth millions. He only owns a part of it. The money is spread out in several different areas. There are investments and a board of directors to deal with. The money is in stocks, also, and they are not doing so well at the moment. You have to understand that he can't just run down to the ATM and make a withdrawal. But you're right, perhaps I am being unreasonable. I'll raise the offer to four hundred thousand dollars. Will that help you?"

"Tajo…Tajo. You think I'm a fool? I know the money is there, I don't care how he gets it as long as he does. This is going to take as long as it takes for you to get us what we want. If you want your package to you soon, you will find a way. But I am feeling generous today. I will lower my invoice to five million American dollars. No less."

"You're a skilled negotiator, Miguel, but I cannot meet such a high price. To do so would attract the attention of several people, and I know that is something neither one of us wishes."

"You play the game well yourself. But I can assure you that the people I represent will never accept such a low bid. The family must do better. I don't know how long they are willing to wait."

"If they want their fee, they will wait as long as it takes. If we are to continue I will need to see further proof of life. Nothing can progress until we have it."

"You already have it. You don't require more."

"Nevertheless, we require it. If that upsets you, I'll remind you that you hate me already."

"You crack jokes, Tajo, but I'm not laughing. I'll call the men who safeguard the package. But they may just decide to send you part of it instead. Good-bye, Tajo."

The connection broke.

Luis ignored the parents' questions and searched the desk for the list of names he had out earlier. Finding it, he ran his finger down the rows until he found the name he wanted.

Miguel.

The father approached and looked over his shoulder.

"I'm sorry, Mr. Perez."

The name was highlighted in red.

Luis smiled as the father turned away. It had gone very well.

KIDNAPPING AND
RANSOM ON THE RISE
February 19, 2009—CNN

—SIXTEEN—

LENNY IGNORED THE MONUMENTS and crowds of tourists clogging the streets as he made his way back across the District from one of its many suburbs. He divided his attention between the view in front of him and the one in his rearview mirror. Every trip to the safe house was preceded by a long drive around the city. Only when he was sure he was not being tailed did he enter that part of town.

He didn't really mind the drives. Time in the car had always seemed to calm him. He had discovered long ago that his brain could take care of the mechanics of driving the car, and yet somehow still allow him to think about whatever case he was working on. He often had ideas that proved to be quite valuable while driving. So he had learned to make the most of travel time.

His thoughts were on Angel and what to do with him next. The interrogations had been going on for a few days now and Lenny and Jack had a team of people working at all hours processing the information. Judges across the country, as well as in Central and South America, the Caribbean, and parts of Europe and Asia, were signing warrants at a record pace. Police, SWAT teams, and federal agents were conducting raid after raid. It was the kind of action that Lenny had only dreamed of. He only hoped that they could complete the arrests before the entire network disappeared. It was rumored that Oscar's brother had taken over in his absence. The file on the man was extensive. While he was known for his ruthless way of getting things done, he did not have his brother's business sense. Lenny did not expect him to last long on the throne. No doubt a competitor, or someone within the cartel, was already considering a move to take over. But that all depended on Oscar. If he survived the transplant he faced prosecution for numerous offenses. But these men had proven difficult to convict. Like a Mafia head, he had the money and the means to threaten, intimidate, or bribe whoever it took. Lenny had no faith in American juries. They could never be counted on to convict such a man.

Despite all this, Angel was a very valuable man for both sides. The feds wished to keep him alive and talking, while the cartel wished him dead as soon as possible. The security arrangement was something Lenny had sweated over since they had brought Angel to the States. He had two options really. One was to hide him with minimal security as they had up till now, the other was to go with the brute force option and place him in the lockup at Quantico Marine base. He and Jack had decided to keep things as they were until the interrogations were over, and move Angel to the base after that. There would be no way to hide him safely once he was forced to travel to and from the courtroom. But if something did happen, they at least had the hours of tapes they had produced in the basement via the video feed. It was their only safety net.

Lenny fired up another cigarette at a stoplight and checked the rearview again—still nothing familiar behind him. Deciding he was clear, he took a right turn toward the row house. After a couple more turns he was on the right street and had to concentrate to make sure he didn't pass it. The homes were all the same. Narrow two-story brick structures with wide front porches and driveways leading to a separate garage in the back. Roof color was the biggest difference, but he looked for a tall tree he had made a note of, and once past that, he slowed to a stop and turned into the driveway. Navigating past the two garbage cans, he pulled past the porch and parked on the side of the house. He looked up to see the curtain covering the window being pulled back an inch. He got out slowly and turned his face to the house so they could see him. The curtain fell back in place as he passed and he flicked the cigarette butt onto the pavement before cutting across the grass to the front steps. The door opened before he reached it, and Jake held it for him as he entered.

"Hey, Jake."

Jake was busy looking out the small window in the door to see if Lenny had drawn anyone's attention. He didn't turn to reply.

"Hey, Lenny. Our boy's napping in the back. Just finished another video speech."

"Good for him."

Lenny proceeded across the room and entered the kitchen were he found Charlie working on a donut and a cup of coffee.

"Morning, Charlie, still on that diet I see."

Charlie stirred more sugar into his coffee and watched Lenny search for a cup for himself.

"Same one you're on, from the looks of it."

"You got it." Lenny helped himself to a donut. "So how you holding up?"

"If it wasn't for the information we're getting, I'd have done the cartel a favor and killed him myself by now."

Jake had entered during the remark. He bypassed the coffee and donuts and retrieved a Gatorade from the fridge. He laughed at Charlie's remark.

"Angel and Charlie aren't exactly getting along," he quipped.

"Oh yeah?" Lenny raised an eyebrow at that.

"Guy's a real ass. Have you been reading the transcripts? Sick bastard's going to rot."

Lenny dropped his donut on the table and sampled his coffee before replying. "I'll agree he's an asshole, but right now he's our asshole. We're making some serious busts just based on what he's given us so far. Evidently Oscar's brother didn't take Angel's capture as seriously as he should have. He didn't move his assets quickly enough and we've been picking them up left and right. The Mexicans raided a house yesterday and found over three million in cash. Three million! They just had it stacked in a back bedroom like wood. They sent me a picture. It was about as high as this table and the room was ten by ten. There was maybe enough room to open the door and that was about it. All American bills."

"All that cash was probably just payroll money, too," Jake added.

"Yup, just operating expenses. The two they caught there were payroll clerks more or less. It was just them and a few guards. We managed to get a list of names and drop points. Some account numbers. The names are code names, so it may take awhile to match them up to actual people, but I'm a patient man. The Mexican president loved it. He's sending more troops to the northern states to fight the drug gangs. Sort of a thank you, I guess."

"That's all great, but what I'd really like to know is when we can get out of this frickin' row house?"

"Tired of babysitting? Can't say I blame you. I just need you to hang on another couple of days. We may be moving him to another house, or just cut it short and go to the base with him."

"Guantanamo?" Charlie asked jokingly.

Lenny had to laugh. "No, I think the brig at Quantico would do just fine."

Charlie's reply was cut off by the sound of Angel's bedroom door opening. They waited silently until he emerged, rubbing his unshaven face.

"Well look who's fucking here," he observed. "Please tell me you're here to take me out of this hole."

"Not yet, Angel. I want to hear every verse of this song you're singing.

Till then, you stay here."

"I'd say I've held up my end of the deal. I want the fuck out of here."

"I decide when you're done shithead. Not you. Better get that through your head real quick."

Angel sneered and searched for a clean coffee cup.

"You making a big name for yourself, are you, Lenny? Gonna get a nice promotion or maybe a little plaque on the wall somewhere? A piece of ribbon with a gold trinket attached?" He turned to offer a shit-eating grin in Lenny's direction. "You're probably busy right now, huh, busting all the guys I'm giving you. Don't you know that their replacements are already hard at work? In a few months, it'll be like you and I never met."

"Ah, but we did meet, didn't we, Angel? You can push my buttons all you want, I don't really care. Your ass belongs to me until I decide I'm done with you."

"What, so I'm just your little slave? Is that it? Just a little puppet you can dangle on a string and make perform?"

"You have choices, Angel. You want to back out of our deal? Fine, I'll give you back to the DEA guys and they can charge you with narcotics trafficking, organ smuggling, and a bunch of other stuff. We'll put you up in one of our nice federal prisons where I'm sure you'll know a few people. Gen-pop, of course, I mean you're just another drug trafficker, right, why should you get special treatment? You'll rot there for a year or so until we get around to the trial, just spending the days with all your friends out in the yard. Hell, I'll even come to your funeral, just to see who else shows up."

Angel sat down heavily and contemplated the box of donuts. Jake and Charlie had found their way out of the room but remained within earshot, enjoying Lenny's verbal smack down of their guest.

"Fuck this, and fuck you, too, Lenny."

"That's what I thought. Don't piss me off, Angel. I get the idea that you're holding back, not telling us the truth, or playing games? I'll end our little deal real quick, and all those things I just mentioned will come true. Don't believe me? Go ahead and try it. I've read all the transcripts of you down in the basement here and I got to tell you, if you had a little accident? Nobody would cry for you, not one little bit."

Angel's eyes rose to meet his and Lenny saw that he'd hit the mark. He lowered his voice.

"What? You think you're the only one who can make a phone call? I know people, too. I can do favors for people on the inside, favors that require one in return. You know how it works, right? Sure you do. Don't fuck with me, Angel. I'm the guy picking out your nursing home."

Lenny finished his coffee and grinned at Angel as he rose to leave. Angel followed him with his eyes, but wisely kept his mouth shut.

"When you coming back, Lenny?" Jake asked as he walked by.

"I don't know yet. You'll get a head's up when it's time to move, maybe tomorrow. Probably just be the three of us doing it."

"Okay."

"Try not to kill the witness, okay?"

"Gonna be tough."

"Try real hard."

"Will do."

Lenny donned his sunglasses and took a good look around before walking down the steps and around the corner to his car. Backing up through the narrow gap between the trash cans and the fence, he made it out into the street without scratching the paint. The nearest approaching car was over a block away, so he paused to light up another cigarette before putting it in drive and pulling away. He headed toward the Hoover Building. He was having lunch with Jack.

* * *

"That's him, right there"

"Slow down, I need to get some pictures. Remember the address."

"Okay."

It was Manuel's turn in the driver's seat. He and Jimmy had been following the signal from Lenny's car for the last couple of hours. They had first visited a few spots Lenny had stopped at in the last few days.

One turned out to be a hotel, but after a check of the registry and a quick walk through, they decided that Lenny had most likely just met someone for a lunch meeting. Jimmy couldn't see them keeping a federal witness in a hotel barely a block from the Capitol Building. The other place had turned out to be a barber shop. About that time Lenny's car had started moving so they had tailed him for awhile from several blocks back, and even caught a glimpse of him when he doubled back and crossed in front of them at a stoplight. The unusual driving activity had them both on edge. The man was obviously going somewhere he didn't want any company. After he had stopped, Manuel had found a place to park and wait. After it appeared that Lenny was staying for awhile Jimmy had decided on a drive-by. They pulled up just in time to watch him pull out and drive away.

"Coming up."

Jimmy thumbed the camera on and held it up against the glass. He silently cursed the bumpy road as they passed. Neither one of them looked at the house as it went by and Jimmy hit the button repeatedly getting about five unaimed shots. Manuel voiced the address out loud and Jimmy repeated it several times to himself. Soon they were at the corner where Lenny had turned.

"Follow him?"

"No, go straight for a while."

"Okay."

Jimmy flipped the laptop back open and watched the signal tracer from Lenny's car move toward the Mall. He was probably headed to the Hoover Building, he decided.

"He's going to the office, I think. Let's go back to the hotel."

"You're the boss."

Several minutes later they pulled back into the parking ramp of their hotel and made a hasty exit to their room. Jimmy walked to the balcony and opened the laptop again. They had a better signal out there.

"He's parked a block down from the Hoover Building again. Why he doesn't park there, I don't understand."

"Maybe security just takes too long?"

"Could be. Anyway, looks like he's there for awhile. Get your laptop out, let's do some recon."

"Okay."

Jimmy pulled the memory card from the camera and stuck it the computer. Soon he had five decent if somewhat blurry pictures of a small row house in suburban DC on the screen. They looked them over carefully several times.

"Looks like a house," Manuel threw out.

"Garage is shut. Maybe a car in there, maybe not. Curtains are all pulled. Grass is a little long," Jimmy added.

"Think that's the place? I don't see any security. No cameras."

"Cameras are so damn small now I doubt we would. The only time you see the big surveillance cameras anymore is if they want you to know that they're there. Let's see what it used to look like."

Manuel's fingers flew over the keyboard and they soon had Google maps up. Typing in the address, he navigated the camera down the street until they had a view of the house. This one was two years old and not blurry. Manuel used the directional features to scan back and forth and see the house from all sides available.

"The door's been changed. There's a little window where there used to be a big one, looks like they added a deadbolt, too. The curtains are heavier. Those shrubs around the basement windows are new, too."

"So what do you think?"

"I think we found our place. Save these pictures and get them printed off."

Jimmy studied the pictures as Manuel's fingers flew across the keyboard again.

"Any ideas?"

"Let's look around the neighborhood a little."

"Okay."

Manuel navigated the computer camera up and down the street several times and they both took notes of things they saw on both sides of the street. Being how the images were two years old, it was difficult to say what it looked like now, but they got the general idea and a good picture in their heads of the lay of the land. Jimmy dug in his bag and pulled out a street map of DC and stuck it on the wall. He called out names to Manuel and he typed them in. They spent the afternoon learning the entire neighborhood without leaving the hotel. After a couple of hours Jimmy sat back and stared at the picture for a while. Manuel waited patiently.

"I think I've got an idea, but we'll need some equipment."

"What kind?"

Jimmy told him.

"And where do we get that?"

"From some friends."

"What kind of friends do you have that would have that?"

"The Italian kind." Jimmy grinned.

* * *

The plane screamed out of the clouds as the pilot took it into another sharp turn, spiraling them down out of the Afghanistan sky in a figure eight pattern to avoid any Taliban missiles that may come their way. The Global Express responded like a fighter and the pilot couldn't help but crack a grin. It wasn't an F-14 like he had flown years ago, but it was fun. The plane responded to every control input as if it was reading his mind. It was one of the few pleasures he could derive out of this job. Knowing that the medics in the back were strapped in as tight as the belts would allow and trying their best to hold down their lunch was even better. The plane came out of the turn right on the approach heading and he leveled the wings to line up with the runway.

"Love this plane," he commented to the copilot.

"The Canadians do something right once in awhile."

"If it flies like this *and* has a bar on board, what more could you ask for?"

"I don't know, hot stewardesses?"

"Got me there, let's put this thing down. Checklist?"

The copilot began the checklist from memory while the pilot voiced his replies to every prompt. He glanced back in the rear to see the two medics looking back from their captain's chairs. They both offered a weak thumb's up. He sniffed the air before turning back to the cockpit.

"No puke in the back, have to try harder next time."

"Long as the wings stay on."

After touching down they taxied to the hangar reserved by their company. A man on a forklift with an empty pallet waited. They would offload the machine and some supplies for appearance's sake to the waiting helicopter before the medics would ride off in it to the base.

Getting closer, they saw another man approach from the hangar office. He was waiting when they finally opened the door. He was one of their men.

"Hey, Steve, what's the word?" the pilot asked.

"No change. You guys are refueling and heading back to the States as soon as they get back." He paused until the forklift driver passed. "Precious cargo heading for Johns Hopkins. I've got all the necessary paperwork."

"Is the heart ready now?" the medic asked.

The man checked his watch, holding it up to catch the sun.

"Almost."

MEXICO: POLICE
CHIEF ABDUCTED
July 18, 2008—The Associated Press

—SEVENTEEN—

MANUEL HAD SAT QUIETLY and watched for the last two hours while Jimmy produced his little black book and made a series of phone calls. Most of the conversations were short and Jimmy often worked his sentences to fit in a certain code word. This would lead to another number being called and another phrase spoken. Finally Jimmy reached who he wanted and the conversation was one of two old friends catching up. Eventually they got around to business, and Jimmy told the man what he needed. A few details were worked out before the conversation ended. Jimmy set the phone down and kicked the chair back.

"So now what?"

"We wait," was all the reply Manuel got.

An hour went by until the phone rang again. Jimmy answered on the first ring and was soon taking notes. Several grunted replies later, he hung up and tore the page off the pad.

"Pack up your stuff. We won't be coming back here."

A few hours later found them cruising through an industrial section of town populated mainly by warehouses and fenced-in lots. Dogs barked from behind fences as they passed and the occasional truck passed them moving another load, but the street was mostly empty.

"Is that it?"

Manuel followed his partner's pointed finger and used his sharper eyes to read the numbers on the side of the building.

"That's it. He said around back, second door."

Jimmy spun the wheel to comply while looking for the welcoming committee. He didn't have to wait long. As the car approached the second corner of the building a man with a sub-machinegun cradled in his arms stepped out in front of them. The barrel didn't waver. Jimmy slowed to a stop and thumbed the window down.

The man approached slowly until he was standing next to the car.

"You Jimmy?"

"That would be me. Tony sent me."

"Pull up to the second door. It'll open for ya."

"Got it."

The man stepped back into the shadow of the building and disappeared. Jimmy did what he had been told. The door opened to reveal what looked to be a truck maintenance garage. Its greasy floor housed a lift, several tool boxes and all the related equipment. Posters of scantily clad females adorned the walls along with a few Nascar items. A glowing Budweiser racing clock kept the time on the wall. Standing below it was a small man dressed in dirty coveralls. Thick glasses perched on his nose and he thumbed them back up with a dirty hand as he squinted into the approaching headlights. He waved them forward with a nervous energy and Jimmy pulled the car in until he was waved still. The man thumbed a switch on the wall and the door began to close behind them, prompting Manuel to exit the car quickly and reach into his waistband.

"Relax, what the hell? Think I'm gonna shoot ya or something? What the fuck? I don't do guns, not my thing. Come on in and lemme hear what you want." The man spoke with a rapid-fire nasal voice and his hands never seemed to stay still. He wiped his nose on his sleeve and gestured for them to follow him. He walked away toward the back of the shop without seeing if he was being followed.

They exchanged a look before Manuel shrugged and stowed his gun. They followed at a distance until they found themselves in a well equipped machine shop. A transmission sat in pieces on one bench, while a tricked-out big block engine sat mounted on a nearby stand. The item Jimmy had requested sat in the middle of the floor.

"Well, here's what you asked for. I don't get it. I mean what the fuck am I s'pose to do with this, huh? Normally I do the occasional restaurant or a car or something. Never rigged one of these damn things. Seems silly. What the fuck?"

Jimmy suppressed a grin. Evidently the man had a favorite expression and they were going to hear a lot of it. Manuel just gazed at the tiny man with the strange mannerism before reaching in his pocket for a smoke.

"You're kidding me right? What the fuck? Just gonna fire that thing up in here with all this gas and shit around? Did you forget why you're here? Stupid kid." He switched his myopic gaze to Jimmy. "What the fuck's this kid's problem? Is he new or something? Trying to kill us! Fucking idiot."

Manuel returned the cigarettes to his pocket, but he'd adopted a look that Jimmy knew well. The little man just didn't see it, so Jimmy broke in quickly to save his life.

"Tony says you got some skills. You want to hear what I need or not?" He waved Manuel back to calm him down.

"Yeah, yeah, sure. I'm here, aren't I? What do you need? Lotta smoke? Lotta fire? Lotta bodies? Something that's gonna burn awhile? What?"

"I need a shape charge. Something that'll take out a guy from say ten to twenty feet. Some fire might help if it can be done. Just need him dead."

"Okay, now you're talking. Command detonate? Timer? What the fuck are you gonna set it off with?"

"I need it command detonated from a long range, and I need a camera mounted on the inside with a wide field of view."

"Camera? How long's it gotta sit?"

"A week maybe."

"A week? What the fuck, man? That's gonna be some serious battery life, unless you got a fucking power source? You got a fucking power source?"

"No, I need the whole mess mounted in that." Jimmy pointed to the object sitting in the middle of the room.

The man gazed at the item for a moment, cocking his head this way and that. He thumbed the glasses back up his nose and adjusted his hat twice before fixing his gaze on Jimmy.

"Well now you're talkin'. I can do that. How soon you need it?"

Jimmy rolled up a sleeve and checked his watch.

"Six hours."

"Six…what the fuck!?"

* * *

As soon as he heard the helicopter approaching, the Major left his office and entered the morgue. He found his partner there preparing the autopsy table and laying out his instruments. The cooler was filled with ice and placed on the ground out of sight. A package of funeral cloth was already pulled from the closet, ready to be spread out on the adjoining table. The man looked up when the Major entered.

"You ready?"

"Let's just do this. The staff will be occupied with the supplies. The only person on the floor will be the nurse at the desk."

"You remember what I told you?"

"Yes, just give me the damn syringe."

With a look of doubt, the man walked to a nearby cabinet and retrieved it. The Major took it and left without a word.

He stopped at his office to retrieve his clipboard before moving to the ward. Looking through the window, he spotted the nurse at the corner desk typing on a laptop. He angled his head to look down the aisle.

Empty.

Pushing his way through, he entered the ward. The nurse looked up from his typing to see who it was, and since it wasn't one of his superiors, he returned to it. He still managed a greeting.

"Hey, Major, not out going through the latest supply run with the others?"

"Nah, I'll pick through the leftovers when they get done. What you up to?"

The nurse glanced at the monitor screens as he spoke. "Just watching the squiggly lines and chatting with my little sister back in Ohio."

"How little?"

"She's twelve."

The Major made a show of checking his watch.

"Past her bedtime a little, Ed?"

"Yeah, I know. She likes to get online after Mom and Dad go to sleep. I used to read under the covers with a flashlight, she talks to her older brother half a world away. Amazing, huh?"

"We're getting old."

"Shit, I'm only twenty-four and she makes me feel old."

A ding announced a new message from the girl and Ed leaned in to read it. The Major saw his chance.

"I'm just going to check on my guys."

"No problem," the nurse replied. His eyes never left the screen.

The Major quickly made his way to the first Afghan soldier. He had minor wounds and was sleeping soundly. He skipped the next and delayed at the third to determine who was sleeping and who wasn't. Fortunately, the wounded who were on ventilators were all in the same area and were all sedated. He skipped two more patients and checked on the nurse. Ed was still absorbed in his chat session. He put his hand in his pocket and felt the cold plastic of the syringe. He palmed it as he moved around the next curtain.

The boy lay as before. The cycling of the ventilator provided a back beat to the drum roll of the gurgling water seal. The suction hissed as it created the bubbles, adding to the noise. The two IV pumps hummed as they pumped fluids into the boy's arms. His skin color actually looked better today, he noted, as he reached out and carefully pulled the bandage back from the boy's neck. The scar tissue was still new and pink, but the swelling had subsided, making it easier to see the landmarks he needed. Listening hard, he heard the nurse laugh followed by the tapping of the keyboard.

Not wasting time, he pulled the syringe from his pocket and stuck the covered needle in his mouth. Biting down, he removed the cap and exposed the needle. It was short and very thin. He felt the boy's neck and lined up the needle. With a quick motion he jabbed it into the carotid artery. Pulling back on the plunger, he was rewarded with a flash of bright red blood. He quickly reversed his grip and emptied the syringe into the boy's neck. Pulling it free, he held a piece of gauze to the site long enough to stop any bleeding. The needle was so small it left no mark that he could see, and the blood was little more than a drop. He watched for any excess bleeding, and seeing none, he carefully replaced the bandage while listening for the nurse.

He tore his gaze away from the boy long enough to recap the syringe. He was tempted to drop it in the sharps box, but that would make a telltale noise. He simply placed it back in his pocket. He grabbed his clipboard and took one last look at the boy and saw it. As he watched, the boy's face seemed to slacken on the right side. The lips around the breathing tube seemed to slide back off his teeth and the skin on his face flowed toward the sheets as if gravity had suddenly increased on that side. A string of drool emerged from the corner of his mouth and slowly trailed down his cheek.

The Major peered around the curtain at the desk, but the nurse was still engrossed in his chat session with his little sister. Stepping back in, he pulled a small penlight from his pocket and checked the boy's pupils. While one was reactive to the light, the other was as large as it could possibly be, crowding out the boy's normally brown eyes.

The ten cubic centimeters of air he had injected had traveled to the boy's brain and was causing a massive stroke. He checked the vital signs monitor. It would not cycle for another ten minutes. He was told the boy's heart rate may change, but so far it remained as it was. The ventilator would overrule any attempt to change his respiratory rate. It was done.

He snatched up his clipboard and moved on to his next patient. This man was awake but still somewhat groggy from his pain meds. The Major attempted a short conversation while he listened for the monitors to alarm. After a minute he moved on. After three more stops he was out of patients.

Nothing. The nurse evidently didn't see anything, or the boy's vital signs hadn't changed enough to trigger any alarms. He was going to have to force the issue.

He walked the center aisle back toward the desk, but made as if to stop and write something at the end of the boy's bed. He looked the boy over. The drool had progressed farther and the teeth showed from a distance.

"Hey, Ed? You want to come look at the kid? He doesn't look so good."

"Sure, one second."

Ed typed off another quick message and hit send before bouncing up and walking down the isle.

"What's up?"

"Something's wrong with his face."

"His face?" Ed flipped on the overhead light and took a look at the kid.

"Oh shit." He pulled a penlight from his pocket and checked the boy's pupils.

"What is it?" the Major asked.

"He's stroking out." Ed pushed past the Major and ran for the desk. He hit a button on the wall before grabbing the phone.

"Eighteen is stroking out…I don't know, sometime in the last half hour…no change that I saw, but his rate is starting to increase… no they're both isotonic…he's not…I don't know…blown on the left…okay…okay."

The Major watched as Ed came back around the desk and down the aisle. He entered the area vacated by the Major and first pushed the button on the machine to get another set of vitals. He then read both bags of fluid that were hanging, and after clamping one he then shut off the corresponding pump.

"What now?"

"Not much we can do for a stroke here. It's up to the doc."

An awkward silence followed until the Major broke it with a question.

"What was in the bag?"

"His sedation meds. Doc told me to cut them off. We need him awake to see how bad it is."

"How long to wake him up?

Any answer was cut off by the doctor throwing the door open. He hurried down the aisle, followed by an anesthesiologist and a couple of nurses. He took one look at the boy and pulled out his penlight.

"One's blown and the other's sluggish. What happened?"

"The Major was visiting his people and he saw the facial droop. There were no changes on the monitor, but his heart rate is up in the last few minutes."

"You cut the sedative?"

"Yes, sir."

"Get a sugar?"

"No, he's not diabe—"

"Get one anyway."

"Yes, sir." Ed hurried off to comply.

The doctor stood up straight and looked to his colleague.

"What do you think?"

"Looks like a big one. Could be air or a clot based on his injuries. Hemorrhagic fits, too. How far you want to go?"

"Shit, question is how far *can* I go? I've got no CT scanner. No way to tell what kind of stroke he's having. I could do a lumbar puncture and look for blood, but even if the CSF is clear, that's not exactly proof that it isn't hemorrhagic. He's got a million places to bleed in his chest if we tPA him. If we do that, he could just bleed out."

"Blood sugar is 86."

"Okay."

"We *have* to tPA him," a nurse spoke.

"How do you justify that? If it's hemorrhagic, it could kill him."

The anesthesiologist answered for her. "If we do and it works, we treat the bleeding after and he still has a chance. If we do it and that's not it, he's brain dead. If we don't do anything, he's still brain dead."

"So it has to be a clot because that's the only thing we can treat?"

"Yup."

"Fuck...Ed?"

"Yes, sir?

"I want tPA, give him...what's he weigh, about 140...58mg. Give ten percent as a bolus and run the rest in over an hour. Draw some labs. I want a CBC, PT and PTT. Has he been typed and screened? Make sure we have some blood and platelets available. And give me pressures every five."

"You want to wait for the labs?" the nurse asked.

"Why? You just said it yourself. We're damned if we do and damned if we don't. The labs are more for me, not him."

They all looked at the boy for a silent moment. The Major watched from the sidelines while the boy's fate played out. The doctor caught him looking.

"We'll know in an hour or so. If it doesn't work I'm just gonna take him off the vent. We don't have room for a brain-dead patient here and I doubt the father would understand what it means anyway. He may be yours in an hour, so be ready."

The Major just nodded for an answer.

The doctor just spun on a boot heel and stormed off the ward.

"Damn it!"

A trail of slamming doors followed the doctor as he made his way out of the building. One of those doors was outside the morgue.

The mortician had a smile on his face when the Major returned.

"What's the score?"

"It worked. The kid stroked. They want to try some tPA?"

"Won't work. it only works on blood clots. Ballsy move when they don't know what kind of stroke it is."

"Yeah, the doc was kind of pissed about that."

"So they're doing some blood work and then the tPA?"

"No, he ordered the tPA before I left."

"No shit? That's an aggressive move. Won't matter either way I guess. Did he say anything else?"

"If it didn't work in an hour, then he wasn't going to keep him on the vent. He'll be coming to us soon."

"Perfect. I'm ready here. You tell the medics?"

"On my way now."

The Major walked toward the door, slipping his hands in his pockets. He paused when he reached it and pulled the syringe free. After a long gaze at it in his bare hand, he reached out and dropped it in a sharps box before pushing the door open and heading for the helicopter.

KILLING OF 5-YEAR-OLD KIDNAPPED FROM MARKET SHOCKS MEXICO

November 4, 2008—The Associated Press

—EIGHTEEN—

FIFTY MINUTES LATER THEY stood over the boy again. Now both pupils were blown and his face still had a prominent droop on one side. They had watched him closely after the tPA had been administered. So far he had not shown any signs of hemorrhage. He had not regained consciousness either, and the doctor was both dismayed and thankful at the same time. They watched as he pinched the boy's legs first and then his arms without getting a response.

"We're going to give him one chance. If he fails either test, I'm going to pronounce him and take him off the vent. Anybody have any problem with that?"

His team shook their heads all around. As much as they had invested in saving the boy, they knew when they had lost.

The doctor moved to the head of the bed and grasped the boy's head in his hands. They all watched the boy's eyes as his head was slowly rotated left and right. The eyes moved from side to side like a child's doll. It was an indication of severe brain injury and they frowned at the result. Ed joined the group in time to see the boy's eyes.

"His blood pressure's still rising, Doc, his inter-cranial pressure's gotta be pretty high."

The doctor just nodded in reply. "This will tell us right here. We'll give him forty seconds."

He reached out and twisted the vent tubing off the endotrachial tube. The vent immediately alarmed before the anesthetist turned it off. They watched silently as they waited for the boy to take a breath on his own. After a long wait, the boy made no effort, and the doctor shook his head as he hooked the tubing back up. A hint of blood began to show flowing from the chest tube. The doctor sighed when he saw it.

"That's it, I'm calling him. Time of death: 1120. Pull the IVs and the chest tube." He nodded toward the Major. "He's all yours now."

"I got him."

The team left one by one until it was just the two of them. The Major watched as Ed removed the equipment and stowed it. Thankfully he removed the vent last. Maybe he was reluctant to, but either way it worked to the Major's favor. Finally, he disconnected the tube. He watched for a moment, but the boy stayed as still as he had before. Ed pulled a sheet over the boy's head before he kicked the brake loose on the bed and rolled him out into the aisle.

"Look, he's dead. No doubt about it, but his heart may go on for a few minutes. Make sure his pulse is absent before you wrap him up."

"Okay. Strong heart on the little guy, huh."

"Yeah, we all thought that's what would pull him through. Not today though."

"I better get him ready."

"Right."

The Major pushed the boy down the ward and through the double doors. Once they had swung shut behind him, he quickened his pace until he burst through the doors of the morgue. The mortician locked the door behind him and then felt for a pulse at the boy's neck.

"Thready, but still there. Let's move him. Gently, we can knock his heart into an arrhythmia real easy right now."

"Then quit talking and let's go."

Lining up the bed next to the stainless steel table they quickly slid the boy across and connected the tubing to a small transport vent they had already programmed. The mortician quickly clamped his head in the block before reaching for the scalpel. The Major turned his back on the scene and began working on the funeral wrappings. The sounds alone were bad enough. He didn't need to see it too.

The mortician worked quickly. The chest was opened with a jet of blood from the severed arteries. The sternal saw buzzed and the grinding noise climbed up the Major's spine. He did his best to ignore it as he readied the funeral wrap.

* * *

Jimmy tugged at the overalls, trying to get them to fit better. While Manuel's seemed to fit perfectly, Jimmy had always been a little wide in the shoulders. The boots were rubbing his feet wrong, also, as they were only hours old and the leather was still stiff. He glanced at his wrist to check the time, but saw only a tan line. He had been forced to give up his Rolex as it would not fit the role he was attempting to portray at the moment. On top of all that, he had a headache from the sunglasses they had quickly bought. His were too tight.

The truck jerked to a stop as Manuel had not yet learned the sensitivity of the brakes. This was the worst part. Every time they were forced to stop, the smell from the back caught up with them. Jimmy's nose wrinkled as the stench of fresh garbage permeated the interior.

"Oh yeah, that's some ripe stuff, huh?"

Jimmy glowered at his partner's laughing face. For some reason he was tolerating the smell with his usual twisted sense of humor. Jimmy just shook his head and did his best to ignore him. His nose wrinkled involuntarily while he glared at the stoplight, they seemed to take forever to change today. Jimmy vowed this would be his first and last day as a garbage man.

"Where do we start?"

"If it's time, we start as soon as we round the corner," Jimmy replied.

"You see the other crew?"

"No, and I hope we don't. They were told to skip a street and that's all. I'm sure they know not to ask any questions."

"Paid?"

"By my friend."

"That's a strong message right there."

"That it is. What time you got?"

Manuel stole a glance at the dash clock as they rolled through a yellow light. He gunned the diesel engine to make it.

"Almost 7:30."

Jimmy performed some quick mental math before replying.

"Let's go."

Manuel turned at the next light and doubled back the way they had come. Within ten minutes they approached the corner Jimmy had mentioned. The truck came to a jerking halt in front of the first house.

"Let's do this."

They both swung out of the open cab and walked to the houses on both sides of the street. Fetching the garbage bins, they rolled them quickly to the rear of the truck and fed them into the jaws of the dumper. Manuel worked the controls, and the hydraulic arm clamped the bin between its jaws before raising it up and over the top of the truck and dumping its contents inside. The smell rose to new heights as it was stirred up by the fresh arrival, and Jimmy cleared his nose forcefully in protest. He rolled his bin back up the driveway and deposited it back where he had found it. He took his time walking back and looked up the street toward the target. While over a block away, he couldn't see any changes from the last time they were there. No new cars out front. Nothing.

He arrived back to the truck just as his partner put it back in gear. The smell left for a brief period while they moved another house closer.

The brakes squealed loudly as they stopped, but there was no way to make a stealth approach in the truck. They repeated the process on the next two houses, and this time Manuel was forced to pause for a passing car. He tugged the hat on his head lower as it passed to hide his face, but it proved to be a working mom on her way to drop off the kids before hurrying on to the office. She was more interested in the phone pressed to the side of her head than the garbage man on the curb. Manuel smiled as she passed. He was on a suburban street in broad daylight, yet he was invisible. His partner was a very clever man. This was going to work.

"Man does that *stink*," Jimmy commented as he worked the controls. "Both of the last porches have been up to about here on my chest. I think we can leave it mounted just like we got it."

"Good, I got a good look at the house, no changes that I can see."

"All right, let's go."

They performed the same task four more times until they reached the house. Jimmy watched the window for any sign that it was still occupied. The noise of the truck guaranteed that their arrival would not go unnoticed. He just hoped they were not too late. As he gripped the handle to swing himself out of the cab, he was rewarded by the curtain covering the front window moving an inch. He checked the smile that tried to appear on his face before walking up the drive. Keeping his head down, he moved directly to the two garbage bins stowed against the side of the porch. Forcing himself not to look at the windows, he walked them quickly to the back of the truck. Manuel had already released the strap holding the new bin and placed it on the street out of view of the house. Jimmy loaded the full one and worked the controls while Manuel returned with his bin from across the street.

"They're still there. I saw some movement."

"I plugged in the battery. It's ready to go."

Swapping the new bin for the one he had fetched from the house, he rolled them behind him back up the driveway. The extra weight of the bin they had altered was evident. Jimmy was counting on them not to move anything other than the lid like most people. The altered bin also had the lid glued shut. He hoped they wouldn't force it and instead just not fight it and use the other bin. Spending an extra second, he made sure the camera in the bin would have a good view of the front door, before turning and walking back to the truck. There he was forced to delay in the cab and breathe in the stench while his partner returned the bins on his side of the street. He wondered if he still had a gun aimed at him while he counted the number of houses left on the street before they reached the next corner. Too damn many. He couldn't stomach the smell for very much longer. He looked for his partner in time to see him swing into the cab.

"Done?" Manuel asked.

"It's in place."

"Good. How many more houses?"

"Five."

Manuel smiled at the quick reply.

"I knew you'd know."

"Just get this rolling cesspool moving, will you? I need ten showers and a bath already."

Manuel cackled as he dropped the truck in gear. It jerked forward for another fifty feet before stopping again. Jimmy cursed his partner's good humor as he walked up another driveway. Sometimes he was insufferable.

* * *

Jake watched through the window as Jimmy and Manuel made their way down the street. He had almost parted the curtain with the barrel of the gun in his fist, but caught himself and switched hands first.

"Same guys?" Charlie asked him from the hallway where he had just emerged.

"Hell, I don't know. They're garbage men. They all look alike in that damn jumpsuit thingy they wear. They didn't seem to be interested in the house."

Jake turned from the window and walked to the kitchen to join his partner. The TV droned as it spewed out an early morning weather report.

"Anything happen last night?"

"No, just a lot of boring television. One good movie though. *The Usual Suspects*. I've seen it a hundred times and still love it."

"Well the daytime TV isn't much better. I'm starting to think you were smart taking the night shift. You get the place without the shithead around. Me? I get him *and* Oprah. It's a wonder I haven't killed us all yet."

"Yeah, well I'm gonna hit the sack before he wakes up. If Lenny calls, tell him to bring some good movies with him next time."

"He texted me this morning. Actually, the bastard woke me up. We're moving tomorrow, sometime in the morning he says. I guess the Marines can watch over Angel for awhile."

"Fine by me. I'm going stir crazy in this place. I haven't run one damn mile in over a week."

"I was just about to say the same thing." Charlie rubbed his ample gut with both hands.

"You should start, be good for you."

"Yeah, I'll get right on it," Charlie deadpanned as he pulled out the coffee maker. Jake just shook his head and made for the back bedroom. He yawned and scratched his ass with the gun as he walked down the hallway. He laughed and slammed the door hard enough to shake the house. Charlie silently cursed him for waking Angel up.

Julio listened to the hushed tones of the conversation with dread. His fellow kidnappers made no effort to conceal their happiness. For them it was all about the money. While he had joined this group for the same reasons, he still considered himself better than his older counterparts. While they wasted their money on liquor and gambling, he saved most of his or sent it home to his family. His parents thought he was in Arizona and had a good job. If his mother ever found out who his employer really was it would kill her, followed quickly by his father killing him.

The girl in the next room was not much younger than he was. Young and pretty, she reminded him of his sister. He had hoped that her time with them would be short. The phone call was ensuring that, just not the way he had hoped.

"We'll be there," his partner spoke into the phone.

He quickly hung up after scribbling some notes on a napkin. He finally set the phone aside and motioned for them to turn up the TV. Carlos twisted the volume higher before flopping down on the couch next to Julio. The man's body odor competed with Julio's cologne and he wrinkled his nose in protest. They both leaned in to hear what Armando had to say.

"We take the girl to the clinic tonight, just after midnight. After that we have two deliveries and then we're done with this one. Payday by next week."

The two of them smiled at the shared news and Carlos held his beer out for a quick toast. Armando obliged and they both drained them empty. Carlos thankfully rose to replace them. Julio sank back into the leather sofa and shook his head. Armando noticed but he waited until he received his beer and sampled it before addressing him.

"What's your problem?"

He looked away, out the window so he didn't have to meet the accusing glare.

"She's just a kid."

"So what if she's just a kid. Not like we haven't taken kids before. They pay more money. What the hell do you think we're doing here?"

"Not to the Butcher."

"That's not your problem either. You do what you're told and you'll like it. You have no problem taking the money, do you? A trip to the Butcher just means we'll get paid quicker. You should be happy. We won't be waiting months now for another payday."

He just grunted and continued to gaze out the dirty window. His partner stared at him for a moment longer before turning away to exchange a look with Carlos standing in the doorway. He just shrugged as if it didn't surprise him before nodding with agreement to the unspoken question. Their young partner was not working out as they had hoped.

"We move her in a few hours. Get your head straight."

"I'll be ready," was all he replied.

Armando launched himself to his feet and with a disgusted last look at him walked to the bathroom with his beer. Carlos just nursed his slowly. It wasn't the first time they'd had this problem. The solution was simple.

* * *

A few hours later Anita found herself once again bound, gagged, and tied to the board. They had said next to nothing to her this time and despite the smell of his cologne, she had not heard the voice of the young one. Her mind struggled to understand what was taking place as the stiff board bounced roughly across the floor of the van. She heard them talking plainly now and even using their names to address one another. She didn't know what to make of it. She cried out through the gag as she and the board were roughly kicked back to the side of the van and held there with a boot. The van lurched through more turns and potholes, bouncing her head sharply against the board. The men talked of what they saw out the windows as the van slowed and turned into a driveway.

"Around back. Get close to the door."

"Can't we walk her in? Those stairs are a bitch."

"I don't care. Just untie her feet. Leave the gag and her hands tied."

The van swayed as the driver made a quick stop before reversing the transmission and backing toward the building. The sounds of several dogs barking could be heard as they got closer, announcing their arrival.

"That's good," the younger one spoke from his position at the back window.

Her heart leaped to hear his voice. Despite the fact that he was one of her kidnappers, he had shown her kindness and she took small comfort in his presence.

The doors opened with a bang barely heard over the din of the multiple dogs. She smelled the presence of the animals and wondered where they had brought her.

A moment of panic gripped her as the older one grabbed her by the throat and spoke into her ear.

"We're cutting you loose to walk inside. If you try anything we'll be forced to kill you. Do you understand?"

Anita managed the smallest of nods against her restraints. Another kidnapper snorted and stifled a laugh.

Knives clicked open and the tape and straps were quickly gone. Two of them yanked her to the edge of the van and she was stood up on wobbly legs. A heavy door opened and the smell of animals entered her nose. The barking got louder as she was walked inside. She heard the banging of cages as the animals jumped against them.

"Shut the hell up!" Carlos yelled. The barking continued.

"Right here. Open the door."

Another door creaked open and she heard one of them descend a set of stairs.

"Step down," she heard as they pushed her forward.

One of them held her from behind by her bound hands as she felt her way slowly down the stairs with her feet. The smell of bleach met her nose and the noise abated some as the door was shut behind them. Bright light penetrated the blindfold around the edges and she heard the sounds of metal on metal. They waited and Anita's fear ratcheted up in the silence. The metal on metal sound continued, like kitchen utensils dropping in a pan. It finally stopped and a new set of footsteps approached. The gag was pulled roughly from her mouth.

"How much do you weigh?" the new voice asked. It was older, and cold, with no emotion.

"I...I don't..."

"How much do you weigh?" he asked again.

"Six...sixty kilos."

Some more sounds she could not identify filled her ears and she started to cry. The hands holding her arms grew tight and she felt her arm exposed once again where the sleeve was torn. The sting of the needle made her cry out, but this time no one hushed her. The needle's sting changed as she felt a cold liquid enter her arm.

The light around the blindfold quickly faded.

Julio watched with distain as his partners caught the girl and lifted her onto the stainless steel table. He hated this place and the man who occupied it. They called him The Butcher, and the man was evil personified. From what little he knew, the man was a former surgeon who had lost his license after he was found molesting his patients, or killing too many of them on the table, depending on who you talked to. He'd developed a drug habit and was now an unlicensed veterinarian. Somehow he had come to be on the cartel payroll. It was not the first time they had come here, and Julio had been shocked at the man's demeanor. He showed no emotion whatsoever, other than to smile when they paid him.

He watched silently as the man arranged her on the table just so, placing her head in a block and deftly inserting an IV in her arm before reaching up and adjusting the light overhead. He placed an oxygen mask over her face and it soon clouded with condensation from her heavy breathing. The tray full of instruments gleamed on the table, and the man quickly tied a plastic apron around his waist before reaching out a gloved hand for a pair of syringes. He held up the first one to the light and examined it, speaking one word as he did so.

"Out."

They needed no encouragement and quickly left via the stairs. Julio took one last look at her blindfolded face lying on the table before swallowing and closing the door behind him.

The Butcher looked down on the young girl on the table before him as he injected the large dose of Heparin. He reached out and pulled the blindfold from her face. Seeing her beauty, he cupped and stroked her face before letting his eyes travel down her still form. If he had more time he would have enjoyed her body before performing the feat he had been hired to do. But time was short. The dose of Etomidate he had given her would only keep her unconscious for a few minutes. It was time to get to work.

Attaching the large syringe to the IV catheter, he slowly withdrew a large quantity of her blood. He then carefully mixed the blood with a crystalloid IV solution until he had a four-to-one ratio. To this he added forty milliequivalents of potassium before setting it aside in an ice bath. A simple recipe for cardioplegia.

Fetching a large pair of scissors from the tray he cut the tape from her wrists and let her arms fall to the side. Working in steps, he soon had the sweatshirt sliced free and her bra also removed, exposing her bare breasts to the bright light. Another pause while he gazed at her form before he grabbed a bottle of Betadine from the tray and coated her entire chest with it. Her muscles twitched at the cold fluid and he cursed his carelessness while searching for the syringe.

He quickly injected 200mg of Succinylcholine in her IV. It would take a moment, but she would soon be paralyzed. He couldn't have her moving around while he worked.

Cold. Anita's brain slowly awoke and this was the first message she received. Something cold was on her. A liquid. On her chest and running down both sides of her to pool under her back. Hard. Something hard was holding her head. She moved to open her eyes and they slowly obeyed to let in a blinding light. She automatically closed them. Where was she? The last thing she remembered was the bleach smell, and there was a man. A new voice.

She tried to raise her hand to block out the light, but it refused to move. Odd. She tried again with no success. The more her mind woke, it seemed her body refused to follow. With a start, she realized she couldn't feel her legs. She attempted to say something, but the breath required to do so was being drawn too slowly.

What was happening to her?

Her eyes slowly opened without her willing them to and she saw the shape of a man standing over her. She clearly heard the snap as he put on a pair of gloves. The bleach smell was strong in her nose. The dogs were still barking.

Who is he? What was he doing to her?

She was quickly both confused and terrified and attempted to take a breath in order to scream. It would not come. She willed her body to draw a breath, but it still refused to respond. Panic griped her, but she seemed frozen in place.

* * *

The three of them paced up and down the hallway while the dogs continued to bark halfheartedly at them. Carlos stopped to blow smoke through the bars of the cage and into the face of one particularly loud dog. It silenced him for a few seconds only. He smiled at the dog's anger before taking one last drag and crushing the butt under his boot on the tile floor.

Julio leaned against the wall with a sigh that drew the attention of Armando.

"It's done, get over it."

Julio met his gaze before letting himself slide down the wall to sit on the cold tile. The gun in his belt stabbed him in the ribs, and he drew it out and placed it on the floor beside him.

"I'm fine. Leave me alone."

Armando eyeballed the gun before exchanging a look with Carlos.

"Okay."

He lit another cigarette.

* * *

The Butcher noticed the slowing of her breathing as the succinylcholine took hold. It was a short-term paralytic. He had a few minutes at best, but that would be more than enough. He noted the pulse from her distended carotid artery speeding up. Too soon for oxygen deprivation, perhaps she was waking up? It didn't really matter either way.

He pulled the scalpel from the tray and made a quick incision down her chest, exposing her sternum. The blood flowed freely and he ignored it as he grabbed the sternal saw. He fired it once with a loud screech before placing it in the incision. Applying steady pressure, he began sawing through the girl's ribcage.

* * *

No! Her mind screamed it repeatedly, but her body refused to save itself. Run! Fight! Scream! All of her thoughts fell away as she stared at the man's face not inches from her own. Her heart pounded in her chest in protest, but the pain was the only feeling she had. She had no choice but to watch this man as he killed her. The pain in her chest increased sharply as her heart began to protest the lack of oxygen. The smell of her own blood and bone overpowered the scent of bleach in her nose. What was he doing to her?! Why can't she move?! He finished sawing and her ribs popped as he inserted a rib spreader and quickly cranked the handle. The pain was like nothing she had ever encountered before. Her vision began to tunnel as her body used up the last reserves of oxygen provided by her killer. Daddy help me! The pain kept her awake long enough to see the large clamp in his hand before the tunnel collapsed and her life ended with it.

* * *

The Butcher was moving quickly now as time was the enemy. He quickly clamped off the aorta followed by the superior and inferior vena cava's. Silently cursing the absence of a surgical tech, he fetched the cardioplesia from the ice bath and injected it into the aortic root. The girl's heart quivered in protest before quickly lying still. He grabbed a small basin of sterile ice and unceremoniously dumped it into the chest cavity. Pulling two suction catheters free he was forced to use his elbow to turn them on before jamming one each in on either side of the heart. He stepped back and forced himself to slow down before again picking up the scalpel.

Working carefully and drawing on a diagram he had committed to memory, the Butcher severed first the aorta. After repositioning a suction catheter he quickly followed with the superior vena cava and then the inferior vena cava. The cuts had to be precise. If the cuts did not look professional, it could arouse suspicion. Working steadily, he soon freed the pulmonary arteries and vein, disconnecting the heart from the lungs. Better able to rotate the heart now, he was forced again by the lack of help to hold the heart in place while he severed some connecting tissue. Once free, the heart flopped into his waiting hand and he carefully removed it from the girl's chest. The suction catheters gurgled loudly as they worked to remove the pool of blood and melted ice from her now empty chest. He ignored it as he checked the heart over thoroughly for any damage he may have caused. All appeared as it should be. The heart was cold, flaccid, still, and decompressed. He moved over to the organ machine and placed it in the tray of cold saline. He made the necessary connections and adjustments before filling the reservoir with blood and closing the lid. The heart was ready. He turned the machine on and watched it circulate the fluid for a moment until he was sure everything was functioning as it should. Only then did he turn back to the girl on the table.

He wasn't finished yet.

*　　　*　　　*

Julio watched them both as they crushed out another round of cigarettes. Evidently they didn't care if they messed up the Butcher's clean floor. Typical.

"How long?"

"Couple more minutes. He has more to do this time, remember?"

"Yeah…forgot."

Julio ignored them and put his elbows on his knees and his hands over his ears. He couldn't stand the barking of the dogs coupled with the words of his partners anymore.

A loud banging was heard from behind the door. The dogs raised the volume in reply. Julio pressed his hands tighter and closed his eyes in a futile attempt to block it all out.

*　　　*　　　*

The Butcher ignored the flying tissue splattering across his apron and repositioned the Lebsche knife for another blow from the mallet. It was harder than he had expected, and the misuse was not doing justice to the knife, but he soon had what he needed lying on the table. He gathered them up and deposited them in an ordinary Ziploc bag before adding some ice and sealing it. Stripping off the bloody gloves, he placed the baggie on the machine and picked them both up. A kick on the door at the top of the stairs prompted one of them to open it. The scene was not what he expected.

Armando stood before him, brandishing a large handgun in his fist.

Julio raised his head when he heard the door open to see the Butcher holding the machine. The plastic bag on top threatened to slide off but the man's attention seemed to be elsewhere. Following his gaze, he saw Armando holding a gun aimed at his head. His hand automatically searched the floor next to him until it dawned on him that the gun was his. Armando cocked his head as he watched the expressions move across Julio's face. His lips parted into an evil grin and his rotten teeth were the last thing Julio saw before Armando pulled the trigger.

They all watched as the blood found its way through the cracks around the tiles. Armando and Carlos stepped back to keep their boots clean. The Butcher said nothing. He simply set the machine down well away from the expanding puddle before standing and holding out his hand. Armando reached into his jacket and removed a large envelope. The man took it and immediately began checking its contents.

"Sorry about the mess."

The Butcher ignored them as they gathered up the machine and plastic bag. He was still counting the money when they left.

*　　　*　　　*

Fifteen minutes later they pulled up to the gates of a small airport outside the city. Armando now wore a set of surgical scrubs and an ID badge from the largest hospital in the area. He picked up the machine and walked through the small FBO to see the flight crew waiting in the crew lounge. He set the machine on the floor in front of them and picked up the clipboard he had balanced on top. One of the crew checked the machine's digital readout as well as the seals covering the lid. Satisfied, he nodded to his partner who was examining the paperwork. He checked his watch before asking a question.

"Harvest was thirty minutes ago?"

Armando shrugged and smiled. "*No hablo.*"

The crewman made a face but just nodded. He signed the form even though he couldn't read it and handed the clipboard back to him. They didn't have time to mess around with paperwork. They only had a few hours to get the heart to Baltimore. The paperwork was someone else's problem. A to B was his and he wasn't going to be the one to hold things up.

The jet engines screamed as the pilot fired them up. The two crewmen gathered up the machine and moved out onto the apron.

Armando just smiled. They would now drop off the baggie and go home. He mentally counted his money, now increased by half a share, as he walked back to the van.

MEXICAN POLICEMEN
CHARGED WITH KIDNAPPING
September 11, 1999—BBC

—NINETEEN—

JIMMY WOKE WITH A start and immediately located his gun as his brain processed the sounds around him. Once he determined there was no threat, he let his head fall back onto the pillow with a sigh. The all too familiar feel of the cold metal in his hand coupled with the view of another hotel room ceiling served to remind him of what he was doing. It was a reminder he was getting quite tired of. But leaving the job he had was not as simple as it was for other lines of work. For now it was something he just had to accept. Besides, it was too early in the morning for thoughts of that nature.

He swiveled his head around to find the clock. The light around the drapes told him the sun was barely above the horizon and the clock confirmed this. He could also hear the morning news on the TV in the next room. Manuel was on duty, and had either fallen asleep or was letting Jimmy sleep past their agreed scheduled time. He doubted it was the former, and the smell of coffee meeting his nose served to support that. Either way, it was time to get up.

He pulled himself to a sitting position before scratching the stubble on his face. He set the gun back down on the nightstand before standing and walking to the bathroom. As he walked by the door he heard Manuel change the channel, confirming that his partner wasn't asleep. After a piss and a mouthful of hotel mouthwash, he put on a pair of shorts and opened the door.

The room was pretty much as he had left it the night before, as was his partner. Manuel looked tired, as expected, and he was in the same position Jimmy had left him in the night before. A room service tray with a fresh pot of coffee sat on the table next to a full ashtray. The remains of some late night meals sat next to him on the couch and Jimmy watched him slowly get up as he entered the room.

"Thank God. I gotta process some coffee. Watch the screen for me. Be nice to not take it with me for a change."

"See anything?"

"Nothing all night."

Jimmy just smirked and nodded while he poured himself some coffee. He hated the waiting, too. Manuel handed him the phone from the pocket of his hotel robe as he hurried past. Jimmy sampled the brew while he walked toward the couch. Not wanting to sit yet, he stood behind it where he could see the two screens. The TV showed a talking head on CNN updating everyone on the latest trouble in the Middle East. The laptop sitting on top of it provided a picture of the row house as seen from the camera they had hidden in the garbage can. Jimmy looked for any changes, but saw nothing new.

Manuel returned from the bathroom and rubbed his face. He also needed a shave.

"You want I should shower first?"

"Yeah, go ahead, I'll order us up some breakfast."

Manuel returned to the bathroom while Jimmy took his place on the couch. He searched for and found the hotel menu on the crowded coffee table before clearing a spot for his feet. They could be here for days. Might as well eat well.

He divided his attention equally between the laptop and the menu. They would only get one shot at this. He couldn't afford to get too distracted.

He heard the shower start.

* * *

Lenny had traded his car for a borrowed FBI Suburban, and he now expertly adjusted the large coffee in his hand as he maneuvered through the DC traffic. At least he could avoid the damn traffic circles today. Something he hated as they always forced him to use both hands while he looked over both shoulders. Last time he'd spilled his coffee as he crossed DuPont circle, burning himself and barely avoiding hitting a man on a bike. The man had smacked his car with his gloved hand before giving him the finger and pedaling off through the traffic. Lenny had returned the gesture despite the man's back being turned. Made him feel better. Anybody dumb enough to ride a bike through DC traffic deserved to get hit, as far as he was concerned. Lenny was a big believer in Darwinism.

This morning he wasn't making the roundabout trip he had forced himself to make in the past. Today was moving day for Angel. He was going to pick up him and his keepers and drive them to Quantico. There he would be housed in the brig with a small number of US Marshals and plenty of Marines outside. No press would get within the base. Lenny hoped it was enough. He had no illusions as to the cartel's reach. They had shown in the past that they were willing to go to any length necessary to silence those who spoke out against them. As a result, Lenny preferred secrecy over brute strength. So far it had worked.

But the evidence had to be presented to the grand jury and Angel would have to start making appearances. Once that started, the word would be out and there was no turning back. With so many people aware of who Angel was and what he was saying, his location could no longer be kept secret, hence the switch in locations. Unfortunately for the grand jury, they were about to be sequestered as well. The whole thing could take months. Lenny didn't envy them.

But his part would soon be over. All he had to do was pick the three of them up and deliver them. Lenny had timed the transfer to fit the DC traffic. By the time they got back on the road, traffic would be lighter, and he wouldn't be heading against it either.

He finished his coffee as he took the last turn. He hoped Jake and Charlie hadn't killed their protectee.

* * *

Jimmy slumped back into the couch and sipped his coffee. He watched the screens but his mind was elsewhere. He wanted out. But how to do it? He had started working for Oscar years ago and he actually thought he had the man's respect. But Jimmy was no fool. He could have all the respect in the world from Oscar, but it wouldn't matter in the least if Oscar considered him a liability. Oscar would think about it for all of two seconds before he took care of business. That was just the way he was, and nothing was going to change it. He remembered a brother-in-law the man had. He'd thought that marrying the boss's sister meant he could conduct business without Oscar's permission. The sister had been told it was a rival who had killed him, but everyone else knew otherwise. If Oscar lived through his ordeal and was somehow found guilty, he would still run his empire from prison. His brother did not have Oscar's abilities, but with Oscar's guidance he might be all right for a short term. It was all up in the air right now, anyway. If Oscar came through all this, Jimmy would ask him to let him retire, but he'd do it from a distance and have an exit plan ready just in case.

His thoughts turned to Jessica. She had no idea what he did and he hoped to keep it that way until it no longer mattered. She thought he worked for a security company and guarded rich businessmen traveling around the world. It worked to explain his sudden departures and absences. He had lied to many women in the past. This was the first time he had felt dirty doing it. But his past was certainly nothing to be proud of, and some things were better left there.

His thoughts were brushed aside as his partner entered the room. A towel clothed him at the waist while he rubbed his head with another.

"Coffee?" Jimmy asked.

"God no. I drank a whole pot last night."

"I got breakfast on the way. Thanks for the extra sleep."

"Seemed kinda pointless to wake you up. No way I'm gonna sleep until this caffeine wears off anyway. No use both of us being up that early. I'll get a nap later, maybe after I use the gym." He smacked himself on the stomach.

Jimmy smiled at that. Most men would kill to have Manuel's abs. He could have been on the cover of a fitness magazine if he hadn't chosen his current line of work. Besides, he tended to get cranky when he missed a workout. He rubbed his head some more with the towel before turning and tossing it over a chair.

"Isn't that our boy?" he nodded toward the screen.

Jimmy looked up to see a figure moving across the grass. He quickly picked up the remote and silenced the TV. He leaned closer in time to see Lenny climb the steps of the row house. He knocked on the door before turning to look up and down the street.

"That's him."

Jimmy reached in his pocket and pulled out the phone.

*　　　*　　　*

Lenny searched the street for any wandering people that looked out of place, but it was post rush hour quiet. The normal setup for this type of security would have been a second security team across the street in another house. One equipped with cameras and lots of firepower. But Lenny had vetoed that as the circle of people in the know would have been too large. Secrecy was still the best policy, in his opinion. After his search for people, he checked every car on the street as he got closer until he was well past the house. He continued on to the intersection and pulled a quick U-turn before parking in front of the house. Should he leave it running? He dismissed the thought as paranoid and shut the SUV off.

Extracting his ample frame from the driver's seat, he adjusted his belt before walking slowly up the walk. Watching the window, he was rewarded by some movement of the curtain as one of the Marshals checked him out. Probably Jake, he thought. Charlie seemed to prefer sitting down to work.

The stairs creaked as he climbed them and he was forced to pause as the locks were thrown open. The door soon opened to reveal Jake's smiling face. Lenny entered and Jake scanned the street behind him before shutting the door. He noted the packed bags waiting just inside. Evidently the boys were more than ready to go.

"Morning. Our boy ready?"

"He's dragging ass a little. Not sure he likes the idea of the Marine base too much. Evidently he doesn't trust the boys in green to take care of him."

"Yeah, well…I don't care. Let's get moving."

Charlie emerged from the kitchen. He had heard the conversation and couldn't agree more. He was sick of Angel and was looking forward to going home. He had an ex-wife and two kids he hadn't seen in some time. The kids didn't know it, but the relationship was undergoing a second start.

"I'll fetch him."

Charlie made the short walk to the bathroom and pounded on the door.

"Let's go, shithead, it's moving day."

The door opened and Angel emerged as he tucked in his shirt. He chose to ignore the remark from Charlie and concentrated on Lenny.

"The Marines? You call that secure? The gangs have all penetrated your military. You telling me you don't know that?"

"Would you prefer prison?"

"I'd prefer something safer."

"Like what? Camp David? It's booked this week. You get what you get."

Angel glowered at Lenny, but kept his mouth shut. He didn't have much of a choice anyway. He stepped into the bedroom to retrieve the small bag of clothes and toiletries they had provided him. They were his sole possessions in the world at the moment, and he didn't want to leave them behind. He stepped out to find them all waiting by the door. Jake stuck his weapon in his belt before giving them a nod. It looked clear. He opened the door and held it for Lenny.

"All right, gimme a bit of a head start."

Lenny stepped through the open door and onto the front porch. He scanned both directions quickly before starting down the steps.

* * *

"There's the cop."

Jimmy hit speed dial number 1 on the phone and watched the number appear on the small screen.

"Doors staying open," Manuel added.

They both watched as Lenny moved across the screen and disappeared down the steps. Less than a second later a young man in the obligatory windbreaker appeared. He did his own scan before stepping forward. Angel's face appeared for a split second before being blocked out by another man.

"Was that him?" Jimmy asked.

"I think so."

They both strained their eyes at the screen until the young Marshal moved to the edge of the porch. The man behind him stepped up enough for them to see half his face around the fat Marshal.

It was enough.

Jimmy's finger came down on the Send button. There was a brief delay before the picture turned to pure static.

Manuel watched as Jimmy set the phone down and picked up the TV remote. He thumbed through the stations until he found a local news channel. Picking up his coffee, he settled in to wait.

Manuel couldn't help but smile at his partner's machismo before retreating to the bedroom to fetch some clothes. After that he would pack. They would be leaving soon.

A low rumble echoed across the city outside the window.

* * *

Lenny's head impacted the driver's side window as the blast picked him up and threw him across the small yard. The heat crawled up the back of his neck and he instinctively rolled himself across the wet grass, thinking he was on fire. Realizing he wasn't, he rolled to a sitting position and looked toward the house. The porch was gone and the house was on fire. Debris still rained down, and he raised an arm to shield himself from it as he got to his feet. Wiping the blood from several cuts on his forehead, he scanned the wreckage in front of him.

"Jake!...Charlie!" His voice sounded faint and distant through the ringing in his ears. He searched his pockets for his cell phone as he stumbled around the burning remnants of the porch littering the yard and street.

"Jake!"

No answer.

He couldn't find his phone and turned back toward the car to search further when some movement caught his eye. He saw a leg sticking out from behind a burning section of wood and stumbled forward. The leg moved again and the man it belonged to began screaming. It was like nothing Lenny had ever heard. He grabbed the burning wood with his bare hands and began pulling, ignoring the pain for as long as he could before it forced him to let go. Rage overtook him and he ripped his shirt off to wrap his hands before grabbing the wood again. Setting his feet, he applied all of his strength and managed to pull the burning boards off the stricken man. He quickly rolled him around to douse his burning clothes. The man's screams continued as Lenny dragged him free of the area.

A siren sounded in the distance and Lenny suddenly had two more sets of hands pulling with him as neighbors joined in to help. His strength suddenly left him and he sank to the ground. His hands were in terrible pain. A man with a garden hose began running water over them and the relief was enough to clear his head. He looked at the man he had pulled from the rubble. People were attending to him. He was badly burned and continued screaming.

Lenny couldn't tell who he was.

2 MEXICAN POLITICIANS SOUGHT;
DRUG CARTEL LINK ALLEGED

July 15, 2009—CNN

—TWENTY—

"LIFEGUARD-NOVEMBER-SEVEN-FOUR-FOUR-ALPHA-LIMA APPROACHING."

"Contact-four-four-alpha-lima, turn right heading two-seven, you are cleared for priority landing."

"Alpha-lima."

The pilot banked the plane to the east until they were on the approach heading, leveling the wings with a practiced skill until the plane was on the glide slope. Their fourteen-hour flight was close to ending. With any luck, the ambulance was on time and they could make the exchange quickly. His mind and body were ready for a good meal, a tall drink, and twelve hours of sleep. Not necessarily in that order.

"Lifeguard-November-four-six-five-charlie-delta. Turn right heading two-seven-six and maintain." He heard the tower speak to another plane.

"Busy day for air-medical," he commented to his copilot. He got a grunt in acknowledgement before the man moved on to the next task on the landing checklist. It was not really a time for chitchat. The pilot returned his gaze out the cockpit window before picking up his scan of the cockpit gauges.

The roar of turbulent air sounded as the landing gear was cycled down. The pilot adjusted the throttles to overcome the additional drag and checked his aim at the approaching runway.

Thirty seconds.

The medical crew in the back divided their time between the view out the windows and the gauges on the POPS machine. The heart had been supported by the machine for the last fourteen hours and looked just as good as when they had received it from the Major at the fire base. They had gotten some sleep by working in shifts. One watched the heart beat in the sterile tray while the other dozed on the bench seat. The pilots would often come back from the cockpit to stretch their legs and fuel up on coffee. Their eyes always lingered on the beating heart. Like a fire, it seemed to draw everyone's gaze.

"I see the ambulance waiting. Two of them. Maybe we can do this quick."

"That would be fine with me. I'm ready to get out of this steel tube for awhile."

The younger one turned his head back to the window without making a reply. The older one didn't bother watching, he had seen enough landings for both of them. He instead watched his handheld GPS as the trip timer counted down to zero.

The gear hit the runway only a second later.

* * *

Jack burst through the double swing doors without slowing down and hospital staff quickly scurried out of his way. Security hurried to keep up with him as he stalked down the hallways, following the signs. They weren't sure why he was here at the moment or what had upset him, but they were not about to ask. They signaled their counterpart waiting at the secure doors over Jack's shoulder and the man quickly swiped his card at the cipher lock and opened it. Jack stormed through without a word.

The two Marshals outside the room rose to their feet quickly and only relaxed slightly once they identified him, as Jack's face had the look of a man ready to wage war. He stepped past them and flung the sliding door open with a bang that threatened to shatter the glass. A Marshal stepped forward to restrain him if necessary, but Jack stopped short of the bed. The lawyer in the chair wisely kept his seat.

Oscar had awoken with a start and instinctively grabbed his chest. Jack glared at him, daring him to die, but he soon recovered and took deep breaths of his oxygen.

"You're too late."

"Now hold on a minute..."

Jack cut the lawyer off with a glare before returning his stare to Hernandez.

"I don't care what your hired gun may have told you, I just want to say we've got all we need. Angel spilled his guts on tape to a grand jury. We've got you on everything you can think of. Right now your little cartel is falling apart and your partners are fighting over the pieces. You're done, Oscar. Even if you survive the surgery, the prosecutors are going for the death penalty. One way or the other, you're finished."

Oscar took another deep breath before smiling at Jack.

"Is this...supposed to...scare me...Mr. Jack Randall of the FBI? The death penalty...As if I have not lived with...the threat of death...my entire life? Make your threats...they mean nothing."

Oscar pulled the mask away from his face and sniffed the air.

"Is that smoke...that I smell?" He smiled behind the mask.

Jack took a step forward until the Marshal grabbed his arm.

"Easy, Jack."

Jack got control of himself, but never took his eyes off of Oscar.

"I hope I'm there to see you go."

Oscar shrugged as if it didn't matter. He took another deep breath before removing the mask again.

"You are…hypocrite. I exist only because…you and your people… wish me to. Americans pay me…and you."

"I don't use your poison," Jack shot back.

Oscar nodded as if Jack already knew the real answer.

"I will bet…you know someone…who does. Are they…in jail? Tell me that…Agent Randall…with the clean white hands."

Jack said nothing. The lawyer sat quietly with his pen poised. The monitors beeped.

Oscar watched Jack's face before he smiled again. He had his answer.

"I cannot wait…to meet this jury."

Jack spun on his heel and stormed out. The crowd of nurses and security men quickly parted. Jack stopped short when he saw Dr. Dayo standing by the monitor banks. His face said he had heard the whole conversation. He and Jack had a silent exchange before Jack walked past him and out of the ward.

Dayo walked through the pathway created by Jack and entered the room.

"Hello…Doctor."

"Mr. Hernandez."

"What news…do you bring?"

"We have a heart for you." Dayo watched as the man's face cracked into an evil grin. He kept his own passive. Without a reply, he turned away and addressed the staff.

"Get him prepped for surgery."

* * *

Senator Lamar sat in the private waiting room at the other end of the critical care unit with his wife. He was unaware of Jack's presence or of any of the drama taking place in the cardiac intensive care unit. Dr. Fong had sent word to them and they had immediately come. They now waited anxiously for his arrival. The nurses had revealed nothing, but one had offered the smallest of smiles and with that, the tension dropped a fraction. His gaze moved around the tiny room, but he did not note any of the objects as he had seen them repeatedly over the last few days. The unread magazines sat next to three-day-old newspapers. Fresh blankets were stacked on one of the pullout chairs that they had been spending short periods in, and the view out the window stayed the same, changing only with the angle of the sun as it slowly counted the day down.

He gripped his wife's hand in his own and she offered the briefest of smiles at her husband's attempt to reassure her. If he only knew. What would he think? Was she a monster for doing what she had done? Or was she a mother doing what she deemed necessary to save the life of their only daughter? Her husband often had to make deals with his adversaries to get things done. Deals with the devil, he called them. If he knew that his wife had far surpassed anything he had done with one brief instance, it could change everything. She swallowed her deeds and focused on her daughter. What did the doctor summon them for? She had an idea, yet she had not received any messages informing her of anything. It was both puzzling and a relief.

A soft knock on the door interrupted her thoughts as Dr. Fong entered with the ever present chart. He strode quickly across the small room and offered a smile. Her husband got to his feet and she rose also on shaking legs.

"I'm so sorry to keep you waiting. I have good news. It looks like we have a heart for Tessa."

"Doctor…that's great. Thank you so much." Her husband replied as he automatically stuck out a hand. Dr. Fong gave it a quick shake before sitting down. They quickly joined him on the facing couch.

"I know it seems very fast, but sometimes these things happen. We actually have two hearts arriving at nearly the same time. I'm told that both are from the same hospital in Mexico. I don't have the details, but this sometimes happens when there are multiple victims, such as in a car accident. I've checked the histo-compatibility and it's damn near close to perfect. Evidently the hospital thought that one staff member was informing us on both hearts and the information got lost in the shuffle. Regardless, they caught the error and faxed the records after the heart had already left. It's already here and on its way from the airport, so we'll be moving your daughter into surgery soon. Any questions that I haven't covered?

He had answered everything they had asked over the last few days as well as provided information for them to read. They had exhausted themselves on the subject.

"No…I guess not."

"Then I better get scrubbed in. Christine will come and visit you in a few minutes."

"Thank you, Doctor."

The Senator collapsed back into the chair in relief while his wife silently cried. She wiped her tears away and walked to the bathroom to collect herself. Once there, she ran the water in the sink. She looked up briefly to see her reflection. Her own eyes were accusing and she quickly looked away.

* * *

Dr. Fong had just offered a reassuring smile before hurrying out the door. His thoughts were on the case already as he moved quickly down the tile hallway. Doing two transplants at the same time was rare, but nothing to be overly concerned about. They had more then enough staff on hand to manage. The sudden arrival of the two hearts was strange, but Mexican hospitals danced to their own drummers and he had long ago given up trying to figure out how other institutions worked. Since the invention of the POPS machine and its ability to keep harvested organs viable for such long periods, they had been getting more and more organs from long distances. He and his colleagues had given up on asking where they were coming from or how they ended up in the system as the answers were always vague and he had enough to worry about on his end. He just trusted in the system they had and did his part.

He and his colleague Dr. Dayo were going to be quite busy for the next six hours.

*   *   *

Jimmy watched another broadcast from the scene of the fire as the talking heads speculated about what happened.

"Move, you asshole," he growled at the screen.

The young reporter refused to accommodate him, and Jimmy was forced to examine the background around him for the information he was looking for. They had watched updates for the last few hours, but once the fire was out, the story just bogged down as the reporters couldn't find anything to add to it. The police had quickly taped off the immediate area and then extended that to the end of the block in both directions a short time later. The only view they had was through the long lenses of the news cameras as helicopter traffic was strictly controlled in the DC area.

The reporter passed the story to one of his equally young colleagues standing outside the ER entrance at George Washington hospital. He just repeated the same thing he had said thirty minutes ago. Two victims brought in. Both men. Both burned. No names for either of them and the police were keeping a tight lid on the whole thing. Back to you Ron.

Jimmy just shook his head and forced himself to be patient. Manuel already had their bags packed and sitting by the door. They just couldn't leave until they had some confirmation. Jimmy put two and two together and was willing to bet that one of the patients at the hospital was the cop. He had been farthest from the blast area, and likely just had a head-ache. If so, that was fine, he really didn't care. He needed to know about the others. If there were two in the hospital and two at the scene, then he only needed to know about the ones at the hospital, as the two at the scene were obviously dead. The lack of urgency by the firemen and EMS workers walking around behind the idiot reporter told him that. He didn't know where Angel was, so he needed to see two bodies leave and hear of one dead at the hospital.

He cussed the TV as they moved on to celebrity dirt and snatched up the remote to find another channel. He tried to keep the noise down. Manuel was sleeping in the chair next to him.

KIDNAPPING BECOMES
GROWTH INDUSTRY
September 7, 2000—BBC

—TWENTY-ONE—

LUIS DROVE AIMLESSLY AROUND the neighborhood and passed the house once, looking for any cars that didn't belong. The drop point was one of six they used. It served to keep the groups within the organization apart. He had never met any of the people who guarded the ones that they kidnapped, and had no plans to ever do so. They were employees and he had one in charge of each group who ran it and took care of any problems that presented. As far as they were concerned, he was just a voice on the phone, a phone that changed its number regularly. If any of his people screwed up and got caught, the most they could give the police was an old phone number.

Last night they'd had a problem. But his man had already taken care of it by the time he had called. The heart was on the way, and the package he had asked for was in the dead drop. He had to simply pick it up on his way.

He pulled his car to a stop under some trees and left it locked. The insignia on his license plate would keep it from harm, unless the thieves were too young or ignorant. But he didn't plan on being away from it for long. Lighting a cigarette, he started on a stroll down the street. It was an old neighborhood with large homes, many of them still grand, but some crumbling under the weight of age and lack of upkeep. Most had walls around them, and this was something he was exploiting.

The walls were for privacy and they worked well. Through a combination of walls and landscaping, a person on the sidewalk was hard-pressed to see the houses behind them. Even the second stories offered only a glimpse. But it also worked in reverse as anyone on the sidewalk was hidden from those inside and, with the exception of the occasional dog walker, the occupants tended to stay inside their walls.

Luis kept his gait slow so as to appear as nothing more than a man out for an afternoon walk. As he approached his target, the wall changed from one of white brick to an older red stone. The stone had several large gaps where the mortar had let a piece slide free and Luis scanned them from behind his sunglasses as he counted his steps. He slowed only slightly and with one quick motion reached over his head and pulled the bag free from the gap. The ice had melted, but the water was still cold. His man had been smart enough to place the Ziploc in a second opaque plastic bag, but he still transferred it to the small paper grocery bag he had brought with him. He swung the bag casually as he continued around the block and made it back to the car without passing another pedestrian.

Once behind the wheel, he fired up the engine and flipped on the air conditioning before examining the contents of the bag. He counted them quickly. Five.

Five little fingers.

He placed the fingers in a cooler full of ice he had brought with him and pulled out the box. It was already addressed and showed a forged processing stamp from the post office. He selected a finger and placed it in the box before adding the letter and sealing it shut. He placed the box on the dash so it would be warm by the time he got there.

Checking his watch, he saw he had over an hour before his appointed time at the house. He decided to grab something to eat first. He would treat himself to something nice. This day would very likely turn out profitable.

* * *

Dr. Dayo sat in his office alone with his hand idly playing with his pager on the desk blotter in front of him. The man in the ICU was on his mind, as were the men he had met in the parking lot of the hospital. The words of the Interpol agent had refused to leave his mind since he had heard them.

He had been to war and seen evil up close. Back then he had been young, and not as wise to the ways of the world. In a way he wished he still was. The photo of his wife and kids on the desk in front of him caught his eye, as did the photo next to it—him and his college roommate smiling into the camera at their graduation. He and Tommy had been best friends for several years, attending the same schools and challenging each other at every turn. An addict in need of his next fix had ended Tommy's life for the cash in his pocket shortly after their graduation. He never got to see his son arrive or even perform his first surgery. Somehow the evil had found its way to him now. There was a police car outside his house every day and his kids had armed escorts taking them to school. He stopped playing with the pager and forced himself to set it down before he threw it across the room.

The phone on the desk in front of him rang and he answered it, already knowing the message.

"Dayo."

"The patient's been heprinized. Should be ready for you in about thirty minutes, Dr. Dayo."

"Okay, tell them I'm on my way."

He cradled the phone and contemplated the pager in front of him. Opening his desk drawer, he rooted around in the mess until he found a small flashlight. He twisted it on before dropping it in the drawer and shutting it. The light peeked out through the small crack, but it would be unnoticeable unless you were sitting at the desk. He stuck the pager back on his belt before leaving his office.

* * *

It took another hour, but the reporters finally had something new to report. A hospital spokesman was coming out to address the crowd of reporters. He had two senior members of the DC police with him and looked a little nervous. It was obvious from the beginning that he was not an experienced public speaker. He had to be led to the bank of microphones and told where to look. He was carrying a pre-written statement and after a go-ahead nod from the police chief, he cleared his throat.

"Hel…Hello, my name is Peter Wosniak and I'm the current head of administration here at George Washington. I have a prepared statement for you, and then I'll attempt to answer your questions."

"Today the hospital received two men who were victims of the explosion that occurred this morning here in the District. We are not releasing any names at this time, pending notification of next of kin. The first patient had injuries to his head and burns to his hands, as well as some inner ear damage from the blast. He is expected to make a full recovery. The second man received extensive burns to the torso, neck, and head, as well as some inhalation injuries. Our trauma team and burn unit worked on him extensively, but were unable to save him and he died approximately thirty minutes ago. I'm afraid that's all I can tell you at this time."

The reporters didn't wait for the man to finish his last sentence. They screamed in unison, trying to be first. The spokesman got a nod of support from the chief before pointing to a woman in front.

"Can you tell us the cause of the explosion?"

The chief quickly stepped forward to field that one and the administrator gratefully stepped back to let him.

"At this time the event is under investigation. I can assure you that both the police and the fire marshal will find the cause of the blast. So far they have ruled out a gas leak. There is no danger to the other homes in the area."

"Was this a meth lab explosion? Were there chemicals involved?"

"We found no evidence so far of a meth lab being on the premises, but we have yet to rule it out entirely."

"Can you tell us the occupations of the people involved?"

The chief smiled at that one. Were they cops, was what he was really asking. He gave them his favorite answer.

"No."

"Can we speak to the injured man?"

The chief turned and looked at the administrator. He reluctantly stepped forward and replied.

"No. He has requested that no press be allowed in and we are bound by law to honor that request."

"Chief, just what can you tell us?"

"Not much, I'm afraid. My office is appointing a liaison to handle all press inquiries. You will need to direct your questions through them. All questions to the hospital will be forwarded to the liaison also. I've been asked to remind you that the hospital grounds are off limits unless cleared to enter by administration. We will update you when we have more information to give. That is all."

The chief ignored the shouted questions and walked back toward the hospital, flanked closely by the administrator. As soon as they were through the doors he turned to his aid.

"Get me Jack Randall at the Bureau on the phone. Now."

* * *

Jimmy had watched the whole thing with satisfaction. He had tied up the one loose end. The other had been taken care of right before the press conference. A clever reporter had knocked on a few doors and with a little money changing hands had found an upstairs window with a view of the crime scene. With his long-view lens he had managed to capture the packaging and loading of two bodies into the waiting ambulance. A group of Federal Marshals stood around in a tight group and the people working around them gave them a wide berth. The reporter eagerly read into the story what he thought it all meant, prompting Jimmy to hit the mute button.

He dug in his pocket for his phone. Making sure he had the right one, he pulled up the contact list and scrolled through the numbers until he realized that he didn't really know who had sent them on the operation. He flipped it shut before contemplating his sleeping partner in the chair next to him. Reaching out his foot, he gave him a stiff nudge. Manuel woke with a start, reflexively reaching for his beltline before realizing where he was. He gave Jimmy a lopsided smile for an apology before his gaze found the screens. He was afraid he had missed something.

"Sorry."

Jimmy waved it away as insignificant before filling him in.

"I think we're done. They just had a press conference at the hospital. They got one dead and one with minor injuries. Won't let the press talk to him."

"That's gotta be the cop Perfect excuse to keep the press away."

"That's what I'm thinking, too. Some reporter at the scene found a perch where he could see over the barriers and fire trucks. He got some footage of them loading two bodies into the ambulances. The cop was farthest from the blast, he's our lone survivor."

"We going to poke around a little and make sure?"

Jimmy sat back and sipped his coffee while he thought about it.

"Who gave us the job?"

"Rico."

Jimmy made a face at that information. Rico was Oscar's brother and definitely the dumber of the two by a long shot. It had always been a combination of Oscar's brains and Rico's muscle that had allowed them to rise through the ranks. Brains always won out in this game, but what Rico lacked in intelligence, he made up for in loyalty and a willingness to do whatever his brother required. But no matter how expensive the suit or how pretty the woman on his arm, Rico always looked like what he was. A street hood with too much money. Jimmy had never liked him, and for good reason. While Oscar had always projected his power through Jimmy with a goal in mind, Rico used his power simply because he could. As a result, Oscar would often cancel Rico's orders after an informative call from Jimmy. Without his brother around to rein him in, Rico could become quite dangerous.

"If Oscar dies, Rico won't last long."

Manuel just shrugged. "You're probably right. He's pissed off a lot of people. Unless he takes care of them first, but I don't see him doing that."

"Has he called you?"

"No, you?"

"No…he probably thinks Oscar is going to make it and hasn't even considered what will happen if he doesn't."

"So who do you think then? Pablo?"

"Most likely. Either him or Nestor, but I'd put my money on Pablo."

They both fell silent while they considered cartel politics for a moment. Jimmy looked for ways it could effect his decision. Whatever happened, it was going to be a mess. He would have to be very careful.

Regardless, he had a phone call to make and there was no use putting it off. He thumbed the appropriate buttons and waited while the call went through. It rang several times and Jimmy patiently waited, it was nothing new. Undoubtedly there was some minion scrambling to get the phone to Rico. No one but Rico or his brother was allowed to answer it. Jimmy counted nine rings before it was picked up.

"Yes?"

"I believe we're done here."

"Jimmy! Is that your work I saw on the TV this morning?"

Jimmy shook his head in disgust. Not only had Rico used his name, he had attached him to the bombing as well. All in one sentence. Jimmy knew there was no such thing as a 100% secure phone, but evidently Rico thought he was untouchable. He was also speaking loud enough that Manuel could hear every word. He probably had someone in the room with him and was showing off. Excuse me while I take a call from my hit-man. Idiot.

"We think the fourth man is the Interpol man. The others were eliminated."

"Good man. My brother will be pleased to hear this."

"He lives?"

"We sent him a new heart last night." Rico laughed.

"You sent it?" Jimmy was confused. Rico obviously had a few drinks in him already so Jimmy threw out the question.

"One of the gangs we deal with in Mexico City has a kidnapping operation. They've branched out into black market organs, you could say. They checked their inventory and found one that would fit. So we had them ship it out last night." He laughed again and they heard the sound of ice moving back and forth in a glass.

Jimmy exchanged a look with his partner. Manuel had a look of disgust on his face and shook his head at Jimmy's silent question. It was the first he had heard of it, also.

"Just like that, huh?" Jimmy fished some more.

"Just like that," Rico echoed. "They have to match it up and do some tests and shit, but it works, they found one. A younger model, too! Some fifteen-year-old girl they were holding. But there's actually two hearts going, I think that one is for him…Anyway, you want to know the sweet part?" More ice in the glass.

"What's that?"

"They still got the parents on the line for the ransom, and the negotiator is one of their people! Clever, no?" He laughed louder.

"Yeah…real clever."

"Hey…hey. So listen. About this cop. If I know you, you're sitting on a pile of information about this guy, right? We may need you to go after him, too. Maybe his family. You know, loose ends. Make an example to the judge and this…what they call it…grand jury? He has family, does he?"

Jimmy looked at his partner, but his face was impassive.

"An ex-wife, that's all."

Manuel was shocked by the answer, but did nothing other than raise an eyebrow. Jimmy had just committed himself to a dangerous game. If Rico found out Jimmy was lying, the result would not be good. They heard the ice rattle again, the drink was obviously empty.

"Okay then. The cop. Be ready for that. I…I will call you soon."

"All right."

Jimmy thumbed the phone off and sat quietly before suddenly throwing it across the room. It impacted a door frame and shattered before falling to the floor. Manuel watched without moving or saying a word.

Jimmy got control of himself quickly. He spoke without turning his head.

"I work for Oscar, not his asshole brother."

"I understand."

"A fifteen-year-old girl? Fucking animal."

"He is."

Jimmy launched himself off the couch.

"Let's get the hell out of here."

Manuel rose without a word and followed his partner out.

DEATH-ROW INMATES 'MAIN SOURCE OF ORGANS IN CHINA'

July 7, 2012—The Bangkok Post

—TWENTY-TWO—

OSCAR WATCHED THE NURSES carefully as they moved around his bed. They were both his caregivers and his captors, but he had no choice but to trust them. He had already answered a number of questions verifying his name, what he was allergic to, what procedure he was having, even how much he had peed the night before. The telemetry unit was removed from his chest for the first time in weeks, and when the signal faded from the screen, the phone immediately rang. The nurse paused briefly to assure the tech watching the screen that the patient wasn't dying before quickly going back to her work. The one who had shaved his chest had refused to make eye contact, as did the other who filled out a never ending pile of forms. The work progressed at a rapid but paced rate, and items were marked off the pre-op checklist.

He slowly raised a hand to scratch his nose. The antibiotic ointment they had swabbed his nostrils with was irritating. The cherry flavor of the blood pressure medication lingered in his mouth, but he had only been offered a small sip of water to wash down a pill and nothing more. He eyeballed the nurse as she approached with a cup of fluid in one hand and a syringe in another.

"What is this?"

"Mouthwash, it's strong, like Listerine. I need you to rinse your mouth thoroughly and spit it out. It's important that you don't swallow it."

"Why?"

"It's to help prevent infection."

"So I…don't die?" he teased her. It was obvious she loathed her patient, but she was too professional to let it show too much.

"Yes," she replied curtly.

He nodded at her blunt answer. "And the syringe?"

"The start of your anesthesia."

He simply nodded and she held the small paper cup to his lips. He took the fluid in and swished it around as best he could before the foul taste and lack of air forced him to spit it out. She expertly caught it in the cup and disposed of it while her patient took several deep breaths. She then uncapped the syringe.

"I'll need you to roll over on your side."

He grunted at the request but made the effort. She pushed him up and quickly sank the needle into his buttock before pushing the plunger. She let him fall back into place before disposing of the syringe in the sharps box. She returned to her paperwork and Oscar switched his gaze to another nurse as she placed a pair of bright red socks on his cold feet. Socks for surgery? He didn't bother asking. He rested and listened as the nurses completed their list.

"Consents all signed?"

"Yes and…yes."

"ID band?"

"Left side."

"Allergies?"

"Codeine and sulfa. Left side."

"Jewelry, dentures?"

"None."

"Ancef?"

"I hung it on the chart."

"Okay...that oxygen tank full?"

"It's good."

"All right, let's roll."

Oscar was quickly surrounded by staff members on both sides of the bed. All of his wires and tubing were gathered and accounted for. He felt the cold stream of oxygen in his nostrils fade for a moment only to come back a second later. His nurse took his arms and placed them on his chest as the sheet under him was pulled free and gathered up in multiple hands.

"On three...two...three."

The sheet became a hammock as he found himself quickly hoisted in the air and placed on the transport gurney in one fluid motion. He reflexively reached out for something solid but it was over before his hand found anything. The staff quickly dispersed and he was soon left with five. The brake on the bed was released with a loud crack and he found himself finally leaving the room he had called home for the last three weeks. One nurse followed, pushing the IV pole and another led with the balloon pump in front of her while yet another toted the thick chart as she helped steer from the front end. The fourth simply pushed and the procession moved out of the ICU. Oscar found himself the subject of numerous hostile looks. He ignored them. They were worker bees, trained to do one skill well. Soon he would have only one man to worry about.

They moved out of the unit and down the hallway to an elevator. The ride down was short as they only dropped one floor. When the door parted they were met with the stern gaze of a hospital security guard and an armed police officer. The guard turned his key, locking the elevator in place before he waved them forward. The nursing team found themselves all alone in what was normally a busy hallway. The guard offered no explanation and the nurses wisely chose not to inquire. He silently led them down the hall and after punching a button on the wall, they entered the pre-op area. Oscar felt the temperature drop drastically and his body responded with an involuntary shiver. His nurse pretended not to notice while the doors swung shut behind them and the guard took up his new post on the opposite side. Rolling past several empty beds, he was deposited in the corner where he was approached by another nurse. He picked up the chart from where it had been left and scrutinized it. The transport team left without a word.

Oscar sized the man up while he waited. He was older, with an air about him that said he had seen it all before. He asked his questions without looking Oscar in the eye.

"Can you tell me your name?"

"Oscar…Hernandez."

"And what are you allergic to?"

"Codeine…and sulfa."

"And what surgery are you having today?"

"A new heart."

Oscar watched as the man read his wristbands and confirmed what he was being told. He then checked the man's IVs before pulling the small bag of fluid from the chart and hanging it on a nearby pole. He flushed it with a practiced skill before connecting it to Oscar's arm.

"You'll be going back in a few minutes."

Oscar did not bother to answer as the man turned and walked back to his desk. He was only there a moment when the doors opened again and a young girl was wheeled past his bed. She was surrounded by staff and equipment just as he had been and he couldn't help but smile as she disappeared behind the curtains.

* * *

The man occupying Oscar's mind was forty feet away, scrubbing his fingers with a stiff sponge. Dr. Dayo worked methodically, ensuring each finger got equal attention. His thoughts were clouded and he didn't notice his colleague approach. Dr. Fong nudged him over without a word before turning on the water and reaching for a sponge of his own. He unwrapped it quickly and began scrubbing his own hands before he addressed his partner.

"Wanna trade?"

"Funny guy."

"I try."

They scrubbed in silence for a while until Dayo finished. He slowed his pace while he watched his partner scrub, rinsing his hands over and over.

"What would you do?" he asked.

Dr. Fong stopped scrubbing and examined the face of his fellow surgeon. Self confidence and the projection of it were repeatedly emphasized in medical school. A surgeon never let his doubts be known to anyone on his team and rarely to a fellow surgeon. Dr. Dayo was widely known and respected as one of the top cardiac surgeons in the country. It was an unusual question.

"I would treat the patient in front of me."

Dayo just nodded before raising his hands and walking toward the O.R.

Dr. Fong stopped scrubbing long enough to watch his friend walk away. He caught his eye as he turned to push his way backward into the operating room.

"Grab a smoke when we're done?"

"Deal."

Dayo offered a lopsided smile before disappearing into the room.

Dr. Fong gazed at the closed door for a moment before shaking his thoughts off and returning to the sink.

*   *   *

Luis parked his car by the front door and surveyed the house and grounds before finishing his cigarette and opening the door. The grass was much taller than before, and the wind had deposited trash on the drive and walkway. He frowned at it, but it served to tell him of his targets' state of mind. Some of his victims kept up appearances, keeping the gardeners, maids, and other staff around while the process played out. Others shut down and ignored the decay they were allowing to happen around them. The current couple were obviously one of the latter and he was glad to see it. Time was short and he would have to push them to make the money come. He felt sure that the box in his hand would work to serve that purpose.

He once again ignored the front entrance and instead walked around the house and past the pool. More leaves covered the surface of the water and the deck, and he had to kick some free of his shoes before entering via the back door. There was no one on site, but he knew where he would most likely find them. Making no effort to hide his arrival, he let his footsteps echo loudly on the tile as he approached the kitchen. Days ago they would have rushed to meet him, asking for anything he may have learned. Now he found them as he usually did, sitting at the kitchen table.

"Hello, Mr. Perez. How are you doing today?"

Mr. Perez raised his head and contemplated the question before answering.

"We are…as well as can be expected."

"Yes, I understand."

Luis crossed the room and fetched himself a cup of coffee from the counter before joining them at the table. He set down the box and their eyes were drawn to it. They watched anxiously while he took a sip.

When he had milked all he could from the moment, Luis cleared his throat to speak.

"There has been some communication."

"But we are not scheduled to talk for a few hours yet."

"I know…they sent you a package. I pulled it from the box on my way in. I need you to tell me if what's in the box belongs to your daughter."

"What is it?"

Luis simply pushed the box forward. Mr. Perez stared at it before searching Luis's face. He got no clue and instead looked at his wife. She covered her face in her hands.

Mr. Perez pulled the small box in front of him and slowly opened the lid. Luis watched his face as it changed from confusion to realization to outrage. He pushed the box away and stood up, knocking the chair over backwards. The contents fell from the overturned box and landed on the clean white table.

"Bastards! Fucking bastards!"

The wife pulled her hands away and covered her mouth in horror as she gazed at the finger lying before her. Her husband raged around the kitchen, punching the cabinets and pounding the countertops. Wood splinted under the blows as he continued his assault. Luis ignored him and instead watched his wife. She slowly reached out her hand and turned the finger over. The sight of the small scar on the knuckle sent her into a fit of sobbing and she collapsed back into her chair. Her wailing pulled her husband out of his rage and he quickly returned to the table and gathered her into his arms.

Luis quietly retrieved the finger and placed it back into the box. He closed the lid and spoke softly.

"They will demand money tonight. How much can you get a hold of today?"

Mr. Perez pulled his head up from comforting his wife.

"I...I will make some calls."

Oscar watched the eyes of the surgical staff as he was rolled across the red line and into the operating room. Everyone's faces were covered with surgical masks, but he made mental notes of skin and hair color, height and weight. The OR proved to be even colder than the pre-op room and some of them sported fleece jackets with the hospital logo on them. His gaze moved around the room and he noted his name on a dry erase board along with his height, weight and age. A list of equipment was written next to it and he took in the unfamiliar names: shods, titus, parsonet, dogs, Bovie tips. It meant nothing to him and he quickly dismissed it. An older man with a skull cap sporting American flags sat at the head of the bed in front of a monitor displaying several colors and numbers, all of which were zeros at this point. He turned to meet Oscar's gaze for a moment, and he recognized the anesthesiologist that had visited him yesterday. Turning his head he spotted Dr. Dayo in front of a machine in the corner. Something was moving in a tray of fluid perched on top, and the surgeon was ignoring the activity in the room as he studied it intently.

Oscar's bed bumped up against the black operating table and there was the brief whine of a hydraulic motor as it was leveled and raised to match the one he was on. Once again, the various tubes and wires were gathered up and accounted for as they made ready to move him.

With a practiced lift and swing he was moved over before he had time to worry about being dropped. The transport bed rolled away and the space was immediately filled by several people, their hands all busy as they prepped him. A tech attempted to guide his arm onto the table's protruding arm rest, but he suddenly fought her and raised it over his chest. The team all stopped.

"I have…a question."

Dr. Dayo rose from his seat and walked to the table.

"What is it?"

Oscar smiled as he looked up at the many faces staring down at him.

"Jonathan Dryer… Raina Sampson… Jennifer Hays… Brian Cleveland… Paula Reed."

Their eyes widened in astonishment as Oscar pointed and called them each by name.

"My question is…do you know… *who I am* ?"

Dayo answered the veiled threat for them.

"Yes."

Oscar simply nodded before relaxing and placing his arm back on the padded rest. Dayo nodded to Dr. Dryer who quickly pushed the syringe in his hand, injecting a sedative. Oscar's eyes closed.

The team sat frozen and exchanged a few looks. Dayo spoke loudly and shook them out of it.

"All right, people, shake it off. This is just like any other case."

The team quickly got back to work, but there was no longer the idle chitchat that usually accompanied their ritual. Dayo controlled his rage behind his mask and watched as Oscar's eyes were taped shut and his freshly shaved chest was exposed before being quickly scrubbed with a Betadine solution. Dr. Dryer's laryngoscope blade snapped open with a loud crack and he quickly inserted it into the man's throat, followed by the endotrachial tube. Drapes were placed and equipment was clamped to them as the hiss of the ventilator announced its presence.

Dayo turned and let his arms be guided into a blue surgical gown, but his gaze never left his patient's face. His head was adorned with his operating lenses and lit without him noticing. He stayed that way until Oscar's face disappeared behind the drape.

Paula broke the silence with her crisp voice.

"Oscar Hernandez, forty-six-year-old male, heart transplant, codeine and sulfa."

A series of mumbled affirmatives answered her from around the table.

Dayo stepped up to the only vacant space and held out his hand as his other automatically probed the man's chest for landmarks. He glanced up at the clock on the wall and then to his anesthesiologist who gave him a nod.

"17:42."

The surgical tech slapped a scalpel into his hand as Paula wrote their start time on the board.

MEXICAN KIDNAPPING
TAKES TOLL ON FAMILY
February 21, 2012—Wall Street Journal

—TWENTY-THREE—

"YOU'RE SURE YOU WANT to do this?"

"Yeah, been thinking about it for awhile actually."

Manuel shook his head and gazed around the crowded terminal over the expensive sunglasses perched on the end of his nose. He hated crowds and couldn't help but look around. But it also served to hide his uneasiness. Jimmy was asking a lot.

"You don't just quit this job."

"I know."

"They'll hunt you."

"I know."

"Come on, man, where will you go? China? New Zealand? You know how far they can reach."

"I'll just have to take my chances."

Manuel shook his head again and shifted around on his nervous feet.

This was highly irregular and completely out of the blue. He had no idea what to say. Jimmy just waited for him to work it out and kept a smile on his face.

"What about me, eh? What the hell do I tell them?"

"Tell them you went out and when you came back I was gone. Rico will bitch, but he can't hold you responsible."

The overhead speakers announced another flight, and Manuel used the interruption to get a good look at his partner's face. He could soon see that it was no use. His partner was done. Quitting and just leaving him on his own.

"I'm keeping your car," he deadpanned.

Jimmy laughed. "It's yours."

The speakers made another announcement, and upon hearing it, Jimmy stooped to pick up his bag.

"That's me, kid. I'm out of here. This makes you number one. Remember everything I taught you…and don't get dead."

"I will…just…just look behind you, all right? Be careful."

They shared an awkward handshake before Jimmy turned and moved away down the terminal. Manuel watched until Jimmy was lost in the crowd. He never looked back.

Manuel turned and walked against the flow of people, not caring who he pissed off. He was soon lost in the crowd, also.

Twenty minutes later he sat in Jimmy's Mercedes, now his, and watched returning vacationers reunite with their cars while the air conditioner removed the heat from the interior. He wasn't sure of what to do next. His thoughts were interrupted by the phone ringing.

"Yes?"

"You think you can lie to me?" Rico hissed in his ear.

"I don't understand?"

"I had someone do some checking. This Interpol man has a family. A wife and daughter! You tell me you did not know this?"

"My partner does the research, not me."

"Where is he? He doesn't answer his phone."

"I don't know. I just returned from getting us some food. He's gone, along with his things."

"Bastard thinks he can ignore me?"

"I...I don't know."

"You knew nothing of this?"

"Nothing."

Manuel's skin crawled while he endured the silence on the other end.

"I believe you. Jimmy never knew his place, but you Manuel, you were always a good soldier. Loyalty is rewarded. You are now the one in charge. Find a partner or work alone, it is up to you."

"Okay."

"And find Jimmy! Find him and kill him!"

"*Si.*"

Manuel held the dead phone in his hand and stared at it. His thoughts were interrupted by the slamming of a car door and his eyes darted to the source. He watched as a young man in a suit gathered up an overnight bag and briefcase before jogging toward the terminal. Manuel watched him check his watch as he hurried off. He shook his head and started the engine before turning it quickly off and pounding the steering wheel with both hands. He contemplated his scarred hands for a moment before reaching into his waistband and removing his pistol. He stuck it in the secret panel before exiting the car.

He followed the man toward the terminal.

* * *

The team rolled Tessa past a wall of X-ray banks before pushing through the doors and into the operating room with a carefully choreographed movement. The multiple tubes and wires were all accounted for and placed well out of the way by each team member. If one were to catch on something it could mean a serious delay or even a stop to the surgery and none of them wanted the criticism that would bring. They rolled her parallel and as close to the black operating table as possible before engaging the brake and arranging the equipment around her. Everything in the room was on wheels and they soon had everything just so.

Kye, the circulating nurse, watched the show in front of her with a critical eye, checking and rechecking each and every action as it was started and completed. She rarely had to speak as the team had been working together for some time and they went about their individual tasks with a quiet professionalism. Once everyone was ready, they all paused and waited for those who weren't. The wait was not long.

While some held tubes or wires, others placed their hands under the young girl, crossing over those of the person next to them to assure an even lift. With a quiet count she was lifted and moved onto the operating table in one fluid movement.

The flurry of activity began anew as the portable connections were all exchanged for the more permanent ones of the operating room. Gas lines feeding a variety of choices hung from the ceiling next to multiple flat screen monitors. As the team worked, the monitors came alive one by one, showing all manner of information on the teenage girl. The various colors made it easy for the team to pick out the reading they wanted and their heads all comically bobbed as they checked their connections. The girl's arms were extended over the matching arms of the bed before being taped in place. The static squeal of the Doppler was heard as a new arterial line was skillfully placed by a tech and secured in Tessa's wrist. Her blood pressure reading popped up on the overhead screens in red, and they all frowned at the number before returning to their work. The glass storage lockers lining one wall opened and closed as team members retrieved equipment and placed it on the trays that had been rolled into place at the foot of the bed. Gleaming rows of gold and stainless steel in all shapes and sizes lay in even rows on the sterile blue towels. Boxes of sterile suture were opened and dumped into the sterile field by the surgical techs as they readied for the surgeon's arrival. The Sarns sternal saw was fired up to assure it was functioning before it too found its rightful place on a tray. Only when everything had found its place and been checked off on the circulating nurse's form did the team relax, their gloved hands clasped in front of them against their sterile gowns. They all watched as the tech began to scrub the exposed chest of the young girl. Her pale skin was soon covered in orange frothy foam. One of the five overhead lamps was adjusted so she could see a little better.

"Anyone see Dr. Jacobs out there?"

"He's running his usual ten minutes late."

The door burst open again as Dr. Jacobs, the anesthesiologist, entered the room and headed immediately to the head of the bed. He muttered his usual apology before entering the small corridor of equipment leading up to the girl's head. This was his domain, and after a quick check that everything was as it should be, he sat down at a small stool and pulled out a pen. The team watched silently as he checked the chart to verify the patient's weight before scribbling out some math on a nearby pad of paper. The team exchanged a look and their smiles were evident around their surgical masks. Most doctors used a computer or phone application to calculate drug dosages these days, but not Dr. Jacobs. He liked to do it the old fashioned way. No one could fault him, as he was never wrong, but it was odd to see a man who stayed on the cutting edge of his field resort to a pen and paper. They silently watched as he performed the calculations twice. Apparently satisfied with his math, he opened a small cabinet and removed some vials of medication. The girl on the table before him was already intubated and on the ventilator, so most of his job was already completed. His only task now would be to keep her paralyzed without dropping her blood pressure so the surgeon could do his work. He donned his stethoscope and checked the placement of the girl's breathing tube before glancing up at the screen.

"What's with her B.P.?" he asked.

"It's been low since we got her here. Her ejection fraction is crap. Low twenties at best."

"Well I'd say she needs a new heart then. Where's that surgeon guy? He stop at Starbucks or something?"

"Scrubbing in."

"And the heart?"

They all just looked at one another.

"Really?" Dr. Jacobs asked, his sarcasm gone.

Kye walked to the small desk in the corner and picked up the phone. She dialed the number from memory.

"ETA on the heart...okay...we're ready here...all right." She hung up and faced the room. "They're leaving the airport now."

"Thank God. Much easier with a new heart."

The team relaxed again with the return of Dr. Jacob's sarcasm. He was a favorite as he always kept the mood light.

"When we get done, can one of you kids fix my iPad for me?"

Any answer to his question was cut off by Dr. Fong entering the room.

"Good evening everyone. Are we ready?"

"We're ready here, the heart's about thirty minutes away."

"I'd like to see it before we start. It's coming from Mexico and I really don't have a whole lot of information on it yet. They faxed the chart on the donor, but all I can really read are the labs and stuff, everything else was in Spanish."

"Isn't there an app for that?" Tony teased.

"Actually there is, but it gets lost in the medical jargon. How about you invent one for us? Make yourself a few million."

"I may have some time this weekend. I'll see what I can do."

Their conversation was cut short by the alarms of the monitor. They all swiveled their heads in unison to stare at the overhead screens.

"She's throwing PVCs," Dr. Jacobs announced.

Dr. Fong stepped forward to see the monitor better. The tracing on the screen that represented each heartbeat was wider than normal due to her injury. He tried to ignore the increasing premature ventricular contractions and pick out the underlying rhythm.

"She's getting wider," he solemnly observed. "Stephanie?"

"Yeah?"

"You better get your stool. We have access yet?"

"Yes," said Jacobs from behind the drape.

Dr. Fong watched a moment longer before turning to find Kye holding his gown and gloves.

"Let's move, she's gonna crash!"

As if on cue, the girl's heart rhythm changed from an irregular mess of lines to a rapidly oscillating pattern.

"V-tach. Get on the chest."

Dr. Fong watched as Stephanie placed her hands on the girl's chest and began pumping. Dr. Jacobs scrambled to open the crash cart. He quickly ripped open a tan box and extracted the pre-filled syringe. It was injected quickly into the girl's central line.

"Epi's in."

Kye tore a form from her pile and wrote down the time.

"What's happening?" Doctor Fong asked the room as he was still completing the gown and glove routine and spinning in a circle to aid Tony who was assisting him with getting it tied. He stopped the spin and his eyes immediately returned to the screen over his head. All he saw was the steady spikes created by Stephanie's chest compressions. She stopped for a moment and gazed at the screen, also. A squiggly line with no organization traveled across the screen.

"No pulse."

"That's V-fib, let's shock her."

Kye produced the monitor out of thin air and slammed it down on the table next to the ventilator before firing up the screen. After changing some settings, the whine of the capacitor charging urged those at the table to place the pads as soon as possible.

"Everybody clear?" She scanned the girl's body, looking for any contact with the team members. Jacobs injected another drug before quickly dropping the IV line.

"Lidocaine's in."

Not waiting for them to answer, Kye pressed the button. Tessa's body responded with a shiver that threatened to send her off the table. The line on the screen flattened out for a moment only to quickly return to its chaotic origin.

"Nothing," Stephanie voiced before returning her hands to the girl's chest and taking up the steady rhythm she'd had before.

"Another epi," Fong ordered. He watched as Jacobs pushed the drug before turning to address his circulating nurse.

"Where's that heart at again?"

"On its way, maybe twenty minutes."

Dr. Fong absorbed the information before turning to his perfusionist.

"Are we ready, Mike?"

"I'm set up for the transplant. What are you thinking?"

Fong was silent as he weighed his options. All of them sucked at the moment. He watched the CPR being performed on the screen. The team sat frozen except for Stephanie who was already sweating from the effort, awaiting his decision. The rest of them were scrubbed in and unable to help her without contaminating themselves.

"That heart isn't coming back, we're crashing on."

"Bypass now?"

"Right now! Mike?"

Mike was scrambling to comply. "I'll be ready by the time you get in!"

"Let's go."

Dr. Fong picked up a bottle of Betadine and Stephanie barely got her hands clear before he emptied it onto the girl's chest.

The surgeon's hands probed for landmarks before one of them shouted out, "10-blade!"

* * *

Luis counted the stack of bills again as he arranged them into piles that would fit in the large bags he had obtained. The father had made several phone calls and repeatedly argued with bank presidents to obtain the growing mountain of cash. Couriers from three different banks had come to the house in the last couple of hours, and there were still two more on their way. Luis suppressed his grin as the pile on the table grew. The wife had retreated to the living room where she continued to sob.

Her husband had finally left her to her grief, and he now impatiently paced the floor. He alternated between watching Luis count the money and eyeballing the driveway for the next armored car.

Luis heard another vehicle pull up outside, but chose to ignore it so as not to ruin his count. He began stuffing another pile into the heavy canvas bag, making room for more on the large table. He heard the footsteps approach, but didn't bother to look up.

"Just place it here on the table," he ordered.

"Packing for a trip?"

Luis stopped. It was a familiar voice. He looked up to see the head of the Mexican AFI standing in the doorway. Another agent appeared next to him, followed by a third in the other doorway. Luis suddenly realized he could hear several engines running outside. More agents moved past the windows, surrounding the house.

"I don't understand!" the father shouted from down the hall as he was being led away by other agents.

"He doesn't understand, Hector. Or should I call you Luis? I can't say I do, either. Perhaps you wouldn't mind explaining to me what one of my agents is doing playing the role of a K and R negotiator?"

"Just a little side job, boss, nothing more."

The man walked forward and examined the pile of bills on the table. He picked one up and fingered it before tossing it back on the pile. He nodded to himself as if considering the explanation. Hector/Luis began to sweat.

"Side job. Is that what you call it?"

"Yes. Their daughter has been kidnapped. I am trying to free her."

"I see. This is the ransom then, or a first payment?"

"A...a first payment."

The man just nodded as he casually reached into his pocket and pulled out the bag of fingers and dropped them on the table in front of Luis.

"And this? Is this your work?"

Luis froze in horror as his brain searched for an explanation to offer. It was cut off by his boss suddenly slamming a fist into his gut. He doubled over and fell to the tile. The man's boots began kicking him and he hid his head in his arms to protect himself.

"You fucking animal! You do this on my watch! I will see you dead! I'll throw you in prison with the rest of your kind and they will feed off you!" The kicks continued without mercy while the other agents watched.

The man's rage eventually subsided and he glared down at his subordinate, both of them breathing heavily.

"Take this garbage away before I kill him myself!"

The others moved in and yanked Luis from the floor only to slam him face down on the table. As he was pinned down and cuffed, the blood flowed freely from his lip and nose and he bled onto the stacked bills he had so gleefully counted a moment ago. He was quickly dragged to his feet and shoved out the back door. His boss followed him as he was led past his coworkers, most of whom glared at him with contempt while some just turned away. Out in the driveway he was led past several police cars. One of them had an occupant he recognized.

Cuffed and bloody much like he was, the detective gazed back at him through the thick glass.

The head of the AFI watched from the doorway before turning and heading back inside to talk to the parents.

He had bad news for them.

* * *

Manuel tapped his credit card loudly on the counter in an effort to speed the work of the rental car employee. Seeing the looks of the passing travelers, he reined himself in. He didn't want to call attention to himself, but he also needed every minute. He had thought long and hard about his options on the plane ride back to Florida, and had come to the conclusion that he was trapped in the situation. He had never dreamed it would come to this. Jimmy was like a father. He had surely done more for him than his real father had ever done. But he had no choice, it was either do as Rico had ordered, or be in the same position as Jimmy was now.

Manuel was a hunter. Being the prey was not something he was prepared for or ever wanted to be.

The card tapping had drawn the gaze of the man's supervisor and Manuel quickly covered by stopping and offering a charming smile to the woman. She had been checking him out since his arrival.

"Sorry, just running late. Damn airlines are never on time at night."

"True. I'm afraid there's not much we can do about that."

Manuel waved the apology away. "Not your fault. I'm just ready to be in my own house for a change."

"I can understand that. How we doing, Nick?"

Nick responded by hitting a last keystroke and reaching for the printout emerging from the printer.

"We're done. If you could just sign here and here, sir?"

Manuel scribbled an illegible signature at the indicated spaces before tearing his own receipt away and returning the paper. Nick smiled as his customer was obviously an experienced traveler. He slid the keys across the counter and the man quickly palmed them before stooping to collect his small bag and heading for the door.

"It's the white Mustang in slot four," Nick called after him.

"Thank you," Manuel acknowledged as he charged through the door.

Nick shared an amused look with his supervisor as they both watched him sprint across the lot through the windows.

"She must be really something."

"Lucky girl," she answered.

She got a snort and a laugh for a reply before they both went back to their computer screens.

ORGAN TRAFFICKING WAS LONG CONSIDERED A MYTH. BUT NOW MOUNTING EVIDENCE SUGGESTS IT IS A REAL AND GROWING PROBLEM, EVEN IN AMERICA.

January 9, 2009—Newsweek

—TWENTY-FOUR—

"CLEAR!" DR. FONG ORDERED and Stephanie removed her hands from over the incision he had just made. They were alternating between chest compressions and opening the chest as best they could. Dr. Fong quickly filled the space with the sternal saw and crammed its hooked point under the girl's ribcage.

The saw cut through the girl's sternum with some steady pressure, with Dr. Fong adding an extra push to get through the sternal notch at the top. He quickly passed the saw into Tony's waiting hands while Stephanie accepted the rib spreader and inserted it into the gap. Dr. Fong silently cursed the device's lack of speed as he cranked the girl's chest open. A Bovie scalpel found its way into his hand as if by magic and smoke rose from the site as he set about opening the pericardium while Stephanie gave the spreader another crank. Instead of the beating heart they were used to finding, the chest cavity was shockingly still.

"We ready, Mike?"

"Close."

"Where we at on the heprin?"

"One and a half minutes!"

Mike adjusted a clamp before double checking all of his connections.

"We're ready!"

As soon as he had the smallest of openings, Dr. Fong stuck a hand in to begin squeezing the heart. As he was pumping with one hand he carefully expanded the opening with the other. Stephanie grabbed the first cannula from the rack clamped to the drape over the girl's chest.

"I'm ready here."

"We're just gonna stab and go. Okay?"

"Okay." She nodded and a bead of sweat crawled down her forehead. She ignored it and tried to slow her breathing as it was fogging her goggles.

Tony was scrambling to stay ahead of the doctor and anticipate his needs, but this was something he wasn't used to. Nevertheless, he had the scalpel ready when the doctor's free hand shot out for it.

Dr. Fong stopped squeezing the heart and quickly located the aorta. Accepting the scalpel from Tony, he expertly flipped it in his hand and made a stabbing incision in the large vessel. Blood poured from the wound and clouded his view, but Stephanie was ready with the suction. She handed him the cannula and he deftly inserted it into the wound.

"Hold," Fong voiced.

Unsure as to who the order was for, both Stephanie and Tony grabbed for the cannula at the same time, and as a result, neither got a hand on it as the surgeon let go. It popped free and the blood jetted across the chest of the surgeon before moving on to the overhead light and over the drape to land on Dr. Jacobs. The whine of the bypass machine changed with the rapid loss of pressure.

"Dammit!" Fong quickly grabbed the errant cannula and stuck a finger in the gushing stab wound just before it disappeared. The chest cavity was now full of blood and he felt, more than saw, his way to what he needed. Stephanie returned with the suction in time to clear the way for him to re-insert the tubing.

"Hang two units!"

He held the cannula in while Stephanie attempted to clear the field, but there was just too much blood. He felt his way around the anatomy and performed the re-cannulation blind.

"Turn the pump sucker way up!"

The blood was clearing, but not quickly enough for the surgeon's liking.

"We're drowning here, give me another one."

"Are you in, John?" Jacobs asked as he opened the clamp on the blood he had just hung, sending it through the IV.

"I'm in. I just can't see anything."

Jacobs stood up and gazed over the drape to see a bloody pool. The surgeon's hands were working beneath its surface with the tubing protruding. As the blood was sucked away the connection appeared.

"We've got some air," Mike announced.

"How bad?" Fong inquired.

"I can walk it out I think."

"Okay...Stephanie, *you* hold this. Tony?"

"Right here."

"Some 3-0 please, forehand. Then it'll be a scalpel and some more 3-0."

"Okay."

Working quickly, Dr. Fong secured the cannula in with the suture as his gloves were repeatedly doused with saline to keep them free of blood. He cinched it down tight for the best seal he could get, but time was short. Ignoring the offered scissors, he left the ends and grabbed the next cannula while he located the superior vena cava, the large vein returning blood to the heart. He made another stab incision before inserting one fork of the cannula in. This one he held in place himself.

"I'm in, Mike," he informed the perfusionist.

"Bypass on," he replied, glancing at the clock.

Dr. Fong glanced at the monitor screen and was rewarded with a climb in the blood pressure.

"Our flow sucks," Mike voiced.

"We got more air?"

"No, it's clear."

"Are you up against the wall?" Stephanie asked.

Fong adjusted his angle slightly.

"No…are we loosing blood?"

They both examined the chest cavity, looking for any bleeding they may have missed.

"We don't see a bleed. She got volume?"

"Should have plenty," Mike replied.

"Pressure's climbing, but it's doing it slowly," Jacobs chimed in.

Fong made a decision. "I'm adding the IVC."

Retrieving the scalpel from Tony, Dr. Fong repeated the stab and cannulate procedure again on the inferior vena cava and quickly connected the other fork. Holding both in place, he again scrutinized the monitor as Stephanie removed the clamp. The red number increased its pace and they were soon within normal limits. The tension in the room ratcheted down slightly.

The surgeon took stock of the situation and determined they were out of the woods for the moment. It was basic plumbing. They had just replaced the heart with a machine, clamping off the lines going in and out of the girl's heart and redirecting them through the bypass machine. The only problem now was that they were committed to the transplant. If there was something wrong with the donor heart, they had no choice but to use it. He pushed the thought aside for the moment. Taking his gaze away from the chest cavity, he examined the faces of his team. Some of them were streaked with blood, sweat, or a combination of both.

"Time?"

"She was down two, maybe three minutes. I think we're okay," Jacobs answered as he whipped blood from his face.

"Okay...let's try not to do that again."

"I'll agree with you there."

"Tony?"

"Yeah boss?"

"I could use that 3-0 now...and some clean underwear."

* * *

Manuel gazed around the parking lot behind the dark lenses of his sunglasses. With no time to change into more appropriate clothing, he was sweating heavily in the Florida heat. Summer had arrived early, and he was the only one in sight wearing long pants. He longed to return to the air conditioning of the rental car, but he had one quick task to perform first. He spotted the car right where he had first seen it and slowed his gait slightly as he approached. While the color was different, the make and model were the same, and that was what was important.

He kept his walk the same right up until he was at the car. Quickly stooping down, he pulled the screwdriver from his pocket and went to work on the screws holding the license plate. The screwdriver was not a perfect fit, but he managed to keep it from slipping enough to get the screws out quickly. Once the plate was free, he swept it under his jacket and into his belt at the small of his back. The screwdriver went into his pocket as he rose and continued his walk across the parking lot. Once across, he circled the store and found his rental car. The air inside was already warm despite the brief stop.

Fifteen minutes later he had found a secluded spot in a park. There was no one around. Evidently it was too warm for even the children to come out. Most likely they were at the beach. He quickly had the plate swapped out and then spent ten minutes carefully scraping the rental car stickers from the window and bumper.

Once the car was sterile, he felt better. Rental cars all carried plates that used specific numbers. Only those with such knowledge would be tipped off, but the man he had learned that from would notice the car immediately. And that didn't fit into his plan. Using his Porsche was out of the question.

A quick stop at a fast food outlet for a gut-burger and another for plenty of drinks delayed him only slightly and he was soon looking at his target through the windshield as he ate. After finishing the food, he wadded up the wrapper before collecting the drinks and one other item from the car. Leaving the rental in plain sight, he walked across the parking lot, stopping at a trashcan before continuing on through the gate and out onto the dock. The sea breeze cooled the air slightly more than it was in town, but the humidity of the harbor kept it a sauna.

Manuel strolled down the docks, returning hellos from fellow boaters as he made his way to the slip he was searching for. He hopped on board the boat as if he owned it and walked immediately to the cockpit. Running a hand around the winch, he reached into the rope well and located the key stuck to the inside. He soon had the hatch unlocked and was inside the boat, closing and locking it behind him.

The dark interior felt at least twenty degrees hotter than outside, but he had no choice. Opening a window or turning on a fan was not an option. He stripped off his jacket and opened the first of his water bottles. Fetching a towel from the head, he found a seat facing the hatch. Making himself as comfortable as possible, he swabbed the sweat from his face before putting his sunglasses back on.

He was here until his friend showed up, or the heat killed him, whichever came first.

* * *

Brian reached out without looking to make an adjustment to his bypass machine, but when his hand failed to locate its target he was forced to look up. The machine he was using today was not his usual one as it was currently out for overhaul by the manufacturer. He would get it back tomorrow, but until then he was stuck with this older model. It was not really a problem as it was the model he had learned on over ten years ago and he knew it well. The hospital had several bypass machines, but most were designated to certain departments, and as much as he would have liked to use a newer model, personal preference did not trump policy. There was another machine sitting in an operating room down the hall, but it was designated to the trauma service, and God forbid he touch anything in their territory. The heart and trauma teams were considered the varsity here at Johns Hopkins, and, as such, they were provided whatever they needed equipment-wise. But bypass machines did not come cheap, so he would use this backup today and not complain. It had been returned from overhaul yesterday, and had so far proven to be reliable. Maybe next year's budget would produce a new one.

He had set it up in his normal configuration. Pumphead 1 was the arterial, number 2 the vent, number 3 was the cardioplegia, number 4 was the suction and number 5 was the backup. He had wall water and an ice bath to control the blood temperature and it had been primed with crystalloid solution and albumin. The bubble oxygenator was such a simple device he seldom worried about it other than to eyeball it every day.

So far the surgery was progressing as planned. Brian had been working with Dr. Dayo for many years now and they knew each other's routines. The bypass had been initiated without any problems and the heart had been cooled to 28 degrees Celsius eight minutes after bypass was established. 750ccs of cardioplegia solution had been infused into the aortic root to stop the heart and now Dr. Dayo was busy removing the man's diseased organ to make way for the new one beating in the tray next to him. Brian only half listened to the conversation at the table as he sat on the stool in front of the machine. He instead divided his attention between the readouts in front of him and the ones on the POPS machine next to him. The first time the machine had been wheeled into the room they had all stared in amazement at the heart beating in the tray on top. He and his colleague, Mike, had wanted to tear the skin off the machine and see how it worked, but the company representative had vetoed the request with a smile. After a dozen visits the rep had stopped coming, and despite the urge to do so, Brian had so far restrained himself from exposing the guts of the machine. He never had time anyway. As soon as the surgeon pulled the heart off the machine it would be shoved out in the hall by the circulating nurse, and the flight team would be gone with it long before they were done with the surgery.

Still, the heart beating in the tray constantly drew his attention, and as a result, it was his nose that first alerted him to the problem.

He smelled smoke.

Turning his attention back to his bypass machine, he saw small wisps of smoke curling out of the control panel. He sat frozen for a moment in amazement as it quickly got thicker and darker. The digital readouts for each pump began to flicker on and off and that shook him out of his daze. The elapsed time meters suddenly failed as did the water circulation readout.

"Paula!"

Paula halted her conversation and turned to see what he wanted. Brian was not one to yell, even outside the OR, but when she saw the smoke pouring out of the console she quickly forgot about it.

"Oh my god! Is it on fire?"

"I don't know, go get an extinguisher!"

"Fire?" Dr. Dryer's head popped up from behind the drape.

Brian produced a multi-tool from his pocket and began unscrewing the clamps on the console housing. He popped it open as they all watched and thick smoke billowed out, obscuring their view of him.

"Is the pump still running?" Dayo's command voice cut though the chatter.

"I'm looking."

Brian did a quick check. To his relief the arterial pump was still spinning and showed no signs of stopping. He quickly checked the other pumps, putting his hand on each. Number 4 was a little warmer than he would have liked, but still seemed to be running fine. He tapped a couple of the RPM readouts with the tool in his hand, but they refused to come back to life.

Dayo bit his tongue as he watched Brian work. He found himself half-hoping the machine would fail.

"Where we at?" Brian asked.

"We're committed! I have to finish at this point," Dayo answered.

"Shit..."

Brian weighed his options while Paula got on the phone and overhead paged everyone. They soon had other staff members looking in the window, and she put them to work opening the doors and fanning the smoke out of the room. An extinguisher hit the floor next to him, but the smoke had already begun to lessen, and he didn't want to use it with an open chest on the table.

"Somebody run down to trauma and get me the other pump!"

"I'm on it," Dr. Dryer voiced. He parked his anesthesia tech in his chair before rushing out the open door. He was the only one, besides Brian, that had some idea of how to run the machine.

Brian reviewed the problem. The loss of the timers was minor, he could do without them if need be. But the loss of the RPM gauges was critical. So was the water circulation. He swabbed his head with his sleeve and rubbed his eyes as they had started to burn from the smoke and the sweat forming on his forehead.

He looked up and saw a tech standing in the door. He pointed at him to remove any doubt of who he was addressing.

"Follow Dryer and tell him I need the portable cooling unit first. Go."

The tech stopped fanning and took off down the hallway after Dr. Dryer. Another took his place and continued fanning the smoke out the door.

"Brian?" Dayo gently inquired to their status.

"We're okay for now. Just...keep going, I'm on it."

He looked for the cheat sheet he always made on each patient and found it on the floor. Snatching it up, he reviewed his math. The patient's body surface area was 1.67m2 so he had calculated the flow to be 3650 milliliters per minute at 2.2 liters per minute per square meter. Okay, so that should place his speed control knob at...

"Tape, I need some tape and a marker!"

Paula scrambled to comply and found the necessary items in the desk drawer. She tossed them over the POPS machine to him. He tore off a strip and stuck it on the machine next to the RPM knob. Making a mark next on both the knob and the tape, he wrote 4LPM next to it.

"How fast is that?"

He looked up to see Dryer looking over his shoulder. Paula was working to clear a path for the second pump into the room.

"150 RPM…give or take."

"Okay…now what?"

"I think the machine is okay for now. Whatever was burning has stopped. Let's hook up the portable cooler to the oxygenator ports so we can control that. I don't want to switch pumps unless we absolutely have to."

Dryer took a moment to think it through, and it soon became obvious that Brian was a few steps ahead of him.

"Okay. If you think that's best, I'm all for it. Anything else failing?"

Brian stuck his hand out and felt the number 4 pumphead again. It was warmer than the last time he had checked it, but not much.

"Four's running a little hot, but nothing serious. I can switch to number five if I have to."

Dryer stood up and surveyed the room. Paula had shut all the doors but one and was attempting to put the room back together. Dayo, Raina, and Jennifer were busy in the chest cavity. Knowing the problem was out of his hands and being addressed, the surgeon had pulled them back into the surgery.

"Mathew? You guys okay?"

Dayo replied without looking up, "Sure, why wouldn't we be?"

His answer was the tension relief they all needed and it produced a nervous laugh. All but Brian. He sat on the stool and glowered at the malfunctioning pump like it was one of his kids and he had caught it misbehaving. He examined the speed of the number 1 pump, looking for any change, but it continued on as if nothing was wrong. Satisfied they were past the initial problem, he turned his attention to the overhead monitor. The patient's temperature had fallen to 22 degrees while he had been busy and he reached out to the cooling unit to make adjustments.

"Temps down a little Brian," Dr. Dryer observed from across the room.

"I'm on it."

After making the adjustment, he checked on the POPS machine. The new heart continued to beat in the tray as if nothing had happened. After that he located his hand cranks and made sure he had quick access to them if the pump decided to fail. Wiping the sweat from his forehead, he felt a chill as Paula shut the door, fanning the back of his scrubs where the sweat had collected. He looked up to see her eyes smiling at him. She gave him a wink before returning to the desk.

They would both have a lot of paperwork to do when this was done.

WHAT'S YOUR
LIVER WORTH?
May 7, 2010—Smartmoney

—TWENTY-FIVE—

"I DON'T UNDERSTAND. HOW long?"

"I can't give you a number...at least a month, maybe more...just to be safe," Jimmy answered.

"Just to be safe? What does that mean?" Jessica wailed back.

Jimmy broke his gaze from her pleading face before sitting on the couch and burying his own in his hands. He'd been struggling to explain since he had burst through the door unannounced a half hour ago. Fortunately Cody was playing down the street with some friends.

"Look, I never meant for this to happen. But in my job you run the risk of making some enemies. Well this time around, I did. I screwed up. I screwed up bad and I pissed off some dangerous people."

"They know where we live? How?"

"I have to assume that they do. These people, they make it a habit of knowing who they are dealing with. I can explain it better later. We need to leave…right now."

"But Cody…his school…all his friends?" She stalled.

"You have to put that aside. Right now is all that matters. Look, Cody's a kid. He'll be confused. But he's still a kid, he'll roll with it. We need to get to a safe place and do it now."

"But…" Jessica cut herself off and turned away from him.

Jimmy rose from the couch and slowly made an attempt to hold her but she twisted away.

"I'm sorry."

"You're sorry? You're sorry! You show up out of nowhere and tell me we just have to pick up our entire lives and leave and that's all I get? I'm sorry?" The tears were flowing now and she stood before him defiantly, a quivering mass of nerves and righteousness.

"It's…it's all I have."

He slowly approached again and put his arms around her and this time she gave in, turning around and burying her head in his chest. He just held her and offered nothing, waiting for her to work it out for herself. After a moment, the sobbing stopped and she raised her head to gaze into his face. He gently wiped the tears away.

"Still love me?" he asked.

"I…yes, damn you." She gently cuffed him across the chin before breaking away and wiping her nose.

"So…an early vacation? What do we tell him?"

"That'll work, to go along with our retirements."

That brought her head back around.

"You're quitting? Really?"

"Yeah, I'm done. You can be, too, if you want."

It took her only a few seconds to decide.

"I think I can live with that."

She returned to his arms and wrapped hers around his neck for a kiss.

They had just come up for air when a noise behind them caused Jimmy's muscles to coil like a spring. He spun them both in a circle as his hand groped the small of his back. He relaxed when he saw the source.

"Mommy?" Cody stood in the doorway, rubbing his head with a towel. His hair was wet from the neighbor's pool. The dog was outside looking in, equally wet.

"Hey, baby, look who's here!"

"Jimmy!" The boy quickly dropped the towel and ran to him.

"Hey, buddy." Jimmy smiled and pried the boy's arms loose from his leg before hoisting him up for a hug.

"How's my little guy today?"

"Good. Are you staying for awhile this time? Please?"

Jimmy exchanged a look with Jessica. She nodded and covered her mouth before flashing a smile. Jimmy got the message. They would tell him later.

"No, I have to leave today."

"Aww, really?" The boy immediately pouted.

"Yeah, but how about this? How about…you and mom come with me this time?"

Cody perked up. "Really!" He looked to his mother for confirmation.

"Really," she echoed.

"Sam, too?"

"Sam, too," Jimmy added.

"When?"

"Right now. Go pack a bag."

"Cool!" Cody squirmed out of Jimmy's arms and ran to the door to share the news with the dog. "Come on, Sam!" He ran down the hall toward his room with the dog hot on his heels. They both watched him go with a smile.

Jessica started off toward her room, but quickly turned around with a confused look.

"What do I pack? I mean…where are we going?"

Jimmy just smiled again.

"Pack for the beach."

*   *   *

"Can I get a wipe please?"

Kye snatched a sterile towel from a nearby pile and carefully wiped the sweat from Dr. Fong's brow without moving the lenses perched on his nose. The fiber-optic light tracked across her face and would have momentarily blinded her if she had not known to look away.

"That's good. Thanks." He turned back to the operating table in time to see Tony retrieve a suture from Stephanie. His physician's assistant gazed into the chest to check her work.

"How do we look?"

"Considering how fast we did it…not bad. Minimal bleeding. The SVC is a little crooked, but it's holding."

"Good. How's our temperature? Did you catch up to us okay, Mike?"

"We're at twenty-five now."

"Okay, labs?"

"Not great. She's a little acidic so I'm giving some bicarb. We may have swung to the plus side on the fluids, also. Should I pull some off?"

"A liter," Jacobs ordered.

"One liter," Mike echoed as he adjusted his clamps. "You going to start the rest now?"

Fong considered the question as he watched Tony lay out sutures on the tray. Fifty-four-inch 3-0 prolene. Several of them. There was a lot of sewing in his future. Fortunately, it was what surgeons considered easy. Unlike a bypass surgery where he dealt with the smallest of arteries and veins, here he was dealing with the great vessels, the big pipes, and everything was large and easy to see. There was just a lot of it. He could begin removing the girl's heart now, as the new heart would arrive before he was ready for it, but it was something he was never comfortable doing, even if they were committed to the new heart as they were now.

"Let's take a break and get all her numbers back where they should be. That way we can scrub out and clean up a little. I still want to see this new heart before we install it."

Stephanie nodded in ready agreement and quickly stepped away from the table. She lost no time in stripping off her gloves and peeling away the bloody gown. Her scrubs were soaked in sweat and stuck to her, and she gave an involuntary shiver in the cold operating room. Dr. Fong quickly followed her example and they were both about to leave when the overhead speaker squawked.

"Heart arriving for OR three, heart arriving for OR three."

Fong stopped at the door and traded a look with his PA.

"You go change. I'll wait for the heart."

"Thank you," she gushed. She lost no time bolting out the door and heading for the locker room.

Dr. Fong watched Kye follow her out to fetch the heart and slowly made his way to the desk in the corner. His mouth was dry. It was against the rules, but he opened the drawer and searched around for the bag of hard candy they kept inside. Finding it hidden in the back in a plain paper bag, he extracted it and searched till he found his favorite flavor, watermelon. Unwrapping it, he quickly snuck it around the edge of his mask and into his mouth. He was barely back in his chair when Kye burst through the doors again, towing a POPS machine behind her. She wheeled it over in front of him and plugged it in. The machine obediently switched power sources without missing a beat, as the representative liked to say, and he leaned in to see the heart in the tray on top.

"Any paperwork with it?" he asked.

"*No habla,*" was Kye's reply.

"Figures," he mumbled.

He watched the heart through the fogged glass as it pulsated in the tray. It was pink and healthy at first glance. His professional eye took in every motion and he changed angles a few times to examine the muscle's movements. The chatter of his staff faded away as his brain and eyes looked for any flaw, any movement that could lead to a problem. There was something odd about the way it moved, something he couldn't quite put a name to. Overall it looked fine, but something…

"Looks good," Stephanie commented from over his shoulder.

Fong jerked slightly as she had startled him, but quickly regained his composure and returned his gaze to the heart. She was right, the heart looked fine. Still, he would check it again thoroughly before they installed it.

"Okay then. Everybody ready?" He got yeses all around while he glanced at the overhead screens. The patient was doing fine despite her rough beginning. Kye was waiting with a new gown, so he stepped forward and let her dress him.

* * *

Dr. Dayo carefully measured a third time before cutting into the aorta to begin separating it from the heart. The instant flow of blood was quickly sucked away by Jennifer and his view was never compromised as his scissors moved across the great vessel. He eyeballed its inner surface as he worked. She retracted the pulmonary artery away from his view while he worked, and he found himself wondering just how much she could see from her station on the opposite side of the table. He measured the placement of his hands in relation to her eyes and wondered if he was blocking her view totally, or if she could change angles and see around him. He tried angling his own head lamp away from his work to see just how much of a difference it would make. Not much. But then he really wouldn't need much, would he?

The aorta separated and the heart settled back into the chest cavity as another of its anchors was cut away. Dayo shook his thoughts off while they repositioned for the next phase. But as Raina rinsed his gloves clean, the thoughts quickly returned, and the surgeon could not let it go.

This man he was operating on had threatened him and his family. He had threatened his entire surgical team right in this very room. He had killed countless people and poisoned millions with his drugs. He had blown up airplanes and assassinated judges.

And at the moment, the man's heart was in his hands.

If he were a young surgeon just beginning his career, he doubted that the thoughts in his head would even be there. He would do the surgery without question, and try to put any thoughts aside afterward.

But he wasn't young anymore, nor was he naive to the ways of the world. He was an established surgeon, at the top of his field. He had built a career and reputation among his peers that was unequaled. Could that reputation see him through this? Could he survive the questions that were sure to follow? What about his team? Would they be implicated, too? Would they agree with him, or find it beyond the level of their profession? What about the man's threats? Were they serious? Was there really reason to believe that a dead man would take such precautions? Was it safer for them all to assume that he would?

"Dr. Dayo?"

"Yes?"

"You stopped?"

"Oh…sorry, uh, metz please."

Raina slapped the scissors into his hand before trading a confused look with Jennifer. She received a shrug for a reply.

The ventilator hissed as they silently went back to work.

ORGAN DONORS MAY BE
DENIED HEALTH INSURANCE
April 18, 2011—The Washington Post

—TWENTY-SIX—

MANUEL TAPPED THE BARREL of the gun repeatedly against his forehead in an attempt to wake himself up. He had already tried several other tricks to stay awake, many of them taught to him by the man he was waiting for. He stopped the tapping and lightly tickled the roof of his mouth with his tongue until it sent an involuntary shiver through his muscles. But that only worked for a few minutes, and he was soon fighting off the sandman again. A drop of sweat crawled down his back and into the already soaked waistline of his pants. If sweating alone kept one awake, it would have been all that he needed, but the sauna-like interior and the gentle rocking of the sailboat made it hard for him to do so.

At least the sun was going down soon, and with it, he hoped, the temperature. He had already exhausted his drink supply, having underestimated his needs by a long shot. Fortunately, a quiet search of the boat had turned up a case of bottled water. It was as warm as the cabin temperature, and far from refreshing, but it served its purpose by replacing the fluids he was sweating out. He was on his second towel, and had given up on staying dry some time ago. He used it on his face and eyes only at this point, as his shirt had long since been saturated. Even his socks were soaked, but he never considered taking his shoes off, he may soon have to move quickly, and there wouldn't be time to put them on.

A voice outside brought him up out of his reclined position and he listened intently, letting his mouth hang open so his ears could perform better, just as Jimmy had taught him. The voice was soon joined by a few others, both male and female, and after a moment he classified them as returning boaters who had obviously had a few drinks. Their laughter penetrated the fiberglass with ease as they walked past, and he found himself wishing he were with them, or at least on his own boat. Anywhere but here.

As he sank back down into the chair his thoughts turned back to the task at hand. He cursed the lack of preparation time. If he'd only had time to go to his storage garage and fetch a rifle. He could have done this from a distance. But there had been no time and now he had no choice but to confront Jimmy face to face. Despite the time alone to think about it, both on the plane and here in the boat, he was unsure of what he was going to do when his teacher showed up.

He shifted on the cabin bench and cursed Rico for putting him in this position. Something he had been doing ever since he had answered the phone in DC. He also cursed Jimmy for quitting on him the way he had. Why did he tell him he was doing it at all? Was it the girl and her heart going to Oscar? They had seen and done some evil things in the years they'd worked together, and while it was true that this was close to the top, it wasn't like they had been tasked with doing it themselves. Was it Jimmy's dislike of Rico? They were all in that club, including him, but like it or not, Rico was in charge now. Manuel knew what happened to those who crossed Rico. They got visits from men like himself. As much as he respected Jimmy, he wasn't about to cross Rico and end up in that position.

Perhaps it was the woman? He knew Jimmy had a woman in his life. He had never mentioned her and Manuel had never asked, but he knew. Any answer he might have received to such a question would have been at best a half-truth. Looking back now, it dawned on him that Jimmy had never spoken of *any* woman in his life. While Manuel would often boast of his many female conquests, Jimmy would simply play along until he had exhausted the subject and then move on to other things.

Manuel smiled in the dark room at the revelation. "That is why he was the teacher and you were the student," he told himself.

He raised the water bottle to his lips and drained it. Soon he would have to piss in the sink again, but he didn't wish to get up and move around until he had to. Moving around meant noise. Noise that might be heard by someone on the dock or a neighboring boat. If there was one thing Jimmy had taught him, it was patience. Besides, he admitted, he was not eager to meet his old partner. Despite the current working conditions he was in.

He opened another bottle of water and listened to the sounds around him while he drank. A car in the parking lot, a young woman's laughter on a distant dock, a passing boat. The sounds were classified and dismissed with little thought. The majority of his brain was still occupied with the one question, and he pondered the thought as the shadows lengthened across the cabin floor.

What would he do when Jimmy got here?

* * *

Unaware of the dilemma playing out in his surgeon's head, Brian sat in front of his malfunctioning bypass machine, watching and listening for further trouble. He was shoulder to shoulder with a man they had all just met and knew only as Joe. Joe was one of the hospital's maintenance men, and he was far outside his comfort zone. He was unlucky enough to have been in his boss's office when the call had come in, and as a result, he'd been quickly dispatched to the OR with some frantically located tools. After being quickly gowned, gloved, bootied, and goggled by the nurses in the hallway, they had pushed him over the thick red line painted on the floor and down the hall. Before he was through the doors, his nose told him the problem. Electrical fire. It had the distinct smell of burning wire insulation. But when he looked around the room he failed to see the source. He froze when his gaze naturally found its way to the operating room table and the people busy over it. Only Brian's call and Paula's prodding had moved him to where he was now.

He now sat on a small stool, holding a timing light in his hands. The cold temperature of the OR failed to overcome his nervousness, and he unconsciously attempted to wipe the sweat from his palms on his pants, only to give up as he remembered the gloves. He instead sat straighter in an effort to see what was happening on the table. It was not his first time in an operating room. He had been here before to service the air handlers and the table hydraulics once. But today was his first time in the room while it was actually in use, and he was a little overwhelmed.

A gentle nudge from Brian's elbow brought him back to the task at hand. Brian didn't say anything, he just pointed to the number one pumphead with his clipboard. Joe obediently aimed the timing light and pulled the trigger to get a reading. The light strobed across the spinning pump until a digital readout appeared on the screen. He silently held it out for Brian to see and watched as he wrote it down on what was obviously a quickly sketched chart.

Joe moved on to the next pump without waiting to be asked. Since he had arrived they had been repeating the process every few minutes. Brian had calmed down once Joe had managed to slap pieces of reflective tape on each pump, while they were still spinning, and get a few readings. Still, he noticed that Brian kept a manual pump handle in his lap in case any of them failed and he had to rotate it by hand. Another reason for his nervousness was that they had switched pump 4 for pump 5 as it had been running too hot for his comfort level. Five was running fine, but using it meant that they no longer had a backup pump. They had to make do with what they had, or switch to another machine. Joe had been told that really wasn't an option at this point.

After getting a reading on each of the four running pumps he exchanged his timing light for his laser temperature gauge and shone it on the cooling unit.

"How's it look?" Brian asked.

"It still matches your gauge."

"Okay."

Brian leaned back in his chair to document the reading and this gave Joe a view of the heart beating in the tray of fluid on top of the POPS machine next to him. He couldn't help but stare at it.

"You okay?" Brian asked.

"Yeah...why?"

"You're not going to get sick or anything, are you?"

"No, blood doesn't bother me. Lord knows I've had to clean up enough of it since I took this job. How people manage to bleed into stuff around here amazes me."

"Really? How's that?"

"Well, remember last month when the air conditioning went out in the ER? We had to set up all these portable units. Well some drunk managed to fall into one of them and jam his hand into the fan. Took two of his fingers off and filled the thing with blood. Took us a week to get it clean enough to put it back in service."

"Sounds fun. They save his fingers?"

"Yeah, sewed them back on. He's probably holding a drink with them right now."

"Could've been worse. At least he didn't puke into it."

"That's thinking positive, I guess."

"It's been that kind of day."

"Yeah...so is that heart really beating, or is the machine just making it look that way?"

Brian turned to the POPS machine and watched the heart pulsating in the tray for a moment before replying. He was too frazzled to give an in-depth explanation.

"A little of both actually. The heart just needs blood and oxygen and some other stuff to do its thing. As long as those things are provided, it *wants* to beat. The machine just gives it what it wants and keeps it happy."

"Amazing."

"That it is."

"So when do they...you know...put it in?"

"Whenever the man says he's ready." Brian nodded toward the table where Dr. Dayo and the team were busy before glancing at the clock. "Should be soon."

"Then how long till we're done?"

"Couple of hours. Are you bored already, or do you need to be somewhere?"

"No, not bored." Joe smiled. "The wife's just gonna start to wonder in an hour or so."

"Just grab Paula's attention when she's not busy and she'll make a call for you. If you can't stay, just show me how to work the light before you go."

"No, I'll stay if you need me. Most interesting thing I've done since I got here. Besides, you can't crank on all these pumps by yourself."

"Okay."

They both sat back and silently divided their attention between the action on the table, the heart beating in the machine next to them, and the spinning pumps in front of them. After another few minutes, Brian picked up the clipboard. The newest member of the team raised the timing light and aimed it at the spinning pump.

* * *

Rico lay on a chaise lounge outside his brother's mountaintop home. He had essentially moved in since Oscar's capture and was taking full advantage of the luxurious space. Oscar's mistress had relocated to the beach house after Rico had moved a few of his girlfriends in with them. He didn't care, he was already thinking of the house as his anyway.

He grunted into the phone and only half-listened to a report from one of his informants in the Mexican AFI. His man Luis had been arrested. It was a small setback, he had many such people like him on the cartel payroll, but combined with the multiple arrests made as a result of Angel's capture, it was starting to sting. The crackdown by the President of Mexico on the cartels had not really made much of a dent in the production or flow of their product. It had mostly served to turn the Mexican gangs they employed against one another as they fought for vacated territory. He didn't really care how much they killed one another as long as lost shipments did not rise above what was considered acceptable losses. His brother had jokingly referred to it as taxes. Import/export taxes, the cost of doing business. Occasionally a gang leader was caught and paraded before the TV cameras like a hunting trophy, but Oscar was usually dealing with his replacement long before the cameras rolled.

It was a lesson that Rico had never really managed to learn.

Rico ended the conversation with another grunt and managed to hang up without taking his eyes off of the very tan and tight buttocks of the girl fixing him another drink. He watched closely as her thong did a rhythmic dance as she stirred it. It produced a leering grin on his face as the drink was delivered and he accepted it while also running his hand up her leg and roughly cupping her bare flesh. She endured the groping with the required smile on her face. Rico falsely read it as an invitation and was about to pull her down onto his lap when they were interrupted by his security man approaching. The girl quickly spun and walked away, this time with a genuine smile.

"What is it?" Rico snapped.

"They've arrived."

Rico made a face. More business. This time a meeting with his top lieutenants. It seemed to never end. He knocked back the drink before pushing himself to his feet. The sudden move, combined with his early start on the bottle that morning, resulted in a wave of dizziness. The mountaintop view blurred and he swayed for a moment before managing to stay on his feet and out of the pool. He turned to find Carlos standing close, his large frame and outstretched hand blocking out the sun.

"I'm fine! Search the both of them and then bring them in."

"Search them?"

Rico glared at his security man. "Yes, search them, and be thorough!" Carlos quickly left without a reply to do so.

Rico walked to the bar to fix himself another drink. He and Oscar had dealt with Pablo and Nestor for many years, and while they had proven to be loyal and trustworthy employees to his brother, they had made it clear to Rico that he was someone to be tolerated. Well, now he was in charge, and it was time to put the two men in their place. He had his own ideas on how to run things, and until his brother returned, the orders would come from him. It was something he aimed to establish quickly, and if they didn't like it? Well, he had a plan for that, too.

Sipping his drink with one hand, he searched for and found his sunglasses with the other. He liked to think he looked more intimidating with them on, but they also served to let him watch things without them knowing.

The two men appeared through the door, closely followed by Carlos. Rico noticed the pissed off looks on both their faces. Nestor was still tucking his shirt back in. Rico ignored their looks and smiled a greeting as fake as the one on the girl who had just left.

"Hello, gentleman, come, sit."

Rico gestured to the chairs opposite the table in front of him, both of them conveniently in the hot sun while Rico's sat in the shade of the umbrella. They glowered but sat without comment and Carlos took up a position behind them, not close, but his enormous shadow advertised his presence as it fell across the table.

Rico watched it all happen with the faintest of smiles before shaking the ice in his glass and setting the drink down in front of him.

"Where are my manners? Carlos, drinks all around."

Carlos left to do as ordered and Rico watched again as the eyes of his guests took in the bodyguard's bulk, as well as the large handgun hanging under his arm. It looked like a small cannon. They exchanged a look before turning back to Rico, who was now making them wait some more while he lit a cigarette. He waved the match out and blew smoke across the table before addressing them.

"So, you asked for this meeting. What is it you want?"

Pablo spoke first. "We wish to know your brother's condition, and when he might be expected to return?"

Rico sat back as if to consider whether or not to respond. He drew the moment out a while as he watched Carlos place a glass of vodka in front of Nestor, and a cold beer in front of Pablo. Neither of them made a move to touch them. When he felt they had waited long enough Rico spoke.

"I arranged for a new heart to be delivered for my brother last night." He checked his watch. "He should have it soon. As for getting him out after he recovers? I…am moving some things into place."

"And Angel?"

"Dead. I sent Manuel and Jimmy to take care of it. They fixed that problem this morning as well. Angel is done talking."

"I see. How?"

"Manuel will be returning soon. You can ask him yourself when he gets here."

"He is returning without Jimmy?"

"He is *dispensing* with Jimmy! The bastard lied to me and forgot his place! Manuel is taking care of it. I put him in charge."

Rico gulped his drink after the outburst while Nestor and Pablo traded a look. Carlos's lurking shadow grew slowly longer as the sun made a rapid descent. They waited for Rico to calm down. Their drinks continued to sweat untouched on the table.

"But the hell with all of that. I'm making some changes."

Pablo spoke up. "We have to replace what Angel cost us."

"You think I don't know that? Now shut the fuck up for a moment and listen."

Neither Nestor or Pablo flinched at the rebuke. Pablo leaned forward and placed his hands next to his beer. His fingers drummed a beat on the glass table top.

"Very well…we're listening."

NEW KIDNEY TRANSPLANT POLICY
WOULD FAVOR YOUNGER PATIENTS

February 24, 2011—New York Times

—TWENTY-SEVEN—

DR. FONG RAISED HIMSELF up in his chair and confirmed the presence of the pathologist through the glass window of the OR room. The man gave him a thumb's up before sitting down in his chair to wait. Fong caught sight of a tablet computer in the man's hands and briefly wondered what video game he was playing.

There was nothing stopping the transplant from moving forward, and while he was well within the estimated time allowed for such a procedure, it was always beneficial to keep the patient under anesthesia for as little time as possible. It was time for the next step.

"Heart's coming off," he informed the room.

Kye checked the time and made a quick notation on her chart. Dr. Fong released the safety mechanism, and throwing a series of switches, shut down the POPS machine. Tony approached with a tray of saline that had been chilled to 4 degrees Celsius. Dr. Fong methodically disconnected the heart from the machine connections one by one and gave it a gentle squeeze to decompress it before unceremoniously dropping it in the saline. Tony carefully carried the tray to the foot of the bed and parked it between the girl's legs. Before the invention of the POPS machine, the heart would have spent hours at this cold temperature, kept on ice from the time it was excised, throughout the hours of transport time, and still longer as the team removed the old heart on arrival of the new one. Referred to as cold ischemic time, it was something to be minimized as much as possible. Now it was not even a factor. The bad heart would be excised in a matter of minutes, and its replacement would be implanted within an hour of that. They would even start re-warming the new heart before the transplant was complete. Everything that could be done to lessen the stress to the new organ had been addressed.

Tony placed a tray of sterile ice next to the one holding the new heart while Dr. Fong resumed his place next to the table.

"Okay, let's go."

Kye scribbled the time once again on her chart as Dr. Fong sought out and grasped the girl's aorta. Holding it firmly, he held out his other hand.

"Potts."

Tony handed the 45-degree angled scissors to the surgeon and watched intently as he maneuvered them around the cross-clamp. He measured carefully before severing the great vessel.

* * *

Jimmy drove the loaded minivan through the crowded parking lot of the marina twice before selecting a spot and carefully backing in. The restaurant crowd was just starting to arrive at the outdoor Tiki hut bar, and boats were still returning from a day spent out on the water. To her credit, Jessica stayed silent and watched as he craned his head in all directions before putting the transmission in park.

The door behind them opened and the dog scampered over Cody's lap and out of the van to explore the marina. Before Jimmy could say anything, the boy was hot on his heels. Jimmy moved to follow, but she stopped him with a gentle hand on his shoulder.

"Calm down, he's just excited. He won't go far."

"I know, but..."

"We need to hurry," she finished for him.

"Yeah."

"Okay, so what do I do?"

He smiled and kissed her before replying, and she felt the tension in the muscular shoulder lessen a bit.

"Take this key. It's that dock over there, slip 42. The blue and white sailboat. Just open everything up and let the heat out first. Maybe turn the fans on. The panel with all the switches is at the bottom of the ladder and around the corner on the right. You and I are in the rear cabin, and Cody can have the forward room to himself."

"On the right. Anything else?"

"No, I'll grab the handcart from the office and start unloading the van."

"Want Cody to help?"

Jimmy grimaced as he watched the boy and his dog explore the dock. He was an inquisitive kid and always full of questions. Questions Jimmy just didn't have time to indulge at the moment.

"No, probably better if you take him with you."

"Okay."

"And Jess..."

"Yeah?"

"Just stay below for now okay?"

"Okay."

She took the key from him and grabbed their two small bags before calling to Cody as she crossed the lot. Seeing where she was headed, the boy made two attempts to get the dog to follow before giving up and scrambling after her. The dog was more interested in the plethora of new smells assaulting his nose at the moment. Jimmy put him out of his mind as he had more pressing matters. The dog never went too far from the boy anyway.

As Jimmy walked toward the office, he watched them walk the dock. Seeing them locate the boat, he turned his attention to the small building. Like most marinas, this one provided a few wheeled carts for its residents' use. There were a few parked on the side of the building and he selected one he knew rolled without too much trouble. The carts hauled everything from groceries to engine parts, and their surfaces reflected the marks and stains of years of use in the Florida sun.

Rolling the cart back to the minivan, he examined the boat again. No windows open, but they were probably exploring the boat and hadn't gotten to it yet. He reviewed the list in his head. He had compiled it on the flight down, and they had made a stop at the local warehouse store for the needed supplies. As a result, the van's suspension was taxed more than usual. They were missing a few items, but nothing they couldn't do without for awhile. Jimmy eyeballed the pile and estimated three trips to get it all transferred to the boat. He lost no time in getting started, and soon case after case of supplies landed on the cart as he bent his back to the task.

Water.

Canned food.

Rice.

A majority of the items necessary were on the boat already, just not in the quantities needed to support three people for an extended sail. Not to mention a dog. The boat had always been more than just a pleasurable diversion. It was one of Jimmy's two bolt holes. A moving safe house should the need ever rise and he had to disappear quickly. He could live on it for months if need be without ever having to visit a port. It held much more than just food and water. A few secret compartments held cash in three different denominations, an assault rifle and a stainless steel shotgun. A few passports. The keys to a few safety deposit boxes scattered across the Caribbean. A makeup kit with hair dye. Everything needed to sail away and arrive somewhere else a totally different person. He had a van that was similarly stocked at a storage unit two towns to the east.

Fruit.

Nuts.

Dog food.

He glanced back down the dock to see the lights on in the boat. Evidently she had found the main circuit breaker okay.

The cart was full and with a whistle toward the dog he set off down the dock. He eyeballed the setting sun. If he wanted to be clear of the jetty by dark, they would have to hurry.

* * *

Dr. Dayo was back on autopilot. Despite the brief terror of the bypass machine fire he had managed to pull his mind, and those of his team, back into the task at hand. His hands moved within the chest cavity and performed the necessary steps of the procedure like a well-practiced dance, accepting the visiting partners of Raina and Jennifer as they came and went. Instruments appeared in his hands without asking, and his gloves were rinsed clean without a stop in their progress.

He was currently working around "the hand," otherwise known as Jake. Jake was one of their surgical techs. His main job was to prep the room prior to everyone's arrival, but on occasion he was called on to hold the heart up while the surgeon worked underneath it. So at the moment he was in his usual awkward position standing next to the surgeon, yet facing the wall, his arm trapped behind him between the surgeon's belly and the chest of the patient. He rarely even saw the heart he was holding. Dr. Dayo would simply guide his hand where he wanted it to go and say "Hold."

Jake was an excellent hand.

It was actually a harder job than one would think. Holding a position like he was in for as long as he was asked to hold it, without moving the slightest, took some discipline. He had to put out of his mind the fact that there were numerous sharp instruments and needles moving around his hand. But Dr. Dayo was a skilled surgeon, and Jake trusted him not to cut or poke him. So far it had never happened.

He may have been a little more afraid today if he knew the surgeon's current level of concentration. Normally talkative during surgery, today he was unusually quiet. The team had all noticed, and most had just chalked it up to the identity of the man on the table, and the unusual number of people in the gallery—people wearing suits, not the usual scrubs. Evidently, there were quite a few people interested in the outcome of this surgery. Fortunately, Jake also knew his way around sound systems, and had quietly worked out a way to kill the microphones in the room if Dayo gave him the signal. Today was such a day. So while the gallery was full of the prying eyes of VIPs, at least the surgical team could all speak without being heard. Not that there was much conversation going on. The room was unusually quiet, and since Jake was the one with the least amount of distractions, he addressed it first.

"Why's it so quiet?" he loudly whispered.

A few laughed before Paula answered in her normal voice, "So Mike can hear his pumps."

"I think we're okay if you guys need some music," Mike chimed in from the other side of the room.

"Okay, Dr. Dayo?"

"Huh?"

"Music?"

"Oh…sure. What we got today?"

"Lemme look." She walked to the small desk and thumbed through the stack of CDs that migrated around the various operating rooms.

"Ummm…Aerosmith, Dave Mathews, Lady Gaga? Don't even go there…Nora Jones?"

"We played that last time," Raina answered as she shot a bulb of saline across Jennifer's gloves.

"Where's my Alex Cuba CD?" Dayo asked.

A collective series of groans was his answer.

"C'mon guys, humor me."

Paula skipped to the bottom of the stack, and as expected, found the disc there. Sliding it in the player she soon had the room filled with the smooth voice of the Latin singer. It wasn't that they disliked the music, it was the fact that the lyrics were in Spanish and Dayo was the only one who understood some of them. He had once tried to convince them that one of the songs was about a meatball sandwich and the singer's debate on whether or not to eat it. His ruse had been defeated by a phone app.

Dayo hummed along with the music while his mind returned to the debate still in his head. If only he could discuss it with the team, but there was no way to do that. His hands returned to the heart and took on a mind of their own, cutting away the posterior wall of the left atrium. Working around Jake's fingers, he severed the last section. The heart fell free yet stayed in place due to Jake's steady hand. Dayo passed the scalpel off to Raina's waiting hand before reaching back into the chest and cradling the heart in both hands. Pulling it free, he treated it like a newborn baby. It was wet and slippery, and it would be bad form to drop it. They all eyeballed the oversized purple mass of diseased tissue with disgust before the surgeon dropped it in a waiting pan.

Jake gratefully flexed his hand and stripped off his first glove so he could shake it without flinging blood about. After he had restored some blood flow, he took the pan and walked it into the next room. There he placed it on the table in front of a waiting pathologist as if he were a waiter delivering a rare steak. The pathologist completed the picture by putting down his book, picking up a scalpel, and carving into the organ. Jake just shook his head and returned to the operating room.

All of this had been witnessed with fascination by Joe from his front row seat next to Mike, and his mouth now hung open behind his surgical mask. The loud gurgle of the suction running dry brought his attention back to the table, and he was surprised to find three sets of eyes on him.

"Think you can roll that heart over here for me?" Dr. Dayo asked.

"Uh…sure."

Dayo clasped his hands over his gown in front of him in the classic sterile posture and sat down in a chair provided by Paula. He wiggled slightly to loosen up his lower back as the heart was rolled up in front of him by their newest team member. Paula gloved up before opening the cover and exposing the heart. Dayo leaned in to examine it without the interference of the fogged glass one last time. It looked pink and healthy and perfect, far different from the one they had extracted only moments ago. He prayed for a defect, something that would make his decision for him, but nothing presented itself.

"That was one ugly heart," Raina voiced while she made ready at her station.

"You can say that again," Paula agreed.

"I'd say it suited him," Dr. Dryer added from behind the drape.

There were murmurs of consent from around the room. Dayo kept his eyes on the heart in the tray, but listened intently.

"You can say that again, too," Jennifer quickly agreed.

It was all that the surgeon needed to hear.

TRANSPLANT DOCS ACCUSED OF ORGAN TRAFFICKING

February 14, 2008—The Associated Press

—TWENTY-EIGHT—

MANUEL LISTENED INTENTLY TO the approaching cart as it thumped its way over the decking toward them. His gaze however never wavered from the woman and young boy sitting across from him. Nor did the silenced pistol in his hand. The woman's own gaze was a mixture of both fear and defiance, and it marred her otherwise beautiful features. The boy's face showed nothing but fear with perhaps a touch of confusion. At least that's what his eyes said as the lower half of his face was hidden by his mother's hand.

Without looking away, Manuel put a finger to his own lips and punctuated it with a wave of the pistol before switching hands and licking his fingers. He reached over his head and unscrewed the light bulb until his corner of the cabin fell dark. He settled back into the shadow to wait.

*　　　*　　　*

Dr. Dayo had removed the heart from the POPS machine much as his partner had in the room down the hall. He now turned it over in the tray of cold saline, examining it further from every angle. He would now basically reverse what he had already done in order to implant it in Oscar's chest.

The human heart had only a few connection points for blood-flow. Two for blood returning from the body, one for deoxygenated blood traveling to the lungs, four for oxygenated blood returning from the lungs, and one to pump that blood out to the body. Instead of severing each connection individually, the surgeon had removed the heart by cutting away the rear wall of the left atrium that held the four connections of Oscar's old heart. Making the necessary connections for the blood flowing into the heart would then be a simple matter of sewing the rear wall of the donor heart to the remaining walls of the old heart. After that, it was just a matter of sewing the two remaining great vessels to their new partners.

Dayo examined the work of the unknown surgeon who had explanted the heart. It was...satisfactory, he decided. The aortic cut was a little crooked, but there was enough of it left that he could deal with that. It wasn't like he had much of a choice in the matter. His fingers probed the valves and he shone his light inside to examine them as best he could. Not finding any faults, he pulled the heart dripping from the tray, dried it with a sterile towel, and set it beside the chest cavity.

Dr. Fong was also pulling the heart free of its ice bath. He had examined it very carefully as its movement on the POPS machine had bothered him. While he had found nothing wrong on his examination, his instincts were still telling him something wasn't quite right. Nevertheless, he had no choice but to proceed. He patted the heart dry and placed it next to Tessa's chest cavity on its anterior side. Receiving a scalpel from Tony, he carefully trimmed a large wedge of fat away before starting on the wall of the left atria. Tony and Stephanie watched in amazement as he cut a virtually identical window to the one he'd made on Tessa's original heart. Dr. Fong worked steadily and without a word as he maneuvered the heart into the teenager's chest. The two puzzle pieces lined up perfectly.

"Every time you do that, it amazes me. How do you get it to fit perfectly like that the first time?"

"Pigs," the surgeon replied.

"Pigs?"

"Yeah, I cheated during my residency."

"I don't get it."

Dr. Fong accepted some 3-0 prolene suture from Tony and began sewing the rear walls together before explaining.

"In med school we used pig hearts to practice on, but there were never enough to go around, so I took a trip out to the country one weekend and drove around until I found a pig farm. I cut a deal with the owner, and every weekend I had a fresh supply all my own. My roommate and I would sit out on the front porch, drink beer, and carve on hearts all weekend. You do something enough times you can't help but get good at it. It was no different than what the trauma guys do, really."

"The trauma guys? Do I want to hear this?"

Dr. Fong smiled before going on, but he never stopped suturing.

"The trauma guys ate a lot of steaks. I knew one guy who put away at least four or five a week. He would buy a big one, slice and gash it up with whatever he could think of, and then sew it up. When he was done, it went on the grill."

"Really?"

"Sure, perfectly good steak shouldn't go to waste. I always did wonder how much suture he ingested while we were there, though."

Tony shook his head while he pictured it. They watched the surgeon sew for a while before Tony broke the silence.

"I wonder what your garbage man thought?"

The thought actually made the surgeon pause for a moment.

"Good question."

* * *

Jimmy nodded to some neighboring boaters as he pushed the cart down the dock. Most of them were recreational boaters, and now that the sun was going down and the darkness was rapidly advancing, it was time to tie up the boat and head for the bar. Some of them had stopped to take in the sunset over the Gulf, and normally he would have joined them. But tonight the sunset was a welcome distraction, and he utilized it to pass people unobserved while they were otherwise occupied. The fewer people that saw them leave the better. There was no doubt in his mind that several of them would soon be asked a number of questions, questions concerning Jimmy and his location.

He looked ahead toward the boat and was glad to see that Jessica had kept herself and Cody below deck. One light was visible in the main cabin, and that was all. His plan was to keep it that way until they were well away from shore and any prying eyes. He wouldn't allow himself to relax until they were.

Parking the cart parallel to the boat, he set the brake before reaching across the gap and disconnecting the sanction line. Loosening one mooring line and tightening another, he brought the forty-two feet of boat tight against the dock. Fortunately, the tide was cooperating and the deck of the boat was almost even with the dock. The hardest part now would be stepping over the rim of the center cockpit and negotiating the five steep steps down into the main cabin with his arms full.

With the sun now down, the marina's solar lights were coming on. They still weren't enough to illuminate the steps, but he was glad Jess was being cautious. She must be keeping Cody quiet as well, something of a miracle itself.

He grabbed two cases of water off the cart and managed to make it over the cockpit rim without falling. Once around the 36-inch steering wheel, he decided it was safer to back down the steps with the bulky load. He carefully felt his way from step to step before reaching the wood floor and turning around.

His gaze immediately fell on Jessica sitting in the corner across the cabin with Cody on her lap. Her infectious smile was gone, and in its place was a look of immen'se self control that was barely holding back her terror. She said nothing, but her eyes pleaded with him.

"Hello, Jimmy."

Jimmy followed the voice to the dark corner opposite Jessica. The light bulb flickered on as it was screwed in to reveal Manuel sitting calmly in the chair under it. He was soaked in sweat and looked exhausted, but Jimmy set that aside when he saw the gun in his hand.

It was aimed right at them.

"Put the water down."

Jimmy hesitated.

"Now...please."

Jimmy heard the tone in his voice and the water slowly found its way to the floor. He used the movement to gather his legs under him in preparation for launching himself across the small room. Manuel watched him closely and shook his head before wagging the gun for Jimmy's attention. Jimmy changed his mind when he saw that the hammer was back. It meant that the trigger would require very little pressure to fire the gun. The barrel was pointed directly at Jessica and Cody, and the round had enough power to pass through them both. He couldn't risk it. Reading the situation quickly, he understood why he wasn't shot already. Manuel didn't wish to do it now, as the noise would attract too much attention here in the crowded marina. It was better for Jimmy to wait and hope for a better opportunity.

Manuel waited until Jimmy was standing again before waving the gun in the direction of the table. Jimmy saw a set of nylon handcuffs waiting for him. No doubt Jessica and Cody were already wearing theirs. He picked them up and slipped them over his wrist before pulling them tight with his teeth.

"So this is how it is?"

Manuel shrugged. "I'm afraid so."

"Rico?"

Manuel nodded. "You know how he is, and you pissed him off anyway. He's never liked you. What the hell did you think he would do?"

"So he sent you?" Jimmy deadpanned.

"He didn't offer it as a choice."

"There's always a choice."

"Not with him. Sit."

Jimmy backed up until his knees touched the curved bench of the navigation station. A small desk at the bottom of the stairs, it held the usual GPS, VHS radio, and radar in a small console. The surface was just enough to spread out a paper chart. Under the table were two objects secured with Velcro holders. One of them was a flare gun.

The other wasn't.

HUMAN ORGANS
FOR SALE?
November 6, 2008—FoxNews.com

—TWENTY-NINE—

DAYO CONTINUED THE SURGERY at his usual steady and unhurried rate. The wall of Oscar's old heart was mated successfully with the window he had cut in the donor heart. Following that, he had placed a catheter through one of the pulmonary veins of the donor heart, past the connection he had just completed, and on into the left ventricle. They were now pumping in saline at 4 degrees Celsius to further preserve the heart while the team labored to make the remaining connections. Jennifer scooped a couple handfuls of ice into the chest cavity to help the process. The heart was starting to look as if it belonged there. The only connections left were the pulmonary artery and the aorta.

The surgeon shoved some stray ice aside before grasping the aorta. Now was the time. He could see Raina's hands waiting with a fresh length of 4.0 prolene suture. It was 54 inches long, usually more than enough to finish the job despite the full-thickness bites he would be taking. Making what he hoped was a casual examination, he leaned over the table and hid Jennifer's view of his work.

"Metz please."

"Metz?" Raina retracted the suture she was holding.

"I just need to freshen up this edge."

Raina had the scissors in his hand a second later, and he carefully began trimming the edge of Oscar's aorta. But as soon as his two assistants returned to their conversation, he changed course.

Leaving the uncompleted edge hanging, he rotated the scissors and inserted them into the aorta itself. Similar in construction to a garden hose, the aorta had three layers. His scissors found and snipped through the first two inner layers in the area he would soon be suturing. After three centimeters he stopped and returned to the edge he was trimming. The conversation around him had not slowed, and he wordlessly exchanged the metz for the waiting suture. He placed the first stitch through the end of the cut he had made and gently brought the two vessels together. After a few more there was no way for Jennifer or Raina to see what he had done.

Switching from a forehand to a backhand grip, he continued the double-armed running suture until the posterior wall was almost complete.

"We can start re-warming, Brian."

"Okay."

With a pause to work his neck around a little, he continued on and stopped one stitch short of finishing the anterior wall before standing straight.

"Trendelemburg?" Dryer asked.

"Yeah, we're ready."

The head of the bed lowered, and Dayo watched as air escaped from the remaining stitch, producing a stream of frothy pink bubbles. They slowly trickled to a stop and he completed the final stitch. Jen removed the vent before removing the last of the melted ice. The heart looked like it belonged to Frankenstein with all the large black sutures crisscrossing its surface. A meat baseball he had heard it called once. Dayo tapped it with a finger and it responded with a faint quiver.

It wanted to live.

He allowed himself a brief grin behind his surgical mask as he finished. He had just doomed the man on the table, and he had done it in front of a room full of people, without them even knowing.

The aorta should hold until Oscar left the operating room. The cut he had made would survive the low pressures it would be subject to when they weaned him off the bypass machine. But once he was upstairs in the CVICU, and the pressure was allowed to climb, the blood would be forced into the cut. At that point it would widen, peeling the layers apart as the pressure increased and worked its way across the vessel. The pain would be excruciating if one were awake to experience it. Unfortunately, Oscar would still be under sedation, and unable to feel the sensation as his aorta was slowly torn apart by his new heart.

He would also be unable to warn his caregivers.

The balloon pump that had been in place to aid in the perfusion of his failing heart would be activated to assist his new one, unknowingly increasing the pressure feeding the fault. Eventually, the dissection would weaken the remaining wall of the aorta to the point that the force would rupture the vessel and seal Oscar's fate. Even if it were to happen in front of a trained surgeon, the man would have little chance of survival. He would bleed out in a matter of seconds.

Dr. Dayo had no intention of being anywhere close by when it happened.

There would be an autopsy. That he was sure of. He would also likely have to present the case at the next Mortality and Morbidity meeting of his peers. But with the first stitch placed where he had put it, it would appear that it had simply pulled through the tissue causing the failure that led to the rupture. He was comfortable that his name and reputation would see him through any scrutiny that followed.

But it would still be a failure for the team, and he already regretted what he was sentencing them to. It would be a no-win situation for both

Jen and Dr. Dryer. Dr. Dryer was an anesthesiologist, not a surgeon. His hands would be tied to what he could do externally, which in this case was very little. Jen was his physician's assistant, and while skilled in most aspects of surgery, she was not allowed to crack the patient's chest without him in attendance. She might, though, if placed in the position he was putting her in. He hoped she didn't step over the line too far, but if she did, he was ready to go to bat for her. But it was done. There was no turning back now.

He deeply regretted the heart he was wasting. Someone had died providing it, and there was a stringent system in place to ensure that they went to the right people. The fact that Oscar was somehow able to lie his way through the process made him wonder where these long-distance organs were really coming from. He had never questioned it before, nor had any of his colleagues. They didn't really wish to know, they usually involved some tragedy, especially with the kids, and his team didn't need that burden on their minds. They saw enough death as it was.

"What's our temp now?"

"35. We really didn't have time to get down too low," Brian answered.

"Okay, let's start weaning him off."

* * *

"Okay, let's air down," Dr. Fong ordered.

"Flow coming down," Mike responded. A simple adjustment to a clamp on the return line started the process. Dr. Jacobs thumbed the hydraulics to lower the head end of the table.

The surgeon watched carefully as the flow of blood returned to Tessa's new heart. The new head-down position of the table worked to push any air that was left in the circuit out through the last remaining stitch in the aorta. Air was the enemy. If left in the heart it could travel to the brain or lungs, causing strokes or a loss of circulation, both of which could be quickly fatal. The frothy pink bubbles stopped and a steady trickle of blood replaced them before the surgeon moved in and completed the closure.

"Done here," Fong spoke through the drape to Jacobs as he released clamps.

"Okay, Mike, let's make her bump."

Mike responded by making further adjustments, and as the flow of blood through the lungs increased, a wave form appeared on the overhead monitor. Small at first, the "bumps" increased in size with the rise in pressure. Dr. Jacobs watched closely, waiting for the numbers he wanted. His hands found the cardiac echo machine he had placed in Tessa's esophagus at the beginning of the surgery. It would allow him to observe the flow of blood through the heart as well as alert them to any air that had failed to vent.

Tessa's new heart chose that moment to wake up. A slight shiver ran over the muscle before it was still again.

"You see that?" Stephanie asked.

"Yeah, give it a poke," Dr. Fong replied.

The heart once again quivered in the chest as it responded to the warmer temperature and the flow of blood.

"That's fib," Stephanie spoke before poking the right atrium with a finger. The heart responded with a beat and a shiver. She poked it again and this time the heart responded by beating. It showed no signs of stopping.

"Magic finger," she announced with an unseen grin. She held it up for them all to see.

"Good flow," Jacobs announced as he played the sensor around. "Little air left in the apex."

"Tony?"

Tony paused long enough from his work in preparation of closing the chest to hand Dr. Fong a 19 gauge needle. The surgeon deftly inserted it through a fatty section covering the left ventricle. He was rewarded with another brief stream of frothy bubbles quickly followed by a pulsing stream of blood. Capping it with his finger, he pulled it clear. The fat worked to seal the puncture.

"Looks good."

Dr. Fong looked up at the screen for only a second before the anesthesiologist began to pull it free. The sensor twisted, and a different view briefly flashed across the screen before disappearing.

"Wait a minute, go back."

"What'd you see?"

"I'm not sure."

Stephanie and Tony stopped their preparations and everyone looked as the multicolored display returned to the screen.

"What...is...that?" she asked.

Dr. Fong offered no answer. He just shook his head and turned to his perfusionist.

"Mike, we're going back on bypass."

* * *

"So now what?" Jimmy asked.

Manuel waved him silent while he listened to some passing boaters. Once their voices had passed, he relaxed a small degree.

"We sit until the marina is quiet. Then we leave."

Jimmy nodded. He could fill in the rest by himself. Manuel would keep them here until the marina was quiet and dark before securing the three of them to something solid. Once that was done, he would cast off and sail the boat out into the Gulf. After he was through with them, he would pick a destination to leave the boat, or just sink it and come in to shore using the dinghy. Either way, he was coming back alone. Jimmy had some time to come up with something.

He had secured the cuffs tight enough to function. They were the type he had taught Manuel to use and they worked well. Police riot cuffs. They weren't just plastic, they had a metal band embedded inside. It prevented the prisoner from chewing through them. But at least his hands were cuffed in front of him. It gave him some options. He felt along the underside of the desk with his knee and located the flare gun. It wasn't loaded, but the flares were stored with it. It wasn't a real option. By the time he would have it loaded he would be dead, noise or not. The only hope he had was next to the flare gun—a snub nosed .38 revolver. Jimmy kept the gun handy for whatever may pop up. Stainless steel to survive the humidity, he had never had any use for it until now. Was it loaded? It had been a long time, but Jimmy was sure that it was. He wasn't in the habit of keeping an empty gun around. An empty gun was as useless as a stick. He felt the Velcro strap that secured it hanging loose, and coughing to cover the noise, rubbed his knee across it. It fell free without a fight. Nothing was holding the gun in the holster now but gravity. He just needed an opportunity to grab it.

"I didn't see my car in the lot."

"I left it at the airport."

"Rico didn't waste time."

"He called before I even had it started. Thought he was going to blame me for a second. Was afraid I might have to run, also."

"You still can."

"I'm not a runner. They always find you."

"Not always."

"*Qué?* Who am I talking to here? Don't bullshit me, Jimmy, they would hunt me down and you know it. It took Rico one second to decide… once he was done cussing you."

"He won't last long, you know that."

Manuel shrugged. "Not my place to decide. I was never cut out to be…management."

"You should call Pablo."

"Or Nestor? Which one, Jimmy? You have it all figured out, do you? How do you know Nestor doesn't want to be in charge? What makes you think Pablo isn't already dead?" Manuel waited, but he got no reply from Jimmy.

"So tell them you didn't find me. They'll believe that."

"And if they don't?"

Jimmy had no reply for that either. They both knew the answer. Jimmy watched him closely, ignoring the sweat crawling down his back. He examined Manuel, looking for an opening. Like him, he was sweating profusely, and Jimmy was blinking the sweat from his own eyes. Manuel's head was glistening in the faint light, and Jimmy could see the sweat gathering there. Sooner or later it would be in his eyes and he would have to wipe it away. Would that be enough time? Even if he got the gun up and around for a shot, it didn't mean Jessica and Cody were safe. Manuel had the hammer back for a reason. It was a lesson Jimmy had taught him. When the human body suffers a gunshot wound it causes the muscles to contract. If he managed to shoot Manuel, his fingers would contract around the gun and cause it to fire, sending the round into Jessica and Cody. The only way to avoid this was to shoot him in the brain stem. It was like flipping a switch. Instead of the muscles contracting, they would instantly go limp. That was the reason police snipers in hostage situations always went for the head shot. It was the only way to keep the hostage alive.

Jimmy would have to get his hands under the table, pull the gun, get it above the table and shoot Manuel in the head across the dimly lit cabin. The first time. The odds of success were slim. But they were all that he had.

He turned his head to Jessica. She held Cody on her lap and the boy stayed quiet. He gave them both a reassuring nod, but it failed to lessen the fear in her eyes. But she was strong, and she was keeping her fear under control. He hoped she would instinctively duck when the time came, but seeing the amount of room she had to deal with in the small space, there wasn't a lot she could do. With Cody on her lap, he knew her first instinct would be to shield him from the gunfire, with her own body if necessary. Something he refused to picture.

He returned his gaze to Manuel. The sweat was growing on his forehead, it wouldn't be long. Jimmy squirmed in his seat as if to seek a more comfortable position. Manuel watched every move.

Some more people walked past on the dock speaking loudly, and they all listened intently. Five people Jimmy counted, and something else he couldn't quite place. He followed the noise until it faded away toward the parking lot. Manuel reached for the sweat in his eyes.

The silence was shattered by furious barking in the form of Sam at the open hatch. Jimmy jumped at the noise, and as Manuel's attention moved to the dog the gun automatically followed. Before he could correct himself, Jimmy had his hands under the table and around the .38. Yanking it free he stood to make it easier to bring up. Manuel saw the motion, but before Jimmy could pull the trigger, he had the gun aimed back at Jessica and Cody.

"Don't do it!" he yelled at Jimmy.

Jimmy stopped himself from pulling the last bit of trigger just in time. His aim however didn't waiver.

"Don't do it," Manuel said again. "You'll kill us both!"

Jimmy exhaled. Manuel was right. The situation had changed, but Jessica and Cody were just as dead if he shot him. Something he had also taught his protégé.

"Shut the dog up."

Jimmy grit his teeth.

"Do it!"

"Jess, call Sam."

Jessica swallowed twice before she could get the words out. The dog obeyed on the second command and scampered down the steps to sit beside them on the seat. He continued to growl at Manuel, instinct telling him who the enemy was.

Jimmy and Manuel just stared at each other across the small room. The lapping of the waves against the side of the boat filled the silence.

ORGAN TRANSPLANT STUDY FINDS WIDE DISPARITY AMONG INSTITUTIONS

October 14, 1999—New York Times

—THIRTY—

"YOU'VE GOT TO BE kidding me!" Dr. Jacobs exclaimed.

"What is it?" Tony quietly asked.

"A septal defect. Looks like it's high up in the ventricles, too. It's letting blood pass from the left to the right on each contraction," Stephanie explained.

"Do we fix it now or later?"

Dr. Fong answered that one.

"Right now. Let's get her back on bypass."

His tone revealed his current feelings. Dr. Jacobs was just getting started.

"How the hell does a heart with a VSD get through the system? Somebody screwed up!"

"It doesn't matter right now, let's just get it fixed."

"I want somebody's ass for this! Who's the Lifelink rep, that blond woman? What's her name?"

"Later, John. Can you tilt her a little my way please?"

Dr. Jacobs cooled off and returned to the task at hand, but not without some words only he could hear from behind the curtain. Dr. Fong agreed with him 100%, but he had to keep his cool. There would be some phone calls and paperwork later. That, he was sure of. But right now they still had a teenage girl on the table in front of them.

He pushed the why out of his mind and concentrated on the current flaw in the donor heart. It had a hole in the wall of muscle separating the left and right ventricles. Its previous owner had no doubt gotten winded after a prolonged exertion, yet the problem, most likely something he'd been born with, had never been detected, or just simply never been addressed. Nevertheless, it was here now, and it was time to correct it.

"Pericardium?" Stephanie asked.

"We've got some core matrix in supply," Kye spoke up.

"I'd rather use that," Dr. Fong informed her as they worked to re-establish bypass. The cardioplegia was reintroduced and the heart once again stopped beating. Kye scrambled to re-supply Raina as they changed from closing the chest and back to another open procedure.

"Refresh me? What's the plan?"

Dr. Fong spoke while his hands moved around the catheters.

"I'll make a transverse incision here just below the pulmonary artery. It's best if you split the muscle fibers rather than going longitudinally. There's less chance of damaging a coronary artery. Then we just have to see how big a hole we're dealing with. If it's small, we can just suture it, but it almost always needs a patch. There's some tricky stitching to avoid the Bundle of His and again on the cephalad edge so you don't damage the aortic valve. But other than that it's just patching a hole. The new core matrix is great. Stem cell coated, it'll grow a new wall to fill the gap. When we're done with the patch we just close with some 4.0 and restart her again."

Kye burst through the door back into the operating room.

"I got your matrix!"

"Good. Tony, we ready?"

He watched as Kye dropped the matrix in his sterile field. "We're ready."

"Okay...let's do this. Knife."

*　　　*　　　*

Dr. Dayo watched from his seat at the OR computer desk while Jennifer deftly ran the heavy sternal wires through Oscar's rib cage. She twisted the wires around one another, passing the heavy Kochler clamps from hand to hand with a practiced dexterity. She paused to cut away some stray tissue with the Bovi scalpel, and the smoke curled up and around her gloved hands. Once the offending item was cut away, she began tugging the wires tighter, drawing the severed sternum back together. Oscar rocked on the narrow table as she increased the effort. Soon the gap was closed and the twisting of the wires began again, the violence of her action in sharp contrast to the previous activity inside the chest cavity.

His gaze moved from the actions of his PA to the monitor screen over her head as Dr. Dryer fired up the cardiac echo machine. Placed in Oscar's esophagus just prior to surgery, it provided a view of the newly installed heart as it worked in its new residence. The anesthesiologist adjusted a medication drip with his free hand and the heart responded with an increase in its efforts. Dayo followed his gaze as it switched to another screen.

"He's showing a little S-T elevation in the V-leads. But the heart seems to like the higher pressure."

"Elevation getting any worse?" Dayo asked.

"No...better actually."

"Air bubble."

"Maybe."

Dayo rose from the chair and walked to the screen to examine it a little closer. The deviation Dr. Dryer spoke of could indicate a possible heart attack, but it was fading rapidly. He was glad to see it as it justified his next order.

"Let's keep his pressure here for now. Once he's settled in upstairs go ahead and let it come up."

"Okay."

Dr. Dryer extracted the echo sensor and began helping his tech clean and stow the equipment. Dayo turned and watched Jen as she placed the last few sutures. Raina and Paula began pulling off the drapes and scrubbing the stray blood away that had found its way under them. Dayo took one look as Oscar's face reappeared before turning away. Brian was still stewing over his malfunctioning bypass machine with their new team member. Dayo quickly determined that he was the only one in the room with nothing to do, so he decided to leave while he could.

"I'll meet you upstairs, John."

"Okay."

With a firm tug, he tore off his face mask before pushing his way out the door. Paula was reaching for the phone as he left.

* * *

Dr. Fong frowned at Tessa's new heart as Stephanie worked to take her off bypass for the second time. The additional line of suture running across the right atrium was just one more insult to a heart that had been through enough for one day. It had already suffered the brain death of its original owner, an act that basically told the remaining organs to line up and get ready to die. Add to that the actions of the Mexican surgeon, who flooded it with cardioplesia before slicing it free of the chest and placing it on a machine for a three thousand mile journey. On arrival, he himself had greeted it by dropping it into a bucket of near freezing water before carving it up for implantation. They had subjected it to two cycles of warming and cooling now with the septal defect repair. If the heart woke up at all he would be surprised.

But wake up it did. This time they needed the paddles as Stephanie's magic finger no longer seemed to be working. After a stutter or two, the heart fell into a somewhat regular rhythm.

They all breathed a quick sigh of relief and gazed up at the overhead monitor. They saw the signature double P-wave of the heart transplant rhythm, and nice, narrow, and peaked R waves, but the rest of the EKG was not what they hoped for.

"The right ventricle's balking," Fong observed.

"Did you expect that?"

"It doesn't surprise me. This heart's been through a lot today."

Their eyes traveled from Tessa's new heart to the monitor and back again as they watched the right side of her heart struggle. After a few minutes and no improvement, Dr. Fong made a decision.

"Let's reestablish bypass and give her a good rest. Say fifteen minutes."

Working together they quickly had that accomplished. This time there was no cross-clamp on the aorta, so Tessa's blood was being circulated by both her new heart and the bypass machine at the same time. This gave the organ the least amount of work to perform, and allowed it a chance to get to know its new owner.

"Everybody take a break. Let's get her numbers the best we can and see what happens after fifteen minutes."

"You think the RV will step up?" Tony asked.

The surgeon shrugged. "No telling at this point. If it doesn't, we can try the RVAD."

Stephanie frowned at that. RVAD stood for right ventricular assist device, and they were seldom used. The chair-sized machine sat in the corner of the room on large caster wheels, and while always present, they avoided its use at all cost. It functioned by intercepting the blood from the vena cava, pumping it around the right atrium and ventricle and directly into the pulmonary artery. This would give Tessa's struggling heart some much needed help. It was well known that surgeons hated resorting to its use, as it usually only worked to delay the inevitable anywhere from a few days to a few weeks. Dr. Fong referred to it as "the road to nowhere."

Mike watched as they scrubbed out and filed out of the room to take a break. Only he and Doctor Jacobs remained. He checked his gauges before reaching for his binder. Inside he found a laminated copy of the RVAD connection sequence. He quietly reviewed it while the pumps continued to spin in front of him.

* * *

Rico swirled the rapidly melting ice in his drink around while he half-listened to Nestor lecture him about production and material costs. He had never had an interest in that part of the business. Oscar had always taken care of all of that. Rico didn't have his brother's gift with numbers, but it was something he would never admit to, especially to these two. He'd been listening to them drone on about this and that for the last hour and he was growing tired quickly. How hard could it be? They paid some peasant farmers double what they would make in a year growing coffee to plant, harvest, and process the drugs. Then they paid the gangs and others to transport it across the borders and into the countries where they had their biggest markets. A few bribes here and a few bullets there, and the money poured in. Simple. Why did these two always want to make it so complicated? Now they were trying to tell him that they had to change things. Why? Everything was working fine. He was thinking about another drink when something Nestor said caught his attention.

"What? What's the problem now?"

Nestor stopped in mid sentence before starting over.

"I was saying that we need to use the routes through Mexico less. It gives too much control to the Zeta's. The longer our product is in their hands, the greater the chances of it being interrupted. The gangs are at war with one another *and* with the army. They are more than willing to inform on each other and let the army do their work for them. Either way, we end up losing product."

Rico smiled to himself and shook his head. They always called it "product." Why couldn't they just call it what it was? Cocaine. They made cocaine and they sold it. Their fancy words just irritated him more.

Pablo spoke up. "It would be better to strengthen our own resources for delivery and move larger shipments."

"With what, more submarines? Bigger planes? They cost too much, and when they're caught we lose too much."

"Not if you look at the numbers and compare them to using the gangs. The product is moved through a much shorter chain of people. Our people."

Nestor jumped in. "That's another thing. We can't have any more men like Angel. He knew too much, and we're paying for that now. We have to compartmentalize the routes and keep the people involved to a minimum. We lost two of our best tunnels in one day because of him. Because of one man we have too many things to change. I recommend we reduce our shipments for four months and raise the street price everywhere."

"Reduce the shipments? Why? You just told me we have enough warehoused for months. There's no reason to ship less!" Rico laughed at them both before draining his drink. The sun had made its way across the table until it was on him also, and he was starting to sweat. It only served to irritate him more.

Nestor sat back with a sigh and shot a look at Pablo before taking another deep breath. Keeping his temper in check had been a struggle since they had sat down. But they had agreed that it was Pablo's decision, and he had not made it yet.

Pablo waited a moment before he spoke and was careful to keep his tone neutral.

"The raise in price is necessary to make the Americans believe they have hurt us badly. If they think this, they will relax once they have exhausted the information they've obtained from Angel. If we don't show a reduction in shipments and a price increase, they will know we have more means than Angel gave them, and they will then expand their efforts looking for them. It is not to our benefit for them to do so. Better to let them think they are winning."

Rico heard the words, but they made no sense to him. Sending less was better then sending more? He tried to see through what Pablo was saying, but he just couldn't wrap his mind around it. The booze was not helping and he felt a headache coming on.

"I don't like it. So what if the Americans suspect we have more ways to get our *cocaine* into their country. What the hell can they do about it? Nothing! The fools have no idea how much we ship in. Their guesses aren't even close! Buy some more of your fancy submarines if you want, I don't care. But we're not shipping less. The Americans are always thirsty for more. Who am I to deny them?"

Rico gestured to Carlos who left his spot behind the two men and quickly retrieved Rico's empty glass. Rico ignored his guests and took in the view of the mountains as the setting sun painted them many colors. It was a nice view. Perhaps he would stay here longer than he had planned.

Carlos set the drink down in front of him and Rico noticed for the first time that his guests had yet to touch their drinks. No matter. He could care less if they died of thirst right now. He really just wanted them gone.

Pablo waited until Carlos had taken up his position behind them again before speaking.

"I think you should reconsider. The wise thing to do is to work around the Americans, not against them. We tried that in Mexico, and now we have an army to contend with. It's bad for business."

Rico's drink was halfway to his mouth when he heard the words and he slammed it back down hard on the table. The whisky splashed across the table and onto the two men. They leaned back, half expecting the glass to follow.

"Listen to me, you skinny little bastards! *I* am the one in charge here! *I* will make the decisions! My brother left me in his place, not you! I say we ship more, and that is what we're going to do! To hell with the Americans! You pencil pushing assholes! If you have a problem with that, I will find new people to take your place, and you can join your friend Jimmy rotting somewhere with a hole in his head! Now get the hell out of my sight!"

Pablo calmly reached out and took the napkin from under the beer in front of him. The beer had been sweating in the sun and the napkin was moist, but it worked to wipe the booze from his face. As he did so, a smile slowly formed on his face.

He raised the beer toward Rico in a mock salute.

"Whatever you say...boss."

On that signal Carlos stepped forward. The pistol appeared in his giant fist and Rico found himself looking straight down its large barrel. The bullet exited the back of his head before he had a chance to figure out what was happening.

The sound of the gunshot echoed off the mountains for some time before finally fading.

"Why the hell did you wait so long?" Nestor asked as he dabbed at the booze on his shirt.

"I felt we owed him a chance. Oscar may just make it to prison alive."

"If he does?"

Pablo shrugged. "Jimmy."

"Speaking of which." Nestor pulled out his cell phone and handed it to his new boss.

U.S. WILL REQUIRE HOSPITALS TO IDENTIFY POTENTIAL ORGAN DONORS

September 6, 1987—New York Times

—THIRTY-ONE—

"C-V-I-C-U, THIS IS DONNA."

"Hey Donna, it's Paula. We're done with Mr. Hernandez. Should be up there in about ten or so."

"Okay, we're ready here. He's going to bed three."

"Got it."

Donna hung up the phone and turned to examine the room. Sharon was placing electrodes on the ends of the color-coded wires in anticipation of their patient's arrival.

"We're ready, right?"

Sharon laughed. "You said we were!"

"I know, just checking. Respiratory here yet?"

"I'll call them."

"Thanks."

Donna checked items off her mental list as her eyes roamed the room and located them. The bed was made, and its internal scale was zeroed. Sharon had prepped all the leads and they were now draped over the monitor, along with the pulse oximetry sensor. Both IV poles and the Gemini pumps mounted to them were in place. Blood tubing and several pressure bags hung ready from the multiple hooks. Both suction units were connected and standing by, and she had syringes and lab tubes sitting next to her I-STAT blood analyzer. Several blankets sat stacked on a nearby chair. All that was missing was the ventilator and the tech to run it.

As if to answer her thoughts, the tech could be heard rolling into the unit, pulling the ventilator with the one squeaky wheel along with her. As she entered the room, her purple scrubs seemed to add more light.

"How long?"

"Any minute."

The doors at the end of the hall hissed open on their hydraulic hinges and Dr. Dryer's voice boomed out across the ward.

"Patient coming through. Make some room please!"

Donna had just enough time to write the arrival time on the board and cross the room before the group pushed the bed into place. It was an impressive display of teamwork despite the fact that they resembled a group of ants working together to haul a leaf across the ground. Dr. Dryer followed along with the chart and a stack of empty forms. The room had gone from virtually empty to overcrowded within a few seconds. Working together, they quickly had all the tubes and wires accounted for before sliding Oscar over and onto his new bed. There was now a flurry of activity as he was wired, vented, poked and prodded. The monitor screen came to life with a stack of colored numbers and waveforms. The ventilator was connected, and its settings were adjusted as Dr. Dryer dictated them. Blood was drawn and passed off for analysis by the waiting machines. Foleys were drained and chest tubes secured. There was a brief lull as everyone double checked their portion of the work before the blankets were applied. Oscar became a cocoon of cotton, with only his face and the breathing tube visible.

Donna helped Sharon work the compression stockings over Oscar's swollen legs while she listened to Dr. Dryer's report.

"Keep him on the Nitro at one mic for now. He had some S-T elevation in the inferior leads, but it resolved on its own. No wall motion changes that we could see on the echo, so we want to bring his pressure up. His new heart seems to like it, and the twelve-lead looks okay."

Donna followed his gaze to the overhead monitor. "That double P-wave always looks weird to me, no matter how many times I see it."

"As long as he's got one I'm happy. I'm gonna go chart. Page me if you need anything."

"Okay...oh, last crit?"

"Ummm...twenty-nine."

"Got it."

Dr. Dryer walked out to the nurse's station, only to find that Jen had beat him to the computer. Dayo already had the one out in the hall. He shrugged and headed off to the on-call room. This late it would be empty and quieter there anyway.

* * *

Dr. Fong backed into the OR with his hands up only to see Dr. Jacobs standing over their patient and contemplating the overhead monitor. Tony rounded the foot end of the operating table with a sterile gown and the two of them did a silent dance as he assisted the surgeon in donning it. Dr. Fong checked the monitor while Tony fetched a pair of gloves.

"Any change?"

"Nope."

Dr. Fong paused long enough to thrust his hands deep into the gloves before approaching the table. He clasped his hands together across his gown as he checked the movement of Tessa's new heart beating in her open chest. An involuntary sigh escaped him when he confirmed what he was just told.

"Okay, let's come off and see how she does."

Fifteen minutes later Tessa's new heart was once again beating on its own with no additional help from the bypass machine. Dr. Fong frowned behind his mask when he saw no improvement. Dr. Jacobs adjusted his echo sensor and shook his head at their unspoken question.

"The RV's still struggling. Septal wall looks okay. Your patch seems to be holding fine."

"So what are you thinking?"

"I played with the wedge pressures and they're a little high. I think the right ventricle just needs a little help pushing against it."

"Did you give her some volume?"

"Yeah, but I don't want to get her up too high. I'm keeping her central venous pressure under twenty."

"You worried about a septal shift?"

"Well, that and I don't want to stress your patch job either."

"Well thanks for that note of confidence."

"Any time."

"So we need to lower her pulmonary artery pressure. How do you want to do it?"

Jacobs picked up his clipboard and scribbled some numbers before replying. "Let's try some Natrocor and see how she responds. I'll bolus her and then run a drip at .01 mics."

"Okay…I'll find myself a chair."

Unable to touch anything without compromising his sterile status, Dr. Fong crossed the room and carefully sat on a stool. He could do nothing but watch as Dr. Jacobs slowly injected the drug into the girl's central line before mixing still more in a small bag of saline. He soon had that running through one of his many pumps. They both settled down to see how the new heart responded.

Tony had heard the whole exchange and was now watching the screens as well.

"So what are you expecting to see first?"

Dr. Jacobs, ever the teacher, answered him. "We think the right ventricle is struggling because the pressure in her lungs is too high and it's having a hard time pumping against it. The drug I just gave her will dilate the blood vessels in her lungs and hopefully make it easier for her new heart to do its job. We should see improvement across the board, but probably on the EKG first. If it works, we can close her chest and hopefully manage her medically."

"What if it doesn't?"

Dr. Jacobs shrugged. "RVAD."

Tony knew what that meant, so he fell silent and found something to do with his tray of instruments.

A minute later they had their answer. Tessa's EKG waveform slowly became less rounded and more upright. Her blood pressure soon followed with a slow but steady increase. Dr. Jacobs once again fired up the echo machine and scanned the girl's heart.

"Better. Good wall movement. Her cardiac output is up, too."

Dr. Fong rose from his seat. They all stepped up to the table and silently waited while he made his decision.

"We've done all we can here. Let's close her up and get her upstairs."

* * *

Dayo looked up from his paperwork as Dr. Fong's team pushed the teenage girl around the corner. Dr. Jacobs hit the door button before he followed them in.

"How'd yours go?" he asked the surgeon as he passed.

Dayo offered a thumb's up for a reply before they disappeared around the corner and into the cardio-vascular intensive care unit. The doors had barely shut when Dr. Fong rounded the corner.

"What took you so long?" Dayo asked.

Dr. Fong just sighed and shook his head before finding a spot to sit on the corner of the desk. He pulled his surgical cap off and tossed it in the trash before rubbing his eyes.

"She arrested as soon as she hit the table."

"Really? Ouch. Get her back okay?"

"No, we crashed-on instead. We got her on bypass with only a minute or so of down time. Good CPR the whole way, so I don't think there was any ischemic injury. But then we had to sit and wait for the new heart to arrive."

"Figures. How was the donor heart?"

Fong shook his head again before replying. "That's a whole other issue I need to talk to you about." He nodded to a passing employee. "Not here though."

"All right. How about the roof in ten? I got another care package yesterday."

Dr. Fong perked up at that. "Cubans?"

Dayo grinned. "Montecito's."

"You got a deal. Let me settle my teenager in and I'll meet you in ten." He stood and patted his waistline. "I left my pager in the OR."

"I'll grab mine on the way up. Don't tell anyone unless you want to share."

"Not a problem."

Dayo watched casually as Fong disappeared into the CVICU, but as soon as the doors shut he was on his feet and hurrying toward his office. He avoided the elevator and looked through the window into the stairwell, as he didn't wish to be seen right now. Seeing it empty, he was quickly through the door and bounding up the stairs. The surgical booties he had purposely kept on served him well by keeping his shoes from squeaking on the tile floor, but they were slippery, and in his haste he nearly busted his ass as he rounded a corner. Reaching his office, he had a momentary flash of panic before determining that Christine had left the door unlocked for him.

Avoiding the lights, he felt his way across the dark interior and managed to reach his office without knocking anything over. Closing the door behind him, he once again left the light off. The lights of downtown Baltimore served to illuminate the interior well enough for him to see what he was doing, and he didn't want someone working late to see him across the courtyard.

Sitting at his desk, he winced as the bottom drawer squeaked in his hand as he opened it. Back behind some files was a new box of cigars, a present from a former patient. A Canadian government employee, the man made the occasional trip to Cuba, and a box of cigars would find its way to his surgeon friend every few months. Being no fool, Dayo let him.

He quickly retrieved two Montecito's, his cutter, and a box of matches before stuffing them in the pocket of his coat and opening the top drawer. Rooting around in the dark, he found the flashlight and placed it on the desk blotter before placing his pager next to it. Taking the cover off, he pulled the good battery from the pager and swapped it for the dead one from the flashlight. It flared briefly before he twisted it off and threw it back in the drawer. Putting the now dead pager back on his belt, he allowed himself a deep breath before sneaking back out of his office and on to the stairwell.

Jimmy waited. The silence was deafening inside the boat and his grip on the pistol was becoming slippery in the heavy humidity. He wished he had chosen a larger caliber of gun. He couldn't count on the .38 making the head shot he needed. He adjusted it without moving his aim and Manuel flinched slightly, drawing a low growl from the dog. His protégé had a dominant left eye. Jimmy knew from watching him shoot on several occasions, so he centered his aim there, the better to give him a view directly down the barrel.

But Manuel's aim was also rock solid, and it never wavered from the center of Jessica's chest. Jimmy knew the power of the small handgun Manuel held as well as any trauma surgeon. While the caliber was small, the penetration power was high. The round would most likely enter her chest before spending its remaining energy bouncing around inside and shredding vital organs. If that happened, there would be nothing to stop him from finishing the job and eliminating any witnesses. Jimmy was not about to let that happen.

But they were at an impasse. Time was on Jimmy's side, but he didn't really want to wait for Manuel to get tired or impatient. The outcome would not be good for any of them.

They all jumped when Manuel's phone rang. Jimmy recognized the tone.

"Your new boss," he stated.

Manuel just grimaced and made no move to answer it.

"Go ahead. I'd like to hear this."

Manuel let it ring once more before slowly reaching in his pocket and retrieving it. He set the phone down on the table in front of him and felt his way across the keyboard.

"Yes?"

Pablo's voice came through the tiny speaker loud enough for them all to hear. "Manuel. You know who this is?"

"Yes."

"There've been some changes. The brothers are no longer in charge. I have taken over for them."

Manuel said nothing, but his face changed. Jimmy waited for what was next.

* * *

Dr. Fong pulled on the cigar repeatedly until he had a nice glow at the tip. Dr. Dayo puffed on his while he watched his friend enjoy the Cuban delicacy. He waited a full minute before his curiosity couldn't.

"So what's on your mind?"

Dr. Fong let some smoke escape before replying.

"You know, its bad enough that the girl's only sixteen and needs a new heart, add to that the fact that she's the daughter of a senator. I know, shouldn't matter, but it does and there's no changing that. But then, not only does she crash on the table, but the donor heart's got a damn VSD!"

"A septal defect? You're kidding."

"Nope, high up, too. Luckily I caught it on the echo just as Jacobs was pulling it."

"Small enough to sew?"

"No, I had to patch it. I was going to just use some pericardium, but Kye pulled some matrix out of the core, so I patched it with that. I swear she has her own secret stash hidden back there somewhere."

"How close to the tricuspid?"

"Close enough. I had to anchor through the base and then on the cephalad edge…well…I always worry about damaging the aortic valve."

"She start back up okay?"

"A little sluggish. The right ventricle didn't want to play at first, but Jacobs coaxed it along. That's why it took me so long. That's not what I wanted to talk about anyway."

"You want to know how a heart with a septal defect got through the system in the first place," Dayo deadpanned.

"Exactly! How did that even happen? I couldn't see it visually, but it was obvious on the echo. What happened to the strict screening process UNOS has? Ever since we started using that POPS machine we get less and less information about these organs coming in. Don't get me wrong, it's an amazing machine, and we need it. It's saving a lot of lives. But when the chart is in Spanish, how the hell are we supposed to know anything about it? Am I just going to have to accept a chart I can't read?"

"The technology is ahead of the system."

"Well the system needs to catch up, and fast," Fong grumbled. "Jacobs is going to write a letter for us. I'll get you a copy before we send it out."

Dayo just nodded and they both puffed for a moment. He wondered what was going on downstairs.

* * *

Jen's fingers flew across the keyboard as she typed up her post-op report. Since her contribution to the surgery didn't vary as much as it did for the surgeons, the words flowed onto the screen with little thought. She had joked with her colleagues many times about just creating a template and choosing the sentences she wanted from a menu, but it had always remained just a thought. The least she had wished for was a function key that would type "in the usual manner" for her.

Her thoughts were interrupted by a loud beeping and flashing light from the monitor screen in front of her. She looked up to see that the arterial blood pressure reading on her patient was erratic. Sharon walked past her and into the room to check on it, so she dismissed the alarm and returned to her report.

She had barely begun the next paragraph when Dr. Dryer hurried past. She got a smile and a wave from him, but he didn't slow, and was quickly down the hall and through the double doors, probably in search of a bathroom, or maybe just in a hurry to get his own charting done. She dismissed the thought and again returned to the keyboard.

She had just collected her thoughts when the alarm sounded again. She looked up only to see the same problem with the arterial blood pressure. This time she watched the waveform more closely as the reading seemed to be stepping down in increments. Looking through the glass wall of the patient's room, she saw Sharon still hovering over him. The frown on her face got her attention.

"Problem with the art line Sharon?"

"Not that I can find."

The reply got Jen out of her chair and she walked into the room. Oscar looked the same as when they had moved him into the room, other than his now exposed arm where Sharon was troubleshooting the problem. Jen checked the monitor again only to see that the numbers were continuing to fall. Donna joined them and eyeballed the equipment.

"Stopcock off a little?"

"No, I just checked. The line isn't pinched either."

"Pressure bag?"

"It's fine."

Jen watched silently as the two nurses checked the equipment again. Her little voice was beginning to speak to her.

"Is it the transducer?" she asked.

Donna checked the device over before replying.

"It looks fine. Can we still draw off of it, Sharon?"

"I don't know, let's find out."

She grabbed a syringe and connected it to the port before working the three-way stopcock and drawing some blood.

"It feels a little resistant, but I can still draw."

"It shouldn't be resistant. Are we still in the artery?"

"We wouldn't get anything if we weren't."

They were cut off by the alarm sounding again. Sharon reached up and silenced it. The screen now read zero and showed no waveform at all. Jen's little voice was screaming at her now.

"Get a blood pressure."

Her tone startled them both as it was out of character for her. Donna complied by wrapping a cuff around Oscar's arm. She donned her stethoscope before placing the bell at his elbow and searched for a pulse before she started pumping.

"I've got no pulse."

"Really? Sharon searched for one also and her face clouded. They all checked the monitor which showed a beating heart.

"I've got nothing."

"A carotid?"

"Yeah…it's there. Faint though."

"It's not PEA…check the other arm."

Sharon scrambled to comply.

"It's here. It matches the monitor."

Jen stared at the screen and watched the waveform that told her the heart was beating fine. No pulses on the right, yet they had one at the neck and the left arm? The voice in her head stopped screaming.

"Page Dayo," she whispered.

"What?"

"Page Dayo! And get Dryer back in here. He's probably in the on-call room."

Donna ran to the desk and grabbed the phone while Jen tore the blankets from Oscar's body. She checked the two drains protruding from his chest and then the screen of the balloon pump before staring again at the monitor.

"Kill the balloon pump."

Sharon flipped switches until the screen was blank.

"What is it?"

"His aorta...I think it's dissecting."

* * *

"So how did yours go?"

"Our bypass machine caught on fire."

Fong choked on some smoke and had a brief coughing fit. Dayo smiled while he waited for him to recover.

"Your bypass machine...caught on fire?"

"Yup. Brian says one of the circuit boards failed. It just had an overhaul and most of the boards were updated. He thinks we got a bad one. Factory defect. One-in-a-million chance, but it happened. I'm thinking of buying a lottery ticket tonight."

"We talking actual flames here? What did you do?"

"Mostly just a lot of smoke. Brian stayed cool through the whole thing. Turns out it was the circuit board for the gauges. The pumps kept running, except for one that got hot. He switched it out."

"Where were you?"

"In the chest. We were committed. Dryer ran down the hall for the machine out of trauma, but Brian just made the broken one work somehow. I haven't gotten the whole story yet. He called a guy up from maintenance with a timing light, and he just sat there giving Brian RPM readings until I got the patient off bypass. Paula had a bunch of people fanning the smoke out the doors. Me, I just kept going, not a whole lot of options really."

"Amazing. How's the patient?"

"Alive."

"You don't sound too happy about that."

"Bastard stopped us right before we put him under and called everyone in the room by their full name. A nice veiled threat."

Dr. Fong didn't know what to say to that, so he puffed on his cigar instead. The rich tobacco soothed him and he turned his gaze to the sky over the city. The full moon competed with the man-made lighting below to illuminate the night. A bat passed by with its broken-wing flight, making impossible turns as it rid the air of mosquitoes. The lights of the baseball stadium could be seen off to the south.

"Who the Orioles playing tonight?"

"Couldn't tell ya."

They smoked in silence for awhile, neither one of them wanting to go back inside.

"So…think we should head back down?"

"Let's stay awhile," Dayo replied. "I think we've earned it tonight. They'll page us if they need something."

"I'll agree with you there."

Fong tapped his cigar and watched as the slight breeze carried the ashes up and over the edge of the roof. It made him think of his sailboat.

"How come you've never come sailing with me?"

Dayo shrugged. Seemed like a good enough time to come clean.

"I get sea sick."

"They say it goes away after three days."

"Oh, well in that case…"

They fell silent again and enjoyed the quiet of the roof.

DRUG SUSPECT WHO FLED U.S. WITH NEW HEART IS CAPTURED

October 24, 1994,—New York Times

—THIRTY-TWO—

THERE WERE NOW FIVE people standing around Oscar, gazing up at the monitors. Donna cycled the blood pressure cuff again, and they impatiently waited for the numbers to flash on the screen.

"Still crap," Jen voiced their collected thoughts.

"What's going on?" Dr. Dryer asked as he was led into the room by Sharon.

"I think he's dissecting. We lost the art line and the radial pulse on the right side. We can't find anything wrong with the equipment, and that arm's getting pale and cyanotic.

"Did it just cut out, or did it kind of step down?"

"It stepped down. His pressures were different in each arm, too, before the right one quit."

"Shit, get me an echo in here. Where's Dayo?"

"We paged him a few minutes ago, he hasn't answered."

"Okay…you stopped the balloon pump?"

"Yeah, what can we do?"

"Just get ready. If it ruptures before we can clamp it off, it'll be over real quick. I'd start by getting some blood and platelets ready. Say, at least six units."

A tech returned with the echo machine and a minute later Dryer had the sensor in Oscar's esophagus. The gray image rotated on the screen until he had the view he needed. Splashes of color showed the blood flow.

"There it is. Call the OR and tell them to get ready, soon as Dayo sees this we're coming back down."

Donna left to make the call and Dryer craned his neck out to look down the hall.

"You sure you paged him?"

"Yeah."

"Call the operator and overhead page him this time."

"Okay"

Sharon cycled the BP cuff again and Jen bit her lip waiting for the number.

"Damn it, he's still dropping."

"That new heart didn't like low pressures in the O.R," Dryer informed them.

"Restart the balloon pump?"

"I wouldn't."

"Then what? We need to stop it."

"*We* can't crack his chest, Jen! We wait for Dayo."

As if to punctuate the statement, the overhead speaker toned out once, followed by the operator's calm voice.

"Dr. Dayo to CVICU, stat, Dr. Dayo to CVICU, stat please."

Jen crossed her arms and scowled at the monitor before turning to Sharon.

"Let's get the Open Chest Cart in here now, and a crash cart."

"500 of saline. Squeeze it in," Dryer ordered.

They both stewed while the nurses acted and the operator continued to page over the speaker, each of them wondering the same thing.

Where the hell was their surgeon?

* * *

Manuel leaned closer to the phone.

"*Qué?*"

"I am running things now. You understand?"

"Yes."

"I want you to ignore what that idiot Rico told you. If you find Jimmy, you tell him to call me, okay?"

Jimmy watched closely as Manuel's thoughts played across his face. Finally, he looked Jimmy in the eye before leaning even closer to the phone and spoke. "You're too late."

"What?"

"I said you're too late. Our friend…he's in the Gulf."

They held each other's gaze as a string of profanity spewed forth from the phone. It took some time before Pablo was ready to speak again. "That fool! He's dead and he's still fucking things up! I should have shot him weeks ago!"

They patiently waited through another string of profanity. Eventually Pablo calmed down and spoke again. "This is not your fault Manuel. You did as you were told. Your partner was a good man. But what's done is done. Stay by the phone, I have work for you."

"*Si.*"

Manuel ended the call, but did not lower his gun. Jimmy watched his eyes. They looked tired. Tired and old. Too old for a man of his age. They were eyes that Jimmy knew. He saw them in the mirror everyday.

Jimmy slowly flicked the safety on before lowering his gun. Manuel hesitated, but soon followed, sitting back heavily in the chair with a loud exhale. He rubbed the sweat from his eyes and pulled the stray hair from his forehead.

He shook his head at what he had just done, barely able to believe it himself.

"Where will you go?" he asked.

Jimmy shrugged. "It's a big ocean."

Manuel just nodded. He really didn't wish to know. He rose on tired legs and walked past Jimmy. The pistol now hung loosely in his hand and bounced against his leg. His sweat-soaked shirt clung to his muscular frame. He ignored the growling dog and slowly climbed the stairs as if all of his strength had left him.

"Hey, kid?"

Manuel tensed and slowly turned, but Jimmy's gun was now resting on the table.

"Be careful eh…don't become an animal."

He got a nod and a lopsided grin for a reply before turning and climbing out of the boat. Jimmy watched him as he made his way down the dock, making no effort to hide the pistol in his hand. A group of drunken boaters gave him a wide berth as he walked through them without even acknowledging their presence. Jimmy kept watching, ready to give a final wave, but Manuel just crossed the lot to the rental car, got in, and drove away.

He never looked back.

"Jimmy?"

He turned to find the boy and his mother at the bottom of the stairs.

"It's over. We're free now."

* * *

"Blood pressure is down to sixty!"

"Damn. Give one milligram of epinephrine and start the blood running," Dryer ordered.

"Get a board under him."

Jen broke the seals on the Open Chest Cart and pulled out a surgical gown sealed in plastic. She tossed it to Donna. "Get some gloves on and suit me up!"

Dryer opened his mouth to say something, but held his tongue when he saw the look on her face. It wouldn't hurt to be ready, he decided.

"Squeeze in another unit when that one's done."

"Another BP."

"Where's Dayo?"

"No answer yet."

"Send someone to find him. Check the office. If he's not there, then page Dr. Fong!"

"BP down to 51 systolic!"

"That's not enough, start CPR."

Ed was the biggest nurse on the floor. He stepped up to the bed and placed his hands on Oscar's chest. Before he could start, Jen spoke up.

"Ed wait…I don't know…just…just be gentle if you can."

"Got it."

They all held their breath and watched as Ed began pumping on Oscar's chest. The crack and pop of his wired sternum was audible, and they half expected the drains to run bright red with blood. But the flow only increased a little.

"The sutures are holding," Dryer observed.

"But for how long," Jen countered.

"Hopefully until Dayo gets here."

Jen let her frustration come out. "Nobody's found him yet? Tell that operator to keep paging him until we call and tell her to stop!"

"Do you want to move him back to the OR?"

"No, they're not ready yet anyway. Better here than on the elevator."

"We have to get it clamped."

"Wait for Dayo!"

"Who's the trauma doc on duty tonight?"

"Dr. Balzano, I think he's in the ER with a gunshot wound. Should I page him?"

Dryer cut Jen off before she could reply. "No, not yet. Dayo will be here."

Jen spun in a circle, her fear level was rising. "Can I get another BP?"

They all fell silent again as the machine did its job. Even Ed followed the numbers as he pumped on the chest. Sweat was already forming on his forehead.

"No change."

"Look at the drains."

The trickle of blood had now increased slightly, and now both tubes showed a small but steady amount flowing to the water seals that Sharon had taped to the floor.

"Hang two more units!"

"Gloves!"

"Jen, you can't! Wait for Dayo."

"He's not answering! You remember what *he* said!"

Only Dryer knew what she was referring to—Oscar's threat in the OR. He fought to keep his face under control.

Ed turned his head to follow the conversation and his shoulders followed slightly. It was enough to change the angle he was pumping at. He felt it more than he heard it. Oscar's chest suddenly offered less resistance.

"Jen!"

Jen turned to look at Ed and followed his gaze to the drains. They both gushed bright red blood as fast as it could flow.

"He's ruptured!"

"Hang more blood!"

"Off the chest, Ed! Drape!"

Sharon threw a sterile drape across Oscar's chest and Jen ripped the sterile dressing off to exposed the sutures she had placed less than an hour ago. She sliced through them without finesse until the sternal wires gleamed back at her.

"Cutters!"

Sharon slapped the instrument into her hand and she made quick work of snipping the wires free. Sharon grabbed each one as it popped loose and discarded it. Blood began bubbling up through the widening gap.

"Spreaders!"

Jen pulled her hands free in time for Sharon to place the device and crank the handle. Oscar's chest was barely open when she reinserted a hand and began pumping on the heart. The pool of blood that was Oscar's chest all but hid her small hand, and more blood overflowed out with each pump to run down the sides of his body.

"Suction! I can't see anything!"

"Keep pumping, it's coming."

"I need a clamp!"

"What kind?"

"I don't care…gimme an Alice."

"Scoop it out!"

"More suction!"

"His aorta's shredded."

"Clamp it."

"There's…nothing to clamp!"

"What the hell is going on here?"

The command voice cut through the chaos like a clap of thunder. They all turned to see Dr. Balzano standing in the doorway.

"His aorta's ruptured!"

"Where's Dayo?"

"We've been paging him and Dr. Fong. They haven't answered."

Dr. Balzano walked forward and took in the bloody mess on the table. Jen continued pumping with one hand while Sharon worked two suction catheters.

"Put the clamp down. There's nothing to work with here."

"But…"

"He's done, Jen. That aorta's unsalvageable. Who cracked his chest?"

"I…I did."

Dr. Balzano just made a face and shook his head.

"Pronounce your patient."

Jen couldn't stop pumping.

"*Pronounce your patient, Jen*."

Jen slowed to a stop before slowly pulling her hand free. She swallowed her fear twice before looking up at the clock.

"Time of death…23:18."

WHITE HOUSE CZAR CALLS FOR
END TO 'WAR ON DRUGS'
May 14, 2009—Wall Street Journal

—THIRTY-THREE—

RITA LAMAR SAT AS she had for the last several days, in a leather chair within arm's reach of her daughter in the hospital bed. This room was new to them, and while still private, it sat in a different hall and lacked the glass wall of the CVICU. The nurses here came and went, but no longer hovered just steps away as they had before. Step-down they had called it. She had finally asked for an explanation for the term, and was told it was for patients recovering from heart surgery. Evidently you started in the operating room, only to step down to the CVICU, and then again to the Cardiac Step-Down unit. She had shrugged it off. Every discipline seemed to have its own language. Evidently the nurses didn't realize that the term had a negative vibe to the people outside their profession. Why not Step-Up?

Her phone vibrated in her pocket and she fetched it with dread. Thumbing the icon open she read the text message. It was a reminder she didn't need, and she quickly cleared the screen and returned it to her purse. She would deal with her own demons later Right now she had her daughter to worry about.

The sun was shining through the window and landing on Tessa's face. She looked better. Her color was good. The majority of the medication drips were gone. A single one remained that would help her body accept the new heart and make it her own. The chest tubes were still in place and poked out from under the sheets, but they held little, and she had been told that the tubes would most likely be gone by the end of the day. The breathing tube was also gone, and they had all held their breath as they waited for Tessa to take her first breath without it. But she had started breathing as if nothing had happened, and Rita now worked to keep the drool from her daughter's face.

Dianne, Tessa's new nurse stuck her head in the door. She scanned the pump and the monitor unit before raising a questionable eyebrow at Mrs. Lamar. They had gotten friendly the minute they had wheeled her daughter into the room, and Rita appreciated the attention she was giving them. The floor was a busy one, but Dianne always seemed to have all the time in the world when they needed something or had a question. Rita smiled and silently waved her away. She only needed one thing right now. Dianne just nodded and left as quietly as she had come.

Their silent communication was not for the benefit of their daughter so much as it was for her father. He sat in the chair next to his wife, but his level of consciousness was on par with Tessa's. Some ever-present paperwork lay in his lap, and his hand still gripped a page or two. It was one of many such naps he had taken over the last few days, but Rita never complained. He was here and that's what counted. The sun was slowly creeping across the room, and when it hit his face it would no doubt wake him. She would intervene with the curtains before that happened.

Tessa flopped slightly in the bed and her hands twitched as if grasping for something. A few mumbled words escaped her lips before she lay still again. Rita sat up and took her hand, but the movements stopped as quickly as they had begun. Anytime now, she'd been told. Rita could wait.

"Anything?" her husband whispered behind her.

"No, she's not ready yet," she whispered back.

They sat quietly until Dianne appeared in the door again. She turned and nodded to an unseen presence and Dr. Fong followed her into the room.

"Did we have a nice nap?" Dianne kidded the senator. She was obviously afraid of no one, whatever their title may be.

The senator, to his credit, took the abuse with a smile.

"Yes, Dianne, I did."

Dianne straightened a sheet and ogled the pump before stepping aside and giving Dr. Fong the floor. She hovered near the door, a polite distance, yet still close enough to hear anything she needed to.

Dr. Fong set the thick chart on the foot of Tessa's bed before sitting next to it.

"Tessa's labs are good. I'm happy to report that her body's showing no signs of rejecting her new heart, which appears to be functioning well. I see the drains are showing little output, so I think we'll schedule to have them removed this afternoon. Stephanie will come by and do that right here in the room. It only takes a few minutes."

"Any idea when she might wake up?"

"There's no telling, really. I would expect her to any time now, but she was under sedation for some time, and some patients just take longer than others. I'm told that she's been moving around some? Even talking?"

"Yes, a little."

"All good signs. Be patient."

"What about the after care?" the senator asked.

"It's involved, but manageable. We have a woman named Milli who will be coming to see you. Very smart. She's been a cardiac nurse for over thirty years now and has probably forgotten more than Matthew and I can remember. She'll give you a class on the proper care and feeding of Tessa's new heart. I'll warn you now, though, Tessa's not going to like some of the restrictions. But they have to be followed. Be strong, Dad."

"I...we will."

"Good. If she follows the plan, there really isn't any reason that she wouldn't be able to lead a normal life."

"...oud"

Dr. Fong stopped his lecture and they all turned to the girl on the bed.

"Tessa? It's Mommy. Can you hear me?"

"Loud."

"What? What did you say?"

"Loud...too loud."

Dr. Fong smiled and translated.

"She says we're too loud."

Rita couldn't help crying. "We're sorry, honey. How do you feel?"

Tessa opened her eyes, but quickly shut them against the sunlight. Dianne was across the room in a second and pulled the blinds shut. The girl slowly opened them again and looked around. Her hand naturally moved to her chest and rubbed the dull ache there.

"Tessa? I'm Doctor Fong. You were in an accident, do you remember?"

Tessa slowly processed the question and Dr. Fong held up a finger to silence her parents, giving the girl time to figure it out.

"A truck."

"Good. Can you tell me how you feel?"

Tessa cocked her head as if contemplating her answer.

"Hungry," she decided.

Dr. Fong shared a smile with her parents.

"I think she's going to be just fine."

He retreated to the doorway with Dianne, and they watched for a few moments as the family reunited. Eventually they realized they were intruding and made their way down the hall.

"Something in your eye, Dianne?"

"Watch it, Shorty."

* * *

Jack listened while Lenny either grunted or spoke rapid-fire Spanish into the phone. After a brief effort to keep up, he quit trying and reread the two secure emails on the screen in front of him. The view out his office window revealed a dark overcast sky that perfectly matched his current mood. They were leaving it up to him. Jack had to weigh out the repercussions before he made a decision.

Lenny ended the conversation and flipped the phone shut with his bandaged hands. Judging by the look on his face, they were more than just tender, but with the help of some quality pharmaceuticals, and his own tenacity, he was enduring the pain.

"Good news?"

"Yes and no. They got him and a few of his henchmen through some eavesdropping help from the NSA. He was loading up a suitcase full of cash. Evidently some form of down payment on the total ransom. He was good, the parents were completely fooled."

"Okay, so what's the bad news?"

"Looks like the kidnap victim may have been Oscar's heart donor. The bastard had her fingers in his car in a cooler. He showed one of them to the parents and that's what produced the cash. He probably had a plan to milk them for all he could get before disappearing. The AFI is rolling up the network now. He'll talk. They won't give him a choice. They'll be raiding a vet's office in an hour or so. Evidently that's where the harvests are taking place."

"Evil."

Lenny just nodded his head in agreement. Some things had only one word to describe them. He sat back in the chair and planted his elbows on the arms before raising his hands. It served to ease the pain. He wished he and Jack could get out the scotch, but it wouldn't mix with his meds. He noticed that his friend was deep in thought.

"How old?"

"The daughter? Fifteen," Lenny answered.

Jack played with the pen in his hands while Lenny watched. He had no jurisdiction in DC, and it was Jack's decision to make. He didn't envy him. He just watched silently while Jack read and reread the computer screen in front of him.

"He give any numbers?" Jack broke the silence.

Lenny took a deep breath before replying.

"Yeah. I see one big problem. The number we got from the kidnapper is twice the number we got from Angel. I'll find out more when I get to Mexico City. Either there's another source of organs somewhere, or one of them is lying."

"Maybe both."

"Maybe both," Lenny echoed. "Either way, I'm gonna be a busy man for the next few months. How about you? Make a decision yet?"

Jack couldn't help but make a face. Lenny only knew about one of the problems Jack was struggling with. The second was worse, and he wasn't ready to share it with his friend just yet.

"Yeah. I need to leave in a few minutes."

Lenny lowered his arms and pushed himself up with his elbows till he was out of the chair. He carefully picked up his hat from Jack's desk and placed it over the bandage and singed hair on his head. Tomorrow he'd see a barber and get it evened out, but right now he was too busy.

"Good luck, Jack. I don't fly out till tomorrow, so give me a call if you need anything."

Take it easy Lenny. You earned it."

Jack watched as Lenny struggled briefly with the door handle before disappearing through it. As it shut with a click, he turned back to the computer screen. He had the two emails side by side. Both of them cell phone intercepts from the NSA. One was from Oscar's brother Rico to Luis the kidnapper. The other was from Pablo to Senator Lamar's wife.

He picked up the phone and called the District Chief of Police.

"Are you ready?"

"Whenever you are, Jack."

"I'm on my way."

Jack opened his desk drawer and pulled out a stack of search warrants that had been delivered only an hour ago. After holstering his Browning, he gathered them up and placed them in his coat pocket. He paused long enough to make one quick call on his cell phone before rising to leave his office. He got as far as the door before stopping. Returning to his desk, he pulled out the bottom drawer. The expensive bottle of scotch went into the waste basket before he turned and left.

* * *

Jack and his crew pulled up to the side entrance of the Capitol Building. He had Larry and Sydney with him and they had just been briefed on what was about to happen.

Larry squirmed in his seat before voicing his opinion.

"This is gonna cost a lot."

Jack just nodded. Larry didn't mean in terms of money, he meant politically. Jack had been both a hero and in the doghouse with the current administration. But he had some cover that Larry didn't know about. And after what he had just learned in his office, there was no way he couldn't do it.

"This is right, Jack," Sydney voiced her support.

Jack nodded a thank you in her direction before returning his gaze out the window. They were stopped on the curb outside watching the last of the tourists leave the building. The chief exited the patrol car in front of them and gave them a signal. Jack followed, with Sydney lugging her case of equipment behind her. They were quickly inside and their collective footfalls on the hard tile echoed down the vast hallway. Heads stuck out of offices on both sides, but Jack ignored them as he was led through the crowd. After a flight of stairs and a couple of twists and turns they stopped outside an office door. A capitol guard outside it nodded in the affirmative to the chief's questioning look. With that, he stepped aside and Jack opened the door.

"Can I help y—" the young secretary spoke before looking up and cutting herself off.

"The congressman?"

"In his office, but he's in a meeting. You can't—"

Jack was already moving toward the door as Larry laid a hand on her intercom with a smile. She had no choice but to watch as the parade of officers rounded her desk on both sides.

Jack opened the door and stepped through to find the congressman sitting at his desk, talking with a lobbyist. He rose to his feet at the intrusion. Jack stopped in front of his desk and reached into his coat. The congressman automatically took a step back as Jack produced the warrants and laid them on the blotter in front of him.

"Mr. Randall? What's all this?"

"Those are warrants to search your person, office, and car."

Jack watched his face closely and saw the tick. He had him. The man quickly covered by smiling his politician's grin and spreading his hands.

"Whatever for?"

"Narcotics."

The Congressman placed a look of outrage on his face and offered it to the lobbyist. The man wisely said nothing before closing his briefcase and leaving the room.

"This is outrageous!" He attempted to watch everyone at once as they began searching his office. "Stop right there, I haven't read this warrant yet."

The Chief of Police chose that moment to speak. "It's a valid warrant, Mr. Foster, I can assure you. I'm afraid I need you to step outside your office...please."

The congressman looked from Jack's stoic face to the chief's impassive one before finally seeing the wisdom of not making a scene.

"Fine, fine! We'll straighten this out later, I can assure you!" He grabbed his jacket from the back of the chair.

"Excuse me, sir, I'll need you to leave that here," Sydney voiced.

Congressman Foster hesitated and another look of panic briefly crossed his face. He set the jacket slowly on the chair, and with a burning look at Sydney left the room. He stepped outside with his secretary and a few capitol guards. He made an attempt to look relaxed, but couldn't help but glance back into his office every few seconds.

Jack and the chief watched carefully as Sydney laid the jacket out on the desk. With gloved hands she emptied the front pocket first. A nice Montblanc ballpoint and a handkerchief were placed in the first plastic bag before she moved on to the inside pocket. There she found a small metal pill box and a glass tube. Larry stopped searching the man's briefcase for a moment to follow Sydney's progress. The box was opened to produce a small plastic bag with several small gray rocks. It was obvious what it was, but she still needed to test it. She opened the bag and removed the smallest rock with a pair of tweezers. Producing a small vial of liquid from her kit, she dropped the rock in before securing the cap and shaking it. The liquid went from clear to a dark blue within a few shakes. She held it up to the light.

"Positive for crack."

Larry shook his head before returning to the briefcase. He pulled a piece of paper free from a pouch in the lid. It was folded several times.

"Syd?"

"Put it on the blotter."

They all watched as she slowly opened the paper to reveal a white powder. She scooped up a sample and dropped it in another vial. A few shakes produced an even darker blue than the first vial.

"Cocaine. Good stuff."

Jack had seen enough. He spun on a heel and walked out to the hallway followed by the Chief. He nodded to the officer babysitting the congressman.

"Congressman Foster, you're under arrest for narcotics possession. This man will read you your rights. I suggest you listen to them carefully."

"Now wait a minute. I have no idea what that is there!" the man began to protest.

"Congressman!"

They all stopped and looked at the secretary. She glared at her boss, and he wisely shut his mouth.

Jack just watched as the man was cuffed and led away. The flash of a camera blinded them as they rounded the corner and Jack looked to see the grinning face of Danny Drake looking back. He offered an innocent shrug before moving off with the congressman and his police escort. Their footsteps on the tile and the practiced recital of the Miranda warning echoed off the walls as the man made his walk of shame out of the building.

Larry stepped up to join Jack as he watched them leave. He pointed with his cell phone.

"Isn't that your reporter buddy from the *Post?*"

"Who?"

Larry ignored the answer. "They found some more powder in his car outside. Looks like a good bust, Jack. You should feel good."

"I should."

"Yeah…me either."

They watched the congressman being led down the hall past a few of his colleagues who had been drawn out of their offices by the noise. Eventually he was gone and the building became silent once again.

"Larry, I need you to come with me tonight. I have a meeting to go to, along with the Director."

"What kind of meeting?"

"It's with Senator Lamar and his wife. Short version is, she's coming to work for us. I'll explain on the way."

"Okay, anything else?"

"Wear your civvies, and keep it to yourself."

That was odd but Larry knew better than to question Jack now.

"Okay."

5 ARRESTED IN KIDNAPPING
AND MURDER OF BOY

September 9, 2008—New York Times

—EPILOGUE—

THE MAJOR TAPPED THE keyboard, sending the information on the three new Afghan soldiers into the database. He had already checked the pending order sheet and determined that one of them was a good candidate for a liver they needed in Los Angeles. He was still waiting on an answer to an email he had sent out the previous day, but for some reason his in-box remained empty. It was odd. Usually he received an answer within an hour of sending the information. But he was a patient man, despite the end of his contract coming up. He was debating whether to renew it for another year. His bank account was in very good shape. He had enough to retire on comfortably once he added his pension to it. But another year wouldn't hurt either. After all, his tastes may change, and another year would guarantee that wouldn't be a problem.

Clicking his way out of his email account he pulled his bank statement up on the screen. The Cayman Island bank he used was efficient and discrete. He saw that the money from the boy's heart had been deposited that morning and he couldn't help but smile. Clicking his way across the screen, he entered some passwords and account numbers before sending the money to yet another bank. This one was in Panama and the name on the account was for a dummy corporation who happened to be owned by a man who looked just like him, yet his name matched a passport he had stowed in his footlocker.

He did some mental calculations while he waited and tried to come up with a ballpark figure of how much the account would total. He smiled again when he realized that he couldn't do it. Having so much money that he couldn't keep track of was a problem that he didn't really mind.

Transaction Denied.

His smile quickly faded when the words appeared on the screen. Had he typed in the account number wrong? He reset the access screen and typed in the password and account number again.

Transaction Denied.

What the hell? Was there something wrong with the bank's computers? Or was the problem at the receiving bank in Panama? He clicked out of the first one and into the second. The password was typed in from memory and his fingers drummed the desk top impatiently while he waited for the balance sheet to appear.

Zero. His account was empty.

He stared at the screen with his mouth hanging open. The account was open, but the money was gone. He quickly typed in the number and password again only to see the same figure appear on the screen. Zero. He snatched up the phone to call the bank. Damn the time zones, this bank was open twenty-four hours a day. He stood up and fumed while the phone began to ring.

Unless…he slowly hung up the phone.

"Is everything all right, Major Willis?"

The Major spun around to see three men standing in the doorway to his office. The large one in front had his head and hands covered in bandages. The two men behind him were dressed in the uniforms of the

Afghan police.

"Yes. What's this? Who are you?"

The big man reached behind him and the Major caught sight of a large handgun strapped to his belt before he produced a wallet. He flipped it open to reveal a badge.

"My name's Lenny Hill. I'm with Interpol. These men are with the Afghan Central Police force. They have some questions for you."

The Major's eyes widened at that. He had heard stories of how the Afghans questioned people.

"I'm an American."

"Oh, I know, and if I had any evidence that you had committed a crime against an American soldier you'd be leaving with me. Since you're a civilian contractor, however, the military has no authority here. So that gives the Afghanis jurisdiction here."

The two policemen stepped around Lenny and seized the Major. They soon had him cuffed and roughly led him out the door. The fear in the Major's eyes was apparent.

It gave Lenny great satisfaction.

"Worth the trip," he told himself before following the three men outside.

* * *

The wind outside howled as it seemed to do most days, and the freezing spray falling from the sky was thrown against the windows with a rattle that threatened to break them. The overcast sky kept the noon sun from shining through the ice coated glass to offer any trace of warmth to the stuffy interior. The TV droned in the room next to the kitchen, providing the only company for the man sitting at the table.

Dressed warmly despite the heated interior, he sat as he did most days. The items on the table in front of him defined his existence and he glowered at them as the minutes ticked by. An ever present cigarette burned in an overfilled ashtray next to his scarred hand. A bottle of bourbon sat center stage with a well used glass holding a few fingers worth.

Several small envelopes were laid out on the table in neat little piles according to their contents. He contemplated the arrangement from under the dark hoodie that served to hide his face.

The TV changed programs telling him it was the top of the hour, and the bubbly blonde in the tight top and perfectly coiffed hair started reading the news from the teleprompter. He half listened until she started the third story.

"Government officials today announced that the average price for cocaine in the United States has spiked to a three-year high. They attribute the rise to a major blow to the Cali Cartel earlier this year that resulted in the capture or death of many of its leadership. While officials were reluctant to release actual numbers or specific names, sources for this network were able to confirm the deaths of Oscar Hernandez, head of the cartel, and his brother, Ricardo. There have also been several arrests within the Mexican, Honduran, and Panamanian governments. While the Drug Enforcement Agency has categorized the efforts as a major blow to the drug trade, some experts disagree. Dr. Issam Halaby of Citizens against Drugs argues that the cartels had a record crop last season thanks to ideal weather conditions, and the price is merely a temporary one and will return quickly to average as demand has not changed. Whether or not the government's actions have made any real success remains to be seen through future prices."

He smiled at the story. They were never going to learn. He ignored the TV as the blonde had now moved on to some political scandal, and instead listened to the wind howl outside. He usually saw some traffic around this time. The house was like any other in this rural town, and he dwelled in one that was in an older neighborhood on the edge. Fortunately it was not far from the new high school. His nearest neighbor was over a block away through some sparse trees. An old retired couple that he rarely saw. He doubted they even went out during the winter.

He rose from his chair and walked to the door to peer out and check the progress of the snow. A good six inches showed on the roof of his car in the driveway, and that was being covered in a layer of ice. The street was still clear as the plow had made a pass about an hour ago. He'd have to go out and clear the end of the driveway before the bastard came around again and piled it even higher. Visibility was down to about a block, and the wind was making drifts against the fence separating his yard from the lot next door. It wouldn't slow down the community much. They were used to weather like this.

He glanced up at the camera mounted to the wall. He had disguised it in a piece of decorative art he had found at a flea market a couple of towns away. He only shopped outside of town. His face was a memorable one, and he didn't want to be seen by the locals too much. The camera was free of snow and ice so far. He'd have to keep checking it if the wind changed.

Returning to the table, he stopped to light up a fresh cigarette before moving to the counter to change the angle of the small TV. Turning it on, he soon had a view of the front yard and the street beyond. The well-packed snow on the path leading to his front door from the street was slowly disappearing under a blanket of fresh snow. He had just sat down when he saw the halo glow of approaching headlights coming through the snow. He watched until he recognized the truck, a brown Ford Bronco that had seen better days. It fishtailed through the icy street as the driver played with the accelerator before coming to a sliding stop on the curb. He rose from his seat and walked to the door.

He could just make out the three teenage boys inside the truck. The passenger collected money from the driver and the backseat passenger before opening the door. Heavy metal spewed forth until he hurriedly slammed the door behind him and headed up the path without a coat. They had obviously snuck away on their lunch break from the high school. He scanned the street behind the Bronco in both directions as the boy ran through the snow to the front door. He was a regular.

Pulling the hoodie farther down over his head, he opened the door. The boy stood shivering in the cold and shuffling his boots back and forth.

"Yeah?"

"Three."

He took the offered money and retreated inside, shutting the door in the boy's face behind him. Locking it, he walked to the table, counting the money. Satisfied, he selected three envelopes from the piles on the table. Retracing his steps he checked the camera's view on his way back to the door. Seeing no change, he opened it and counted out the envelopes into the boy's hand. He caught the boy staring when he looked up, and he quickly broke his gaze and looked away before retreating down the steps and back to the warmth of the Bronco.

The man muttered a curse as he closed and locked the door. Returning to his seat, he added bourbon to what remained in the glass and slugged it down. He drew on the cigarette forcefully and blew the smoke across the room. The blasts of cold air had started his nose running so he heaved himself to his feet and made for the bathroom. Pulling some toilet paper off the roll he cleared his one good nostril as best he could. Straightening up, he contemplated his hooded face in the mirror. His hands found the hood and he slowly pulled it back to reveal the scarred face and head, the missing hair, the misshapen nose. He rubbed a scarred hand over his bare head, feeling the rough texture of the burnt skin covering it.

Angel gazed at his own face reflected back at him and cursed it.

* * *

"Turn now! Keep turning! Keep turning!"

The bow responded to the turn of the wheel and the sail snapped taut as the boat fell off the wind. They heeled over and Jessica grabbed hold of the sanction as she watched her son spread his feet and keep his balance. His eyes moved from the water ahead to the compass in front of him and back again. Jimmy's muscles bulged as he worked the winch to tighten the sail further.

"Heading?" he asked Cody.

"One, eight…six!" he answered.

"Perfect, steady as she goes."

"Steady as she goes!" the boy sang back.

Jimmy exchanged a look with Jessica and got a smile in return. The boy was a natural. Despite his young age, he had taken to sailing rapidly, quickly developing his sea legs and absorbing the language of the craft by instinct. Halyard, sheet, jib, mast, bow, starboard, stern—his mother was struggling to keep up. But she would learn she promised herself. The boat was their home now.

Jimmy tied off some loose line before taking a seat behind her where he could watch the boy's progress, yet still be close enough to assist. She scooted back and settled into his arms and he held her close as they glided over the water.

"You're sure?" he whispered the question in her ear.

Her answer was a nod before her lips found his. He drank her in like the sweetest of wines.

A cresting wave sent water over the bow and they were brought back to the present by the salty spray and Cody's giggling laughter.

They settled in and divided their attention between the boy and the setting sun. Jimmy sighed and let himself relax as he hadn't in years. He had made it out alive, unscathed…and free.

They had their whole lives before them.

Randall Wood is the author of the novels *Closure*, *Pestilence* and *Scarcity*. After a life spent in occupations such as paratrooper, teacher and flight paramedic, he eventually listened to the little voices in his head and now writes full time. He currently resides on the Gulf coast of Florida with his wife, their three children, two cats and one Great Dane puppy.

He welcomes readers, and fellow writers, to his website at: www.randallwoodauthor.com

I welcome any comments, feedback, or questions at

mail@randallwoodauthor.com

I also welcome any input as to mistakes I may have missed, not necessarily typos or grammar, as they are self-explanatory, but mistakes pertaining to procedures or content. Mistakes of this nature tend to pull the reader out of the story and make it less enjoyable. If you should find such an error please fire off an email in my direction. The beauty of e-books and print-on-demand physical books is that they can always be updated to fix such things. I'll post the mistake on my website with full credit to the person who found it. If you wish to remain anonymous, that's fine too, the help is always appreciated.

I also welcome any and all reviews, with one small request. With the controversy over fake reviews garnering so much attention, it gives your review greater credibility if you do so in your real name and with the verified purchase icon. Doing so helps all readers call honest attention to their favored writers, and helps keep the integrity of the online review process intact.

Who knows?

Your review may end up on the back of the next book.

Please visit my blog at www.randallwoodauthor.com to learn about current and future projects.

www.TensionBookworks.com

Made in the USA
Columbia, SC
20 March 2021